WRATH OF THE FAE

BOOKS 1-3

ALESSA THORN

Copyright © 2021 by ALESSA THORN

All rights reserved.

No part of this book may be reproduced in any form or by any electronic or mechanical means, including information storage and retrieval systems, without written permission from the author, except for the use of brief quotations in a book review.

Cover Design by Damoro Design

Editing and Proof Reading by Damoro Design

PROLOGUE

No one was ready when our world ended.
   The year had been so bad that everyone had started making jokes about it to stop themselves from going insane.

In the first six months, the world had seen massive fires that chewed through billions of acres in the Southern Hemisphere, where the Northern had freak snowstorms that had iced Europe over. There had been hurricanes, monsoon flooding, and landslides in Asia.

Volcanos were rumbling, and we figured it was only a matter of time before they exploded and blackened the sky with ash once more. We thought it was global warming.

And magic? We didn't even believe it was real. We couldn't have known that the freak nature events were magic rushing back into our world.

England was one of the few countries that had yet to suffer a disaster. The rest of the world made jokes that our weather usually sucked enough to be classed as a natural disaster.

We didn't stop to think it was because something worse was coming for us.

We should have known that those events were warnings, precursors to the oncoming scourge.

We thought the worst thing was whatever freak climate event was happening. It wasn't. The worst thing was finding out how much mankind deserved it.

We should've put as much effort into preparing ourselves as we did into joking. Not that you could have been ready for England's calamity when it did arrive.

No one could have been ready...not for him.

1

Elise knew the day would be a nightmare when a guy in a posh suit bumped into her on the train and spilled his coffee down the front of her work uniform. He tried pawing at her with a handkerchief to mop it up as he apologized, to the point Elise had to slap his hands away for having a grope.

"Bloody Mondays," she muttered, buttoning up her coat to hide the stain as she got off the train. Tottenham Court Station was packed with commuters this time of morning and was humid with humanity's fug.

Outside, the winter wind was paralyzing, blasting Elise full in the face and making the people around her hunch inward to brace against it. The coffee was already freezing and sticky against her skin.

Just perfect.

Elise would need a pick-me-up before she spent the day surrounded by dusty boxes in an airless basement office. She checked her phone. 8:30 am. Plenty of time to indulge in her favorite sanity saver.

Instead of going on the usual route to her work building on Morwell Street, Elise hurried up Great Russell Street and headed to her happy place. The British Museum's columns came into view, and she let its unique kind of magic work on her.

She calmed down even as she dodged the tourists and bought a coffee from one of the vendors who liked to take advantage of the Museum's traffic.

One day, Elise, that's where you are going to be working. She sat down on a damp step, sipped scalding coffee, and let herself fall into her favorite fantasy. In it, Elise poured over ancient manuscripts, carefully restoring and digitizing their words for future generations. She would wander the archives and find lost treasures, forgotten about in their depths, be an insider advocate to help repatriate treasures and assist Interpol in hunting down black market antiquities.

She had completed a degree in history and a master's in restoration, and where did she end up after graduation? Working in HR for a fucking real estate firm. It didn't matter how good her grades had been or how highly her academic papers had been praised. She still had to pay the bills, and jobs at the British Museum didn't come up often.

You'll get there. Baby steps, her father's voice echoed in her head, and her chest ached. Last summer, he had finally succumbed to cancer that had been eating away at him, and Elise still missed him every day. She had taken a month off to sort out his estate, and then, her boss had mentioned if she needed more time, Elise should quit.

Like I'd give her the satisfaction. She should have probably sold the house in Salisbury and moved closer to the city but hadn't had the heart to do it.

"Hey Elise!" a cheerful voice shouted across the green space and hurried towards her. Chrissy was an eyesore to look at on a gloomy day. Wearing an offensively bright yellow jacket and beanie, her curly brown hair corkscrewed in the wind and tangled with her massive pink earrings.

"Morning," Elise said, standing up and taking one more wistful glance at the stately columns of the museum before they began walking to work.

"I thought I was going to be the only one running late, but this is brilliant. We can say the train was delayed," Chrissy said breathlessly. "Come to worship at your fave shrine?"

"Yeah, something like that. Couldn't bear going into work just yet," Elise replied, giving her a smile. It was not that Elise didn't like Chrissy, but she was high-intensity first thing in the morning, and Elise tended not to feel alive until 10 a.m.

"I hear you. Goddess, I'm hungover. I went to an early winter solstice party yesterday, and I hit the homebrew beers too hard," Chrissy replied, stuffing half a croissant in her mouth. "The energy was off the charts, though. I'm buzzing even with the hangover."

"Share some of those good vibes around. I think we all need them at the moment," Elise said, smiling because it was impossible to stay in a bad mood around her.

"Oh yeah, I heard on the news this morning that Yellowstone Park is going to blow in America. Seriously, with this year, nothing would surprise me. Gaia is kicking about and pissed off, I tell you. We did a ritual last night to try and calm shit down, but the Goddess wants what she wants." Chrissy was keen on her New Age spirituality, but thankfully, she didn't push her 'love and light' brand of it onto Elise too much. She was a jaded Lutheran raised kid, but Chrissy was more concerned with her preference for wearing only black and never getting laid than her spiritual beliefs.

"A winter solstice ritual sounds like a really cold orgy in the woods," Elise teased. Chrissy's pink lips smirked.

"Well, there was a bit of that, but don't mock it until you try it. I'm gutted that the Solstice falls on a fucking Monday, or I would have gone to Stonehenge and really soaked up the energy," she replied as they walked into the blissfully warm foyer of Highland and Pierce.

"And no doubt, I would have gotten a call to come to pick up your freezing ass because I conveniently live twenty minutes away from it," Elise said, giving her a playful nudge with her shoulder.

"Probably, but to be fair, your cottage comes with tea and a fireplace. Do you think Umbridge will be wearing the beige cardigan or the cream with the beige spots?" Chrissy asked, stepping into the lift. 'Umbridge' was their name for Susanna, the manager of the HR department who was a total troll, just like the Harry Potter character, but with a worse taste in clothes and desk knick-knacks (creepy dolls that Elise occasionally moved around to mess with her).

"What about the one slightly more beige than standard beige, but less beige than mocha beige?" Elise said, and they both giggled.

As it turned out, Umbridge was wearing the one with spots because she was standing outside of the elevators, waiting for them.

"Where have you two been? You're ten minutes late, and I need you to watch the phones so I can go to the manager's meeting upstairs," Susanna demanded.

"Sorry, the train was delayed, something about ice on the tracks," Chrissy lied and gave her a harried smile. "You know what the bloody tube is like in winter. You better run. We can take it from here." Susanna's eyes narrowed behind her glasses, her lips pursing together as she stepped into the elevator. "We will discuss this later."

"Should have farted in the elevator before I got out," Chrissy said once the silver doors shut.

"You'll get her next time," Elise replied with a laugh and headed for her corner of the office.

Elise had a standing desk with a computer and scanner next to the storage compactors that housed all the hard copies of employee contracts and files. A half-dead succulent and a picture of her Dad were the only decorative touches she had bothered with.

What's the point of decorating when I'm going to be out of here in two months? She had said over a year ago. *I really have to get out of this place.*

Elise dumped her coat over a chair, found the clean shirt she kept for emergencies in a drawer, and headed for the bathroom to change.

By the time she got back to her desk, Chrissy was waiting for her, shuffling her deck of faerie creature oracle cards and looking at her curiously.

"What? Is there still a coffee splash on me somewhere?" Elise asked.

"No, your aura just looks a bit ramped up today, like way more than usual," she said.

"I tried a new cereal today, if that counts? It's bran heavy," Elise replied. Chrissy rolled her eyes.

"Trying to stir me up today won't work. I'm too charged with dark energy."

Elise turned on the computer. "Hmm, sounds dodgy."

"We are made up of both light and dark, Elise. You have to accept both sides whether you like them or not," Chrissy replied, unperturbed. She fanned out the deck and held it out to Elise. "Pick one."

Humoring her, Elise shut her eyes and ran her fingers over the deck. This was a fun thing they did at least once a week, so Elise was surprised when she pulled a card she'd never seen before.

It was of a tall male fae, with long scarlet red hair and a set of antlers like a stag rising from his head. He had two swords strapped to his back, with his torso covered in woad tattoos. His golden eyes were savage, with a sensual mouth curled in a smile the kind a wolf gave you...right before it tore your throat out.

"Please tell me it means I'm going to win the lottery," Elise teased. Chrissy was frowning at the card, deep in thought. "What?"

"Nothing. This card is a heavy masculine energy card. I've never seen a woman pull it before." Her voice deepened, and her eyes glazed over. "You're going on a journey, and you're going to face darkness and hardship. You will have a protector from the shadows, but you're never going to be safe." Chrissy shook herself. "What did I say?"

"That I'm going to meet someone. Hopefully, he's hot and not like... Barry from Accounting," Elise joked. Barry had drunkenly groped her at the last Christmas party, and since then, he had kept asking her out once a month like clockwork.

No, thanks.

"No, it won't be Barry."

"Then the only other man I see regularly is Glenn down the pub every Monday night," Elise said, determined to make her laugh. Glenn was her Dad's old drinking buddy and best mate that wanted to keep an eye on Elise and make sure she was doing all right. It was nice to hang out with the old guy and have someone to talk to about her Dad. Besides, Monday was Cheap Night at the local pub, and Elise could never say no to a pint and meal deal.

Chrissy shook herself and propped the card next to Elise's succulent. "I don't know, honey. I'm probably just jittery or hungover. You can hang onto the hot fae warrior for the day," she said with a smile.

"I'm going to go with hungover. Maybe get some water into you with all the pastry you're inhaling."

Chrissy flipped her off. "I drink heaps of water, asshole."

"You have crystals in your water bottle. I worry about you."

"Whatever. I'll see you at lunch."

Elise frowned as she watched her walk away, her eyes eventually drifting back to the card.

"Looks like it's just you and me and the adventure of all the scanning from the last Staff Quarterly Review."

The vicious fae only smiled a little wider.

2

As Elise predicted, the day was a drag. The sandwich roll she bought from the building's cafe had hair in it, and the coffee was cold. Her computer shut itself down twice for updates. The scanner alignment stretched all the writing on the pages, forcing Elise to do them again. Chrissy got more anxious as the day went on, her buzzing from the night before wearing off, leaving her nauseous and twitchy.

"What the hell did they put in that homebrew?" Elise asked, passing her some stomach tablets that she always kept handy. With a two-hour commute every day, you learned to always be prepared.

"I don't know, maybe someone put fun mushrooms in the salad," Chrissy complained, looking gray.

"Not so fun now, are they?"

"Eat a dick," she groaned and downed the tablets. "It doesn't feel like a hangover. It feels like dread and really bad juju."

"That's a typical Monday for you," Elise said, rubbing her back.

By the time five o'clock rocked around, Elise was packed up and ready to go. The stag fae on the card looked at her with enough judgment that she stuck her tongue out at it.

Stupid Chrissy is making me paranoid now. Elise just wanted to go home and have a hot bath.

The footpaths on the way to the train station were already packed with people. Elise had her arm tucked through Chrissy's to help keep her upright.

"I need to sleep for a week," she said.

"Drink some electrolytes and feel better," Elise replied, letting her go once they reached the bottom of the stairs and heading for her platform.

Three women and a man walked past Elise dressed as some kind of crazy forest nymphs. They wore leather leggings and their long hair in braids decorated with feathers. They had dark blue war paint all over their arms and face in intricate spirals.

Looks like these guys managed to get the Solstice off work. They were probably off to a party at a pagan convention.

"Cool costumes, guys," Elise said with a smile. One of the women hissed in reply, flashing her fangs. The others merely stared at her before walking away. *Weird*. No one else was looking at them as they walked the opposite way through the crowd; people just got out of their way. Honestly, it wasn't the oddest thing Elise had seen on London public transport.

Elise had to stand for the first thirty minutes next to a guy with a nasty body odor and a woman who wouldn't stop talking on her phone. Still, by some miracle of the transport gods, she managed to get a chair in the front of the carriage once they got to Woking. Elise pulled out her eBook reader, but it refused to turn on. She tried resetting it, and still nothing. She could have cried out of sheer frustration.

This day can't get any worse. Then her phone died.

"You've got to be kidding me," Elise muttered. It had been fully charged when she had left work. She looked up at a man cursing across the aisle. As she stared around, she realized everyone's electrical devices had died.

Elise didn't have a chance to contemplate it because the lights flickered and turned off next. People complained as the train ground to a halt, and the side doors opened, sending icy wind into the carriage.

That was when the screaming started.

"What the fuck is going on?" a woman said somewhere in the dark. Elise looked through the glass panel in the door that connected to the next carriage just as a man's face got slammed against the glass, his blood spurting everywhere.

Elise could make out a flurry of movement of passengers brawling and women screaming and clawing each other's eyes out. A man was stomping on the head of another, blood spilling out onto the floor. Through the chaos, there was a flicker of a figure in gold. The people moved out of his way, and Elise covered her mouth to hold back her scream. The asshole from her fae card was staring right at her.

Someone grabbed Elise by the hair, and she turned quickly to shove the woman off. People started shouting in the carriage. A man used his laptop to smack the passenger in front of him hard in the back of the head.

Elise crouched down on the floor, shaking like hell and hoping no one would see her. The doors connecting to the carriage opened, and she held her breath, dreading what was coming.

Ivory stag antlers smeared with gold appeared, and the tallest man she had ever seen stepped into the carriage. He was wearing golden armor in delicate interlocking designs. His long white hair hung in a braid down his back and ended in red tips.

He turned to face her, his eyes vivid scarlet under the golden mask he wore. He had twin swords hanging from his back, and eying them, Elise crouched down lower on the carriage floor, pushing back against the wall to get away from him.

Everyone was too busy killing each other to notice the world's scariest fae cosplayer in their midst. His armor got splattered with blood as a woman knocked her own head against the bar on top of the chair.

Golden light shivered out of him, and then all the screaming stopped as everyone in the carriage slumped dead. Elise gagged, terror clawing at her, and waited to meet the same fate. Death by the hands of a creature she hadn't believed existed. When the killing light touched her, it only made her skin tingle before moving back to the fae staring at her, scarlet eyes wide with confusion.

What the actual fuck is happening?

Another fae covered in woad and blood climbed up through the side door and said something in a guttural, Gaelic sounding language. He noticed Elise cowering and drew a wicked-looking blade.

There was a sharp clang an inch above her head, and Elise peeked an eye open. The golden one's blade slid the other one's away. He hissed out something, an order, judging by the tone, and the black-haired fae drew back in surprise and horror.

The golden fae moved out of the way, and the other fae sprang into action, pulling Elise out of her hiding place. Elise kicked and punched out at him, but it was no use. He dragged her out and pushed her to her knees in front of the golden fae.

His red eyes shone behind the mask as he observed her. Then he cut his thumb on the edge of his blade and smeared his blood along Elise's forehead before sticking it in her mouth and running it against her teeth. Elise tried to spit it out, but he gripped her face, holding her jaw shut until she swallowed. Elise's stomach churned, her mouth tasting of honey and flowers.

With that done, he jumped lightly out of the train and onto a white horse that was waiting outside of the carriage. The black-haired fae bound Elise's hands with a strap of leather, then she was thrown over the front of a saddle. The fae climbed behind her and pressed a dagger to the back of her neck. He muttered something Elise didn't understand but got his meaning clear enough. *Don't try and escape, or I'll slit your throat.* Elise nodded, too scared to do anything else.

She turned her head and saw the army of mounted fae surrounding the train. As they passed the open carriages, she caught glimpses of what remained of the people who had torn each other apart in the horrifying fit of madness. Elise gagged violently at the sight of so much death and carnage. The people had done it to themselves; the army hadn't left their mounts, only watched.

The golden prince looked at Elise again, his eyes cold. "Take her back to the camp," he said, and she jolted, realizing she could understand him. "I'll deal with her when I return."

"Yes, my prince," the warrior behind her said.

With growing horror, Elise watched the golden prince make an elegant gesture with his hand. The train hummed back to life, doors shutting automatically, as the train started to move back towards London, carrying the vicious madness with it.

3

Elise had always thought of herself as a brave person. She'd nursed her father as he had slowly died without breaking. She'd dealt with her shitty mother trying to crash his funeral, kicking her out of it with as much grace as possible. She'd worked a job where managers frequently demeaned her and had taken it on the chin.

Dangling over a monstrous fae horse, dealing with the fact that mythical creatures had come out of hiding with an army and she was their prisoner...Elise wasn't brave. She vomited in fear as the ground churned beneath her, knowing with every step she was riding towards torture and death. She sobbed, the relentless speed and position she was in making her ribs flare in agony.

It was so dark that she couldn't make out where they were in this countryside she knew so well. Every time she tried to raise her head to look around, a hard hand would push it back down.

The horse eventually slowed its pace as lights came into view. Elise risked turning her head and saw hundreds of torches burning around monoliths.

Stonehenge.

The fae army had turned it into a war camp. They roamed everywhere, erecting tents, whooping war cries, and lighting fires. The stones themselves were lit up with glowing runes and designs.

For one wild second, in the middle of her breakdown, Elise thought how much Chrissy would love to see it glowing with magic.

Fucking magic is real.

She thought about all the times she had teased Chrissy and felt like a total asshole. *God, I hope she's okay.*

The fae stopped the horse in front of a large red and gold tent, erected closest to the humming energy of the stone ring.

"Back with spoils already, General Fionn?" a voice called.

"Not my spoils. The prince's. Though don't ask me why he chose *this* one," the fae warrior behind her said.

Fionn jumped down from the horse and dragged her off. Elise stumbled on numb legs and sagged to her knees, struggling to breathe, her ribs hurting so bad, they had to be cracked. Fionn didn't care. He dragged her roughly into the red and gold tent and slammed her to the ground next to a tall pole.

"Don't move," he hissed, and taking her bound hands, he tied Elise to it like a stray dog. Grabbing her chin in his strong fingers, he lifted her face to the torchlight. His blue, curved eyes were filled with disgust and violence.

"Pray to your gods, pathetic human. I can't wait to see what the prince has planned for you." Elise didn't get any time to process that before his fist struck her, and she hit the dirt.

WHEN ELISE WOKE, it was to an aching head and the rumble of hundreds of hooves slamming into the earth and making it shake. She curled into herself as much as she could, knowing the army had returned. The tent flaps opened, and the prince came in.

Elise pretended to be unconscious and tried to watch him inconspicuously. His black and gold boots walked past and went to a table where a basin of water had been placed next to a stand.

The prince slowly unbuckled his blood-splattered gold armor and hung it up piece by piece. Underneath his breastplate was a black leather jacket and shirt, damp with sweat and blood. He lifted a hand to the golden mask, and Elise's breath caught despite her fear.

He had a straight nose, a sharp jawline, and high cheekbones. His scarlet eyes were large and curved slightly upward at the ends. His mouth was the only soft feature he had, with full lips that were stained with blood.

The gold cuffs on the tips of his pointed ears flashed as he turned and started to strip off his jacket and shirt. He was somehow bigger without the clothes to hide how muscular he was underneath. Lean and broad shouldered, he radiated strength.

Blood had soaked through his clothes, staining his pearl white skin with red smears.

Elise was horrified and couldn't look away from him washing his face and chest. She thought about the train heading to London and the towns in between them that he could have raided with his army.

Fionn's words came back to her, *I can't wait to see what the prince has planned for you.* Ice filled her belly.

Would he torture me with those long knives? Would he rape me? Elise shut her eyes, having to look away as fear clogged her throat.

Footsteps came closer, and a long finger poked her shoulder. "I know you are awake, human. I can smell your fear."

Elise opened her eyes and scooted away from him, her back hitting against the pole. The prince crouched down in front of her and studied her like a bug. Up close, his antlers were about as long as her arm, their pronged black tips still smeared in gold paint. Elise could suddenly taste his spicy honey and spring blood again and tried not to swallow.

"What's your name?" he asked, his voice deep and lilting.

"E-Elise," she said and then remembered the stories about never giving the fae your real name. "Fuck, no, it's not," she tried to blunder on, but it was too late. The prince's brow lifted a little.

"Elise," he repeated slowly like he was savoring the taste of it in his mouth. A knife appeared in his hand, and she flinched, turning her face away. Cold metal brushed against her hands, and the binds slid away. Elise clutched her freed hands to her chest, rubbing feeling back into them.

"Thanks," she mumbled, figuring being polite might stop him from cutting pieces off her.

The prince's head tilted a little, staring at Elise's dirty face and hair. He looked like he was trying to figure something out. She wasn't dumb enough to meet his gaze for long. Elise tried to look away, but he took her face and tipped it up. He was close enough that she could now smell his scent of fir trees and sweet smoke, alluring and dangerous at once.

Elise stared at his mouth, not daring to raise her eyes higher, and she caught a glimpse of his fangs as he repeated, "Elise." He let go of her face with a growl of frustration and pulled one of her hands away from her chest. Elise tried to stop him, but his grip held her like a vice.

"Be still," he commanded, and she froze as he ran his blade along her palm.

It was so sharp, Elise didn't realize she had been cut until blood started to well up. The prince tugged her bloody palm to him and lowered his soft mouth to it. Too shocked to move, Elise watched as he drank her blood, his scarlet eyes flaring with gold.

His warm tongue lapped at her skin, and goosebumps skittered down her arms. With one gentle scrape of fangs against her, he let her hand go. Elise held it close, the cut closing over like magic.

What. The. Fuck.

"Unusual," he murmured. His eyes shifted back to scarlet again as he licked his bottom lip. Reaching over, he twirled a lock of Elise's hair around his finger and let the dark curl spring back up.

Fae arriving outside of his tent made him snap out of his intense concentration and stand quickly. He pulled a scarlet shirt from a chest, sliding his arms into it, before crisscrossing the panels around himself and fastening them. He snapped his fingers, and golden cuffs appeared on Elise's wrists. Magic curled around them and runes danced on the gold before fading into black markings.

"Don't try to run, Elise," he warned and tapped the golden band around his own wrist. "I'll know." The prince took a black crystal the size of her hand from the chest and opened the door of his tent.

The roar of the crowd of fae outside was deafening as they made a path for him. Elise crept to the door, too scared to step out of it, but too curious not to look. The prince crouched down and buried the crystal in the churned-up turf. Golden light illuminated his face like some kind of fucked up pagan god, magic exploding out of him.

The crowd was shouting again, but Elise could barely hear them. She was struck dumb at the sight of his magic - real, terrifyingly powerful magic.

The earth shuddered, and the black crystal began to shoot up out of the ground like the trunks of demonic trees. The crystal was alive as it took form and grew higher, twisting and molding together into a castle. The prince turned, flashing a fanged smile while his magic continued to feed the crystal and the land. The fae were going wild, shaking spears, hitting drums, and drinking from horns. They let out war cries and screams for their prince as his power washed over them.

The golden wave of magic hit Elise, and she swayed. It burned through her, making her skin hot and blood rush to her head. Elise backed away from the doors as the heady power knocked her down. Her human body couldn't handle the potency of it, of *him*. His feral golden face was the last thing she saw before blacking out.

4

The human was unconscious again by the time Kian returned to his tent before dawn. Exhausted from the amount of power that had been riding him for days, and all he wanted to do was sleep.

Arawan knows I deserve it.

He, Kian the Blood Prince, had managed the impossible and brought his people from where they had been banished to Faerie and through the stone circle back to Albion. Fifteen hundred years of imprisonment were finally over.

The humans had built the stone circle as a warning that it was a gateway to Faerie, one they didn't know how to open or close. Now it was Kian's, his castle growing beside it, forever to be a part of this land that was taken from them. He had no intention of showing mercy to any of the humans, and yet, on his first night of war, he had taken one captive.

"Why you?" Kian murmured softly, staring at Elise on the ground. On the steel contraption he had found her in, she was the only one who saw him. No human should have been able to. Not only that, but the spell he had worked on them had no effect on her either.

Kian's own damn curiosity had made him stop Fionn from killing her, but maybe he shouldn't have. Kian had taught the fae that humans were worse than beasts and should be treated as such, but he hadn't been able to crush this bug. It was worse than embarrassing. He crouched down, trying to find an answer to what about her had him so thoroughly puzzled.

Sleep had taken the fear from her face, and with some horror, Kian realized that she was beautiful. She was the opposite of the fae females, softly curved and clearly no warrior. Her long hair was a messy tumble of looping dark curls that were silky soft to the touch.

When her eyes were open, they were big and blue, and as soft as the rest of her. Her full lips were open a little, and Kian had drunk enough mead that he didn't stop himself from running a thumb over them. She sighed in her sleep, her lips closing over him. Something about it made his long-dead desire flare to life. Kian pulled his hand away with a hiss, hating the sudden emotion.

"I should kill you," he said, hand going to his dagger and incisors lengthening. The thought of drinking the human dry made his desire flare hotter, and Kian rocked back from her.

Usually, the curse only made him hunger for blood on the full moon, which brought him right back to what the fuck was different about her.

Elise.

It couldn't only be that her blood was delicious. It was a flavor like something Kian felt he should be able to identify and couldn't. Like he had tasted it in a dream once and forgotten it. It was liquid magic and joy and warmth.

He thought it might've been because she was human, but he had tasted others that day in battle, and none of them was like hers. It was like drinking liquid light that warmed his coldest places. That one small sip from her hand was enough to replenish his strength and power to grow the castle easier than Kian imagined.

What in Arawan's name was she?

Kian was a scholar first and a warrior prince second. He would figure out what made his body and power react to her so strongly, and then, he would kill her when he was done.

Kian could do what he wanted with her. His gold shone on her wrists, a sign that she belonged only to him. That he was her master filled Kian with a dark and delicious delight. He had never had slaves before, abhorred the practice, but the first thing he did when he saw her was make her one so she would never escape him.

"All mine." Kian ran a hand down her side, letting his power creep over her. When he reached her small rib cage, he detected cracks in her fragile human bones and growled at Fionn's rough treatment of her. Without hesitating, Kian's magic healed her, and she began to breathe more deeply.

What are you doing? Kian stood up and stepped away from her. He had only possessed her a few hours and was already fighting impulses that he wasn't in control of.

If my brothers were here, they would tease me mercilessly for being so ridiculous.

He hated not being in control almost as much as he hated humans.

Kian gripped the hilt of his blade again, strode back to where she was, ready to drive it into her flesh. Elise murmured softly, a frown on her face, her fingers stretching and clenching like she was reaching for him.

"Fuck," he muttered, unable to do it when she was as helpless as a babe. There was no victory in that. Disgusted, Kian threw the knife at one of the tent posts where it embedded itself.

You just need to sleep. The curse is taking its toll on you, that's all.

He looked at the end of his braid and the remaining two inches of red in it. It was all the time he had left in the world. When the red turned white, he would die. He had fought the curse for fifteen hundred years and would barely have a handful of years left.

It hardly mattered. It was enough time. Kian would get his revenge on the humans for killing their babies before banishing them. He would laugh at the shade of the dead sorceress who had cursed him and his two brothers to horrid fates. They would die in a firestorm of death and burning blood, freezing ice and endless darkness, and go to Arawan's halls with righteous smiles on their faces.

Kian kicked off his boots and collapsed onto his large bed covered in furs. It was already colder there in Albion than it had been in Faerie. No sooner had the thought occurred to him than Kian was up again, putting a cloak over the human.

"By all the gods, you must be a witch," he grumbled and went back to bed.

5

Elise woke the next day, curled up underneath a black cloak that smelled of fir trees and smoke. It was past dawn, but the camp was barely waking from the night of partying. Someone had put some fruit and a jug of water near her. Sitting up, Elise realized her ribs no longer ached. In fact, there wasn't a bruise on her.

How is this possible? She had been covered in scratches and bruises the previous night from the ride. Had the wave of the prince's magic healed her? She had watched the cut on her hand close over, so anything was possible.

Elise sniffed the water and figured the fae could just stab her with one of their weapons if they wanted her dead. Her throat was parched, so she risked it. The water was the best thing she had ever tasted; cool and clear, she drank it all down. She was munching a mouthful of grapes before remembering the warnings about eating fae food.

Fuck, you really should've paid closer attention to Chrissy's warnings and stories.

Elise stilled when she spotted the prince, sprawled out on his bed, sleeping deeply. His hair was out of its braids and fanned out around him in silvery, red-tipped waves. He was, without a doubt, a beautiful monster.

Elise glanced up at the dagger in the post beside her and back to the sleeping prince. How many humans had he and his warriors killed yesterday? How many more would they kill when they woke? They were all drunk and hungover. Maybe she could get away and not be noticed. The gold on her wrists warmed as if it sensed her thoughts and made to warn her. Elise was bound to the prince, but if he were dead, he wouldn't find her.

She stood up, and grabbing the knife, Elise wiggled the blade until it came free of the wood. It was long and sharp, its hilt a polished cherry colored wood with gold designs. A prince's weapon. She swallowed hard, staring at the still sleeping fae.

Did she have it in her to plunge it into his chest? Elise licked her lips and gripped the knife tighter. She thought about a Bible story she'd liked when she was a kid, about a woman who had seduced and then cut off the head of an enemy general. He had been hell-bent on killing her people, and she wasn't going to sit back and let it happen.

It's not like you haven't taken a life before. A chill snaked through Elise's gut at the horrible memories the thought evoked. She fought them back, refusing to think of that night.

This could be the only chance she had to kill the prince and get away, no matter how much the act destroyed what was left of her battered soul.

Elise trembled as she crept closer, watching the rise and fall of his bare, muscled chest. With every step, the taste of his blood grew stronger in her mouth, the scent of fir trees emanating from him. She had the sudden terrifying desire to bury her face in the crook of his neck and breathe him in. It had to be some kind of fae self-defense trick, and damn if it wasn't working on her.

Fight it, Elise.

Her palms sweat and heart raced as she reached his bedside. Human's fucked up fascination with beauty was working against her as she looked down at him. Even with the antlers, he was the most handsome man she had ever seen. It was an eerie, alien beauty, but no less lovely.

Think of the people on the train. The blood and screams rattled through her. The horror of watching people tear themselves apart. *All because of this beautiful monster.*

Elise turned the dagger down, its wicked blade pointing at the center of his chest, and gripped it tighter. The taste of him in her mouth was overpowering, but she swallowed it down, fighting the impulse to climb in beside him and kiss his sleeping lips.

You can do this. He's going to kill you in some horrible way, you know it.

Elise lifted the dagger above her head and drove it down as hard as she could. Strong hands grabbed her wrists, the blade stopping an inch from his skin. Red eyes opened, and a violent smile spread across the prince's face.

"Too slow," he hissed. He moved, and suddenly, Elise was pinned to the bed, his massive body between her legs. Elise tried to wriggle and kick out at him, but he pressed in harder so she couldn't connect with anything. The knife was still between them, so she tried to shove it up. The prick only chuckled at her efforts.

"So you have some fight in you after all. That's good to know."

The tip of the blade pressed into his chest, and golden amber blood dripped onto her. At the sight of it, Elise let the dagger go in shock. The horror of seeing his blood sent a strange panic through her, drowning out all of her burning, violent thoughts. She wanted to put her lips over the cut and kiss it better so badly that her mouth watered.

"I-I'm sorry," Elise stammered, putting her hand over the cut as if it could somehow stop the bleeding. The prince frowned down at her and drove the dagger into the mattress.

"You really are a terrible assassin, Elise. You're not meant to apologize for a scratch."

"Do I get points for trying?" she asked. That made him laugh and shake his head.

"No. You get punished," he replied and gripped her wrist, pulling it away from his chest and onto the bed. Elise tried to struggle again and throw him off, but it was futile. With one hand, he pinned her hands above her head, and the other gripped the front of Elise's shirt and pulled. The buttons popped open, revealing a black lace bra. It seemed to surprise and distract him, his red eyes heating the longer he stared at it.

Elise wriggled again, but a warning growl in the back of his throat made her freeze. He pulled out the dagger from the bed and pressed the tip to the skin of her chest.

Panic raced through her. "I promise I won't try and kill you again, even though you kidnapped me."

"Oh, I know you won't. I'm going to make sure of it."

"Please don't cut my tits off," she begged.

"Why would I do that?" he asked, his lips lifting in a sensual smile. "They are pleasing to look at." Elise held her breath as the tip of the blade touched the skin on the curve of her breast, making a small cut. "You cut me, I cut you."

"So we are even?" she asked, hopefully.

"Not even close. I've killed people for slighter offenses, but I'm going to make sure that you don't ever try it again." The prince lowered his head to the small amount of blood beading up from the cut and licked. Elise shuddered underneath him and not from fear.

What the hell is wrong with you?

He hummed against her skin, his sharp teeth scraping against it but not breaking it. The sound turned to a growl, and he flipped her so Elise was on top of him. She managed to scramble backward an inch before his hand clamped on her bicep and held her in place.

"Drink," he commanded. His other hand went to the back of Elise's head, pushing it towards the still bleeding cut on his chest. She pulled away, but his fingers tightened in her hair.

"No-" Elise couldn't fight him as her lips mashed onto his hot skin.

"Drink, or I'll have no choice but to kill you," he said, and she stopped fighting. Sweet liquid spring flooded her mouth, and Elise whimpered and swallowed. Burning heat and magic raced through her veins as her lips moved against his skin, savoring it. He swore when she tongued the cut again, high on the taste of him.

"Elise," he said, sitting up and loosening the grip on her hair. Elise's mouth came off him with a pop. She stared up in wide-eyed horror at what she'd done, at the desire tightening her chest. She could feel his dick hard underneath her and knew she wasn't the only one suddenly turned on by the enemy.

"Look at me," he commanded, and her eyes automatically opened, looking directly at his. "Say, 'I, Elise, will never raise my hand in violence to Prince Kian ever again.'" His magic inside of her took hold of her tongue without consent.

"I, Elise, will never raise my hand in violence to Prince Kian ever again," she whispered, her tongue curling around the feel of it. Kee-an. She had his name like he had hers. Elise raised a brow. "Your name is Kian?"

"Yes."

"And that's what I'm meant to call you?"

"Not if you want to keep breathing." He lifted her off him and did the buttons back up on her shirt. "You call me Master like everyone else." He got up and put a shirt on, the cut on his chest already closed.

And licked clean. She shook her head, still unable to believe what she'd done. *What the fuck just happened?*

"Are all fae vampires?" Elise asked, and his head snapped up. "You drink blood. Do the others?"

"No. Only me," Kian replied, pulling on a leather holster over his shoulders that contained a sword hanging down his back and a variety of mean-looking daggers. "And I'm not a vampire. I'm cursed. There's a difference."

"Good to know I'm not going to be cut and sucked on by everyone-" Elise began, but he was suddenly standing next to her, his hand gripping the golden cuffs around her wrists and eyes blazing with fury.

"These say you belong to me. *My* slave. If anyone lays a hand on you, they lose that hand." She nodded, and he let go. The prince lifted the cloak off the ground and wrapped it around her. For someone who had just claimed she was a slave, it was a strangely considerate thing to do. Elise must've looked as confused as she felt because he cursed.

"It's cold outside," he said irritably and pulled on a fur-lined black jacket. "It's time I find a use for you so you're too busy to plot ways to kill me."

"I'll make time for that," Elise whispered under her breath, but he still heard.

Kian's smile was sharp like the blades he carried. "You're always welcome to try again."

6

It was sleeting outside, and the ground was frozen solid. Elise clutched Kian's cloak around her shoulders, wishing she had proper boots on and not the fashionable ones that she only ever used for office work.

Elise stared up in terrifying awe at the hulking castle that had grown up overnight. It had six towers and looked like it had been carved from a single block of obsidian.

"Don't dawdle," snapped Kian ahead of her, and she hurried to catch up to his long strides. The small smile he'd worn in the tent was gone, and only the terrifying prince she'd met on the train remained. She still couldn't believe that she had tried to stab him, and he hadn't killed her. She had seen how ruthless he could be.

Be smart and stay alive, her father's voice echoed through her head.

The few fae that were awake bowed to the prince and stared at Elise with a mixture of curiosity and disgust. She tried to keep her eyes focused on Kian's back, his words about no one touching her oddly comforting.

Not that Elise trusted him not to kill her whenever he wanted. Just because she tried to kill him and stayed alive didn't mean she was dumb enough to think he wouldn't choose to get his revenge whenever he wanted.

I cut him. He cut me. Elise hoped that it would work the same way if she didn't try and kill him, he would let her live. It was a fool's hope, but she had to hang onto whatever kind of hope she had.

Behind the high castle walls was a large stable yard, already full of fae warriors attending to the horses. The horses were the biggest Elise had ever seen, with shaggy manes and feet. There were stone troughs next to the stalls that were big enough that she could've used them as a bath. The warriors bowed low to the prince, who gave them a nod as they walked past and in through a wooden back door.

Inside, the kitchen was a flurry of activity. Unlike the warriors, who looked more or less humanoid despite the pointed ears and horns here and there, the fae in the kitchens were more what Elise had imagined from the stories. They looked like nature had sexy liaisons with humans and ended up with wild children with leaves for hair or butterfly wings. She tried not to stare but couldn't help it.

"Oh, master! What are you doing coming in through the back door?" A short, squat fae with bark skin and unruly hair made from vines and budding flowers stood with clawed hands on her wide hips.

"Forgive me, Hedera, I didn't want to cause a fuss," Kian said, giving her a dashing smile that seemed to pacify her, at least until she saw Elise.

"Master, what is *that* behind you?" she said, her face screwing up like Elise was something he had stepped in.

"I was hoping you could find a use for her."

"It's a human, so it'll have plenty of meat. I could make something with pastry-"

Kian chuckled. "No, Hedera, she's my new pet. Not for eating," he clarified and then flashed his fangs at Elise. "At least not yet."

The kitchen tittered with laughter, and she tried not to tell them all to go fuck themselves. Elise's bravery had its limits, but her anger was abundant.

"Well, master, I suppose we have to find some use for their kind in general when you conquer Albion."

Conquer Albion? She couldn't be serious. Albion was the ancient name for England, and the humans wouldn't allow anyone to conquer it. Elise risked a glance at Kian and wished she hadn't hesitated so much with the dagger. Her cuffs heated again, and the vow she'd made never to hurt him made her tongue ache.

Oh, you fucker. The prince seemed to know precisely what Elise was thinking because his smug smile widened.

"I'm sure she's good at something," he said.

"Well, you were a bit too enthusiastic with the castle building yesterday, and most of the rooms are a mess. I'll make her clean them," Hedera replied, wiping her hands on an apron.

"Excellent. Don't worry about her running away. If she leaves the castle grounds, I'll know." This was more of a warning for Elise than a reassurance to Hedera. His scarlet eyes flashed as he looked over her. "Keep her out of the northern tower. I don't want it smelling like a human. I get enough of their stench on the battlefield." He left the kitchen without a backward glance, leaving Elise alone with his frowning servants.

Hedera looked her over again like she was assessing Elise's usefulness for hard labor. "Can't imagine why he'd want you except for food."

Maybe because I saw through his glamours, and he likes to have someone to torment. Elise didn't dare mention that. The fact she saw him on the train seemed to confuse him, and maybe it meant she could see through any of the glamours that the other fae tried to trick her with. Elise didn't say anything, so Hedera grunted and shoved a mop and wooden bucket into her hands as well as some cloths.

"This way, slave, and don't spill that water, or I'll beat you bloody," she said and opened another door.

Elise followed her into a series of long hallways with archways and high ceilings made of obsidian. She didn't dare stop and look at the strange and beautiful murals on the walls. The same insignias were repeated all through the castle; a pair of antlers, a blade of ice, and black wings. At the center of each was a cluster of roses.

Hedera might have been short, but she moved quickly, and Elise had to work to keep up and not drop everything. Hedera pushed open a set of wooden doors covered in vines of bronze. They had small white flowers blooming from them, and when Elise passed them, she saw that they were real. She went to touch one, and Hedera slapped her hand away.

"Hurry up!" she barked. They went through the doors and into a feast hall with one long massive table. Chairs, candlesticks, cutlery, and china were scattered about the room as if it had been in a snow globe and shaken.

"Put this room back together, dust and mop it," she said, and with one final glare, stomped off.

Elise stared at the chaos around her. She fucking *hated* cleaning, but maybe she'd be left alone to figure out a way around the castle. Just because she had magical cuffs around her wrists didn't mean she wasn't planning on running away as soon as possible. If the prince really was trying to conquer England, then he would be too busy to worry about what a lowly slave was doing. *Here's hoping.*

Elise studied the cuffs around her wrists. The gold was in one entirely forged piece, not a catch or hinge that could be used as a weakness. Gold was a soft metal, but she needed tools to cut or saw through it. She wasn't going to hang about and let the prince use her before he got bored and decided to bake her into a pie.

Elise started to lift the heavy, carved wooden chairs and arrange them around the table, all the while making plans on how to get the hell out of there.

7

Elise needed to pee so badly that her stomach was aching. The sun had only just set, but she couldn't wait for her regular late-night visit to the outhouses.

Move quickly, and they won't see you.

Checking outside the kitchen door, Elise took a quick, cautious step into the shadows. Fae warriors had returned earlier and were drinking around their tents. If she was careful, she could avoid them altogether. Elise thought she'd soil herself by the time she finally made it, locking the door behind her so no one would accidentally walk in, and breathed a sigh of relief.

It had been weeks since Elise was taken from the train, and she had learned a lot in that time. Mostly, how to hide.

In the beginning, she had been naïve enough to think that if she did as she was told and behaved, she would become an invisible fixture in the castle and be ignored. That was impossible because the fae were in equal parts disgusted and intrigued by Elise and weren't about to forget she was there for a minute.

Elise had taken to sleeping by the fireplace in the kitchens at night wrapped in Kian's cloak that still seemed to smell more like him than her. She had woken up more than once from someone poking her with long implements to see if she was real. Elise was polite enough not to do the same to them, even though no two of them were alike in appearance. They all smelled differently, too, especially the ones with the flowers growing on them. The food they prepared, while recognizable, was often created using magic as another utensil. It was hard not to watch them work, even if they snapped and snarled at her.

When Elise was awake, she was stared at by every passing fae and occasionally spat on by the warriors. The lesser fae stayed out of the way of the warriors for good reason. They were fierce and beautiful to look at, but they were assholes one and all.

Elise had tried to leave the castle grounds only once. She wanted to see what her limits were and if she'd be stopped at all. She had waited until the dead of night and made a run for it. She had managed three steps out of the castle gates, and the cuffs had burned so severely, Elise had almost screamed and woken everyone.

She had run back through the gates, sobbing and stomach heaving in pain, even though the skin under the cuffs wasn't burned. She hadn't tried it again but refused to give up on finding some kind of a tool to get the cursed bloody things off her.

Elise's days turned into a blur of scrubbing, dusting, and arranging. Her hands were red and dry from the hours spent trying to clean up the disarrayed castle. She would collapse on the warm stones by the fireplace at night with whatever crusts Hedera tossed her if she remembered to feed her at all. It was the worst diet she had ever been on.

Elise knew where all the best hiding spots were about the grounds and only used the communal washhouses and toilets when everyone had gone to bed. She tried to keep her clothes clean but learned that you really could wear the same pair of underwear four times before washing them.

Elise also did her best to eavesdrop on conversations, desperate for news of the outside world. The fae warriors would come and go sporadically, and the castle staff would titter with gossip.

"Londinium is burning!"

"The bloodlines have been discovered!"

"Hung them along the banks of the river!"

"Justice!"

They would cry in their variety of harsh and soft voices. Londinium was what London had been called during the Roman period, and Elise realized that most of the fae were ancient as the stones.

That London was burning filled her with gut-churning terror. Elise had seen what the prince's screwed up magic had done to the people on the train. She hoped and prayed that Chrissy was safe, that she had somehow gotten out of whatever fighting was going on there.

Elise wanted to know what they meant by 'justice' but was too scared of asking when their blood was up and cheering for the death of humans.

Did they really think humans wouldn't retaliate? What could their swords and battle woad do against tanks and machine guns? The fae would be slaughtered, the castle bombed by a drone and her along with it.

But the fae had *magic*, something humans had long stopped knowing how to use or believe in. And the fae had the prince. Every fae was loyal to him, no matter their station. Thankfully, Elise never saw any sign of him. She had gathered from overheard conversations that he was moving with the army.

Elise also heard whispers of his brother in the north of Scotland, who had turned it into another ice age for all of the winter fae to live in. There was a third brother, but he was the Voldemort of the lot. Everyone was too scared to talk about him; even a passing mention got hushed like he lived in the air and would be able to know if anyone was talking shit about him.

For all Elise's sneaking about and listening in on conversations, she didn't learn the one thing she really wanted to know. Why did they want to kill the humans in the first place?

Now she was waiting for the prince to return or for the humans to attack. Every night, she congratulated herself for surviving another day.

Elise was scrubbing her hands and face as horses thundered into the castle grounds, their powerful hooves making the earth shake. She crept out of the outhouses and into a nook in the obsidian wall of the castle to make sure none of the horses trampled her.

The army is back. That can't be good.

Hot, golden light started to burn in Elise's chest, her mouth flooding with honey and spring, and she knew the prince was close by. Elise's treacherous brain remembered him pinning her down underneath him, the hot feeling going straight to her core. Disgusted at the thought, she spat on the grass, trying to get rid of the taste of him, pissed off that whatever magic he did to her still hadn't worn off.

One day it will, and I'll get that knife into his heart.

A man's cries cut through the night, and Elise moved from the nook, slipping like a shadow along the castle walls' jagged stone roots.

A human was on his knees, a ring of fae warriors around him. Standing before him like a golden god was the prince in full armor. Elise hadn't seen him since he dumped her with Hedera, and now he was in front of her. A twisted part of her was relieved to see him in one piece.

It's only his magic fucking with you, Elise. Get it together.

"Please, please don't hurt me," the man begged.

"Did the female fae that you were caught trying to rape plead for her life, human?" the prince asked, his voice cold. "She was collecting water by a stream, not hurting anyone. Innocent. What gave you the right to attack her?"

"S-she bewitched me and—" the man on the ground screamed as his hand hit the dirt in front of him. Elise didn't see the prince move, but his sword was suddenly out and dripping blood. She gagged, her hands clutching the edge of the wall so she didn't collapse.

"I know the female, and she isn't strong enough to bewitch anyone, you lying filth. You ambushed her, and you put your disgusting human hands on her," the prince continued, and the other hand came off the man's body.

He was writhing and wailing on the ground, covered in his own blood. The prince's expression didn't change, devoid of all compassion, and his sword took off the man's legs with one swipe. Elise vomited at her feet, unable to hold in her horror.

The man's cries were silenced as the prince took off his screaming head.

"Deliver that to the nearest humans with a warning that if anyone touches a fae, they will meet the same fate," he said to the warriors. He sheathed his sword, and then his head twisted towards Elise's hiding place. She ducked, terrified he had seen her.

How did he even know I was there? Elise looked down at her bleeding palms from where she had clutched at the wall. *Can he smell it?*

After a few terrifying minutes, Elise risked peeking around the wall again. The prince and the warriors were gone, leaving only a wide pool of blood steaming on the ground.

She ran back to the kitchen door, stumbling in the dark and landing hard on her side. Her knees barked in pain, but she scrambled back to her feet without stopping.

The kitchens were full of activity when Elise came back in, shaking and pale and stomach hurting. One of the chefs with ram horns hissed at her when she accidentally bumped into him.

"I'm sorry," Elise said quickly.

"Get out, slave!" he shouted. She did as she was told, hoping to find a quiet place in the rest of the castle to hide until everyone had gone to bed for the night. Elise hugged her arms around herself, fighting the urge to throw up again for the man's fate, even though she didn't know why. He had been a rapist. It wasn't like he was some innocent, but she couldn't seem to stop the pity clawing at her.

"Well, well, I thought I smelled something," a harsh voice said behind her.

Shit. Elise turned slowly to see a fae warrior standing behind her. He had a horn of mead in one hand and was looking at her with a vicious light in his eyes. Two other laughing warriors joined the first.

"What prey have you sniffed out, Aiden?" one of them said. Elise took a step back, getting ready to run, but suddenly, Aiden was standing behind her.

"Where are you running, human?"

Don't say anything. Don't provoke them. If they are bored, they'll go away.

"Maybe it's mute," one of the warriors said, reaching out a finger to poke at her. Elise knocked his hand away, her fear turning to anger.

"Oh, look out, Owain, she doesn't like that," Aiden said. He held out his hand to her, a small, glazed cake in it. "Maybe you'd like this instead?"

Elise's stomach cramped again, and when she looked at the cake, its perfection blurred, and she saw a rotting piece of moldy bread. The fae warriors laughed and Aiden moved towards her.

"Come on, it's delicious," he said, in a gently mocking voice. Elise clenched her fists, re-opening the cuts on her palms. The pain kept her mind focused as the glamour hit her again.

No! Get out! Elise shook her head, trying to step away and bumping into a warrior cutting her off. He grabbed her hands, holding them behind her back. Elise squirmed, trying to shake him off.

"Let me go!" she shouted, and they all laughed.

"She can talk after all," Aiden said and held out the rotting bread. "Time to eat up, slave."

Elise pulled her head away, but the fae holding her yanked her arms up. Aiden shoved the bread against her mouth, its disgusting moldy taste hitting her tongue as he forced it past her lips. Elise spat it out, flecks of soggy bread hitting Aiden in the face. He wiped it off his cheek before backhanding her hard.

Elise sagged, lights dancing in front of her eyes, and the fae holding her arms dropped her to the floor. Blood was pouring out of her lip and nose, the cruel, laughing faces blurring as they stared down at her.

"You're going to pay for that," Aiden said, pulling her legs apart and throwing his weight on top of her.

Oh, hell no. Elise screamed, lashing out at him with her fists. He battered her away and pressed a knife to her throat. She stilled, her anger vanishing and fear returning like a switch had been flicked.

Aiden chuckled, and with his free hand, he gripped the front of her shirt and tore it open. His green eyes glowed with a combination of madness and lust. He grabbed her left breast and squeezed it.

"What is going on here?" the prince's voice said, his tone cutting through the warrior's revelry like a cold blade.

"Nothing, just having a little fun with this human," Aiden said, not looking up. He was too far gone to notice that his friends had backed away. "You're welcome to join in. Maybe we should strip her and make her run around the castle while we hunt her."

Aiden lifted his hand to grope Elise's other breast. Blood showered over her as the hand came off. Aiden cried out, the prince's boot kicking him in the shoulder and off her. Elise was too scared to move, head still ringing and sight blurred.

"Are you having fun yet?" the prince asked, in the same terrifying voice.

"She's just a filthy human!" Aiden said, clutching his bloody stump.

"But she is *my* filthy human, or did you not see the gold around her wrists? If anyone is going to torment her, it is going to be me." The prince kicked the amputated hand at him. "You will wear that around your neck so everyone will know what happens when they touch my things. Now all of you get the fuck out of my sight."

Aiden was wise enough not to argue, picking up his hand from the floor and bowing to the prince before hurrying away.

"Hedera!" The prince's voice bellowed through the halls, and the housekeeper popped out of the air beside him.

"Master." She jumped when she saw Elise lying on the floor, covered in blood.

"I told you to take care of her. Why is my slave in such a state?" he demanded.

"With respect, master, you told me to find her work to do," Hedera replied.

"I thought keeping her clean, fed, and clothed would be obvious."

"She's just a human."

"I don't care. Even my slaves are representatives of my household. There are over a hundred rooms in this castle, give her one. Make sure she has a bath and some fresh clothes. I have to look at her too, and I want her presentable as I want all my servants," the prince snarled, and Hedera flinched.

"Yes, master."

"Arawan damn me, it's like I have to do everything myself in this place." He turned on his heel and strode away. It wasn't until he had disappeared that Elise dared to sit up.

Don't throw up again. You can do this.

Hedera didn't bother to help her up. Her black, beady eyes glared as

Elise struggled to her feet. She might hate her, but Hedera wasn't about to anger the prince.

"Follow me, girl. Try not to ruin the floors by dripping all over them."

Biting her tongue, Elise clutched what was left of her dirty shirt and hobbled after her.

8

Hedera led Elise to a room in the southern tower, opening the door with a touch of her hand. Lanterns on the wall flicked to life, revealing a room as trashed as the others had been. She raised her hands and clapped three times. The furniture righted itself, the dust and cobwebs swirling in the air and out of the open window.

Get fucked. Elise had been breaking herself to clean the rooms by hand, and Hedera could do this? It gave Elise one more reason to hate her.

"I'll return shortly with food. Get cleaned up," Hedera said. She gave Elise a disapproving look. "What's so special about you that you deserve such attention?"

"Absolutely nothing," Elise said honestly. She was just a girl who had been unfortunate enough to be on the wrong train at the wrong time. If she hadn't squeezed herself onto that train and waited for the next one, she would never have been in this situation. Hedera grunted and pointed to a door on the other side of the room.

Inside was a bathroom and a toilet tucked away in its own space like a big wooden closet. When Elise turned the taps on in the deep tub, she was surprised to find hot water rushing out of it. She peeled off her filthy clothes and went to the basin.

Elise's reflection stared back at her in the large, polished mirror. She barely recognized her gaunt, blood-splattered face. Her split lip was already swollen, nose seeping blood, and her long brown hair was a snarled, oily mess. Elise turned on the taps, hissing through her teeth as she cleaned the cuts on her palms. Drinking handfuls of water, she tried to get the taste of blood and rotting bread out of her mouth.

When Elise opened a basin cupboard, she found an old-fashioned toothbrush with coarse bristles and a bar smelling of mint beside it. Wetting the brush, she rubbed it against the bar before using it to clean her teeth for the first time since she was taken.

Elise dragged her hands through her filthy braid, and satisfied that most of the blood was off her, she stepped into the bathtub. Biting back a sob, she sat down into the hot, clean water. It was the first time she had been properly warm in weeks.

There were small vials and soaps in a carved shelf beside the tub. Elise opened them and sniffed experimentally. Fir trees and smoke. *The scent of the prince.* She put it down and tried another. Fir trees and smoke. They were all exactly the same. Elise didn't know if it was magic or just his preference because it was his castle. She didn't want to smell of him but was more interested in getting clean. Giving in, she tipped the contents of one over her greasy hair.

It took a long time for her to feel really clean again. The water in the tub stayed hot the whole time, even though Elise knew she'd been in there for at least an hour. It was the color of the water and not the temperature that made her get out. She dried herself with one of the linen towels and went back into her room to find something clean to wear.

Hedera must have returned while Elise was in the bath because a tray of food had been left on a small table. The smell of hot food reached her nose and her stomach grumbled.

Elise opened a carved wooden wardrobe that looked like it could have Narnia hiding in the back of it. Unfortunately, like all the wardrobes she had searched as a child, there was no doorway into another world. There were shirts and trousers and a blue robe that she wrapped herself in to keep warm. She pulled open a drawer and found underwear and socks. Creepily, everything looked like it was her exact size.

Elise pulled out a pair of black pants and a shirt and put them on. If she hadn't seen the prince get dressed, she doubted she'd have been able to figure out the wrap-around style of the shirt and its multiple ties.

Elise was combing out her knotty hair when the door opened, and the prince came in. His armor was gone, his hair still damp from his own bath. When he was like this, she could only think of him as Kian, not the prince, and Elise hated the intimacy of it. He crossed his arms and stared at her.

"How are you feeling?" he asked gruffly.

"Fine." Elise stopped herself from thanking him.

Fuck him.

She might have a room now, but she was still a slave and couldn't trust a single damn act of kindness.

"You look sick."

Elise had an overwhelming urge to hurl the brush at his perfect face. His lips lifted in a snarl like he could read the violence in her face.

"You don't have the strength to take me on, Elise, even if the vow you took allowed it," he said. A thrill swept over her when he said her name, and it made Elise hate him even more. Kian sat on one of the stuffed velvet chairs opposite her.

"Show me your hands," he commanded.

Elise put the brush down and held them out, the golden cuffs shining in the lamplight. He turned her hands over, inspecting the ragged slices and dry, cracking skin of her palms. Kian pulled a small jar from his pocket and opened it. Inside was a pale-yellow balm, and he began rubbing it into her skin.

What the hell.

Elise had watched him decapitating people with all the emotion of a glacier, and now he was gently tending to her wounds. *This guy has some severe split personality disorder.*

"Why haven't you eaten in the weeks I have been away?" Kian demanded, not looking up from her palms.

"You're assuming I have been fed," Elise replied, trying and failing to keep the anger out of her voice. Kian growled in the back of his throat but didn't look up. He turned her hands over and continued massaging her aching wrists. His long fingers moved against her skin in small circles, making her tongue stick to the roof of her mouth. She looked away and focused on the curves of his antlers instead. That was a mistake because she got the urge to touch them to make sure that they were really there.

Just his stupid magic inside of you making you enjoy this. Remember the man's screams and London burning.

"You're quiet. I thought you would be yelling at me," Kian said.

"I didn't know I was required to talk to you, master," Elise replied obediently, if a touch sarcastic. She couldn't help it.

Kian's scarlet eyes flicked up to hers, filled with a heat that wasn't anger. A touch of excitement danced up Elise's spine like she had poked a bear, and now it wanted to eat her.

"I suppose you shouldn't. Familiarity breeds contempt, and I'm still determined to kill you," he replied.

Elise had plenty of contempt without the familiarity. "Like you killed the people in London?"

"I killed those who deserved it."

"What did they do to you? Fight back when you tried to turn them all mad?"

His fangs flashed. "They were the bloodlines of the betrayers. Betray a vow to the fae, and it doesn't matter how many years pass, the fae will make you pay for it."

The anger in his voice made Elise shut her mouth against the hundred questions that burned on her tongue. She had been hit enough for one day to want to push her luck with him.

"What is your trade?" Kian asked, releasing her hands.

"What does it matter?"

"I need to find a use for you because hard labor doesn't suit you. Your body isn't built for it."

"Books," Elise answered reluctantly. "I'm trained to restore and preserve books."

"You can write too?"

"Of course, I can write."

"Don't sound so offended, Elise. Not many of your kind could when I last interacted with them. Only the Thorn King's priests were really proficient in the art, and there wasn't many of those in Albion."

The Thorn King...did he mean Christian priests? She didn't ask. Elise was torn between wanting to talk to him and wanting to remain defiantly silent.

Kian's fingers stroked Elise's jaw, making her lift her head. She held her breath as he dabbed some of the balm on her busted lip. His thumb moved slowly over her lips, and Elise didn't think of the stinging cut or how much she hated him. She thought about gently sucking that finger into her mouth. The air charged between them, and Kian let his hand drop.

"Go and eat," he said huskily.

Elise got up, needing to put some space between them. She shook her head, trying to clear the crazy out of it. What the hell was wrong with her? She lifted one of the silver covers and found roasted pheasant meat and vegetables. Her hand closed around the knife, and she slanted a look in Kian's direction. His face lit up with amusement.

"You could try to kill me again, little slave, but it will end the same way with you helpless beneath me." His cockiness filled Elise with rage, and she threw the knife at him. She didn't get a chance to see where it landed before magic burned through her, driving her to her knees.

Kian stood over Elise, laughter bubbling out of him. She glared up at him and realized she was at the same height as the ties on his leather pants.

Great, now I have his dick bulge in my face.

"Forgot about that little vow you made, did you?" he asked.

"Fuck you," she snarled.

"Don't give me ideas." His hand cupped her cheek. "Fight me as much as you want, Elise. I like seeing you on your knees in front of me with your pretty mouth open." She shut it so quickly her teeth hurt. He ran his fingers through Elise's hair, staring mesmerized at the dark strands as they fell.

"Why are you killing my kind?" she asked. His dazed look sharpened, and Kian stepped back from her.

"The oath-breakers killed mine first," Kian replied. He moved towards the bedroom door. "Make sure you eat."

As soon as he was gone, the magic released her, and Elise slumped forward onto the floor. Shaking from the after-effects, she managed to get onto a chair and pick up a fork. Elise wanted to throw the tray out the nearest window, but she was too hungry. Cursing the prince, she did as she was told and ate.

9

The next day, Elise didn't wake up until the milky winter sun was high in the sky. For some reason, Hedera had let her sleep and left another tray of food. Elise washed her face and, through bleary eyes, saw that the cut on her lip was almost fully healed.

"What was in that balm?" Elise murmured. Her hands were the same, fine scars crossing her palms from where she had gripped the obsidian wall. She wasn't going to question it. The prince could have left her to suffer but hadn't, so she grudgingly counted her blessings.

Elise was finishing off the pastry and tea when Hedera appeared out of thin air again.

"I have a new job for you," she said stiffly, folding her arms.

Elise pulled on a pair of warm, knee-high leather boots and a jacket from the wardrobe. "I'm ready."

Hedera only grunted at her, and Elise followed her through the castle. It was eerily quiet, and when she stared out of the windows, she saw that the army was gone and probably the prince with it. Something inside of Elise clenched in concern, but she ignored it and tried to get her bearings.

They were in a part of the castle that she'd never visited before.

Leaves and vines grew from the walls, white roses blooming and filling the air with their sweet fragrance.

"What is this place?" Elise asked, running her fingers along a row of blooms.

"This is the northern tower, and if you value your pathetic life, you will only go to the room I show you to," Hedera snapped. "Being his favorite won't stop the prince from killing you if you trespass into his rooms."

"Understood," Elise replied.

She was instantly curious to go through all of his stuff and fantasized about trashing his room and life the way he had done to hers.

All malicious thoughts died when Hedera opened a pair of carved green and black doors. Lanterns flickered on with a snap of her fingers, the two massive chandeliers hanging from the cavernous ceiling glittered with glass birds and woodland creatures.

Elise's hand came over her mouth as an excited, delighted laugh escaped her lips. She was in a library. It was trashed like the rest of the castle, but God, it was beautiful.

The shelves were all carved like trees, with unfamiliar animals and birds dancing in their branches. The books were in piles where they had fallen off the shelves, but most of the furniture was upright.

"The prince wants you to clean this up and get the books in order," Hedera said and vanished, leaving her alone.

Elise had a bit of a *Beauty and the Beast* moment as she wandered through the aisles of the library. It wasn't hers, and she wasn't about to break into a song, but she was giddy as she bent down and picked up a codex, bound in green leather. Elise flipped it open and was dazzled by the paintings inside of eerie and alien landscapes. *Faerie.*

Placing it down on the table, she picked up another and was surprised to find it written in Koine Greek. It was a copy of Hesiod's *Precepts of Chiron*. Elise's Greek was a bit rusty, but she knew the significance of what she was holding. The poem was composed to record the wise centaur's lessons that he had taught to heroes like Achilles and Jason. It had only survived in fragments, but there was a whole and completed copy in a fae prince's library.

"Breathe, girl, don't let it go to your head," Elise whispered, clutching the book to her chest. She put it down on the other end of the table and reached for another. This one was written in a language that she'd never seen before. Figuring it was probably fae, she placed it on top of the book of paintings.

Elise lost herself in the books she was picking up, her piles growing as she tried to sort them out into languages. She cleared one pile off the floor and started on another finding more books in Greek and Latin that she could recognize.

Elise forgot she was a slave. She forgot that the world outside the castle was burning. She forgot everything except the treasures she was discovering.

She was so caught up in her own head that Elise overlooked the weird thrumming some of the books were giving off. She picked up one held together with a strangely shaped iron latch and opened it.

Shadows exploded out of the pages, and Elise dropped it with a startled shout. Clouds formed into tentacles, wrapping around her ankles and dragging her to the floor. Elise screamed, fighting the grip the ethereal force had on her. She grabbed one of the table legs and hung on as it yanked her hard. More tentacles slithered up her body and tightened around her waist. Her fingers started to slip, nails tearing before it pulled her free.

Books scattered as Elise was thrown across the floor, the shadows dragging her towards the flapping, black pages of the tome. Golden light flashed above her, and the carnivorous book screeched. The tentacles holding her turned back to smoke, and the book shut with a resounding crack, Kian's foot holding the cover down as he bent and latched it again.

"What in Arawan's name are you doing?" he hissed, tossing the infernal book on the table.

"Cleaning," Elise groaned, one hand rubbing her bruised ribs. "What the hell was that thing?"

"A book you had no business touching. You should know better than to open books of magic when you have no experience with them."

Elise pulled herself up on wobbly feet and brushed the dust off her pants. "Well, I didn't know it was magical, did I?"

Kian made a frustrated sound at the back of his throat.

"What are you doing here, anyway?" Elise asked before she could check herself.

"I can go where I please in my own castle, slave," he hissed. He folded his arms, highlighting how broad his chest was and how deep the open V of his shirt. *Stupid, handsome fae.*

"It was lucky I happened to need a book; otherwise, you would be suffering a fate worse than death right now."

"Because being a slave to a fae prince is such a dream come true," Elise muttered.

"There are worse fates than being my slave, or have you forgotten Aiden's attentions so soon?"

Elise quickly bit her tongue, determined not to provoke him further. The library was better than cleaning the rest of the castle, even with its psychotic, sentient books.

"Is there a way to know which books I shouldn't open?" she asked as politely as she could manage.

"How about none of them."

Elise put her hands on her hips. "Then how am I supposed to organize this place? By color?"

Kian's scarlet eyes narrowed, and she raised her chin. *Insufferable bastard.*

"I can do a spell so that you will know which ones are normal books and which ones are magic. It will also allow you to read every book in here no matter the language," he said through gritted teeth.

"Then do it."

Kian shifted, looking uncomfortable. "It's not that simple. Language belongs to the tongue. I would have to kiss you to do it."

Elise's stupid stomach flipped. "Thanks, but I'd rather get eaten by a monster book."

"You and me both. You think I want to kiss a disgusting human?" he snarled in her face.

"About as much as I want to kiss an arrogant fae dick."

"I don't want you anywhere near my dick."

"Does it have horns too?" Elise retorted.

"You'll never find out." Kian looked at her shirt and rolled his eyes.

"Gods, you can't even dress properly. How did I get cursed with such a useless slave?"

Elise looked down at how she'd laced her shirt and shrugged. "It's closed." He reached over and pulled two of the strings out of their bows. Elise smacked his hand away, and he hissed at her so feral she halted in shock.

Kian undid the laces of Elise's shirt until it was hanging open, and she was flashing the red bandeau that passed as a bra amongst the fae. He stared at her bare skin, making heat climb up Elise's chest to her cheeks. Muttering something under his breath, Kian pulled the shirt closed again, tying them the opposite way to what she had them.

"Happy now?" She couldn't resist asking, humiliated that a grown man had decided to dress her like a child.

"Not even a little. You need to be useful, and I need this library fixed, so as much as I hate it, you're going to need magic to assist you," Kian said, stepping forward into her space.

Elise stepped back and bumped into the table. His arms came down either side of her, trapping her. "Stay still. This will be over before you know it."

Kian bent his head and put his lips softly to hers. His magic rushed over her tongue, tasting of spring and honey, blood and smoke. A small groan caught in her throat as heat and desire shot up her spine. Elise's mouth tingled, moving against and craving more of him.

Kian's hands went to her hips, gripping tight before lifting Elise up on the table. Her legs wrapped around him, holding him close, her hands moving over his chest and into his hair.

Kian grabbed Elise's braid and pulled her head back so he could control the kiss, deepening it until her lips and body ached. His tongue brushed up against hers, and Elise was swamped again by the taste of his magic. Her teeth closed on his bottom lip, and a low growl rumbled through Kian's chest.

"Infernal human, you disgust me," he panted against Elise's mouth. Her hands were bunched in his white hair, and she pulled on it, making him hiss.

"Good, because I fucking hate you, you arrogant fae dick," Elise replied, her lips moving against his. Kian's eyes flashed with emotion, torn between anger and desire.

"I can't wait to kill you."

"Do it, then you can clean up your own fucking library."

His lips hovered back over hers. "Don't wish for death. It will come for you soon enough. Now, get back to work, slave."

"Let me go, and I will, master," Elise replied.

Kian released his grip on her, and she unclenched her fingers from around his silky hair. When Elise managed to tear her gaze away from his flushed cheeks, she saw some of the books were shimmering with light.

"Wow," she whispered, jumping down off the table and hurrying over to where the closest one was buried under a pile of others.

"The ones that glow are magic. The ones that are wrapped in shadow, you aren't to try and open under any circumstance," Kian said behind her.

"Ah huh," Elise murmured. She picked up another and ran her hands over the red cover. She opened it and the words cleared out into English. Elise laughed, reaching for another from her 'Greek' pile, and found it had changed too.

"Why do you have books in Latin and Greek?" she asked, but when she turned around, Kian was gone.

10

Infernal human.

Kian didn't need to kiss Elise to pass on the magic; he didn't even need to touch her. He *wanted* to kiss those angry lips that he had thought about for weeks. It had been so easy to lie, to take the opportunity that presented itself, because he needed to know what she tasted like.

Weeks ago, Kian had run from his own castle because of her. He had a war to start and knew the castle's location was ideal as a base to harass Londinium. He had explicitly planned it that way. Then those plans had changed because Kian was nervous around a human slave.

I should have let Fionn kill her when we found her.

He should kill her right now. The thought made Kian nauseous, which was the most suspicious thing of all. He had no problems killing. He was the bloodthirsty prince. Arawan, the God of the Dead's chosen warrior. The one who came alive on a battlefield. Except after the curse, Kian didn't feel alive even then.

As soon as Kian's mouth touched Elise's lips, gods, he felt alive. His blood had been on fire, her treacherous mouth torture. Angry, greedy, delicious torture.

I fucking hate you. Elise's words had rocked through him. Kian could feel her body responding to his. Her body didn't hate him; it *wanted* him. Elise had no magic from what he could tell, but she could feel whatever this cursed thing was between them. It was like a terrible hunger for a poison he knew was going to kill him.

It was madness.

Kian had all but run from that library before he stripped her down, fucked her right there on the book strewn floor, and drained every drop of her blood. It wasn't until he was outside of the door and heading towards his private chambers that he saw the red seeping into the roses.

"Impossible," Kian murmured and plucked one of the blooms. The castle roses had been white for the past fifteen hundred years. Were they changing now that the castle was back in Albion? There was too much strangeness going on. Kian needed to talk to someone that would piss him off enough to think clearly.

Kian headed straight to his workroom, put the rose in a goblet of water and went to the scrying mirror. It was as tall as he was, its silver frame woven in decorative knotwork and full of spells trapped inside of them.

Kian cut his finger on a fang and drew a line of ogham runes along the glass. They shivered into the surface and disappeared, the magic calling out to its counterparts. He didn't have long to wait before a fae male appeared in the reflection. He was leaner than Kian, with long, straight blue-black hair. Both of his pointed ears were full of piercings, arms and bare chest covered in dark blue tattoos.

"Hello, brother," he greeted.

"Kian, what the fuck are you waking me up for?"

"Nice to see you too, Bayn. How goes the northern invasion?" Kian asked, folding his arms. Bayn ran a hand over his face.

"Fine, big brother. Covered in ice as promised. The humans have started to move south, unsure of what the fuck is going on. A few have been seen, but the sight of my ice castle has sent them running," Bayn replied. His sapphire eyes cleared of sleep and then focused on Kian with their characteristic sharpness. "Beira's tits, what's happened to you?"

"I don't know what you mean."

"You look different. Something's changed. What is it?"

Kian should've known better than to talk to Bayn. He could always tell when he was hiding something. Kian lifted the rose to show him.

"This happened today."

Bayn's dark brows drew together, instantly recognizing the significance. "Change of location?"

"I thought that, but I've been here for weeks, and it's only just started."

"What other variable has altered?" Bayn demanded.

"What do you mean?"

"What else has changed within the castle, you idiot. What has been taken out or brought in? Apart from it growing from Albion soil with your magic, what has altered."

Kian thought back to when he performed the magic. It had been intensely potent because he had...drunk Elise's blood.

"I fed off a human right before I built it," Kian said finally. "The magic rushed out, and it left the castle a bit of mess."

"Was she a witch?"

"No. She has no magic."

"I suppose she's too dead to be sure," Bayn said. Kian hesitated before he tried to shield his expression. *Too late.* "The human isn't dead? Why? What the fuck have you done?"

"She's my slave."

Bayn's angry scowl was wiped clean with shock. "You have a human slave? *You.* The one fae who hates them more than anything in all the worlds."

"She tastes good," Kian replied and regretted it instantly.

Bayn's laugh was filthy. "Oh, brother, I bet she does."

"Not like that, idiot. Her blood gives my magic an edge. I'll take any edge I can get. It's a tactical decision. And she could see through my glamour, so I couldn't leave her for the humans to use as a weapon," he argued.

"You should kill her."

"I know."

"But you won't." Bayn's grin widened. "She's your variable, Kian. She's the reason the roses are turning."

Kian slumped down into his chair. "Have you ever thought about

Aisling's loophole?" Aisling and Aoife, the twin sorceresses who had both saved and ruined the lives of his brothers and the fae.

Bayn reacted as Kian expected. His sapphire eyes filled with ice, his tattooed skin breaking out in frost patterns.

"No. The three of us agreed that it wasn't ever going to be a possible solution. We shouldn't waste our energy, magic, or efforts in bothering to pursue it," he said, and his gaze sharpened. "You think this girl could be your loophole?"

"I don't know. I doubt it. I always thought that Aisling only said it so we wouldn't lose hope because we were stuck in Faerie. The roses bother me, though. As you said, Elise is the only thing that's changed." Kian ran his fingers along the petals of the bloom. "What would you do?"

"I would torture her until she spilled every secret she had to find out what made my magic react to her."

Kian placed the rose back in the water and looked at the fading red in his hair. "I don't think I can. I... like her."

Bayn's laughter made Kian lift his head because it was so damn rare to hear. "Kian, you hate everyone, and you haven't been interested in sticking your dick into anything for so long I'm surprised it hasn't fallen off."

"Fuck you. Just because I like her, and I can't seem to kill her doesn't mean I want to fuck her."

"Yes, it does. Maybe it would be good for you. You can always kill her after. You've always enjoyed killing more than sex anyway."

"And if I can't?"

"Give her to me. I'll get the truth out of her."

A growl so deep and primal came out of Kian that it rattled the mirror. Bayn's laughter died on his lips.

"Kian. You can't be serious."

"I-I'm sorry. I don't know what came over me." *Gods, what was happening?*

"Deal with the human, Kian. We have gone through too much and come too far for you to go soft on us now," Bayn snapped.

"Speaking of us, have you spoken to Killian?" Their eldest, most troublesome brother hadn't checked in with Kian, and it was starting to piss him off.

"Not since we crossed over. He was supposed to follow and never did. Perhaps he got waylaid in Faerie. It's not the time for his part of the plan anyway. He's probably too busy stalking his night castle and pouting dramatically."

"True. The betrayer's bloodlines have all been dealt with, and I have warriors beginning to collect the debts owed," Kian reported, needing to keep the subject off Elise and his fucking act of territorial aggression.

"Why aren't you with them? Can you really trust such an important task to the likes of Fionn? You know he's just waiting for you to die so he can take your place."

"I can't go. It's less than a week away from the full moon. I need to be here, not around younglings," Kian argued.

"I forgot about your time of the month," Bayn mocked. "Perhaps you should let your more beastly side deal with the human because clearly your judgment is clouded by your dick finally waking up after its eternal sleep."

"Fuck you. I'm going. Let me know if you hear from Kill."

"Yeah, yeah." Bayn yawned. "Deal with the human, Kian. Or I will."

Kian stayed in his chair long after the magic in the mirror had faded and his brother with it. He couldn't remember the specifics of what Aisling had said so many years ago, and he didn't know if searching for them would make it better or worse.

The twin human sorceresses. They had been friends to the fae before Aoife had joined with Vortigern and their other enemies. Aisling had stayed with the fae, unable to fathom what her sister had done for power. Aoife had used her magic to curse and banish the fae through the gateways of the Otherworlds.

Aisling, her twin in magic as well as blood, weaved into her sister's curse a possible way to save them all. Something about the blood of the kings being the key... Kian looked up at the delicate crystal vial that sat on a high shelf.

It had held Aisling's blood for the last thousand years. The gift was given on her death bed so that if Kian ever needed her, he could use the magic mirror to summon her shade to have council with.

Kian had never used it, not once. Aisling deserved her peace in the Afterlife, and he'd never felt the need to take it from her.

"You're too close to the full moon to think clearly," Kian told his reflection. It made him restless, so he got up and headed to the stables.

Tending to the horses always soothed Kian's moods. He needed to keep his hands busy so he didn't think about wrapping them around Elise's beautiful neck.

11

Elise didn't leave the library until dark, a few books tucked under her arm for reading. No one said she couldn't borrow any, and the prince wasn't around to stop her. She had done her best to throw herself into work and not think about the blistering kiss that she could still feel against her lips.

You haven't been kissed in two years, that's why you think it was so good. Don't forget you hate him, no matter how your treacherous body feels about it.

Elise followed the vines and roses on the walls back to her room, stopping to smell them. They had been white that morning, but now their petals were tipped in red like they had been brushed with bloody fingers. The thought made her shiver, so she hurried back before shutting the bedroom door firmly behind her.

Elise was curling up in a window seat with Hesiod and a cup of tea when she looked through the glass and saw lights at the castle walls. It wasn't the flaming lights of the fae, but the sharp beams of torches. Figures were climbing down the walls with ropes, and she spotted the unmistakable shape of helmets and guns in the clear moonlight.

Soldiers. Hope filled her chest. She was saved. She just needed to get to them.

Elise grabbed a jacket and stuffed her feet into boots. She took the knife from the dinner tray and shoved it into a pocket.

The castle hallways were empty, the staff off in their own beds, and the warriors hadn't returned yet. The kitchen was dark, the ashes burning low but giving Elise enough light to see. She crouched down, hiding behind benches and in nooks that she had become acquainted with in the past few weeks.

Outside, the ice-covered ground crunched under her feet, the bitingly cold winter air slapping her in the face. Elise stuck to her usual hiding places and made her way toward the stables where she'd seen the soldiers in tactical gear.

"Hold it right there!" a deep voice commanded, and she froze, hands in the air.

"Don't shoot. I'm human," Elise said, and a light shone on her face.

"What's your name?" the soldier demanded when he had checked her over.

"Elise Carlisle. I was taken as a slave about a month ago... Actually, I don't know how long it's been," she stammered as the light lowered.

"Six weeks since the incursion," the man said through his balaclava.

"We have him!" a voice shouted near the stables.

"Stay down and out of the way, Elise. We'll deal with you after that fucker with the antlers is dead." He hurried off, his gun raised.

Elise knew she should stay, but she couldn't. She went after him, her feet carrying her forward of their own accord. A spotlight switched on, and Elise hid as it shone directly on the prince. He wasn't in armor and had no weapons. He was just standing in front of the stable with a horse brush in one hand.

Elise's heart pounded so loudly she couldn't hear what the soldiers were saying to him. She stepped out of her hiding place and the prince's eyes flicked in her direction.

For a second, Elise thought she saw fear in them before it was gone again. She didn't know if it was his magic inside of her, but her guts and chest were burning in fear of them killing him.

This is what you wanted. He'll be dead, and you'll be free. But she only wanted one of those things. The thought of seeing him gunned down in the freezing mud was unfathomable. Small red dots appeared on the prince's body, and he touched them curiously. Elise's terror turned to panic. He had no idea what they meant. She was running before she could reconsider.

"Get down!" she shouted and tackled Kian. They sailed over the stone water trough and into the hay of an empty stall as bullets flew around them. Searing hot pain sliced through Elise's bicep, and she landed hard on top of Kian. Her arms went around his head, careful not to get one of his antlers in her eyes. "Stay down!" Kian was staring up at her with wide, surprised eyes. "What? You don't know what bullets are? Idiot fae!"

The guns stopped firing, so Elise shouted, "Stop shooting at me! I'm human!"

"She's protecting that creature. She's a sympathizer!"

"Shoot her too!"

Kian's hands went around her bleeding bicep. "You're hurt, Elise."

"That's what happens when you're shot at," she hissed through clenched teeth.

"You protected me. Why?" he demanded.

"Because if anyone is going to kill you, Kian, it's going to be me," Elise snapped. His face lit up in a devastating smile like she had just told him that she loved him, and he had won the lotto and was invited to a threesome with Harry Styles, all at the same time. He was ecstatic, and it was disturbing as hell, considering Elise had admitted she wanted to murder him.

"I can defeat them, but I'm going to need something from you," he whispered.

"What?"

Kian looked pointedly at the blood seeping between his hands. "I haven't fed, so my power is weaker than the curse that's killing me. They are going to kill us both if I don't take your blood, Elise. Once they are dealt with, I can heal you."

All Elise had was shit options now that the soldiers would kill her too. "Okay, but be quick because they won't hold back much longer, and I'm *not* dying for you."

Kian's smile turned wicked, and he flipped them so he was on top of her. He removed his hand from Elise's throbbing bullet graze and tore the sleeve off her jacket and shirt to expose the wound. His smile vanished as he put his mouth over it.

Time slowed, his eyes flaring with golden light. His fangs sank into Elise, and her wounded arm went numb. She gasped in relief and strange, horrifying desire as she stared at his beautiful lips on her skin. Elise's hand brushed the hair from his face, fingers tracing his cheekbones and jaw like he was her lover, not her master.

Kian's magic slammed into Elise again, before curling around him in a golden haze. He lifted his head, and his tongue gave her wound one last, slow lick.

"Stay down," he said, pressing a warm, magic-fused kiss to Elise's surprised mouth. He vanished in a blink, the cold air rushing over her. Guns fired and men screamed. Elise gripped the side of the stone trough with one hand and tried to ease her way up.

A horrible silence settled over the night, and she peeked over the edge. The stable yard was covered in the torn-off limbs and the heads of the soldiers.

Kian's bloody mouth smiled at Elise, and he dropped the last dead soldier to the ground. Horror slammed through her at the carnage he had wrought in seconds.

"What have I done?" Elise whispered, sagging back into the dirt.

She had no energy to fight him when Kian picked her up, holding her close to his chest and carrying her back into the castle. Elise's face fell against his neck, her mouth on his bare collarbone. She pulled it away, and pain shot through her.

"Stay still," Kian said.

A wooden door swung open for him, and he set her down on a velvet chaise lounge before taking off her jacket and exposing her blood-soaked clothes. For the second time that day, he unlaced her shirt and tossed it to the ground. Elise's skin was red with blood, and Kian's eyes were lingering over it like he wanted to lick it clean. She still had enough blood in her to blush, so she snapped the fingers of her good hand at him.

"Focus! You said you could heal me."

"Maybe I brought you here so I could watch you die slowly," Kian said, even as he pulled bandages out of a cupboard.

"Don't be a dick, just for once. I saved your life tonight," Elise replied, resting her spinning head on the back of the couch.

"Debatable. I'm sure I could have healed from whatever damage the humans did to me." He came back to her side with a basin of steaming water, laying out cloths, bandages, and other items Elise didn't want to look at too closely.

"Don't make me regret it even more," she said, tears pricking her eyes.

Those soldiers thought she had sided with the fae. *What a nightmare.* She had thrown away her one chance to be free. Elise had done plenty of dumb shit in her life, but that would have to be the dumbest. Still, she couldn't find it in her to regret saving Kian's life. "Honestly, you should just let me die."

"You only get to die when I decide to kill you."

"You really are an asshole, Kian."

"You say my name like it's a curse," he replied and started to clean the blood off her in warm, smooth swipes of the cloth. "I like it."

"It's because you are one," Elise murmured, the warmth and blood loss starting to drag her down again. "You're my curse."

She was almost asleep when his lips brushed against her knuckles. "I know."

12

Elise spent the next two days with her arm in a sling and instructions to change the dressing and use the balm that the prince left her. She really needed to stop thinking of him as 'Kian.' It was terrible for her brain. That familiarity wasn't breeding the amount of contempt Elise would like. Mainly because she had been having more than one filthy dream of his sweaty body pressed up against hers. She blamed the pain pulsing from her wound and her severe lack of judgment.

The human soldiers had come to the castle for one reason only, and that was to take him down. It wasn't to shake his hand because he was such a good guy. The prince was their enemy, so Elise didn't like that he had stopped feeling like hers.

Elise spent most of her time in the library, organizing books, setting aside ones that needed repairing, and trying not to get lost in between their pages. Weirdly, she had gotten her dream job. She only wished it didn't have a fae dick overlord to go with it.

Speaking of which...Elise hadn't seen the prince since the night she'd been shot. Some of the army had returned, and there were patrols of warriors roaming the grounds at night to ensure that no other humans tried to get into the place.

You really did blow your only chance, you dumb ass. Elise's wound throbbed in agreement. She didn't know much about medicine, but she knew that a bullet wound shouldn't heal as quickly as it did. The scab was gone in two days, the skin healed, and she only had some deep muscle soreness. It made her wish she had some fae magic up her sleeves when she had to watch her father die slowly.

Don't think about it. She had enough to worry about in the present to not get dragged down in the painful past.

Elise was lost in her own head. She didn't notice that all of the castle's usual staff were in a celebratory mood. It wasn't until Hedera pulled her aside that she even looked up from the book she was reading on the walk back to her room.

"You need to get ready to leave," she snapped irritably. Her hair was blooming in small red flowers, and she was in a purple dress.

"Why? What's going on?" Elise asked.

"It's a full moon, and the prince is in residence. It means we all leave for a night off. There will be drinking and dancing at the henge tonight, and no one is allowed to stay behind." Her face screwed up in disapproval. "Not even you."

"Why? Does the prince like to walk around naked and howl at the moon or something?" Elise didn't get what the big deal was. Kian could walk about naked any time he liked. He didn't need everyone to leave. *Maybe he is trying to be a nice boss.*

"Stupid human. You have no say in the matter. Now—"

"Brownie! Let the human stay. A fae party is no place for the likes of her, especially with how *protective* the prince is of his little pet." Fionn was standing in a stone archway, a lazy smile on his face and one hand stroking the hilt of his sword.

"But the master—" Hedera's protests trailed off at Fionn's glare, and she backed down. "Yes, sir."

"I'll be fine on my own. I still have work to do." Elise didn't know why she felt the need to reassure her. Hedera nodded at her and walked away.

"I should have killed you when I had the chance," Fionn said, looking Elise over slowly. "Watch yourself, human. The prince won't always be around to save you."

Elise held her ground, not wanting to turn her back on him. With a grunt, he turned around and walked away, leaving her clutching the book so hard her knuckles went white.

∽

It was almost midnight when hunger drove Elise out of her room. She figured that the place should be empty enough for her to walk around unhindered for once.

The castle hallways were still lit with candelabras and lanterns, so Elise took her time to admire the murals on the walls and the woven tapestries. When she wasn't worried about getting harassed by the fae, the castle was a beautiful place. She had a strange urge to ask Kian about why he chose individual paintings or carvings in the obsidian.

Elise wondered if he was enjoying his night off doing whatever it was he did when the fae left him alone. A graphic image flashed in her brain of him reclining in a bubble bath, and she tried not to giggle.

Elise made a pot of tea down in the kitchens and helped herself to the bread and honey. Balancing everything on a small tray, she made her way slowly back towards her room.

A tingling sensation crept over the back of Elise's neck, and she turned. There was no one, only shadows behind her.

"Creepy old castle," she muttered. A rush of wind whipped past her, making the tea pot rattle. Elise tightened her grip on the tray and quickened her footsteps. "Just a draft of wind, Elise. Nothing to get worked up over." The quaver in her voice meant it was too late for that. The fae were all partying. She was on edge because she'd been on edge every day for the last six weeks.

Elise's shoulder was starting to throb with the tray's weight, so she focused on keeping everything on it and ignored the tingle between her shoulder blades. A warm breath tickled her ear, making her whip around.

Nothing.

I am finally losing my mind.

Elise took a deep, slow breath and tried to steady her heart rate. Her imagination was rapidly filling with ghosts and ghouls and monsters that would haunt a fae castle. When she was younger, she and her father had toured all the castles in the United Kingdom, and she'd sworn that she had seen a ghost more than once. She had nothing to fear from the dead. It was the living she needed to be worried about.

"Can't hurt you," Elise whispered and started walking again. Moving shadows danced in the corners of her eyes, and the feeling of being followed made the hair on the back of her neck stand on end.

No, not followed. Stalked.

Elise's tray swayed and she tried to get a grip on it. She could see the bedroom door; she just needed to keep her nerve until then. The teacup pinged as something dropped into it. A perfect golden drop of blood was staining the porcelain.

Don't look up...

Heart pounding, Elise looked up. The prince was crouched on the wooden beams above, his face wreathed in shadows. He moved, and the edge of his face hit the light. His fangs were out, and there was nothing like recognition in his feral eyes.

"K-Kian?"

A deep, low growl echoed off the obsidian walls and his muscles bunched to leap. The tray hit the ground, and she ran.

Elise didn't turn as the pounding of footsteps raced after her. She was only a few meters from the bedroom door when he appeared in front of it. Elise screamed, dodging his outstretched hands and tore off down a set of stairs, trying not to slip.

The prince bounded over the mezzanine and onto the banister, something sharp scraping Elise's cheek on the way past. He jumped onto the obsidian wall, his hands gripping it as another unearthly growl rattled out of him.

Elise dashed across a walkway and into a ballroom, slamming the heavy wood door and dropping the locking latch. She was halfway across the ballroom floor when the door burst into splinters, and the prince's heavy body slammed into her. Elise lashed out, hitting and kicking. He dropped her on the polished floor with a chilling laugh and disappeared into the shadows. Elise got back to her feet and pulled a heavy unlit torch from its brackets, gripping it like a baseball bat.

"Little human thinks she can hurt me with that?" the prince mocked, his voice distorted from its usual timbre. "Food can fight as much as it likes. It's still food."

"You really are the worst," Elise replied, hands tightening on the torch.

"Yes, I am." In a gust of wind, the torch was knocked out of her hands, and she was slammed up against the wall. The prince gripped Elise's wrists in one hand above her head, his face full of wild excitement.

He leaned in and slowly licked the cut on her cheek. "Delicious little human."

"K-Kian, you don't want to kill me before I get that library sorted out, do you?" Elise babbled, heart pounding in terror. He pressed up against her, moving his lips along her jaw.

"But I *do* want to kill you. It will make the dreams stop. Make the hunger stop," he purred against her neck, and goosebumps broke out down her skin. "So soft, so lovely." The prince lifted Elise high, and with one finger, he undid the top laces of her shirt, exposing her bound breasts.

"You said I disgusted you, remember? You don't want to eat me," Elise tried to reason with him. His face broke out into a brilliant smile that said, yes, he really fucking did. The somewhat reasonable Kian she knew wasn't home. Not even a little.

"The most disgusting thing about you is how much I crave you," he snarled softly. "After tonight, I won't, and all will be well again." His hand traced along Elise's chest before gripping her braid and exposing her neck. Elise struggled, trying to kick her legs up, but he only laughed and pressed his big body between her thighs. Elise's legs tightened around his hips to try to leverage herself up to yank her hands away.

"Keep fighting. It excites me," the prince said, grinding her up against the wall so Elise could feel his excitement right against her core. Elise's body lit up in response, and she wriggled, trying to stop the horrible pressure building inside her.

"Kian, I'm warning you. If you bite me, I will bite you back, and you won't enjoy it," Elise threatened angrily, her voice shaking.

The prince brushed the tip of his tongue against her lips. "Yes, I will."

And the fucker sank his fangs into her neck, sharp pain turning to ecstasy as his mouth sucked hard. Elise cried out, wet heat rushing through her, and pooling in a painful throb where his hard dick was digging into her. He whimpered and dropped Elise's hands so he could grip her hips, holding her tighter against him. Her hands tangled in his hair, and she grabbed one of his antlers.

"Fuck...you," Elise gasped and bit into his shoulder as hard as she could. He cried out, momentarily letting go of her neck. He pulled his head back, eyes burning. He ran his thumb over his gold blood dripping from her mouth.

"How does it feel, asshole?" Elise snarled, breath coming in sharp pants.

"Like you're a nightmare I'll never get enough of," Kian replied reverently. Elise didn't know who moved first, but their mouths locked together, teeth and tongues fighting with burning rage and want.

Elise's fingers pulled at his hair and antlers, and they ended up on the floor with Kian on top of her. His mouth moved from hers, fangs nipping at her throat before latching onto the bite again. Elise made a choked sound, pleasure exploding through her like a burst of drugs and magic. She was wild with need, rolling her hips against his, burning for more, for release. Wanting him touching her and inside of her.

The prince's hand reached down between her thighs and cupped her, making her writhe and rub against him. His fingers tore at the laces of her pants, skimming under her panties and plunging into her wet folds.

"Kian," Elise groaned against his shoulder. He slid two fingers inside of her and started thrusting them hard and deep.

"Perfect. So fucking perfect," he murmured, his tongue licking at her ear. "Give me your pleasure, my nightmare, let me have all of you."

Elise didn't recognize her voice when she begged, "Bite me, Kian. Please, bite me again."

His fangs pierced the curve of her breast, his fingers curling inside of her while his thumb moved to circle her clit. Elise screamed, white light bursting through her vision, and her orgasm exploded through her. Kian's arm gripped her to him, Elise arching up against him. She licked the sweat from his neck, before kissing him deeply, stealing his taste of honey and smoke and iron.

"Ass...hole..." Elise murmured. Her hands slipped from his antlers, darkness taking over and robbing her of his beautiful, surprised face.

13

The red haze of Kian's madness cleared, and he found Elise slumped lifeless in his arms. Blood stained her chest from the bite at her throat, and his fingers were still inside of her. He removed his hand quickly and set her down.

"Elise?" Kian touched her face, trying to rouse her. "Wake up, Elise!" Cold panic raced through him. He pressed an ear to her chest and found her heartbeat dim but still there. How much blood had he taken from her? Kian hesitated, staring down at her too pale face.

Let her die, his voice of reason commanded.

She's the nightmare you've never asked for and always wanted, his heart replied.

For the first time in Kian's two thousand years of life, he listened to his heart. Kian scooped Elise up in his arms and ran, her blood making him stronger and faster than he'd ever been. He kicked the door of the tower off its hinges and carried her into his workroom. Kian laid her down on a couch and ran his hands through his hair, the panic taking over.

"Think, Kian!" He opened a cabinet of glass vials, searching for a potion that would help Elise. Would fae medicine work on a human? He had to try. He popped the cork of a healing elixir open and tipped it into her mouth.

"Swallow, Elise," he commanded, gently rubbing at her throat until it went down. Kian grabbed another vial for wounds and tipped it over the ragged bite on her throat. He hadn't lacked control like this since the first month he had been cursed. In saying that, the victims Kian encountered when it was the full moon usually ended up in pieces. He hadn't killed her outright because she had been able to make the madness controlling him subside.

"What in all the hells were you doing in the castle on the full moon anyway?" he muttered.

Kian's eyes caught on the blood on her chest, and swearing, he pulled the edge of her bandeau back and revealed another bite mark on her full breast. Kian smeared the potion on it with his fingertips, rubbing it into the wound until it closed.

Kian got up and fetched a wet cloth to clean her up. Something he had to do far too often of late. *Because of you.*

Elise didn't rouse as Kian removed her shirt and dressed her in one of his own. When she still didn't wake, he picked her up again and carried her to the bedroom.

Kian laid her down on the bed, the beast in him waking up again at the sight. He kissed her eyelids, her cheeks. Fuck, she smelled so good he wanted to wrap himself around her and breathe her in. He could still smell her blood and arousal, and his dick hardened again. Something felt wet and wrong, and Kian belatedly realized he'd come in his pants earlier like a fumbling faeling. He ripped himself off her in disgust and went into the bathroom.

Kian pressed a sigil in the obsidian wall, and hot water shot out of it in small jets. He wanted to scrub his skin until it hurt just to get the feel of her off him. Elise's blood was pounding in his veins, messing with his own scent, and he bit back a scream.

Blood streaked through the ends of his hair, and he washed it, growing more and more frustrated when it refused to come out. Kian stopped, wiping water from his eyes. It wasn't blood that was soaking the ends of his hair. It *was* his hair.

"Not possible." There was at least an inch more red in it. He sagged to the floor as his world tilted.

Shutting his eyes, Kian tried to breathe through his panic and instead was hit with the image of his most hated enemies; fair-haired, arrogant Hengist. He and his bloated brother Horsa had been Saxon kings that had sided with Vortigern, High King of the Britons. Fae and human relations had become irreparable soon after.

Kian's stomach shuddered and he fell forward, throwing up blood on the floor. He needed help and knew Bayn and Killian would be no use.

"Aisling." Kian hauled himself upright and tried to pull himself together. *I am the Blood Prince, for fuck's sake*. If Elise died, then it would be one less human to worry about.

A sharp pain pierced Kian's chest, enough that he doubled over at the agony coursing through him. He had taken no vow not to harm her.

"What has that witch done to me?" he groaned, pain lashing his insides.

Kian strode back into the bedroom, ready to confront Elise, to shake her awake and demand answers. He took one look at her, and all his anger vanished. She had curled onto one side and was cuddling one of his pillows. Her color had returned, and relief coursed through him. Instead of snapping her neck, Kian placed a blanket over her.

Disgusted by his own weakness, he put on some fresh clothes and went into his workrooms, making sure all the doors were shut.

Aisling's blood glowed ruby red in its vial of crystal and silver. Kian turned it over in his hands, contemplating whether or not to use it. He had violent recollections of Elise underneath him, his hands and mouth on her, and the sounds of her screaming in pleasure. Kian swore and took ten deep breaths. He had to get answers before he drove himself mad and took Elise with him.

Kian opened the vial and tipped some of Aisling's blood on his finger before sketching runes on the mirror. He waited, not knowing how quickly the magic would work. Summoning from Arawan's realm of the dead was risky and unreliable, but Aisling wasn't about to let him down. She appeared through the mist, her black hair floating in an invisible breeze.

"Kian. How long has it been, my prince?" she asked, blue eyes dancing with mischief.

"Too long. The curse hasn't killed me yet."

"I can see that. Why have you summoned me after so long?" The mischief turned to concern, her brows drawing together. "Kian, what's happened? You don't look like yourself."

"I'm back in Albion. My brothers and I finally found a way to open the portal back and are getting our revenge before we die," he admitted. Aisling had always advised against it, and he could tell her opinion on the matter hadn't changed.

Aisling crossed her arms. "You are getting what you want then. What is your problem?"

"I found a woman. A human. And I can't kill her. My glamours don't affect her. I caught her on a full moon, and she lived through it. I hate her. I want her. I can't kill her, and I need to." Kian was babbling, and it made him want to punch the mirror. "Advise me, Aisling. You always did it best. Tell me what to do with her."

Aisling burst out laughing. It was high pitched, joyful, and absolutely grating. Kian didn't know that a shade could cry, but she laughed so hard that tears ran down her cheeks.

"Are you finished?" he demanded coldly. "I need your help, and you're braying like a donkey."

"I'm sorry, my prince. I didn't know if my magic actually took hold when Aoife cast the curse," Aisling said, trying to get a hold of herself.

"So this is your fault," Kian ground out between his teeth.

"Yes and no. You were destined to find her. I just made sure you would if you returned to Albion before the curse killed you." Aisling wiped at her eyes. "You forgot my part of that magic, didn't you? Typical. You want help and never pay attention to it."

"Speak plainly, woman. I don't have time for gloating."

"Oh, very well." Aisling gave him a patient smile. "She's one of the king's descendants. Either of Vortigern, Hengist, or Horsa's line. All of your curses will be unlocked by the blood of your enemies in this time. You were the prince controlled by bloodlust, so you were cursed to drink blood. If she offers you her blood willingly, it will lessen the power of your curse, and if you don't fuck everything up, she will be the key to breaking it entirely."

Kian held up the red tips of his hair, thinking about the night. *Bite me, Kian.*

Elise had offered her blood in the heat of the moment, but would she agree to help him when she woke?

"The magic is fading, Kian," Aisling said, pulling him out of his thoughts. "Please, I know the depth of your anger, but if you hurt this woman, it will destroy you in ways you can't even imagine. Don't pass up this opportunity because she has some of your enemy's blood. Heal the past. Create a future for the fae."

"I don't know if I can," Kian replied honestly. His hate had sustained him for over a thousand years, and he didn't know how to live without it.

"You can. I wouldn't have followed you in the first place if I didn't believe you were capable of it." Aisling's form started to slip away, her words fading, but her smile remained brilliant. "Summon me to meet your mate sometime. I bet she's wonderful." Then she was gone, leaving Kian gasping for air and clutching at the mirror frame.

"Come back, Aisling! What do you mean my mate?" he shouted. Mates were rare for the high fae like him and his brothers. The cases of mates had been reduced to myths amongst their people. Even in the stories, mates had been something to be feared. They became something *else* when they found each other. Their power magnified, and their bond was impossible to sever.

It made them loyal to each other first, everything and everyone else second.

Kian shook with rage and fear. He had seen a vision of Hengist's face. Did that mean Elise had his blood? Even a drop? Gods, the horror of it.

Aisling had always been a powerful seer, and she had tried to warn them all that there was only one way to break their curses. He and his brothers had laughed it off because mates weren't real, and there was no way they would suffer the kiss of their enemy's descendants. They had boasted about killing every single one of the bastard king's bloodlines as soon as they could.

Closing his eyes, Kian tried to use his power to search out any magical bindings. It hit him square in the chest as soon as he uttered the spell. A rope of gold and scarlet was wrapped around his chest and constricting his heart. Kian had never seen magic like it, and all it took was him surrendering to the dark desire to make Elise his as soon as he saw her. Now it was starting to change him like the bond would start to change her.

Fuck.

Kian cracked open the bedroom door to watch Elise sleeping. Almost instantly, warm emotions bloomed in his chest. The desire to check on her and to keep her safe was overwhelming. It suddenly made sense why he had lost his shit when another fae male touched her and why he couldn't handle seeing her a half-starved wraith.

Up until that moment, *he* had been the most significant danger to her.

Kian had tried to kill her. He had wanted to hate her. He had fought not to like her.

Blood of my enemy. My slave. My salvation...My mate.

14

Elise woke up slowly, sleep still holding her in a soft, downy embrace smelling of fir trees. Her brain started firing, alerting her that something was wrong. Why could she smell the prince? *Oh, God, the prince.* The recollection of fangs and fear and desire hit Elise in the face like cold water, and she sat bolt upright.

The familiar surroundings of Elise's room were around her, but she could feel something wasn't right. She was sleeping with a pillow that wasn't hers and wore a shirt that swam on her. Elise lifted the front of it to her nose and smelled fir trees and knew who it belonged to.

Elise jumped in fright as something shifted on the other side of the room. The prince was stretched out on her couch in front of the fire, a book open on his chest and fast asleep. Elise was about to poke him to see if he was really there when he woke. He focused on her, and relief filled his eyes.

"You're awake," he said huskily, his smile showing the tips of his fangs.

Elise squeaked in fear and dashed to her bathroom, bolting the door behind her. She swayed, too much blood rushing to her head.

"Elise, you don't have to be afraid...I am myself again," Kian's voice echoed from the other side of the door.

"Like that's a comfort! What are you doing in here?"

"It's my castle, woman. I'll go where I please!" Kian mumbled something she couldn't catch, and when he spoke again, he was calm. "Elise, we need to talk. Come out of there."

"No. I need a bath. Go away and come back later," she said and cringed. *So stupid*. Elise turned on the taps so whatever he said was drowned out. She struggled out of her clothes and climbed into the tub. Starting to shake, she pulled her knees up to her chest.

The prince had *hunted* her. *And bit me, and...oh God, had he really gotten me off?*

There was an ache in her lady parts that told her she hadn't imagined the earth-shattering orgasm. Elise had been begging him to bite her so she could feel that sweet rush. She groaned, covering her burning face with her hands.

Just when you think you can't sink any lower.

Elise turned off the taps to the tub when the water reached her neck. Silence from the other side of the door. Maybe he had gotten the hint.

"Elise?"

Nope, nope, nope. She slid under the water and held her breath until her lungs were burning. When she emerged again, the prince wasn't saying anything. Good. He had proven last night that he was strong enough to bust open doors when motivated. Maybe he was exhausted from the crazy bullshit he had pulled.

Trapped with a schizophrenic fae prince because life can't get worse.

Elise washed thoroughly, wondering how she was ever going to face him again. She had kissed him, asked him to *bite* her, while his fingers had been inside of her. She wanted to throw up. She wanted to do it again. She wanted...

I can't be hot for the prince. He was a horrible bastard, and she deserved better. Elise's taste in men had always been pretty bad, but not violent psychopath bad.

It had to be the effect of his magic. Elise clawed at the golden cuffs on her wrists, soaping them and trying to pull them off.

When Elise had calmed down enough to think straight, she got out of the bath and wrapped herself in a soft robe. Her body was screaming for food and more sleep. She opened her door and found Kian sitting back on the couch with a tray of food on the table in front of him.

"Come and eat, Elise," he said, closing the book he had been reading.

"Don't you have better things to do than hover about my room?" Elise asked, sitting on a chair opposite him.

"Yes, I do. Some things need to take priority, and today, that's you." Kian poured out tea for her, and Elise's eyes narrowed. Something was seriously up.

"Really? Felt like chasing me around the castle again like a crazy monster?"

Kian's lips lifted in a small smile. "You seemed to enjoy that game too in the end."

Elise's face flamed and she picked up a pastry. "I was faking it."

His smile widened. "No one can fake being that wet."

He did not just say that.

"Why are you here, master?" Elise said through gritted teeth. She needed him out of there so she could die of mortification in peace.

"I have a proposal for you."

"I'm not having sex with you," she blurted out.

"I don't want to have sex with you either," said Kian, his smile slipping a little. "This is about your freedom and how badly you want it."

"My actual freedom? Like you'll take these gold cuffs off, and I can walk out and never see you again freedom? Or freedom as in death?" The fae loved to twist words, and Elise wasn't about to get screwed because of word usage.

A muscle in Kian's jaw popped. "Yes, true freedom. You will be able to leave."

"Forever?"

"Yes," he replied through gritted teeth.

"Okay, and what would I have to do to get away from you?" Elise asked, sipping her tea. It was perfectly doctored to her tastes though she had no idea how he knew them.

"I want your blood."

Tea splashed on her hand, Elise almost dropping her cup. "Excuse me?"

"I want your blood. Freely given."

"Why freely given? You didn't seem to have any problem taking it without consent last night."

Kian shifted in his chair, visibly struggling to look at her. "I apologize for that. I am not myself on a full moon."

"No, shit. Something to do with this curse, right?" He nodded, looking even more uncomfortable. "And my blood is helping you somehow?"

"Yes." He showed Elise the tips of his hair. "I have more red in it today, which means the power of my curse has lessened. That's never happened before, and I've had to drink a lot of blood over the last fifteen hundred years."

"So what makes mine different?" None of this was making any sense.

"I don't know."

Well, that was a lie. "Yes, you do. Otherwise, you wouldn't be here asking me for it instead of just taking it."

"I don't know all of the specifics, only that you need to offer it to me freely. Like you did last night when you asked me to bite you while you were riding my-"

"Please, stop, I was there. You don't need to repeat it," Elise interrupted him. She hated that he could embarrass her so quickly, and one look at the mischief in Kian's eyes said the prick was loving it. "Tell me why you're killing humans."

His smile vanished. "You're in no position to make demands," he said.

"Actually, I am. You just said that my blood needs to be given freely, and I won't give you a single drop unless you tell me about what the betrayer's bloodlines mean and why you want to kill them."

"It's a long, complicated story."

"I have time."

Kian leaned back in his chair with a sigh. "It will make you hate me."

"I already hate you. We have an agreement, though, or we will have if you tell me about the curse and what the war on humans is about. It doesn't matter if I hate you even more, I'll still freely give my blood."

"A promise to a fae is binding," he warned.

Elise held his gaze. "So are mine."

It was true. She had kept the promise to her father, and it had almost destroyed her. But she still went through with it. *Don't think about it, Elise. It's not the time.*

"What just happened?" Kian asked, head tilting, and his eyes narrowed. "Your face changed for a moment."

"None of your business," she snapped.

"Why do you want to know about the curse?" he asked, wisely changing the subject.

"I suppose I want to understand your motivations. If I hold out on you and don't give you my blood, then the curse will kill you, and you can never hurt humans again. I want my freedom, but maybe I can live with giving it up for the greater good."

Elise had never thought she'd be one for self-sacrifice, yet here she was. She was probably the only human he couldn't kill without consequences, and that had its own power. Despite her bravado that Kian believed, judging by the scowl on his face, Elise really did want to know what made him hate humans so much.

Elise had jumped in front of bullets to knock him out of the way. As much as a part of her despised him, she had pesky *other* parts that would probably do it again, and that kind of liked him and wanted to know him better. It made no sense, but it didn't make it less true. Maybe she could find a way to convince him that all humans weren't terrible.

The prince and Elise were locked in a stare-off. "If your goal is to try and find something about me that's redemptive, you are wasting your time."

"I'm your slave, Kian. All I have is time." Elise brushed her damp hair behind her ear, and his hands clenched. "And I'm not about to start thinking better of you."

"No, we wouldn't want that, would we?" he replied, his small smile returning. She may have smiled back. "Eat something. You've lost too much blood in the past few days, and my healing potions can only go so far."

"If you keep bringing me food, I'm going to think that you're trying to be nice," Elise teased.

"I'm trying to keep you from dying on me before I can get enough blood out of you to break my curse," he corrected her.

Of course.

Elise slathered honey on some of Hedera's freshly baked bread and ate it only so he'd stop staring at her like he wanted to start shoving food down her throat. Some of the tension left his shoulders when she finished one piece and moved onto the next.

Elise smiled smugly at him so he would know that she'd noticed. He glowered back at her. "So how did you get cursed?"

15

Kian poured more tea for himself before he got settled. It was a new kind of strange to see him almost relaxing around Elise, drinking tea like they didn't want to stab each other with something.

"Do you know who Vortigern was?" Kian asked. Elise didn't have to search her memory too hard.

"He was a king in the Dark Ages. In some versions of the story, he was King Arthur's great uncle, I think?" she replied.

"I'm not sure who King Arthur is, but Vortigern was King of the Britons the last time I was here in Albion."

"God, so you must be what? Fifteen hundred years old?" she asked.

Kian looked uncharacteristically bashful. "Older. But that's irrelevant. The fae had decent enough relations with the humans, even the Romans, before Vortigern. When he started to lose control of the warring kings beneath him and was unable to keep up with the raids by the Picts and Scots, he recruited two Saxon kings to help fill out his army, Hengist and Horsa."

"I've heard of those guys too. They became the kings of Kent," Elise said, and Kian made an exasperated sound.

"Do you want to hear this story, or do you want to keep interrupting?" he demanded.

"Sorry, master," she said, holding her hands up in surrender.

"Hengist and Horsa were the ones that stirred up discontent with Vortigern and the other kings. They felt that the fae were holding out on them, especially when it came to magic. We didn't want to get involved in their squabbles with the raiders. The fae were always fewer in numbers than humans, and our birth rate much lower. Despite that, my brothers and I decided that we should protect our homeland." Kian smiled grimly. "I should have listened to Killian. He told me that humans were too greedy to be trusted. That once we gave them what they wanted, they would turn on us. I have never been able to live it down that he was right."

"We became Vortigern's allies. In return for our help, the fae would never be attacked or harassed by the humans. This land we are on now would be ours forever because it held the gateway to Faerie. I saw it as a way for our young ones to always be safe, and because they didn't have to hide, they would be able to thrive," Kian said, his voice cracking. Elise didn't dare say anything. He wasn't faking the pain in his eyes, and her breakfast sat uneasily in her stomach.

"With the help of two powerful sorceresses, Aoife and Aisling, we eventually pushed back the raiders, and Albion knew peace for the first time in years," he continued after a while. "After two winters, Hengist and Horsa engaged in warmongering once again. They didn't think that the fae deserved the lands that had been promised us, and the raids started against us.

"When we got enough evidence to confront Vortigern about the Saxons, the treaty fell to pieces. When the fae make a bargain, they are bound to it forever. The kings forgot that when they decided to attack us." Kian's expression grew feral with violence. "They promised to protect the fae or their bloodlines would be cursed forever. They swore vows on their family lines.

"My brothers and I were invited to meet with Vortigern and Aoife, a ruse to distract us. Aoife sided with the humans, but her sister Aisling sided with the fae. It broke her heart that Aoife sold herself for power, but even Aisling couldn't imagine the depth that Aoife would sink to.

While we met with Vortigern, Hengist and Horsa led a raid on the fae under my protection here in the south. There weren't enough warriors, and that night the humans killed one hundred and seventeen faelings. An entire generation was gone."

Kian's eyes had glazed over, lost in the horror of his memories. Elise wanted to say something, take his hand...but didn't. There wasn't anything she could do that would make him feel any better.

"Nothing could have prepared us for that tragedy. The shock was bewildering, surreal almost. The humans used that distraction to their advantage. Aoife had gathered other human magic users to her side, and together they had enough power to hold us. My antlers were hacked off, a trophy for the kings, and we were cast through the portals and into Faerie."

Elise dared to look up at the antlers that had regrown, feeling sick at the pain and humiliation he must have felt to be reduced to a trophy. Kian noticed her staring, and in his eyes, she could see the memory was still carving pieces out of him.

"My brothers and I were all cursed on top of it. I was the warrior, bloodthirsty prince, so I was cursed with the need to drink blood," he continued, his voice husky. "Bayn, the winter prince, always had ice magic, and he was as cold as his power. His curse is a heart that's slowly freezing solid. Killian is the night prince and ruler of all things that happen in it. Now, if he so much as touches another being, they die.

"We have spent the last fifteen hundred years trying to get back to Albion to get our revenge. Aisling tried to counteract the curses that her sister had placed on us. She told us that she had seen loopholes, but we didn't believe her because it would require the help of certain humans, and we hated them all so much." Kian's heavy gaze rested on Elise, and her heart thumped painfully in her chest. "Turns out, I should have listened to her."

"You think I'm your loophole?" she asked.

Kian held out the tips of his hair. "I know you are. This is an hourglass, Elise. I had a few years left at the very most before it turned completely white. That was when I was due to die, and now there is more red. More years. All because I drank your blood last night."

"But...I'm no one." Why her? Why, of all the women in England that might be okay with being bound to a fae, did Fate have to choose her?

"My hair says otherwise, Elise. I couldn't kill you when I first met you. Maybe this is the reason why." Kian looked as pleased about it as Elise felt.

"The humans you have been killing, are they from the families of the kings?" she asked, hazarding a guess.

Kian nodded slowly. "The kings and the warriors who were there the night of the massacre who killed the faelings. Do you know less than fifty of the original families of those murdered children still live? The rest died of grief or killed themselves. I promised them all justice, and I won't stop until I get it. Bargains with the fae are forever, Elise. The kings bartered on their future descendants, and I'm bound with magic and honor to carry out the consequences."

Elise didn't realize she was crying until tears streaked down her cheeks. She brushed them away, hoping Kian hadn't seen them. She couldn't imagine the horror of carrying out such a vow or the weight of responsibility to his people. Elise couldn't argue about the innocence of those human descendants to him; the lost fae babies were innocent too.

"If I help you break your curse, will you consider another alliance with the humans? Times have changed, and no one wants a war where more innocents could die," she said.

"Just because I am merciful enough to spare you doesn't mean I should spare them," he replied. His sly faerie smile returned, the kind that Elise needed to be careful of because it could convince her of just about anything. "But if you break my curse, it might encourage me to look favorably towards at least one human."

"Humans might have more to offer than we used to. I could tell you about it...maybe show you some of this new world. You might like it."

Did I just ask him out on a date?

"I suppose you will have to break my curse to find out if I'm interested in learning," Kian replied, his sly smile widening.

It wasn't a no. If Elise could get through to Kian, maybe he could convince his brothers that slaughter wasn't the only answer.

Elise selfishly wanted her freedom most of all.

"Okay," she whispered.

"Okay, what?"

"I'll help you break your curse." Elise stuck out her hand for him to shake. Kian stared at it and shook his head.

"You seem to have already forgotten how fae make a deal," he said. He took Elise's outstretched palm, pulled her out of the chair and onto the couch beside him. A knife appeared in his hand, and she knew what was coming.

"Blood again?" Elise complained.

"Just a little."

Kian's smile was so damn charming, her brain hazed. Elise didn't feel it when he cut the tip of her finger. He lifted it to his warm mouth, the brush of his tongue, making heat prickle up her back.

"I, Kian, the Blood Prince of the Fae, vow that if Elise offers her blood freely to me and breaks my curse, I will free her from all bondage and ensure her safety for the rest of her life."

The magic in the vow tugged like an invisible rope around Elise's chest and bound it tight. He cut his finger and held it out to her.

No going back now.

With her heart pounding, Elise took his hand and brought his finger to her lips. His golden honey blood swirled across her tongue, his eyes flaring hot when she sucked softly. Elise quickly removed it from her mouth.

"I, Elise, vow to offer my blood freely to Kian, the Blood Prince, in exchange for the freedom of all bondage and safety for the rest of my life," she said, gasping when the knot around her chest tightened even further.

Kian groaned, leaning forward until their foreheads touched and hands entwined, the magic dragging them down.

"Now, we have a deal," he said. He brushed his mouth lightly against hers before letting Elise go and getting up.

Kian turned back when he reached the bedroom door and gave Elise a once over that was so filthy her thighs squeezed together.

"Rest up, Elise. I'll be back tonight to get another taste of you."

16

There was no way Elise would be able to sleep again after Kian's visit. She dressed and went to the library, her mind full of ancient kings, sorcerers, and the screams of dying fae.

Elise should have known that Kian wouldn't be interested in starting a war over something as simple as vanity or power. He was too calculating for that. She had no idea how deep the pain ran.

Elise hugged her arms around herself, her mind turning over all the times he had looked at her in confusion. Some kind of higher power had stopped him from killing her when he had so desperately wanted to. Elise was so fucking grateful for that, even with the gold cuffs of slavery around her wrists.

Kian had proven more than once that he was protective of her. Elise had jumped in front of a kill squad to save him. Was the impulse because of Aisling's magic? It would explain a lot. The real question was, would they be able to kill each other once his curse was lifted?

A treacherous voice whispered, *Would you still want to?*

Elise rubbed at her chest. The ball of tension that she always put down to Kian's magic was feeling bigger and hotter, pulsing like an extra heartbeat when he was near. It was one more thing she would like to be rid of as soon as she was free.

If Elise broke his curse, Kian might let her show him humanity had its good bits amongst all its really shitty ones. *Or he could be telling you that to get what he wants.*

Once Elise was back amongst the books, she started to feel better. She was still working through different piles, separating the magic books and the dangerous ones away from the normal ones. It was slow going as she put books on the shelves in alphabetical order, always having to rearrange as she went.

Elise opened one from a new pile, almost dropping it in surprise. Kian's face was looking at her from the page. He was painted standing next to two other fae that she assumed were his brothers. *Pre-curse princes.*

The biggest surprise of all was seeing Kian's deep red hair and black and gold antlers. He was wearing his golden armor with a crown of leaves on his head. He was handsome as hell the way he was now with silvery pale features, but he was downright heart shattering in the picture. It was the kind of beauty that inspired awe and fear.

The picture on Chrissy's fae card flashed in Elise's memory, and she tried not to laugh. Oh, boy, she had no idea the 'masculine energy' that card had been warning her about.

Kian's brothers were also exceptional in the handsome and terrifying department.

Painted on Kian's right was Bayn with frost patterns decorating his armor, and a crown made of ice on his blue-black hair. He looked like a god of winter, ready to smite at the least provocation.

On Kian's left was Killian. He was the tallest of the three with tousled black hair, green eyes, and a grin that promised all kinds of sin. Sable wings rose from his back, with silver talons at their arches. His black armor shone, and a crown of silver stars sat on his hair.

Something moved in the corner of Elise's eye, and she spotted Kian sitting on one of the high windows alcoves, pretending to read a book. She, in turn, pretended not to notice him. She closed the book she'd been looking at and shelved it. Elise didn't know why he was up there and didn't want to. He was probably working himself up to lecture her about not resting.

Elise did her best to ignore him and the heat between her shoulder blades when he was watching her. She was starting to get used to the magic that always made her know when he was close by, even if it still unnerved her. Hopefully, it would stop once Elise was finally free and the golden cuffs around her wrists gone.

Elise focused on her tasks as much as she could, letting herself think about what had happened to her cottage for the first time since she was taken captive. Salisbury was only a short drive away, and she really hoped that the fae hadn't burned it to the ground.

Elise could ask Kian, but they didn't need any more animosity between them right when they had come to a peace agreement. An agreement that involved a certain kind of intimacy, so she didn't want to have the urge to stab him with something the whole time. Elise stilled, an uncomfortable thought occurring to her. Every time he had drunk her blood, she had been turned on like crazy in the heat of the moment. Would that happen every time?

I'll be back tonight to get another taste of you.

Elise dropped the book she was holding. *I am in such deep shit.* She didn't want to get sexy feelings over the prince every time he tried to suck on her neck. Just thinking about it made her sweat.

Elise snapped out of it and bent down to pick up the book she'd dropped. The warm heat of Kian's gaze traveled over her ass, and she straightened slowly. Maybe she wasn't the only one struggling with the conflicting desire and hatred for the enemy. He might have been able to use the full moon as an excuse, but he had been as aroused as her the night before. Shutting her eyes, Elise could feel his hand on her again as it slid inside her pants.

Bite me, Kian. She gripped the book until her fingers hurt, delighted and disgusted with the idea as usual.

Girl, you have issues, Chrissy's voice said in the back of her mind. Elise wished she was there so she could get her advice. Knowing Chrissy, her advice would be, *Bitch, how is this even a problem? Get some of that hot fae D while you can.*

That was no help.

Elise had no doubt that last night had gotten as far as it had because it was the full moon. She had told Kian right to his face she wouldn't have sex with him, and he had agreed that he wasn't interested either. Remembering that was the psychological cold shower she needed.

Elise shelved another three books, determined to keep her eyes on her freedom and not on what she would have to do to earn it.

～

Elise's anxiety had built to the point that she was a nervous wreck by the time Kian knocked on her door later that night. He looked as calm and controlled as ever. It really sucked knowing that she was the only one bound up in knots. Maybe because she was the one losing the blood, and he was taking what he wanted as usual.

"How are you feeling this evening, Elise?" he asked politely, sitting down on one of the lounges.

"Fine."

"And you've eaten?"

Elise rolled her eyes at him. "Yes, master."

"It's for your well-being, not mine, slave," he replied, annoyance already creeping into his tone. Good. Elise needed the reminder of their status because she didn't like how comfortable she was getting with his presence. Elise hated thinking about all the questions she wanted to ask him about his past and Faerie and what the Dark Ages were like.

"Can we get this over with?" she asked, fiddling with the cushion she was holding.

"Elise, look at me," Kian commanded. When she finally did, his face was concerned. "I'm not going to hurt you. You don't need to be afraid of me. I'm not even going to bite you."

"You're not?" Elise didn't know if she was relieved or disappointed.

"Not unless I have to. I don't think the curse will know the difference, but let's be sure." Kian produced a knife and took a goblet from the dinner tray. He gestured at her. "Wrist."

Elise held it out to him and shut her eyes. "Do it quickly."

"I'm not so uncivilized to just cut you without anything for the pain."

She peeked open an eye. He tipped something from a yellow glass vial onto her skin and gently rubbed it into her wrist.

"You did the first day you captured me," Elise pointed out.

Kian's nostrils flared in annoyance. "That was different. You were trying to stab me with my own dagger."

"Yeah, that was me," she said and choked back a nervous laugh.

Kian lifted the knife. "Look away if you need to."

Elise focused on the dark tips of his antlers. Cool metal ran against her skin, but there was no pain as promised. The rim of the goblet pressed into her arm and released.

"It's over," Kian murmured, wrapping a cloth over the cut on her wrist.

"That's it?" Elise asked, surprised by how quickly he'd gotten what he needed.

"I suppose we will find out." Kian removed the cloth and placed two fingers over the cut. He whispered under his breath, and golden light glowed where he touched her. When he let her go, the cut had vanished.

"That's amazing," Elise whispered, touching the skin. Not even a scar remained.

"No, what's amazing is *you* being the key to my curse. Aisling is probably laughing her ass off in the Afterlife." Kian picked up the goblet and lifted it to his lips. "Here's hoping this works."

"Bottoms up," Elise replied.

Kian drained it, his eyes changing to gold for a second and then back again. She was reminded of the picture she'd seen of him. He had golden eyes before, not red. Elise hadn't fully believed it, but now she did...her blood was fighting the curse inside of him.

"Do you feel any different?" she asked when he put the goblet down.

"Not yet," he replied. He studied the red in his hair grimly.

"Maybe it takes a little while to work?"

Kian's frown deepened, and he rose to his feet. "Good night, Elise."

"Night," she managed to say before he was gone again, leaving her staring after him.

17

It didn't work. Kian knew it wasn't going to the moment he drank from the goblet. It wasn't the same. The spark of magic and fire wasn't there. *Why* wasn't it there? It made no sense.

Up in his tower, Kian went through all the notes he'd made on what Aisling had said. He didn't know enough about mates, and the books in the library weren't going to help him.

Kian cut a finger and sketched more runes on the mirror. He needed to talk to someone older than him, and there was only one fae he knew.

Shadows grew in the mirror and transformed into a flurry of black feathers before Killian appeared.

"Finally! Where the fuck have you been?" Kian demanded.

Killian's green eyes glowed, and the shadows and feathers cleared away, leaving only Kian's hulking big brother with his smug smile.

"I've been busy. Out and about. Seeing the new England before we destroy it," he replied before drinking from a bottle. "You look like shit. I thought you would be ecstatic by now, running about, bathing in the blood of your enemies and whatnot."

"I need to ask you a question about...about mates," Kian said, hating that he had to ask him anything at all.

Killian's eyes narrowed. "What have you done, Kian?"

"I think - I mean, I know-"

"Spit it out already."

"I have found my mate!" Kian shouted over him. He was as hysterical as he sounded. Killian's frustrated expression vanished, his green eyes wide, all traces of his mocking brother gone. He drained the bottle he had been drinking from and produced another.

"How can you be sure?" Killian asked finally.

"I summoned Aisling because I captured a girl. A woman. She's turning me mad, Killian, and I don't know what to do. I can't kill her."

"Then fuck her." Killian laughed at his expression. "Don't look at me like that. My advice is always going to be to fuck her because I haven't been able to touch anyone for over a thousand years."

"Be serious, Kill. She can lift my curse. Do you know what that means? You and Bayn could have your own mates out there too."

"You forget, I don't want to be saved. I want to die and have this all be over, Kian."

"So did I! That's what this whole war on the humans was about. Get revenge. Freeze Albion. Cover it in darkness until all the humans left and the fae could have the country. We could die in peace, and it would finally be over," Kian said, running his hands through his hair. "But that's changing. I'm changing! I can't stop it, and I don't know how to deal with it. I didn't search for her. She found me. Fate or the curse pushed us together, and now, I don't know how to be free of her."

"Calm down, little brother," Killian said with a sigh. "Mates. Gods, as if we weren't cursed enough. Let me think." He drank down another half of a bottle before coming up for air again. "You're fucked. Sorry, but you are. You can't be free of her, and she won't be able to get free of you, no matter how bad you both might want it. You started being an overprotective bear yet? Trying to make sure all of her needs are met? Trying to kill anyone who looks at her wrong?"

Kian didn't need to say anything. Killian knew and sniggered. "Shut up, Kill. This isn't funny."

"It really is. You were always so in control. The stoic. I would've made you the king of us all if you had taken the crown because you were always the most responsible. It's great to see you're not so perfect, after all. She must really be an amazing woman," Killian replied.

"She's got Hengist's blood." It was the wrong thing to say. Killian stopped laughing.

"I'm sorry, Kian. Aisling really was right with that loophole of hers. Maybe we have to re-think our plans a little," he said, surprising Kian.

"What do you mean?"

"Well, your mate is human. She's not going to want you to wipe everyone out, is she? Aisling always talked about trying to make a formal treaty with the humans again. You and Bayn were the ones that were always so against it. Humans are fucked up, but they have their good bits." Killian lifted his bottle. "Their alcohol has gotten better, and the *music*. Gods, so much music. If you stopped rampaging and started exploring, you might find things you like about this time."

"You sound like Elise. She's trying to convince me of the same thing," Kian said, feeling side-swiped by his own brother.

"She sounds like a smart woman, your mate."

"She is." Kian crossed his arms and uncrossed them again. "I think I like her too. It's disconcerting."

"Well, if you don't want her as your mate, maybe you could introduce me? The bond might work interchangeably with brothers."

Kian's fangs dropped, and he snarled viciously at him. Killian choked on his drink, trying to hold in his laughter.

"Oh dear, you're definitely mated. Have you told her yet?" His eyes glittered with all kinds of mayhem.

"No. I've only gotten her to agree to give me her blood to lift my curse. I had to use her freedom to barter it out of her," Kian replied.

"You made your mate a slave?" Killian's mirth was gone. He looked horrified, a rare expression for him.

"The other way around, Kill. I took her as a slave on a raid and then found out she's my mate."

Killian pinched the bridge of his nose. "I know being an asshole comes naturally to you, little brother, but this is beyond unacceptable."

"Fuck you. You have no idea what I am going through. She hates me, Kill. She's tried to murder me, and I have no doubt when the cuffs are off, she will try to do it again. I need to keep her bound to me until the curse is lifted," Kian argued.

"Maybe she would stop trying to murder you if you stopped being a fucking prick," Killian shouted back. "Mates are connected to each other in ways you can't imagine. You need to accept there is no going back from any of this. She belongs to you. You belong to her. Unbreakable. That's how it works. You're never going to want anyone else, so you need to pull your head out of your ass and treat her like you should. It doesn't matter if she's got Hengist's blood. She's yours, not his. If she hates you, then you need to fix it, Kian. Seduce her, charm her, cherish her. It won't matter if she lifts the curse for you. If she leaves you afterward, it'll kill you."

"I feel like it's already killing me," Kian admitted. Elise had twisted him up inside, and nothing was making it feel better.

"Well, if it does, I'll make sure she's well taken care of," Killian teased, knowing just what to say to Kian to piss him off.

"You're terrible at giving advice," Kian muttered.

"No, shit. You should know better." Killian's mood shifted again, the terrible prince of the night that all fae kind feared coming to the surface. "Don't let this opportunity pass you by, Kian. Out of all of us, you're the one our people look up to. A better life for them has always been our goal. Don't forget that."

"I never will."

"Good to hear it. Kiss my new sister-in-law for me." Killian shot him a wink and then vanished.

"Useless," Kian muttered. It didn't make him less right, though. It was okay for him to suggest seducing Elise. Before the curse, Killian had been able to seduce anything that caught his attention.

A human woman shouldn't have the power to make Kian feel so awkward and helpless. Elise was going to drive him to his knees and walk all over him. And he was going to let her.

∼

Kian managed to avoid Elise for the whole day. He steered clear of the library where their bond told him she was working. He enjoyed watching her expressions change from curiosity to delight whenever she opened a book, but he had more pressing matters than ogling a woman who didn't know she was his mate.

Fionn looked at Kian from across the table like he was trying to figure out what had changed about him in the past few days.

"Have the young ones crossed over yet?" Kian asked, trying to get the meeting over with as soon as possible. The sky was darkening, and his anticipation of seeing Elise was gnawing at him.

"All of them went through the portal last night and have been placed with the families. They have sent their thanks to you for honoring your agreement and will hold a feast on your return to Faerie," Fionn reported.

"Thank you, you may leave," Kian said, dismissing him with a wave of his hand.

"Forgive me, my prince, but you should know that rumors are circulating amongst the warriors."

"What kind of rumors would those be?" Kian asked through clenched teeth. Now was not the time to deal with insubordination or disruption within the ranks.

"There are concerns about your attachment to that human slave of yours. You maimed one of our best warriors over her, and that hasn't been taken lightly by the others," Fionn replied. He had enough sense to look nervous.

"My human slave should be no one's concern. Aiden was punished for touching that which didn't belong to him. I won't have my warriors disrespect me in my own house. The human is nothing but food. I like the way her blood tastes," Kian replied coldly. "Shut them up, Fionn. You're my general, after all. I shouldn't have to reprimand my warriors like unruly children."

"Master." Fionn bowed low and got out of his sight. He was smart like that.

Kian had too much to think about to deal with gossipy warriors. He had been going over Killian's words in his mind all damn day. He was obsessing, and that was never a good sign.

Kian had measured the red in his hair to be sure of what he already knew. Drinking Elise's blood from a cup wasn't going to work. He needed to get her to trust him enough to take it directly from her, but Kian had no idea how he would manage it. Elise had been nervous the previous evening like he'd never seen before. It made sense that the encounter on the full moon had scared her. It had scared him too.

Kian was drinking wine and arguing with himself in front of the fire when he heard a tentative tap on the door.

"Come in," he called, expecting Hedera or Fionn back again to bother him. Kian didn't know how to react when Elise stepped through the door and into his chambers. Her hair was out in a long wave of dark curls over one shoulder, and Kian's mouth watered as her floral and sex scent hit him.

"Hey," she said. She was nervous, but she was there.

"Would you like some wine?" Kian asked, desperately trying not to show her how happy he was to see her.

"That would be really nice," she replied. Kian pointed at a chair, and she sat down with a small smile. "I thought I would come to you. I didn't see you today, and I wanted to know if there was any change to your curse?"

"No, unfortunately not," he said, passing her a full goblet and sitting down on the chair beside her. She didn't flinch or move away, so he stayed where he was, careful not to touch her. She drank her wine, her bright blue eyes taking in Kian's chambers, her curiosity palpable.

"Do you know what went wrong?" she asked finally.

"I spoke to my brother, and he proposed that it was because I didn't drink from you directly," Kian lied. Better to throw Killian in the shit than himself.

"I thought that might be the case," Elise said, surprising him again. "I don't know anything about magic, but I know how yours feels and tastes when you use it. I've felt it whenever you drank from me, but I felt nothing last night."

"Clever little human, aren't you?" Kian smiled at her, unable to stop himself.

"I might surprise you."

"You continually surprise me, Elise," Kian said, and she laughed. "You walking straight into my chambers without a care surprises me most of all."

"I know I shouldn't be so bold, but I wanted to see where you lurk, and you can't kill me at the moment, so that makes me braver," she admitted. "And if you're going to bite me, I wanted to get it out of the way, so I'm not so worked up waiting for you to come and visit."

"Careful, Elise. You keep talking like this, and I'm going to think that you *want* me to bite you," he warned her. She was so beautiful when she blushed, he could barely stand to look at her.

"I'm eager to be free," she said primly. Elise drained her goblet and put it down on the small table beside her. She arched her lovely pale neck to him. "Do it. I'm ready."

"Not one for foreplay, are you?"

"This is biting. It has nothing to do with sex," she was quick to point out.

Oh, Elise, how wrong you are. Kian wasn't about to correct her or scare her off. "Of course not. You don't have anything to fear from me. I've never been one to go where I'm not wanted, and I'm not about to start now," he said and brushed a stray lock of hair away from her neck. Her skin was so warm and soft under his fingertips, he wanted to run his hands all over her. Elise's eyes fluttered closed, and Kian gently took her by the shoulders.

Killian's words whispered to him, *Seduce her, charm her, cherish her...*

"Relax, Elise, I'm not going to hurt you," Kian whispered and ran his lips down her throat.

"I know you won't," Elise replied, her hands going to his chest. So trusting. She could fight it all she wanted, but when Elise was in Kian's arms, she knew she belonged to him. Like his own, Elise's body knew it right down to her bones, even if her mind and heart rebelled against it.

In that blinding second, Kian knew he would do anything to possess all three; her body, mind, and heart.

"Kian, are you going to do it or not?" Elise asked.

His fangs pierced her skin, making her whimper. He sucked her sweet, glorious blood inside of him, and Kian fought not to fall into the madness of it, to have her pinned in such a primal way made the predator in him come alive. It demanded more.

Elise's hands moved up to his shoulders, and she leaned further back into the soft couch, surrendering herself to him. Fire and honey and damnation roared through Kian as he swallowed her down, the power in her blood burning the roots of his curse.

Kian needed to stop. He didn't want to take too much and leave her weak, but he didn't want to let her go. He swirled his tongue over the bite, and her small hands pushed their way into his hair. Elise's shallow, hot breaths were panting against his ear, and he could smell her arousal. This mad, reckless desire was burning Kian alive, but he wouldn't force her. He was a bastard, but even he had lines he wouldn't cross.

Kian gently licked the blood away and reluctantly lifted his head, Elise's fingers dragging through his hair. "Elise? Are you okay?"

"Yes. Just...give me a second," she replied, not opening her eyes.

Kian got up, found some healing balm, and gently rubbed it over the bite marks. She made a sound in the back of her throat that he wasn't sure was pain or pleasure.

"It'll be gone by morning," Kian assured her. Elise's long lashes fluttered, and she opened her eyes. Her pupils were blown out with desire, and it pierced him straight in the gut. She had no idea how dangerous it was to look at Kian like that.

He didn't think *anyone* had ever looked at him like that.

"Are you sure you're feeling okay?" Kian asked, needing her to leave while he was still willing to let her.

"Yeah. I don't know if anyone has told you, but it's an overwhelming experience getting bit like that."

"No. I haven't been told that." Mostly because she was the only one he had bit. Everyone else had been a cup and a cut wrist, or a mouthful from a dead enemy. She didn't need to know that.

"Well, it is. I feel a bit high or drunk. Hard to explain."

"Take as long as you need." Kian got comfortable beside her again, their knees touching.

"Careful, master, you don't want to get too familiar, remember?" Elise said, her eyes drifting close again.

"A little too late for that, slave. I keep waiting for my contempt to return, but alas, it hasn't."

Elise chuckled softly, a husky sound that streaked through him. "I know the feeling. I'm starting to think it was easier to hate you."

"You don't hate me anymore?" Kian asked, hope squeezing his heart.

Elise opened one eye. "Not nearly as much as I should. God, what did you put in that wine? I shouldn't have told you that. You're just going to use it against me later."

"Want to know a secret?"

That got her interest. "Yes."

"I don't hate you as much as I should either," Kian admitted. Her answering smile was the most beautiful thing he had ever seen.

18

Elise hadn't planned on seeking Kian out that night. She had been restless and started to wander the castle and ended up going straight to him. She had begun to recognize magic more and more as it manipulated the world around her, and she'd definitely been feeling influenced since the full moon.

What is happening to me? She was hurtling blindly towards something that she couldn't see and wasn't sure she wanted to feel. Elise was also certain she could feel Kian moving about the castle. If she shut her eyes and spun around and around, she knew she'd end up walking right into him.

Elise didn't know him all that well, but Kian had changed too. He had a carefulness around her that hadn't been there before. He needed Elise on his side to break the curse and was doing his best not to piss her off.

Lying in bed and staring at the canopy of silk, Elise allowed herself to let go of some animosity and try and sort out the jumble of emotions inside of her.

She was starting to feel like a different person. Cut off from the rest of the world, Elise was disconnected entirely from her past and was becoming something...else. She didn't have family, except for a cousin in

Norway that would be safe because she was so far from there. She missed Chrissy, The British Museum, espresso coffee, and her eBook reader. But everything else? Not so much.

The pragmatic in Elise had taken control of an impossible situation to survive it. She was a slave but wasn't mistreated anymore, other than being unable to leave. Even before the full moon, Kian had been protective of her. She had tried to stab him and couldn't do it. When he wasn't trying to provoke her, Elise enjoyed his company. A part of her knew he was a scary bastard, capable of violence that would give her nightmares forever, but everything he did, he had a reason for doing.

Kian also kissed like a demon and had given her an orgasm so intense that it scared the hell out of her.

I can't be crushing on him. He was a psycho. Maybe she was too. He had hunted her down on the full moon, and the bastard had been right. Elise had liked that game in the end as much as he had.

She buried her head under the pillow and groaned in sexual frustration and embarrassment. Elise wasn't a prude but had never been one to get excited over biting and dominance games. Not that she'd had a partner that adventurous.

As if it knew Elise was thinking about him, the place Kian had bitten on her neck pulsed, sending little jolts of pleasure through her. She knew what an out-of-control Kian bite felt like (terrifying, exciting, painfully hot), but when he did it gently? It hadn't hurt. The pain had come from what it did to her. Elise's insides had melted with the need to touch and taste him.

With her arms around him and face pressed into his hair, it was like Elise could breathe properly for the first time since the full moon. Kian had relaxed, his muscles under her hands loosening. She couldn't be the only one feeling this way.

I don't hate you as much as I should either.

How many more times would he need to drink from her before his curse had lifted? Elise trembled under the sheets, knowing that she wouldn't be able to hide how she was feeling for much longer.

I am such a fucking mess.

Maybe this was why there were so many stories about being aware of the fae because they will make you want them so badly that you would cheerfully follow them into Faerie and never return.

～

THE NEXT DAY, Elise was bleary-eyed and slow to wake up. She had been up late tossing and turning in her usual conflicted state of hating and wanting Kian.

The corner of the library, however, was looking neater and better every day. Elise was proud of how it was coming together and had a list of materials to ask Kian for so she could start restoring some of the books that had gotten broken.

Elise might have been conflicted about her feelings for Kian, but the love growing for the library was real. She loved how the bookshelves were carved with beautiful trees and creatures and how at certain times of the day, the birds would sing haunting songs.

She loved the way the books of magic smelled spicy and floral instead of like ink and paper. The books made in Faerie felt alive and watchful compared to the ones made in the human world, which felt dead in comparison. Elise wanted to ask Kian if it had something to do with how the paper was prepared, from what kind of trees, and how they made their inks and paints. She wanted to know more each day.

If they hadn't killed each other by the time Kian's curse lifted, maybe he would let her finish the library? It was a short drive from Salisbury to the castle every day, so it would be the ideal commute. It was a ridiculous thought seeing how outside of the castle walls, humans and fae were fighting each other. It could have turned into world war three out there, and Elise was none the wiser.

Rough hands grabbed Elise's arms, slamming her down over the worktable so quickly, she didn't have time to cry out.

"Fucking human," Fionn growled, the tip of his blade resting under her ear.

"P-Please don't hurt me," she mumbled against the table.

"Tell me the truth, human. What are you to the prince?"

"A slave as you can see."

"Lies. You've been going into each other's chambers at night. Is he fucking you?"

"No!" Elise tried to lift her head, but Fionn pressed it back down. "We aren't fucking. He's drinking my blood to help with his curse." The cold blade pressed tighter against her skin.

"Lie to me again, and I'll slit your throat," he hissed. His body was pressing over hers, revulsion prickling against Elise's skin. "I have seen the prince drink blood for centuries, and it hasn't helped his curse at all."

"You'll have to ask him! All I know is that he drinks my blood, and he's got more red in his hair the next day. That's it. I am nothing to him."

"You're breaking his curse." Fionn's confidence was gone. He sounded spooked. "You tell him that we talked, and I'll kill you in ways you can't imagine." He gave Elise a final, hard shove and then was gone, leaving her shaking.

"You should be careful of that one," Hedera said, appearing from behind a bookshelf. She placed a tray of tea and fruit on the table.

"I should be careful of all of you," Elise snapped, straightening her clothes.

Hedera grunted. "True. We have reasons to hate your kind."

"I know, but I didn't do anything to any of you. I never asked to become a slave and be threatened to be baked into a fucking pie."

Hedera smiled, showing rows of sharp pointed teeth, and made a wheezing sound. It took Elise a second to figure out she was laughing at her.

"I still think you should be. The master feels differently, and even though I don't like you, I'll obey his wishes," she replied and put her hands on her hips. "Fionn is getting too big for his britches. He's getting impatient under the master's boot, especially because he's becoming more interested in you than killing humans. All fae warriors can't be trusted, but that one most of all."

"Why do you even care what Fionn does to me?"

"The master would care, so I care. The master is the smartest, deadliest fae of them all, and if he's interested in you, then he's got good reason." Hedera wheezed-laughed. "Though I doubt it will be good for you in the end."

19

"Why are you lying to me, Elise? What you're saying isn't possible," Kian argued later that evening.

"No, really. They are from an ancient culture from Assyria. Winged lions that used to guard the entrance to a temple. There is also sarcophagi from Egypt, one of the oldest cultures in the world. I can take you and show you if you like. That is if your warriors haven't burned the British Museum down," Elise replied.

Kian shook his head. "I told them that there will be no looting. It will be there. When I trust you more, perhaps I will consider taking you."

Kian had been trying hard not to be interested in the things she had been telling him over dinner. Elise had the best chance to appeal to his curiosity, and she could see it was working by the multitude of questions he kept asking. He was going to *freak* when she took him to a museum. He had been interested in the concept of public libraries and the symphony and art galleries. That was another story about the fae that was true; they loved art, music, and beauty.

As they argued about modern medicine techniques (which Elise didn't know much about), she decided that she was getting dangerously close to liking this Kian. He was funny when he wanted to be and deadly smart. His mind quickly turned over massive concepts, and Elise wondered how much information overload he could handle. She wished desperately for a tablet and an internet connection so she could *really* blow his mind.

Hanging out like this, Elise could forget he was 'the prince,' the male eager to wipe humanity out of England. This was, she decided, the most dangerous version of Kian she had seen.

They sat in a small private dining room that was connected to his chambers. It was strange to be sharing a meal with him, talking about human history and culture. Good conversation. Nice candlelight. It was suspiciously like a date.

Elise wanted to tell him about Fionn's threats. It was burning on her tongue, but at the same time, his warning about killing her held her back. Fionn wouldn't hesitate like Kian. Elise had nothing that he needed. Fionn might be trying to overstep like Hedera said, but Elise had no doubt that Kian would squash him like a bug if he tried.

"How much more red do you have in your hair today?" Elise asked. Kian's long mane was tied back in a braid, and she itched to pull it out of its bindings.

"Two more inches. I had given up ever finding a cure for the curse that I had resigned myself to death. Now that it's receding, I'm feeling adrift."

Wow. A real confession out of the Blood Prince.

"Don't you have things that you've always wanted to do? Things you regretted not trying? You can do all of those things now. The human world has changed so much. You have limitless things to explore and do."

Kian smiled at Elise, a touch sly. "It sounds intimidating. I may need a guide, someone to help me navigate this time."

"You will find someone. I'm sure plenty of people will put their hands up to help. If you stop trying to kill them, that is," she replied. A small crease appeared between his brows.

"I was implying that perhaps *you* would show me?" he said.

A small vibration of happiness unexpectedly fluttered through her. "Oh? I thought I disgusted you."

Kian's smile returned. "You do. Just less than all the others."

"Don't hurt yourself with all this flattery you are showering me with. I thought the fae were supposed to be master seducers."

"My brother Killian got all of those abilities. I have...other skills."

Elise wanted to know what those skills were. Badly. She refused to give him the satisfaction of asking.

"Then maybe Killian will have a better chance of convincing me to play tour guide," Elise teased. Kian went very still, anger and magic rolling out of him. The armrests under his hands crumbled under his grip. *Shit.*

"You are mine. Not Killian's. You will go nowhere with him," he growled, fangs dropping.

"Kian, I was joking," Elise said, trying to keep her voice steady. "But when I'm free, I'll go wherever I want, with *whoever* I want."

"Is that what you think?" She didn't like Kian's entitled tone one little bit.

"Yeah, it is. You promised to free me from being your slave. Fae promises are unbreakable."

Magic pulsed hard in Elise's sternum, tugging towards him like it was going to try and break free.

Kian snarled softly, gripped the armrest of her chair, dragging her over, so their knees were touching. He clasped her face in his warm, hard hands.

"I am bound to release you from slavery," he purred, rubbing his cheek against hers. Warm breath tickled Elise's ear as he pressed his lips to the space behind it. "But you are *never* going to be free of me." While he was distracted, Elise grabbed his knife from beside his plate and held it to his throat.

"Why?" she demanded. Kian didn't try and pull back even though one slip of her hand would open him up.

"You *know* why, Elise. You're ignoring it, fighting the feeling, but you know," he whispered.

Kian lifted his head back so that she could look him in his gold streaked, scarlet eyes. The magic in her core pulsed again, reaching for him.

"I hate you," Elise ground out between her teeth, pressing the blade tighter to his throat.

"You might want to, but you don't. You crave me," he said with that all-knowing smile of his.

"I do *not* crave you," Elise hissed in his face. A trickle of gold seeped out of the small cut on his neck. Panic stabbed her at the sight of his blood, but she held her ground. Kian's large hand rested on her belly between her ribs, over the ball of magic that burned like a sun. Tears filled Elise's eyes as he took her other hand and placed it on his chest in the same place. Gone was the smug smile and arrogant fae dick persona that was his normal state.

"Yes, you do," he said.

"It's just the magic of our bargain that's fucking with me," Elise replied in a painful breath. She pressed her forehead to his. "This is just another part of your curse. You don't feel this horrible thing burning me up inside because you did it to me."

Kian grabbed her hand, pulling the knife away from his neck. Elise was leaning over him, her knee resting on the chair between his thighs.

"I feel it too. It's not my magic, and it has nothing to do with my curse," he said, drawing her closer. "Tell me you don't want me, Elise. That you're repulsed by my touch. That you don't dream of my mouth on your skin and my dick buried inside of you. Tell me you don't want me to make you scream in pleasure as my teeth pierce you."

The knife fell from Elise's hand and clanged to the floor. Her fingers traced his face and hair before gripping the base of his antlers. Their lips were almost touching, eyes locked on each other.

"No. I won't tell you that," Elise snarled softly.

Surprise, fear, and desire flashed in Kian's eyes. He pulled her down onto his lap so she was straddling him. His arms held her tight, preventing her from running.

"Kiss me like you mean it," he begged.

Elise's lips obeyed and weren't gentle. She bit and sucked, releasing her pent-up frustration. She pushed her tongue up against his, sucking it into her mouth. His hands gripped her thighs, dragging her up against the hard length in his pants. Rolling her hips, Elise got it right against the spot that was aching for that sweet friction.

Elise tugged at the laces on his shirt until they came loose, unwrapping him like a present she always wanted. She dragged her nails over him, leaving faint red marks on the curve of his pecs and down his abs. Kian let out a sexy little gasp as Elise bit her way down his chest and sucked his nipple. She closed her teeth on it, and Elise was suddenly in the air, Kian hoisting her up in his arms.

"Infernal human," he growled, pressing her up against the nearest wall, stripping off her shirt and tearing her bandeau in half. Elise's breasts bounced free, and he leaned back so he could stare at them for a long moment. With prodigious strength, Kian lifted her higher, his pelvis pinning her hard against the wall so he could free up his hands to cup and squeeze.

Licking his thumb, he ran it over Elise's nipple in slow circles. He held intense eye contact with her as he rolled the tight bud between thumb and forefinger. He squeezed slowly, tighter and tighter, until a startled cry escaped her lips and warm, wet heat flooded her panties.

"That's it, my lover. That's your sweet point," he said smugly, grinding hard up against Elise's pelvis, the pressure on her breast not easing up. She was going to come without even getting her pants off.

"Kian," she whimpered and kissed him, nails dragging down his spine. He pulled her off the wall and carried her into his room.

Dropping Elise on his bed, Kian pulled off the rest of her clothes until she was naked and sprawled out in front of him. He didn't join her on the bed, just stood at the edge of it, studying every bit of her. His gaze dipping between her legs where Elise couldn't hide how wet she was for him.

"Fuck," he whispered, almost reverently, his expression full of awe before it turned savage. His big hand pressed down on Elise's chest between her breasts, her heart fluttering like it was going to burst under his palm. His lips lifted into a sharp smile full of fang and possession, his hand moving slowly down from her chest, over the curve of her belly before resting on the mound of soft curls between her thighs. His palm pressed down harder, turning his hand and curled his fingers through her slickness. Kian thrust two fingers inside of her, hard and fast, making Elise cry out.

"Mine," he said, eyes blazing at every one of Elise's reactions. She grabbed his forearm with both hands, nails breaking his skin. She thrust her hips up, riding his hand, needing release. He pulled his hand away from her, and she let out a strangled cry of loss and anger. Kian stared at his glistening fingers before licking them slowly one at a time.

His eyes fluttered closed, and he hummed in pleasure at the taste of her.

"Delicious everywhere," he said.

Elise got up on her knees, tugging the laces of his leather pants loose with shaking fingers. A deep growl rolled up from the pit of his stomach as she gripped his dick and pulled it free. Elise knew it would be big, but it actually made her pause and stare.

"No horns after all," she said, looking up at him.

Kian chuckled huskily. "Disappointed?"

"Not at all." Elise tightened her hand and stroked him hard. Kian's expression darkened, and he pulled her hand away and turned her around. Instead of bending Elise over, his strong arms came around her, holding her so her back was pressed up against his chest. His hands cupped Elise's heavy breasts, gripping and releasing, stroking and teasing. One hand went back down, and he pressed a slow hard circle around her clit.

"Delicious, perfect, infernal human," Kian said against Elise's shoulders. Her hands went up around his neck and gripped hard on his antlers, giving him a full view of her breasts. She turned her head, and he kissed her roughly, biting her lip hard enough to draw a drop of blood and suck it off.

"Fuck me like you mean it, Kian," Elise said, throwing his words back at him.

Kian's hands slid down her hips and pulled her thighs wider. He rubbed his hard dick between her folds to wet it down, the delicious friction making her push up against him.

"Don't let go," he commanded, and Elise's grip on the base of his antlers tightened. The breath was sucked out of her lungs as he thrust his dick into her in one powerful move. He was so big that her thighs tightened to slow him down.

"Breathe, Elise. Every single part of you was made for me to plunder and pleasure," Kian whispered darkly. His hands tightened on her hips, rolling them back and pushing his dick the rest of the way in, holding her there until she adjusted to him.

Elise could barely get enough air as Kian started to rock his dick moving back and forth, hitting secret places deep inside of her. She was dancing on a delicious line between pleasure and sweet pain, Kian instinctively knowing just how hard and quick he could push her. Elise surrendered to him, letting him lead, knowing that he would get her to a place she had never been before.

"Fuck, Kian, you feel so damn good," Elise managed to gasp, his hands stroking and teasing her body.

"So do you. Better than I could have ever dreamed of," he whispered, kissing her shoulder. He placed his foot on the edge of the bed and lifted Elise's leg over his bent knee, spreading her wider. She pulled herself up, the change of position overwhelming. His hand went between her legs and underneath where they were joined, stroking firmly up and down over both of them and pressing a circle over her clit whenever he reached the top.

Even in her pleasure hazed mind, Elise knew it wasn't just fucking. Kian was breaking down every hidden part of her and putting his mark on the pieces. He was taking things and replacing them, and she was doing the same to him.

He's mine, a voice Elise barely recognized chanted like a mantra.

Every cohesive thought went out of her head as Kian began to thrust again, Elise's orgasm building so hot and tight that she was almost weeping. He shifted, pushing in and out harder and faster until she was shaking, struggling to hang on.

"Bite me," Elise groaned, her head dropping back on his shoulder.

"So perfect," he growled.

She screamed when his teeth sank into her, Elise's orgasm exploding so violently she lost her grip on his antlers.

Kian held tightly onto her, guiding her down onto her stomach. He laid his massive body over hers, resting on his elbows, his lips on her neck. He was still hard inside of her, pushing slow and deep, dragging her orgasm out until Elise was sobbing into the mattress. He had broken her entirely and still wasn't done.

Kian lifted his mouth from the bite and kissed Elise's shoulders. Hoisting himself up, he licked the trickle of sweat from her spine. Fingers traced her sides before reaching the curves of her ass, gripping it until Elise gasped and pushed it up higher for him.

"Greedy girl wants more," he purred approvingly, and goosebumps broke out over her skin. He pulled her ass roughly back up against him, making her cry out again. Elise went up on her elbows, her breath coming out in shallow gasps as their sweat-slicked skin slapped hard against each other. Kian kneaded her ass, setting a torturous pace and guiding her back down over him again and again.

One hand went underneath Elise to grip her breast, pinching her nipples again and making her scream. His breathing became labored as he bit her again, hurtling them both through a climax with enough force that they ended up on the bed in a tangle of arms and legs and struggling breaths.

The small ball of magic inside Elise was burning like a supernova as she climbed on top of Kian. As soon as her chest was pressed to his, the magic rushed out of her. Their skin lit up in shining golden runes, making them both jump in alarm.

"What is this?" Elise asked in wonder, twisting so she could study the runes better.

Kian's hands gently stroked the wild hair from Elise's face before dragging her up further to cup her cheeks in his hands.

"It's just magic reacting, that's all. It's not going to hurt you," he assured her, even though his own voice was shaky. He kissed Elise softly, his scarlet eyes shot with so much gold that they looked luminescent, his face full of wonder.

20

Kian couldn't breathe. He couldn't think. His skin was lit up with strange magic he didn't recognize, and Elise's face was glowing with light. He didn't want to worry her that he had no idea what was going on.

The mating bond.

Kian thought it had already clicked into place, but maybe he had been wrong, and it had taken a sexual bonding? Elise's finger came up and smoothed his frown away.

"Stop thinking so hard, or I'll have to fuck you again," she said, her full lips red from kissing.

"Are you...threatening me?" Kian replied with a wolfish grin. Elise only grinned back with no fear of him whatsoever, a string of runes glowing over her soft cheeks.

My mate. A warm feeling flooded Kian's heart, and that scared him almost as much as the sex that had shaken him down to his soul.

Elise squeaked in surprise as Kian sat up, taking her with him and carrying her into the bathroom. She was a soft, tousled bundle in his arms, and having her pressed up against him felt like the most natural thing in the world. Kian lowered her to her feet and pressed the sigil to get the water flowing.

"Oh, I love that," she said, studying the holes in the stone curiously. He had to stop staring at her but couldn't look away if he tried. She undid the tie around Kian's braid and slowly unraveled it.

"It has more red in it already," Elise said, lifting the scarlet ends and brushing them across her cheeks. Kian's heart fluttered, and to hide the ridiculous feelings coursing through him, he stepped under the warm water.

Kian reached a hand out to her, and without hesitation, Elise let him pull her close again.

Taking a soft cloth, Kian carefully washed the smeared blood away from the bite on Elise's neck, wanting to take care of her. He should've been gentler with her, but the woman knew how to break his control every time.

"I didn't hurt you, did I?" Kian asked, worried that humans weren't built for aggressive fae lovemaking.

"No, of course not," Elise replied, running her small hands over his chest. Reaching higher on her tiptoes, she touched his antlers and started to giggle.

"What?"

"They have more black on them, but...they look like my handprints."

Kian laughed with her, a joyful sound that he'd forgotten how to make. "Well, you were hanging on rather hard."

Elise touched his cheek. "I like this new smile."

"Don't get used to it," Kian replied, running his hands down her warm, wet back to her perfect hips. He could spend days worshipping her body.

Elise only rolled her eyes at him. "Don't worry, master. My expectations when they come to you are meager. I'm sure this is another part of your madness, and tomorrow you will be back to growling and hissing at me."

"Is that so?" Kian guided her back against the stone wall, his hands resting on the walls on either side of her. He lowered his mouth to hers, making her heart rate spike. "You think this is me mad?"

"Yes, but maybe I am too," she whispered and kissed him. Her mouth was soft and intoxicating, and he needed more. He would *always* need more.

Kian sat down on the stone bench, bringing Elise onto his lap. Her ass and thighs were soft against his hard body, and his embrace deepened. Her hands glided over his chest, never breaking the kiss.

Kian had always hated to be touched by others, and it was one more thing that was different about Elise. He loved her stroking and exploring him and never wanted her to stop. Kian's dick was hard again, and he did nothing to hide what she did to him. He cupped her full breasts, and Elise made a hungry sound against his lips, sending fire through his veins.

Elise took his dick in one hand, rose up on her knees, and guided him slowly back inside of her. The dominant side of Kian wanted to take over, but he held it in check. His mate had a dominant side of her own, and he would let her use him in any way she needed.

So dangerous. These feelings would burn him up and ruin every responsibility Kian had because he would always put her first.

All Kian's thoughts vanished as Elise rolled her hips and began to ride him, setting a slow and deep pace that would kill him in the best way. Runes were dancing on their skin again, Elise's face full of wonder and wicked delight.

"One day, you are going to tell me what these marks mean," she panted.

It means you are my mate. Kian bit his tongue so he wouldn't tell her right then and there. He didn't want to frighten her and wasn't going to ruin this moment for the world. Kian gripped her hips, pulling her up harder against him, needing to be deeper inside of her, closer to her body.

Elise kissed Kian roughly, biting at his lips. With a groan, she began to come again, her head tilting back. His mouth watered, but he wouldn't take any more blood from her, so he kissed and nipped at her until her breathing steadied. Elise moved to rest her forehead against his, her blue eyes full of emotion Kian didn't know how to interpret.

"You are going to be the most dangerous mistake I've ever made," Elise admitted, making Kian smile.

"Infernal human, you took the thought right out of my head," he replied.

Kian's dominant side won the fight and quickly had her back up against the wall, fucking her until they both couldn't breathe.

Once they finally got out of the water, Kian wrapped a towel around her before taking one for himself.

"I don't suppose you know what happened to my clothes?" asked Elise.

He frowned, confused by the question. "And what would you need clothes for?"

"I can't run bare ass back to my room, Kian," Elise pointed out. His hands stilled from pressing water from his hair.

"You're not staying?" He tried not to sound as desperate as he felt. Kian had just mated her properly and didn't think he would be able to let her go.

Elise bit the inside of her cheek. "I didn't think that you'd want me to."

"You thought this was only about sex?" Kian demanded, trying to hold back the anger inside of him.

"Well, yeah. Wasn't it?"

Arawan, damn me, she's serious. His hands were shaking as he rested them on her shoulders. "Did it *feel* like only sex to you?"

Kian could see the questions and uncertainty in her eyes. Fear that he was trying to trick her. He deserved that. Kian had taken her as a slave. He hadn't told her a thing about the fierce bond growing between them. He was too scared to.

"No. It didn't feel like only sex. That doesn't mean I'm going to presume you wanted me to stay the night," Elise replied. Her eyes went steely. "You want me to stay? Ask me, politely."

Kian could feel her foot on his neck, their roles slipping as she became the master. It should have scared the shit out of him. It should've made him snap her beautiful neck.

Instead, Kian lifted her hand, brushed the back of it against his cheek, and kissed her knuckles. "Please, Elise, stay with me."

Elise smiled, her cheeks turning pink. "Fine, but if you snore once, I'm out."

DESPITE HER THREATS, Kian woke the next day with Elise still curled up in his arms, her fingers in his hair and lips pressed into his side. He had to get up. He had a morning meeting with Fionn to get reports on the army and couldn't give up his responsibilities to lie in bed staring at his mate. *My fragile, human mate.* His arms tightened around her.

Your mate is human. She's not going to want you to wipe everyone out, is she?

Fuck, he hated it when Killian was right. Kian needed to think of a way to change their plans to create a safe place for their people. Elise seemed to believe that she could convince him that humans had evolved, that they had things that would interest the fae and vice versa. She talked about going to London to prove it to him. Perhaps, he should let her try.

Kian was interested in much she had told him so far and was finally willing to be convinced. His hands stroked her arm that was flung over his chest. The golden cuffs he'd put on her were gone. He didn't know how, but it hardly mattered. If Elise ran, he'd be able to use their bond to find her.

The thought of Elise leaving him struck a resounding blow inside of Kian's chest. He had made so many mistakes with her that he couldn't blame her for wanting to go.

You have to give her reasons to stay.

Kian couldn't think straight with her curled up next to him, so he climbed out of bed. She made sleepy sounds of protest but thankfully didn't wake. Kian couldn't face her feeling this raw.

Kian dressed quickly and was about to leave when he returned to the bedchamber and pressed a kiss to her lips.

Such weakness.

Fionn was already waiting for him by the time Kian made it to the council room. Not for the first time, he wished that his brothers were there, sitting in their chairs. It would mean that Kian wouldn't feel like the only one making the decisions.

But he was.

Both Killian and Bayn had little interest in ruling, their once packed courts slowly disbanding in the past thousands of years. Like Kian, they were tired and were fully prepared to die. That was before Elise. How could one woman cause so much disruption in his life?

"My prince," Fionn said with a short bow. He was frowning as he looked at Kian. Had he changed so much?

"What are you staring at?" Kian asked.

"Forgive me, but your hair has changed."

"I am aware. The curse is finally lifting."

Kian knew that Fionn had imagined himself as his successor when he finally did die. Nothing had been announced because it was a fae tradition for all would-be rulers to fight it out until only one remained standing.

"How is that possible?" Fionn asked.

"Magic," Kian replied, shutting the conversation down. "How is Londinium?"

"The army has retreated back as requested, and there are scouts everywhere to report any movements. The humans have set up an encampment halfway between Londinium and here. It was where their warriors came from when they broke into the castle. I still think we should burn Londinium to the ground and be done with it."

"I appreciate the suggestion, but it's not the size that it used to be. Burning it down would take more resources than we have, not to mention we are grossly outnumbered. I'm reluctant to waste our warrior's lives."

"You could release your madness curse and let them tear themselves apart, my prince."

Kian raised a brow. Had he always been this mouthy?

"I could, but I don't think that would be best for the fae right now. We have taken our revenge on the betrayer's bloodlines, and child compensations have been provided." Kian steepled his fingers, ignoring the confused expression on his face. "I would like to go to Londinium and see things for myself before I make a final decision."

"Master, you shouldn't put yourself at risk. We no longer have the element of surprise that we did when we attacked the bloodlines," Fionn argued.

"I will glamour myself, and I will take my human slave to be my guide," Kian said, secretly relishing the idea of Elise showing him all the marvels she had spoken of.

"You can't trust the human! She will betray you as soon as you are free of the army!"

"Do you think me helpless, Fionn? That I'm some mewling faeling who can't protect myself against one woman?" Kian demanded, his temper flaring. "Well? If you have something to say to me, now is the time."

"You are a mighty warrior, my prince, but I fear she has bewitched you. You are different with her, and she will be the death of you if you allow yourself to be blinded," Fionn replied steadily.

"I am not bewitched. What I am is a prince who has fought for too long to create safety for my people. The betrayer's bloodlines had to be terminated. I was blood sworn to do so. Now that we are back in Albion, I can see how much the human population has grown. I know that starting a war won't end the way we imagined," Kian said, trying to see Fionn's concern from his point of view. "I'm going to Londinium to try and come up with a new strategy. My human will attend to me. I need you to support me or challenge me. Those are your options." It was enough of a threat that Fionn bowed low in submission.

"My prince, I will talk to the scouts and find a route to get you to Londinium," he said before backing slowly out of the room.

Kian pulled out all the maps and original plans. If Elise managed to convince him that making a treaty with the humans was a good idea, he needed to be ready with his demands and a plan should the humans try and betray them again.

21

Elise turned the pages of an atlas and tried her best not to think about Kian. It was a task easier said than done because her whole body was feeling him. Intimately.

Elise had woken up late in his bed, but Kian had already disappeared for the day. *Was he weird about the sex?* She didn't want to be weird about it but knew better than to try and predict what mood Kian would be in. Hopefully a good one, considering how well her blood was fighting back his curse.

Elise had seen for herself how quickly the new color had stretched out in his hair the previous night. Was it because of the sex as well as the blood? She didn't know if her poor human body could handle that level of intense lovemaking every night to speed up the curse breaking.

She bit back a laugh. *Who am I kidding? I would cheerfully hang off Kian's antlers whenever he asked me nicely.*

Every time Elise was with him lately, something else between them changed. It was a good thing...and probably a terrible thing in the long run. Elise could already imagine all the years she would spend in therapy in the future when she was free, and this temporary Stockholm Syndrome shit she was feeling had gone away. It had to be Stockholm, right? If it wasn't, it meant that what she was starting to feel for him was real, and that was another kind of disastrous life choice.

Speaking of Elise's freedom, her golden cuffs were gone. Her wrists were curiously light, and she couldn't stop touching them. She got a brief rush of adrenaline, thinking about sneaking out of the castle and running for her life. Then Elise woke up properly and realized that just because the cuffs were gone, it didn't mean that Kian and his fae warriors wouldn't hunt her down if she tried to get out of their bargain.

Elise had experienced the power of a bargain firsthand, and if she tried to escape, it wasn't only her life at risk. She needed to prove to Kian that if he could trust one human to keep their word, he could have the capacity to trust more.

Elise smiled, imagining the awe on his face when she finally did get the chance to show him the British Museum. Not to mention her favorite books and music. She had never wanted to share so much, so badly.

Elise was putting the book back into a shelf when a cold blade pressed to her throat.

"Make one sound, and I'll gut you," Fionn hissed. Elise held her hands up to show she was unarmed. When Elise tried to turn, he put a heavy hand on her shoulder to stop her. "Walk, bitch. I'm done putting up with you."

With the blade never leaving her throat, Fionn guided Elise out of the library and into the ballroom. He pulled back a heavy tapestry to reveal a door and shoved her through it into the darkness.

"I thought that it was only about your blood, slave, but I could smell you all over my prince this morning. I can smell him on you right now. That he would debase himself with a human like you makes me sick. He might not believe that you have him bewitched, but I know him. I know he's not himself, and I will cure him of you forever."

Fionn was ranting, and Elise let him. He sounded like a jealous, spurned ex-lover, not a general. Unlike Kian, Fionn wouldn't hesitate to slit her throat and leave her to bleed out in the dark.

Fionn knew the passages well enough that he didn't light any torches to guide their way. Thankfully, they hadn't found any stairs. They were moving down in a slow spiral, the air going stale and cold.

"Are you throwing me into a cell?" Elise asked, her voice echoing off the stones.

"No."

"Are you going to kill me?"

"I wish I could, but fae don't kill each other's slaves."

Elise opened her mouth to speak again, and Fionn slammed her hard against the wall. "Enough talking." Pain flashed down her side, and Elise cradled her bruised arm to her chest. Uncaring, Fionn shoved her roughly through the bowels of the castle.

It had been mid-afternoon when Fionn had snatched Elise from the library. When the tunnel finally ended, the sun was gone. They were outside the castle walls, the entrance covered in brambles. They parted for them and revealed a horse tethered to a peg in a small glade.

Elise didn't see the blow coming. Fionn hit her hard in the face and head in a series of quick punches, driving her to her knees. He bound her hands up and tossed her over the horse. Blood dribbled out of Elise's mouth and nose. He mounted behind her and kept her pinned with one hand as the horse lurched forward.

The fae might not kill each other's slaves, but they were smart enough with words that Fionn could throw Elise off a cliff and blame the rocks for killing her. Elise thought that she would be used to getting smacked about and traumatized, but apparently not. She did the most useless thing she could and started to cry.

It wasn't all about the pain. Kian would think she had run from him and their bargain. He trusted Fionn, and he wouldn't ever suspect him. But Kian still needed her blood. He would try and find her, wouldn't he? That brief flash of hope died as lights came into view, and Elise could make out some kind of military encampment. *A human one.* What the fuck was Fionn playing at?

Magic rolled over them, and a pale blue shimmer surrounded the horse as Fionn slowed to a trot, riding them up to the tall metal gates.

"Hold it right there, fae!" a human commanded over a megaphone. Soldiers lined the walls, their guns pointed at them. Fionn only laughed. He grabbed Elise by her hair, yanking hard, so she fell off the horse and onto the freezing mud.

"Enjoy your freedom," he hissed at her nastily. The fae mount shimmered and was gone in a flash. Elise was crying again, sobbing as the pulse of magic that always told her when Kian was close faded away.

"Don't move," someone was shouting at her. Like she could. Elise was hurt and aching everywhere, blood still running from her face.

"We need a medic!"

Strong arms lifted Elise up and carried her into the camp, the tall metal doors shutting behind her with a clang of finality.

22

The tea that Elise had been given tasted like shit. She felt like this was a strategic move because, really, this was England, and there was no excuse for a lousy cup of tea. She refused to even get started on the cold cheese sandwich they had thought she would want to eat.

Elise's bloody face had been cleaned up, with temporary stitches holding the worst of the cuts together, and her arm had been put in a sling until they could get it x-rayed for a fracture. If she ever saw Fionn again, Elise was going to kick him in the balls. Or ask Kian too. She rubbed at her chest, heart aching and empty from the missing ball of magic.

Elise should've been happy and grateful to have gotten away. Instead, she was nauseous and emotional. She'd try and blame her Stockholm Syndrome later, but right then and there, Elise missed Kian. Seeing humans on phones and other technology felt alien after so many weeks away from it. She wanted her quiet library back.

Once Elise had stopped leaking blood everywhere, soldiers had taken her to a small building, and she was put in an interview room with a stainless-steel table and mirrored windows. That wasn't even the best of it. Some guy had turned up and put a necklace over her head that was made of iron rings. Elise tried not to laugh at him. While she didn't see any iron in the castle, she couldn't confirm its efficacy against the fae. She sure as hell didn't know what they thought an ugly necklace would do.

Elise was about to lay her pounding head down on the table and go to sleep when the door opened. A stocky man in uniform came in. He had to be the boss. A few months ago, Elise would be pissing her pants seeing a guy like that glaring at her, but after dealing with Kian, the guy was...small.

"What's your name?" he asked, sitting down and taking out his phone and tablet. He pressed record and looked at her expectantly.

"Elise Carlisle. I'm from Salisbury."

"Elise, I am General Gatesbridge. Can you tell me how long you were with the fae?"

"I wasn't 'with' them. I was their slave," she corrected. "I was taken from my train home from London...maybe eight weeks ago? It was the first night the fae returned."

"I see." General Gatesbridge tapped on his tablet and held up a picture of the train's interior filled with blood splatters, but thankfully no bodies. "This look familiar?"

"Painfully. I was pulled out of a carriage where people were trying to kill each other or themselves," Elise replied.

"You mean the fae were killing them."

She shook her head. "No, they were doing it to themselves. They were caught up in some kind of magic. The fae didn't even get off their horses."

The general brought up another image. It was out of focus, but the antlers were enough for Elise's heart to trip.

"You know who this is?" he asked.

"That is the prince," she whispered, not wanting to give them his name.

"Can you explain your relationship with him?"

Elise frowned. "I don't have a relationship with him. I was his slave, as I said."

"So you can explain this then?" Gatesbridge held up his tablet that showed black and white camera footage of the castle's stable yards.

There was no sound as the guy filming aimed a gun at Kian. Elise flashed across the scene, moving unnaturally fast and tackling Kian behind the stone trough.

"I can explain that," Elise said calmly, thinking of a lie. "As the prince's slave, I was bound by magic to protect him if he should come to harm. Look how fast I ran. That's the magic because, as you can see, I'm not built like a track star."

"Are you still under the magic's influence?"

"Not that I'm aware of."

"I see. And if you were a slave, why were you tossed outside of our gates this evening?"

"I'm not sure. Maybe the prince had enough of me, or he's returning me as some kind of peace offering. I was the only human held at the castle," Elise replied. She was still hoping to salvage something of her plan to stop the fae and human aggression.

Gatesbridge actually turned purple-red in anger. "Does this fucker look like he's interested in peace?" He tossed the tablet at Elise, and she lifted it to watch the silent footage. The dry cheese sandwich rose up in Elise's throat.

The video was a bloody montage of the fae roaming the streets of London, hunting fleeing humans. Along the Thames, trees had grown out of the embankment and were decorated with swaying, hung bodies. Small babies, all younger than two, were being loaded into padded baskets and given to warriors to transport.

And everywhere, calmly watching, was Kian in his blood-stained armor. His face, the few times his mask was removed, was the coldest Elise had ever seen as he watched the fae hanging people, snatching babies from weeping mothers, and lighting houses on fire.

Elise dropped the tablet and vomited on the concrete floor. She sucked in breaths, trying to get air into her lungs, her panic attack tearing her apart.

Elise knew by the rumors that the army had been in London for the first month of her imprisonment. She knew they had been killing people. *The betrayers*. But babies? She vomited again, retching up yellow bile.

"That's the monster you saved that night, Elise. We had one shot at him, and it was blown because of you," Gatesbridge snarled, leaning over the table towards her.

"I told you it was because of the magic," Elise panted.

"You better choose what side you want to be on and get ready to give up every little bit of information you know on these assholes. I don't want to have to torture it out of you, but I will do what I have to save England from-"

The door to the cell banged open. "Stand down, Gatesbridge."

A woman entered the room in a suit, her graying, red hair pinned neatly in a bun. She wore pearl earrings to soften the severity in her face, but Elise wasn't buying that female trick for a second. This was the *big* boss. She hadn't raised her voice, but both the general and Elise flinched. "Thank you, general. That will be all." He turned purple again but didn't argue as he stormed out of the room.

"Can someone please get Elise some water?" she said, and there was suddenly a man with two water bottles.

"Thanks," Elise replied, opening one and taking a mouthful.

"You'll have to forgive the general. He lets his passion overrule his reason at times. You may call me Ruth."

Elise nodded, the water sloshing uncomfortably in her stomach. The video was still playing on the tablet, and every shot of Kian was like a knife burying inside of her. She had slept with him, and worse, Elise had started to get feelings for him. Painful, real emotions.

The prince in the video was his true self. The other one, who she had drunk wine with, talked about books, and had taken to bed, was only working on getting her blood out of her without a fight.

The worst part was that Elise *knew* he was killing humans. She had seen him calmly decapitate someone with her own eyes. That knowledge hadn't stopped her from falling for him, so what did that make her?

"I can't imagine what you have been through, Elise," Ruth said, breaking the silence. "The fact that you have survived so long amongst the fae tells me how resourceful you are."

"Yes, I have been through hell, and I would like to go home now," Elise replied, her voice small.

"That is an option if you help us. Gatesbridge went about it the wrong way, but the truth is we don't know anything about the fae, why they are invading us, and what their weaknesses are. You have lived amongst them, and that makes you uniquely qualified to tell us about them."

"They are invading and killing people because they want revenge for what British kings did to them," Elise replied.

"And the prince? Anything you can tell me about him?" Ruth pressed.

"He's ruthless." *And cursed. And cruel. And I'm in love with him.* "He's got a lot of magic. The only way you can save England is to try and make a peace treaty with him. He can be reasoned with. He's not some mindless beast. He's strategic, and he wants to have a safe place for his people."

Ruth was frowning, no doubt reading on Elise's face the conflicting agony she was in.

"Out of everyone on that train, why did he take you?" she asked.

"I don't know. I'm no one." *I'm the key to the curse that's killing him. All you need to do is wait, and he'll be dead.* That didn't fill Elise with any kind of comfort. It made her feel worse.

"Did he hurt you? Rape you?"

"No. He didn't rape me, and neither did any of the others. They don't mess with other fae's slaves in that way."

"I see. Anything else?"

Elise looked her in the eyes, let her see the hollowness and pain inside. "No."

Ruth's lips thinned. "Don't force me to give you over to Gatesbridge, Elise. I'm the only thing standing between you and him, and withholding information is the worst possible thing you can do for yourself right now. Protecting the prince, sympathizing with the fae, won't serve you."

"I'm not protecting him." It tasted like a lie, but Elise held eye contact. "Give me to Gatesbridge. It won't change the truth."

"And what truth is that?"

"The prince has no weakness, and he will kill you all if you don't try and bargain with him," she replied, the hollowness in her chest growing wider.

Ruth let out a long sigh before banging on the cell door. It opened, and Elise heard her say clearly. "She's all yours."

23

The sun had set hours ago, and Elise still hadn't come to find Kian. He didn't know what she was feeling about their night of passion, but she was all he had thought about all day. Elise had made parts of him wake up from their centuries-long sleep, and every day, Kian was feeling more like the male he'd been before the curse. The one that was capable of things like love and affection before Aoife's magic had stripped it away. It was thrilling...and terrifying.

Kian waited until midnight, anxiously drinking wine. He was torn between wanting to give Elise space and needing to see her like he needed to breathe. Kian had resisted using the mating bond between them because he didn't want to invade her privacy in such a way.

Was she doing this to tease him? To infuriate him? Because Elise didn't want him now that she had slept with him?

None of those were pleasant to think about, and he was done waiting.

Kian strode out of his chambers and headed for hers, lesser fae scattering in fright at the anger and determination in his aura.

"Elise?" Kian pushed open her bedchamber doors, but there was no fire burning and no lights on. He turned around and headed for the library. She sometimes liked to work late, getting caught up in whatever books she was reading.

The library was dark and silent. Hot panic and rage fought for dominance as Kian tried to think where else she could be.

"Master?" Hedera popped out of thin air, her brownie magic sensing that her master was in need.

"Where the fuck is she?!" Kian shouted, grabbing her by the shoulders.

"I don't know, m-master. I delivered her food in here this morning." Hedera clapped her hands, and the lights all came on at once. Elise's tray of tea and food was untouched on her worktable. There were no signs of a struggle, but that meant nothing. Elise was so small and human, she would be powerless against any of the fae.

"Oh no, he didn't-" Hedera began and shut her mouth with a snap.

"Who. Did. What?" Kian growled, grabbing her around the throat, his anger a living flame.

"I saw Fionn enter the library not long after I did. He has taken an interest in your slave and has visited her more than once. Not friendly visits."

"And you said nothing of this to me?" he demanded.

"Would you have listened to a lesser fae over your general? Or any fae warrior?" Hedera replied. Kian quickly let her go, and she rubbed at her neck.

"Find him for me, and don't be seen," he commanded, and she vanished.

Kian closed his eyes and breathed deeply, searching for Elise's scent. The library was covered in it, so he singled out the most recent ones. He tracked it to a bookshelf, where her usual warm scent sparked with sour notes of fear. Mixed in that fear was Fionn.

Kian gripped the bookshelf, his vision turning black with rage. Murderous magic was boiling up inside of him, so powerful the library shook. The magic called for battle, and his armor responded, appearing piece by piece on his body, swords crossing over his shoulder blades.

"Master, Fionn is near the stables. His mount looks exhausted and is damp with sweat," Hedera reported, appearing at a safe distance from him.

"Thank you, Hedera. Keep the lesser fae inside tonight," Kian said, the warning in his tone palpable. Fionn's complaints were rushing back to him like a flood, and he didn't know what other poison he had spread amongst the warriors.

It had started to snow outside, and Kian tried not to think where Elise would be in the freezing night. Fionn was speaking with Aiden and Owain, the former still wearing his rotting hand around his neck. Every single warrior in the castle grounds turned their attention to Kian.

"Where the fuck is she, Fionn? Where did you take her?" he demanded, his voice a whip crack in the silence.

"Who, my prince?" Fionn replied. As Kian drew nearer, he caught the strong, intoxicating smell of Elise's blood. He followed it to Fionn's horse and found a dark stain on its front flank. Kian touched it, and through their bond, he could feel Elise's pain and terror. He caught a glimpse of a human encampment, and then it was gone.

"Tell me where you took her," Kian repeated. He let loose some of his power, and the three warriors groaned in pain. Their feet froze to the ground, and the compulsion magic started to strip their minds.

"I gave her back to the humans at their camp where she fucking belongs!" Fionn shouted, blood dribbling from his nose. "I did it for you, master. She has bewitched you and broken your resolve-" He didn't get to finish the sentence. Kian roared in anger, and Fionn exploded in a shower of blood and gore.

"Did you help him?" Kian turned to where Aiden and Owain were twisting on the bloody ground in agony. They shook their heads. There was no way they could lie to him under such compulsion. He let them go, and they stilled, sobbing loudly.

Kian turned to the terrified warriors that were still watching. "Does anyone else believe I am bewitched?"

No one moved. No one breathed.

Kian mounted the nearest horse, channeled some of his magic into it, and raced out of the yard and into the darkness.

The nighttime landscape blurred around him, Kian's rage only fading a little as his fear for his mate took over. He searched for their bond. It was agonizingly weak, but it was there. It told him that Elise was still alive, at least. She had been hurt and bleeding when Fionn had carried her away, and that thought was enough for the dark fury to return.

It didn't take long for the bright lights of the human camp to come into view. The bond grew warmer with every step.

Maybe she doesn't want to be rescued? The thought jolted Kian so sharply, he halted the horse. Elise was finally back amongst her people. What if she now felt happy and safe? As her mate, her wellbeing was Kian's highest priority. He hadn't considered for a moment that perhaps letting her return to her old life would be the best way to provide that.

Kian shut his eyes and tried to get a fix on Elise's location and feelings. The shaky bond suddenly opened wide, and a jolt of screaming pain roared through it. Kian couldn't breathe. He couldn't think. The pain stopped only long enough for him to drag in a breath, and it started again.

Kian! Elise's voice screamed, and then the bond closed off again.

"Elise..." He raced towards the camp, throwing up a magical barrier around him to stop the human's projectiles. Kian couldn't hear anything except the fear and pain in Elise's voice.

As he neared the camp, magic whipped out of him, tearing off the tall metal gates and flinging them aside. Warriors were shouting, filling the yard with their loud weapons. Kian's power knocked them back, wiping out the metal boxes they traveled in. He followed the bond to a building and ripped the roof off, tearing apart the walls. People were screaming as they were crushed and shoved aside until he found Elise. She was on her knees, barely conscious and soaking wet. A man was holding onto her by the hair with one of their weapons to her head.

"You dare touch my mate and do violence to her?" Kian snarled, pulling one of his swords loose. "Release her, or I'll kill every single one of you."

The man looked wide-eyed at the destruction all around him. He let Elise go, turned, and ran. Kian wanted to go after him and tear him apart piece by piece, but she needed him more.

Elise whimpered as Kian crouched down and lifted her up with one arm, holding her tightly and scanning around them for oncoming attacks, sword ready.

"You came for me," she whispered against his neck.

"I promised that you would never be free of me," Kian replied, and her hot tears dampened his skin.

"Hold your fire!" a woman's voice commanded, and the humans all froze. "Let them go." She was holding a weapon too but had it lowered. She was the only human in the place that had any sense. The soldiers backed out of their way, making a path for them as Kian headed back to the horse.

"Fucking fae loving traitor," a soldier spat. Kian's blade was ready to lop his head off when Elise touched his face, freezing him mid-swing.

"Don't hurt them, Kian. Please, just take me home," she begged. Kian's very nature warred against it, but he removed the blade from the human's neck.

"She has only ever tried to convince me to show your kind mercy. This is how you repay her?" Kian spat out the words before mounting the horse. He sheathed his sword, and without a backward glance, Kian got his mate the fuck out of there before he slaughtered them all.

Elise clung to him and they raced towards the standing stones. Kian couldn't trust his own warriors or the safety of the castle. He wouldn't take his mate back there when she was dying. Kian needed to get her to a place where his power was most potent to heal her.

Kian charged towards the standing stones, his magic roaring as the portal exploded with light. Hanging tighter to Elise, they bolted through the burning, golden magic and into Faerie.

24

Elise's lungs ached with every breath she took. Her wounds were bleeding, and she struggled to hold on, but she trusted Kian not to let her fall.

He came for me.

Gatesbridge had thought they could waterboard her to get the information they imagined she was withholding. They were getting frustrated enough with Elise to break out the pliers when Kian had thrown their world into chaos. Elise thought she was hallucinating as golden magic had torn open the building she was being held in.

And there he was. Golden armor shining and a look of such fury on his face that the guy holding her had actually pissed the front of his pants. Elise never thought she'd see the Blood Prince and think of salvation, not damnation. Kian had come for her, and Elise's shredded heart pulsed back to life.

Despite all the confusing anger and pain Elise felt towards him, she was now clinging to Kian and weeping with relief. His scent of fir trees and smoke wrapped tight around her, and she knew she was safe. Runes glowed faintly where their skin touched, and the sun of magic was burning inside of her once more.

Dark forest and strange glittering lights flickered on either side of Elise's vision. She had no idea where they were, but it was nowhere around Salisbury.

Kian finally slowed their pace, and the sound of running water trickled through the rocks and trees.

"It's okay, Elise, we are almost there," he murmured. They crossed through a group of trees and into a glade full of glowing flowers. Their luminescence was nothing compared to the turquoise water of a deep, steaming pool. It pulsed with power that even a human like Elise could sense.

"Where are we?" Elise asked, her voice a scratchy whisper.

"One of the healing pools...in Faerie." Kian slid off the horse and pulled her down. Elise's mouth opened and closed again, speechless. She barely had the strength to stand, let alone undress, but Kian took care of their clothes and carried her gently into the warm water.

"Just keep breathing, Elise, the power in the pool and I will do the rest," he said, holding her to his chest. Elise rested her cheek on him and closed her eyes. The water made her skin tingle, and heat slowly returned to her body.

Very softly, Kian began to sing. It sounded like Gaelic, and the runes danced and pulsed brighter on Elise's skin. His magic poured into her, and she stared in fascination as the cuts and bruises on her hands healed. Within minutes, her breath stopped rattling and wheezing, her lungs and sinuses clearing.

"I need to put your head under the water just for a moment," Kian said, and her nails dug into him. "Shh, Elise. I know what they did to you tonight, but I won't do anything to hurt you." Elise's eyes filled with tears, but she nodded, holding her breath as Kian lowered her slowly back. The water closed over her face for barely a moment before he lifted her out again. "There we are. Your face should feel better soon."

Kian held Elise, humming softly under his breath and soothing her as all of her hurts healed. Well, most of her hurt.

When Elise was feeling steady again, she let him go and swam to the other side of the pool. She couldn't think straight enough to have the conversation she needed to while he was touching her. Kian was watching her so closely like he was afraid she would vanish on him again. The tension and rage that he had been humming with had barely dampened, and Elise saw how close he was to losing control of himself.

"They showed me what you did in London," Elise managed to croak out, her arms going around herself so she wouldn't start shaking.

"I've never hidden what I am from you," Kian replied stiffly.

"You've never been really open about what you were doing either!" Elise swallowed back tears, trying to reason with herself. *You are his slave. He owes you no explanations.*

Kian's expression didn't shut down like Elise thought it would. "I told you what the kings did to my brothers and the fae."

"So what? You killed innocent people for revenge? I saw the babies, Kian! They were innocent like the faelings were!" she shouted, unable to hold in her anger and horror.

Kian drew back like she had struck him. "You think I killed the children?"

"I saw videos of the warriors carrying them away. What else am I meant to think happened to them when there are magical hanging trees now lining the Thames covered in the bodies of their parents."

"No harm has come to those children, and no harm ever will. The fae cherish their children, and those humans will be safe with their new families," Kian replied. He took a step towards her, anger burning in his eyes. "You want to know the whole ugly truth, mate? Then here it is."

Kian put his palm to Elise's forehead, and she was suddenly standing in a forest glade. Bayn and Killian stood with her, and opposite them were Vortigern, Hengist, Horsa, and their fifty elite soldiers. Bastards one and all.

"As promised for receiving your assistance in pushing back the Picts, we hereby swear on our blood that no harm shall come to the fae while we rule Albion. If any of us break this treaty, may it be paid in kind with our bloodlines," Vortigern declared, Hengist and Horsa echoing him. They cut their palms and waited as the three fae princes repeated the vows, and they all shook hands.

The forest glade vanished, and Kian was running through a burning settlement. Everyone was screaming, the ground littered with the bodies of fae women and children. Kian's agony and terror coursed through Elise as he coughed up smoke and tried to search for any survivors in the burning houses. The roof started to collapse and Killian pulled Kian out of the building in a rush of wings.

They didn't have time to recover or retaliate before magic latched about them like manacles of iron. Through the smoke and flames and blood, a beautiful woman walked toward them. Aoife, the sorceress, held them in her power, driving them to their knees in the blood of faelings.

"You really should have taken me as your queen, Kian, and this would have all been prevented," she said, stroking his cheek.

Then the physical pain began as they were tortured and beaten bloody. Elise suffered through his humiliation as soldiers tore off his antlers. She felt his fear as the fae were led in chains to Stonehenge and forced through at spear point. Aoife's curse flayed the prince's insides, turning them into unfeeling shadows of their former selves.

In Faerie, the wailing of their loss lasted for months. Elise watched as Kian swore to all the hollow-eyed, fading fae that he would find a way back to Albion. That the blood promised curse would come down on the lines of Vortigern, Hengist, Horsa, and their elite that had been responsible for the slaughter. They would pay compensation for their crimes with a child given over to the families who were robbed of theirs.

Then came the years of guilt, a part of Kian always wondering that if he had relented to Aoife's advances, all that death could have been avoided. His brothers had stopped trying to comfort him as the years dragged on and on, their own curses cutting away at who they once were piece by piece...

Elise jolted out of the memories with a cry of agony. Kian's hands dropped to her elbows to keep her from slipping under the water. He was shaking, tears falling down his cheeks.

"I did what I was blood sworn to do, Elise, and I won't ever regret it," he said, his grip tightening. "I still hear their crying in my sleep. I smell their blood and feel their little broken bodies in my hands. The only night I haven't was when you lay by my side. Now, you know the horror of my life and mind and burden of trying to fix all that was broken. I can't undo what I did in London. I won't give the children back even if I could. I'll always be a monster, but I'm their monster."

Elise took his face in her hands. "And mine, Kian." His face went slack in surprise and relief. Kian dragged her to him, wrapping his arms so tightly around her that her ribs groaned.

"My Elise, I'm so sorry for every wrong I have done to you. I'm sorry for Fionn and those fucking humans," Kian said, burying his face into her neck. It was unnerving and amazing to watch a being so powerful finally break down and be so vulnerable. It hurt to watch and to feel, so they both clung to each other until they calmed.

"I'm sorry if my actions in London have frightened you. You have no idea what it's like to be bound by magic and honor to such a promise that only leads to death," he said, his grip easing around her.

"Yes, I do," Elise replied and her own horrific past tore itself free.

Kian's hands stroked her back in small circles. "Tell me, Elise. Whatever it is, you know I won't judge you."

He'll understand where no one else will.

"My mother left my father and I when I was about four years old. He raised me, and we were as close as you could get," Elise began, a lump forming in her throat. "When he got sick, my whole world stopped. I put aside every dream or ambition to look after him. He hated it but got too unwell to fight me about it. He made me promise him that if his quality of life was so bad that he couldn't talk and move, that I would…assist his death."

The chemical smell of the hospital rooms hit Elise, and she fought to steady her breath. She hadn't told anyone.

"He got bad really quickly. When he could only blink and plead with his eyes, I waited until the nurses were on rotation, and I…I smothered him with a pillow." Elise had never said the words out loud before, and the horror of that hospital room would never leave her.

"You honored your promise even though you were not bound by magic. You did the right thing, Elise. Not one should live like that," Kian said, kissing the top of her head. He really believed it too, and somehow that made her feel a little better about it.

"I was still struggling to get my life back together, trying to find what I did with those dreams and ambitions when you attacked my train."

"Destiny intervened," he replied, and Elise gave him a sharp look. It only made him smile. "I have no regrets. It brought you to me."

"And the cure for your curse with me. How convenient for you." Elise gathered her courage together and asked, "Did you only rescue me because you need my blood?"

Kian's expression softened, and he pushed a lock of wet hair behind her ear. "No, it's because you're my mate."

25

Elise's frown told Kian to watch his step because she wasn't up for any lies. He could see her mind trying to piece together what he had just said.

"What do you mean I am your mate?" Elise asked slowly.

"It's hard to explain."

"Try."

The night had already ripped Kian apart on the inside, so what was one more thing? It was too late to try and talk around it.

"It has to do with Aisling's magic so that only our mates could break the curses on us. My brothers and I thought it was her trying to give us some hope. Then she told us our mates would be human and of the king's bloodlines," Kian explained.

"You think I'm a descendant of Vortigern or something?"

"Not Vortigern. Hengist. And I know it because the night of the full moon I saw his face after I had drunk your blood." Elise hadn't shoved him away yet, so Kian continued. "Mates are rare amongst the fae. They are like...two halves of the same whole. Bonded mates make each other stronger. Magic binds them. It was that bond that I tracked tonight."

"They showed me footage of the night I saved you. I ran faster than I thought I did to knock you down. That's because of the bond?" she said, chewing on her bottom lip. Kian nodded.

"Yes. It's not unheard of that mates can share attributes like strength," he explained. Kian didn't dare bring up the other fae traits she might start to manifest. Their short tempers and quick passion were already similar enough.

"The mates thing is the reason I couldn't watch you die. I couldn't let them shoot you. I didn't even have a choice." Elise's expression went from curiosity to fury. "I didn't have a choice. It doesn't matter that the cuffs are gone. Being your mate is just another kind of slavery, isn't it?" she demanded, letting Kian go and swimming away to put space between them again. It was like a kick to Kian's balls to have her compare the two that way.

"Only because you're now holding my leash and not the other way around," Kian replied, folding his arms. "I lost my fucking mind and all reason tonight because you were gone. I went to the humans and hesitated to rescue you because a fae only wants their mates to be happy and safe. But you aren't happy or safe with them. You called out my name through the bond, and I would have slaughtered the whole damn world to get you back. I'm one of the strongest fae in all of our long history, but I'm powerless when it comes to you! So yes, I am your slave in every way that counts."

Elise's mouth had dropped open in surprise. "Have you known I'm your mate since the full moon?"

"Yes. Aisling confirmed it, but I didn't want it for either of us. I made the bargain with you exchanging your blood for your freedom. I didn't know I had already fallen for you, and the bond was already there. I wanted you. I'm never going to *stop* wanting you."

"I see." Elise smiled a little, and Kian was suddenly afraid. "As your mate, who has all this supposed power over you, I could ask things of you, and you would have to do it?"

Fuck. He didn't like where this was going one bit.

"Like fuck you until you pass out from pleasure? Absolutely," Kian said, trying to distract her. Her cheeks turned pink, but she saw through his attempt.

"Nice try. I was thinking of something else." Elise squared her shoulders as she fixed her piercing blue eyes on him. "As your mate, I ask that you give me one night with you in London to convince you humans have things to offer the fae. If you are convinced, then you will talk to your brothers and make a new alliance with the humans."

"And if I'm not?"

"I am confident it won't come to that." Elise's stubborn little chin rose. "They are my people, Kian. After everything fae and humans have done to each other, the answer can't be more bloodshed. We have to be better than that. Don't you see? We could be the bridge our people need."

Of course, Kian would end up with a mate that was clever and dominant, and idealistic. In other circumstances, he would've appreciated that fire. He tried to remember that he was the negotiator, the diplomat, and he needed things.

"As your mate, I would be inclined to grant your request," Kian said, inspecting his nails. "But you haven't agreed to accept the bond between us, so I don't have to consider anything you ask for."

"Fuck you," Elise hissed.

Kian's eyes narrowed. "Excuse me?"

"I said, fuck you, Blood Prince. I was *tortured* for you tonight because I refused to give them anything they could use against you. I took a bullet in the arm for you when people tried to kill you. I went to your bed willingly. There was no magical coercion in that part of our relationship. God! The balls on you to try and say that I haven't accepted the bond between us," she snarled. "Fuck. You."

"Fuck me?" Kian had her out of the pool and on her back in the bright star flowers in the blink of an eye. "You mouthy shit of a mate. Are you ever going to stop being an infernal human?"

"Are you ever going to stop acting like an arrogant fae dick?" Elise asked, grabbing handfuls of his hair and pulling him closer.

"No, but I will teach you to show your mate some proper respect," he growled.

"Try earning it for a change, you -" Kian kissed her, his lips and tongue silencing her while he devoured her lovely, wicked mouth. Her sweet taste drove out all the darkness that had been tearing at him since he'd found her gone.

"All mine," Kian purred, running a hand down her side and possessively clasping her breast. Elise wrapped her warm thighs around his waist, her hand taking hold of his hard dick.

"Prove it," she said, her grip tightening as her thumb ran over the tip. Kian snatched her hand away and thrust inside of her. She was so hot and wet, he bit his tongue hard enough to taste blood. Her intimate inner muscles clenched, and she shifted her hips up, pushing Kian deeper. She kissed him, sucking his lip and letting him know how impatient she was becoming.

Kian began a torturously slow and deep rhythm, their skin lighting up with runes again, and she broke the kiss to gasp his name. It was a sound he'd never get tired of, even if he lived another thousand years. Elise grabbed onto his antlers, and Kian rolled on his back with her straddling his hips. As he knew she would, Elise took the opportunity to speed up their pace, hands traveling down to scratch his back.

"My mate," Elise said, holding him close.

"Yes," he replied, fangs dropping. Elise touched them, unafraid and uncaring as they pricked her fingertip. She ran the bloody tip against his bottom lip while circling her hips. Kian cried out, fighting not to come before her.

"Naughty, infernal human," he growled, making her laugh and tipping her head to the side for him. Kian could resist no longer. He bit into her making them climax together. Her sharp teeth and nails gripped him, and she rode him relentlessly through it, dragging it out and making him hold her tighter.

The magic flowed between them, the final tie securing their mating in place. There would never be anyone or anything else that would take priority over her.

Elise sighed happily and kissed him. "So when are we going to London?"

Kian laughed. She was definitely his mate, ready to negotiate. "When it's safe, Elise. I promise to do my best to be open to what you wish to show me, but I can't guarantee that I'll be convinced."

Elise's arms tightened around him. "That's all I ask. You know I won't stop until you see things my way."

Kian kissed the top of her head. "You wouldn't be you if you didn't."

For the first time in fifteen hundred years, he thought of the future with some hope and was willing to do anything he could to keep her in it.

26

Kian's mate. Well, fuck.

The more Kian told Elise about it, the more her behavior in the past few months made sense. She had been changing a little more every day, and now she knew why. At least partly. The runes glowing on her when they were skin to skin were only the beginning of the weirdness she would likely start experiencing.

They had been back at the castle for two days, and Kian had spent most of the time investigating how far Fionn's treachery ran. Elise had stayed out of it, spending her time back in her beloved library. She didn't know what to think about the riot Kian would cause when he decided to announce that she, a humble human, was their prince's mate. Maybe she'd just stay in the library until it all blew over.

The healing pools in Faerie had worked their magic in more ways than the physical, and Elise was feeling lighter than she had since before her Dad got sick.

There were moments where Elise would freak out about the thought of being the other half to someone like the Blood Prince. *What does it say about hidden parts of my personality?*

Then Kian would appear suspiciously quickly, kiss Elise's forehead, and with a smile, would leave her grinning every time. He really knew how to play her like a drum. *The clever prick.*

"Are you sure that you're dressed warmly enough?" Kian asked Elise for the third time that afternoon.

"Stop being a pushy ass mate," she complained, mounting his horse.

"Never," he replied, pulling himself up behind her, one arm curling around her waist to hold her tightly. Kian was trying to look annoyed but failed. Every time Elise called him 'my mate,' her psychopath prince turned into a puddle of goo...or she got pounced on in the best way possible.

Warriors lined the gates, with Cora, the newly appointed general, giving them a stern nod as they passed. She didn't like the idea of Kian going to London without an escort after the shit they had caused last time with the hanging trees. Kian assuring her that he would be glamoured to look human didn't change her mind.

They were finally going to London, but they had one stop to make first.

For a town so close to Stonehenge and the castle, Salisbury was remarkably untouched by the presence of the fae. Kian had told Elise that his warriors had only been concerned with London. Still, she didn't quite believe it until she saw the familiar streets for herself.

They stopped in front of Elise's cottage, and it was a surreal feeling to encounter her old life. The gardens desperately needed tending despite the winter snow, but otherwise, it remained in one piece.

"I won't be long," Elise told Kian and slid off the horse.

Digging around under pots near the front door, Elise found her spare key. The cottage smelled heavily of the jasmine-scented candles she loved and musty dampness from being locked up for so long. She was relieved to find that no one had broken in and taken anything. Elise picked up her wall phone and dialed Chrissy's number. She held her breath as it rang and rang and...

"Hello?" Chrissy sounded like she had just woken up.

"Hi, it's Elise," she replied, suddenly feeling awkward as hell.

"Elise! Where the fuck are you? Where have you been?" she demanded, moving from shock to anger. "I thought you were fucking dead."

"I'm okay, really. I've been with the fae," Elise hurried to explain.

"With. The. Fae." Chrissy sighed through her nose, and Elise could see her pissed off expression in her mind's eye.

"Yeah. The prince, specifically."

The prince, who was now standing in her lounge room, looking at school portraits of her with missing teeth and pigtails.

"Goddess, have mercy. What is going on, Elise?"

"Look, I don't have much time. I just wanted to hear your voice and make sure you're alive. I have to take care of some things, but I wanted to offer you my cottage to live in. I know you are tired of living with your sister and her kids, and I won't be needing it anymore. I'd like you close by," Elise pressed on.

"I don't know what to say...but yes, yes, I will come and take over your cute as shit cottage in the country, near Stonehenge, which was as magical as I've said for years. Where are you going to be?"

Elise glanced at Kian, who was trying not to smile while he eavesdropped on their conversation.

"At the castle, working for the prince. The library is as filthy as its owner," she said, and Kian gave her a look that told Elise he was willing to explore just how filthy he could be.

Sweet Jesus, have mercy.

"I don't know if you are aware that you've gone crazy, but bitch, you be crazy. The politicians are arguing about when to nuke that goddamn castle, and you're going to go back there willingly!"

"Yes, and don't worry, I've got a plan to work on the situation with the politicians too," Elise said. As Chrissy spluttered, she added, "The key will be under the pot plant with the blue base. I'll come and visit you soon, so don't hock any of my stuff. Bye!" Elise hung up and found Kian behind her, arms folded.

"Why didn't you tell her we are mated?" he demanded.

"Probably the same reason that you haven't told the fae. There are only so many shocks a person can get, and I don't want to upset her." Elise squeezed past him and headed up to her bedroom.

Elise grabbed a backpack and filled it with lingerie because the fae version of bras were seriously inadequate for dealing with her breasts. She also chucked in some skincare, a framed picture of her Dad, and her laptop. She would have to be careful about the battery life and come into the village to charge it, but she wanted to show Kian...well, everything. Elise wanted to create him playlists full of her favorite music. She wanted him to read her favorite books. Most of all, Elise wanted to show him the world outside of England.

Stop getting ahead of yourself. You have to stop a war first, remember?

"I'm ready. Let's get going," Elise called. She tried to get down the narrow staircase and found him blocking it. She walked down until they were at eye level. "What's wrong?"

"You are giving up your home to stay at mine. That means a lot to me," Kian said, visibly struggling with the emotion that was battering him. Feelings he had started to get back since they had mated. Elise kissed him hard and quick.

"I'm not giving it up. I'm lending it to a friend. I can always move back in if I get sick of you glowering," she replied flippantly.

"I don't know whether you are joking or not," Kian said, eyes narrowing. "You test my patience."

Elise smiled sweetly, batting her lashes at him. "We had best be going, *mate*." Kian's mouth twitched at the corners, but he let her pass. Elise grabbed a set of car keys off the hook. "If you are going to fit into the Jeep, you had best show me how human your glamour can be. Otherwise, you're not going to get inside of it."

The transition happened eerily fast. Kian's antlers disappeared, his hair shortened to his shoulders, and his clothes turned into a long black overcoat, a white button-down shirt, pressed dress pants, and shoes. Elise gaped at him.

"What? Too much?" he asked.

"No, you should be fine," she said. He was devastating, even dimmed down. She stood on tiptoes and ran her hands through this hair. "You don't look right without your antlers," Elise lamented.

"Don't worry, I'm going to have you hanging onto them by the end of the night," he replied, kissing her. They really had to get going because if he kept looking at her with heat in his eyes, she wouldn't leave the cottage.

Elise crossed all her fingers and toes as she turned the Jeep's ignition. After three tries, it started, and she sighed with relief. They had barely made it out onto the street before Kian started throwing up protective shields around the car.

"Hey, my driving isn't that bad!" Elise teased.

"It's not you hitting things that worry me. It is other things hitting us," Kian replied, gripping the door until his knuckles turned white. Elise tried not to laugh at the novelty of him being unnerved. She had spent the last months of her life being in a state of awe or terror, and she liked that the tables had turned. As soon as Elise put the radio on a classical music station, Kian forgot all about the cars and traffic, his attention lost in the music.

Despite the fae army attack and the strange oaks lining the Thames, London was as busy as usual. Elise had expected roadblocks at the very least. It would take more than the return of mythical creatures to slow business down.

Driving in London was a special kind of torture that didn't get much better after the sun went down. Elise parked illegally in the street near the British Museum, and Kian did a glamour on it so it wouldn't get towed. Being the mate to a fae prince had its perks, including having the night security guards open the doors for them with a smile and a nod.

"Try and keep that big brain of yours open," Elise said, taking Kian's hand. Because he hadn't believed her about the winged lions' statues, Elise took him straight to the Assyrian collection.

"I had no idea that humans were capable of such artistry," Kian said, ignoring the 'no touching' signs and running his fingers over a flank of a sculptured lion.

"Wait until you see the Egyptian collection," she said with a delighted laugh. Elise wisely didn't take him anywhere near the Sutton Hoo exhibits or anything else Anglo-Saxon in case it triggered him.

Elise loved watching Kian and his reactions when something really delighted him. He would light up and want to feel and study it. He was fascinated that the Egyptians had lived as long as the fae and helped himself to a book from the gift shop.

They only had a night, so Elise moved him on from the museum to the National Gallery. There were plenty of stories about how much the fae loved art, but Elise wasn't ready for the utter joy on Kian's face as he looked at paintings and sculptures. His eyes seemed to glaze over when he really loved something, like he was lost within the picture or whatever emotions gripped him.

They stopped in front of Artemisia Gentileschi's 'Judith beheading Holofernes,' and Elise was reminded of the first night they had spent together and her failed assassination attempt.

"You are smiling rather deviously, mate. I do hope this picture isn't giving you any ideas," Kian said, raising a brow.

"Not anymore," she replied, trying not to giggle. Kian put an arm around her shoulders and kissed the top of her head.

"We need to think about getting back soon," he murmured against her hair. "I do want to explore this place again, so you will have to bring me back."

"I promise. I have one last place to take you," Elise said, steering him towards the gallery exits.

Elise only knew about their final location because of Chrissy. Her sister Lou had trouble conceiving her second child and had gone through doctors to help her out.

Kian stood outside the pale blue and silver clinic, reading the signs and information, his frown deepening.

"Why are we visiting here, Elise?" he asked.

"You told me that faelings are so rare because the fae have trouble conceiving. Maybe human science can help with that?" Elise tried her best to explain what IVF was and how it might be used to assist the fae population grow once more with some modifications depending on anatomy. It would be a way for them to make up for the lost generation of faelings, and ensure that the pregnancies weren't so dangerous in the future.

Then Kian, the Blood Prince, the fiercest fae general in their history, the scourge of London, began to cry.

27

Kian waited for his brothers to appear in the mirror before him, all the while wondering how he'd find the words to tell them what he had learned.

"Little brother, you are starting to make a bad habit of summoning me when I'm otherwise preoccupied," Killian grumbled, his raven wings and hair appearing through the gloom.

"This had better be good," Bayn added through the mists before he stood next to Killian. "Where the fuck have you been?"

"Enjoying myself, little icicle, like you should be doing. After centuries stuck in Faerie, we've earned it," Killian said. "How's your pretty little mate, Kian? Still your slave?"

Frost broke out over Bayn's skin, his magic giving away his emotions. "What fucking mate? Not the roses girl!"

"Please," Kian said hoarsely. "Please don't fight. Just listen to me."

That seemed to shut them up. Now they both look concerned for him, and Kian didn't blame them. The red in his hair now reached his shoulders, and black curled around his antlers. He couldn't hide that the curse was lifting.

"What has happened, Kian?" Killian prompted, his green eyes seeing all the raging emotions inside of him. Killian was the one that had always been the most passionate, not Kian.

"I am mated, and my curse is lifting," Kian began. He told them about Elise, the full story, from taking her as his slave, how he wasn't feeling like himself, what had happened on the full moon, and how Fionn had betrayed him.

"I told you that fucker was getting too confident in his own abilities," Bayn muttered.

"Is your mate safe now?" asked Killian, black brows drawn together.

"Yes, I retrieved her and completed the bond."

Killian's frown vanished, and he chuckled. "Well then, I suppose congratulations are in order."

"The fuck they are. He's hiding something, Kill." Bayn was starting to ice over in places with impatience.

"Not hiding. My mate took me to London and showed me many things..." Kian tried to explain the wonders in the museum and gallery, saving the biggest surprise for last. They both ended up as speechless as he was at the concept of science helping infertility.

"That doesn't seem possible," Killian said eventually.

"Even if it is, I highly doubt the humans will want to help us. They are going to want to wipe us out, not help our females breed," Bayn argued.

"We don't know that until we ask," Kian continued. He drank some wine, trying to fortify himself. "Elise has convinced me that we should try and make an alliance with the humans."

Kian didn't hear what growling insults Bayn came out with or the sarcastic replies from Killian. Elise had come into the workroom, her hair out in a shining wave of curls and blue eyes glittering with trouble. She saw his brothers in the mirror, and her face lit up in surprise. She could hear them arguing and cursing, and a wicked little smile crept across her lips.

Arawan, damn us all, she's going to take them on.

Elise joined Kian, sitting on the side of his chair and putting her arm around his shoulders.

"Good evening! You must be Kian's brothers!" she beamed brightly. Both of them shut up and stared. Probably because no female had ever been game enough to approach Kian in such an affectionate manner. "Which one is Bayn, and which one is Killian?"

"My lady, I am Killian, the only brother worth knowing," he said, bowing deeply. Killian threw her a smile that Kian had seen wipe out entire courts in fits of lust and longing. "You are more lovely than I imagined, and Kian doesn't deserve you."

Elise laughed. "You're right there."

"So what makes you think that humans are going to want an alliance. They tortured you, girl, and you still think that it's a good idea?" Bayn demanded. Kian tensed at the tone he dared to use, but Elise stopped him from tearing Bayn's head off.

"Yes, I do. Both peoples have a lot to offer the other, and while you might still be thirsting for revenge, Bayn, you have to consider the other fae that aren't as powerful as you. *You* are dying. They are not. You won't be around to protect them and make the humans fear you. As soon as you are dead, the remaining fae will be targeted. Do you seriously not care about their future at all?" Elise challenged, staring the Winter Prince down with a glare cold enough to rival his own. "And don't you call me 'girl' in that tone ever again."

Bayn flushed, something he hadn't done in centuries. Killian threw his head back and laughed hysterically.

"Oh fuck, Kian, she's definitely your mate," he said, trying to catch his breath. "I'll support whatever you decide. I've always wanted what's best for the people before us. As our new sister just pointed out, we have a date with Arawan and his halls of the dead. The other fae do not. I trust what you're doing. Summon me if you need me, but avoid it if you can. I want to spend my last years in Ireland, too drunk to care when my end comes." Killian blew Elise a kiss and vanished.

"I'm not giving up the land I have taken here in the north," Bayn said, folding his arms. "Take that into calculations when you bargain. Let it be known that I'm still eager to turn Albion into a frozen wasteland if they want to be stubborn about a treaty. I won't settle for a few hanging trees either if they provoke my anger. Take care, sister. You're going to need all that fire inside of you. Kian? Try to remember who you are and not let your mate rob you of your balls as well as your spine." Bayn shook his head in frustration, and then he too disappeared muttering a parting, "Lovestruck dickhead."

"They seem nice," Elise said, making Kian laugh. He buried his face into her neck.

"Over a thousand years old, and they still act like fucking children," he complained. "You were very good with them just now. I would have been arguing with them all night."

"That's part one of the plan done. Now we have to do part two," she said. Elise slid from the arm of the chair and onto his lap.

Kian's arms came around her, holding her tight. "You know I don't like part two."

"I know, but it's the only way." Elise kissed his jawline, making heat flow through him like her touch always did. "You talk to your people, and I'll talk to mine."

Kian didn't know which he was going to hate more.

∽

ELISE NEVER WANTED to see the military camp again. Cora sat on her horse beside her, golden eyes scanning the area. Kian had insisted on her joining Elise as an escort because he trusted no one else with her safety.

Cora was intimidating as all hell, her black skin covered in luminescent blue battle woad, and hair pulled back in a mohawk of braids and raven feathers. She carried a golden spear and shield and looked more than ready to take on the entire camp with them.

"Let me cast some protection shields around you, my lady, before we go any further," she said, her eyes not leaving the nearest patrol of soldiers.

"Thanks, that would be...wait, you just called me 'my lady,'" Elise replied.

"You are the prince's mate. It would be disrespectful to call you anything else."

"Did he tell you?"

Cora shook her head. "He didn't have to. I was present the night he killed Fionn, and I've never seen a mating rage quiet like it."

"But...none of the warriors have said anything! I didn't think anyone knew about it."

"They know better than to ask. New mates can be volatile. It's better to stay out of their way until they settle and announce it themselves," Cora replied with a slight shrug. "The warriors are giving him space, especially after Fionn. That idiot should've seen the signs that the prince was mating with you. Ridiculous male." Cora's magic shimmered with orange light as it arched over them and the horses.

"And they don't care that I am human?" Elise asked.

"Oh, no, they absolutely hate it, but also it gives some...hope."

Elise didn't expect that. "Why hope?"

"Mating is a gift from the gods. It has become almost unheard of in the last fifteen hundred years. Perhaps it's because we stopped being connected to Albion. The fae have hope to find mates of their own," Cora explained. Elise wanted to hit her with more questions, but Cora shook her head. "There will be time enough for that later. Now, we see what your human leaders have to say."

Elise nodded, schooling her face in a way that she hoped looked as imperious as Kian, and not just her squinting. They didn't make their presence known by thundering down the road through the camp's still ruined gates. They came at a slow walk so that everyone could take note of a white flag of parley, emblazoned with Kian's rose and antler insignia.

Gatesbridge and his men filled the space where the gate used to be, all of their guns pointed at them. Elise prayed to whoever would listen that Cora's shields were as strong as Kian's had been. Otherwise, they would be riddled with holes before they even hit the ground.

"I come bearing a message from the Blood Prince of the Fae. Where is Ruth?" Elise demanded, looking down her nose at Gatesbridge. She would never forget the feel of his big hand on the back of her neck, holding her down in a tub of water. One day, she would get her revenge, but the alliance had to take priority.

"We don't want to hear anything that you have to say, traitor! Get out of here before I put a bullet in you myself," he snapped.

"Move aside," Ruth commanded behind them, and they parted for her. "Gatesbridge. Enough."

Ruth looked tired and still steely enough to make Elise want to bolt in the other direction.

"Elise Carlisle, I am surprised to see you back here," she said.

"Believe me, I don't want to be, but I have been tasked to invite you and two advisors to the castle to parley with the prince in three days. Do you have enough authority to speak on behalf of England?" Elise asked her. She never did get given her title or her last name.

"I will be able to get it. What are the prince's terms?" Ruth asked.

"That you come to Stonehenge and talk peace if it's something that you are interested in. All other terms he and his brothers have will be laid out for you there."

Ruth actually paled. "He has brothers."

"He does indeed, and they have all had to put aside their dreams of pushing the humans out of England and making a fae country because they believe that there might be a chance for us all to work together," Elise said and then took great satisfaction in smiling menacingly.

"Do not waste this opportunity. It was hard enough for me to convince Kian to have this one talk with you. The other princes are still undecided until he is sure that a treaty is possible. I know what weapons we humans have, and there is no way that we could win a war against them. Something for you to take into consideration for the next few days."

Elise didn't say goodbye. They didn't deserve any extra courtesy after how they had treated her. She turned her horse and rode back the way they had come, Cora riding a few paces behind.

"Do you think they will come? The idea of peace looks confusing to them," she said once they were out of sight of the camp and breathing a little easier.

"They are scared, but not knowing what else the fae are capable of will be enough to bring them to the table. Kian will convince them of the rest."

"Or take the opportunity to kill them all," said Cora.

Elise hoped it wouldn't come to that.

28

The courtyard on the second level of the castle had been turned from snow-laden dead plants into a lush summer garden. Roses and other sweet-smelling flowers bloomed alongside a fountain of a proud forest stag and dancing nymphs. The fae loved a good show, and Kian was going to make sure that even though they were going to be talking peace, he would find subtle ways to let his power be known.

Warriors dressed in their finest clothes and armor were stationed around the gardens, and a short distance from the table and chairs that had been set out. Just close enough to be a threat and intervene if necessary.

Kian and Elise both wore all black clothes stitched with golden thread. She thought he would bring out some kind of fancy crown made of gold, but instead, he wore a crown of green leaves. Despite the humbleness of it, she couldn't forget for a second that he was the prince. He exuded so much power and authority that everyone was on edge when his gaze landed on them.

The red in his hair reached the golden cuffs on his pointed ears, and Elise had to stop herself from running her hands through it. Kian had also gifted her with a dagger that matched his own and asked Elise to wear it.

"I would feel better having you armed in some small way," he said, kissing her softly. "It's not like you haven't had experience trying to stab people."

"But I only like trying to stab you," Elise teased, and he nipped her lip. Elise's heart rate jumped, and her pupils dilated. "Stop trying to turn me on. You're not getting out of talking to the humans."

Kian's smile could have made an angel take off her pants. "I'll have to keep the talks quick then."

Elise took his hand and kissed his knuckles. "Thank you for doing this for me. Try and keep your temper."

Kian was about to reply when Cora came out into the courtyard leading Ruth, Gatesbridge, and another man Elise didn't recognize...until she did.

"They have brought the Prime Minister, Mark Holbrook," Elise whispered to Kian. "He's the ruler of Britain. Not a king, but still in charge."

"They are at least taking it seriously," Kian replied.

"I present to you, The Blood Prince of the Fae and his mate and consort, Lady Elise Carlisle," Cora announced formally, bowing to her and Kian before joining us.

"Thank you for meeting with us. My name is Mark, and I'm the Prime Minister of Britain. I understand that you have already met my associates Ruth and General Gatesbridge," he said. He didn't look nervous like the other two, but meeting intimidating people was his day job.

"Yes, we became acquainted when I found them torturing my mate," Kian replied with a deadly sharp smile. Elise wanted to smack him. "She has convinced me that we could move past such things. It is not the fae way, but I'll honor her request."

"Thank you for that. I want us to be able to move past all...unpleasantness."

Elise gestured at the table. "Let's all sit and make things more comfortable," she said, trying to stop the deadly staring competition Kian and Gatesbridge were engaged in.

Then the hours of talking started. Elise tried to remain alert, her hand resting on Kian's thigh under the table as they discussed terms.

Kian wanted to remain at Stonehenge, with a vast stretch of land around it in which he could grow a forest and settle a small fae population. They would be answerable to the land's laws, and any judgment or disciplinary action would be overseen by Kian. Bayn would keep his castle and an area in the north of Scotland for the winter fae ill-suited to southern climates.

The humans and the fae would learn to co-exist, trade together in knowledge and skills, and the most crucial part of all, the world would be told the real history of the Dark Ages' battles and the atrocities carried out against the fae. Kian told them exactly what had happened and why he was so driven to carry out the revenge he did.

In return, all hostilities against Britain would cease. No, he would not return the children. They would be well cared for, and perhaps, when they were adults, if they wished to return to Albion, it would be permitted.

The Prime Minister would have to speak with Scotland about Bayn's presence, but the other requests were not unreasonable.

"You are all talking about this like we have no choice in the matter!" Gatesbridge exploded, and they all looked at him coldly.

"You don't," Kian replied. "Know this; our plans were to freeze this land and cover it in darkness until the humans had no choice but to leave. It's only because of my mate that I sit at this table. You only have your life because of her."

"Pull yourself together, man, you're meant to think of the good of Britain, not just your own personal grievances," the Prime Minister chastised. Gatesbridge shook his head like he couldn't believe what he was hearing.

"No! This is our country, and I won't allow it to go to ruin because some tart decided to open her legs to the enemy," he snarled. Elise didn't see the gun before he had fired, and she was thrown to the ground with Kian on top of her.

People were shouting, but all Elise could see was Kian's eyes above her and feel the hot wetness that was soaking her clothes.

"Kian?" She rolled him over on the grass and cried out. His chest was soaked with amber blood.

"Had to keep you...safe," he whispered, his hand reaching for her face. Elise put her hands tightly over his wound, panic and pain tearing her apart.

"You're going to be okay. Just breathe. Somebody help!" Elise shouted. She looked around to see the fae warriors surrounding them. Gatesbridge was pressed on the ground with Cora's spear at the base of his head.

"Elise, I'm sorry," Kian whispered. "This peace isn't going to work. Brothers will want revenge."

"Shh, stop talking like that. You can heal from this," Elise said, tears dripping on him. Kian's hand dropped from her face.

"Kiss me, Elise."

She pressed her trembling lips to his. "I'm so happy to be your mate."

"Me too," he replied and sighed.

"Kian?" Elise shook him hard. "Kian!" She was pulled back by Cora as an amber casing started to grow over Kian's body.

"My lady, please," she begged, but Elise struggled against her. With mounting horror, Elise saw the amber cover his face and hair. The ball of magic inside of her, the bond to him, was starting to dim and fade as Kian slipped away to a place she couldn't follow.

"No!" Elise shouted, and a blast of magic had Cora flying off her. Elise rushed over to Kian and smashed her fists down onto the shell around him. It cracked and broke like wax, and she pulled it off his face, neck, and chest to reveal Kian transformed. His hair had turned back to a deep wine red, and the wound in his chest had closed over.

"You don't get to die on me today, you arrogant fae dick!" Elise put her mouth to his and blew in a deep breath before starting chest compressions. She had to learn CPR when caring for her Dad, and Elise wasn't about to lose another man she loved. *Not this time.*

"Wake up, you bastard! We aren't done yet," Elise panted. She blew another breath into his mouth. Runes were lighting up on her skin as she did another round of compressions. "I can't believe you're going to give up this easily. If you don't come back, it will mean I finally won an argument against you. God damn you!" Elise brought her fists down hard over his heart, and magic surged out of her and into him. Kian woke with a sharp inhale.

"Did you just yell me back to life?" he wheezed. Elise threw her arms around his neck.

"I told you, you only get to die when I decide to kill you," she replied. The bond was like a hot sun inside of her, so she kissed him, and kissed him, and kissed him some more.

"Impossible," Cora mumbled.

"That's my mate," replied Kian. He looked at the mess around them. "You broke me out of my death shroud? What disrespect."

"Punish me for it later."

They were interrupted by Cora banging the butt of her spear on the ground.

"My prince, let me kill this would-be assassin," she demanded.

"I assure you, he will be punished," the Prime Minister said. He and Ruth were on their knees with their hands on their heads, fae warriors guarding them. "Prince, as you asked to be in control of the judgment of your fae, I ask that you allow us the same courtesy."

Kian and Elise slowly stood, her arm around his waist to support him if he needed it. There was fury and bloodlust in his eyes as he stared at Gatesbridge.

"Twice you have tried to kill my mate, a defenseless woman," he growled and walked towards him. His knife slashed through the air carving two lines across Gatesbridge's cheeks. "You have no honor, and you will wear this shame on your face until the day of your death. You, Mark, will punish this man according to your laws, but do not dare heal these cuts."

"Understood, thank you," the Prime Minister replied. Kian nodded to his warriors, and they let him and Ruth stand once more.

"I am done talking for the day. You may leave now and give me your answers tomorrow. I died today and had a curse broken," Kian said. He looked down at Elise with his now golden eyes filled with love. "I need to go and be alone with my mate."

29

At Elise's insistence, there was no bloodletting or magic to seal the final agreements, even though Kian didn't think signed paperwork made a formal treaty. She had convinced him that at least this way, he would be free to make his own choices on how to act should the humans break their truce. After being under a blood bond for so long, Kian quickly saw the sense in it.

Kian couldn't stop staring at his red hair and smiling. They were going to see Chrissy at the cottage that afternoon, but first, they needed to contact his brothers again to tell them of the agreement.

Elise was curled up on one of the chairs in his workroom, pretending to read, but really watching Kian. She wasn't ever going to get over the trauma of having him die in her arms. She was still waking every couple of hours to check he was still breathing.

"Did I ever tell you that I have a thing for redheads," Elise said, with a teasing smile.

"Not with as many words, but your body was very expressive about it last night," Kian replied, sketching runes on his mirror. Elise joined him, and he slid an arm around her waist.

Bayn was the first to appear, and Elise leaned a little further into Kian. The Winter Prince looked as pissed as ever.

"Baby brother, it's nice to see you," Kian greeted with a smile. Killian joined him in the mirror, and his face cracked into a massive grin.

"Your curse is broken! Wow, I forgot how bright your hair is. Well done, Elise. How did you do it?" Killian said. His exuberance made up for the glare that Bayn still wore.

"I brought him back to life," Elise replied.

Killian laughed. "I bet, lass."

"She's being literal, Kill." Kian told them all what had happened in the last few days, his voice filling with pride when he got to the part where Elise had broken his burial shroud to give him the kiss of life.

"The treaty with the humans has been signed," Kian concluded.

"I know. I saw the human news. This age has some wild kind of science that Elise can show you. It's a weight off my mind that I can die in peace somewhere without having to expend all my magic and energy turning Albion dark," Killian said.

"I wish I could feel so joyful and flippant about the idea. You both are insane," Bayn snapped. "The humans will keep the peace only as long as it takes to figure out the best ways to kill us."

"And if they do, we will respond in kind, Bayn, but peace is worth a chance. Your mate could be out there somewhere," Kian argued.

"I don't want a fucking mate! I would rather die of my curse than lie down with the spawn of my enemies. Do whatever you want, Kian. When it all goes to shit, you know where to find me. I won't fail in freezing the whole fucking lot of them out of existence!" Bayn vanished, part of Kian's mirror icing over as he did.

"Don't worry about him," Killian said with a sigh. "You did well, both of you. Elise, I hope to see you in person shortly. Don't forget to give Kian a hard time any chance you get."

"I will," Elise promised. Killian blew her a kiss and faded away. "Is Bayn always that angry?"

"Yes, though don't expect him to understand or react normally. His heart is slowly freezing after all," Kian replied.

"I wonder if there's a way to free him of his curse without a human? Maybe there is something in the library that will give us a clue." Elise wanted to help both of Kian's brothers if she could. A new set of eyes on an old problem might help. Kian pinched her hip.

"Ouch! What was that for?"

"Don't you dare think about my brother so hard," he said, drawing her close. "I love you, infernal human."

Elise slipped her arms around his neck. "Fae dick."

"You love me and my fae dick," he said, rubbing his nose against hers.

"One definitely more than other," Elise replied. She yelped as he picked her up and bit her shoulder. His laughter was a deep rumble in his chest, as he carried her back towards their bedroom.

"I love you too," Elise said and kissed him, their bond burning hotter than ever.

EPILOGUE

No one was ready for when the world ended. Despite the pain, it needed to end to make way for a new beginning.

It didn't take the government long to agree to all of Prince Kian's terms. It wasn't a hard choice to make, and at least this way, the fae and humans could both have a better chance at surviving a war with each other.

No one could know the future or predict if the humans would ever accept the fae fully, but they had made a start towards a better life for everyone.

We would have to hope that they could all hold true to their agreement this time, not to mention monitor the Winter Prince's continued anger, but at that moment, the future had never been brighter.

HEART
OF THE
WINTER PRINCE

ALESSA THORN

PROLOGUE

It had been two years since the fae returned to England, and no one could have predicted the aftershocks. Six months after signing the peace treaty, other magical beings had started to show themselves to the world. Light and dark elves had come out first in Scandinavia and then the werewolves in Germany. The Blood Prince and his consort had become ambassadors, helping settle disputes and create treaties with any magical beings who wanted peace.

Then there was the magic.

Its return had been the reason for all the seasonal disruptions and ongoing earth tremors. It had flooded back into the world as the fae did, and the humans had to rely on them and other magical adepts to understand and stabilize the phenomenon. It was one more thing that kept the treaties secure.

There were other kinds of humans, though, who now that they knew magic and creatures were real had decided that there was profit to be made from finding relics and weapons that they could use to *protect* themselves should the treaty ever break.

So far, there had been no reports of such weapons being used against the fae.

But there was a fae prince, far in the frozen north of Scotland, who was waiting for them to try.

1

Bayn's phone was ringing, and he was contemplating freezing it over to make it stop. He saw who was calling and hesitated. *Elise.*

Bayn still wasn't sure how he felt about Kian's new mate. The curse that was slowly freezing his heart solid shredded his ability to feel, and it was beating slower every day. One day soon, it would stop altogether. Under the dark blue tattooed designs on his chest, pale white lines stretched like roots to circle his heart. It wasn't a complete circle just yet, which meant he still had time.

Elise wasn't going to let him give in to the curse, even if he wanted to. He tried to growl and hiss at her. He couldn't. Not because he was afraid of his brother, though Kian in a rage was something to behold, but because Elise was so damn *kind*. It was like being angry at the clouds. Totally pointless. Growling at her didn't work either because she could manage Kian, which gave her too much experience dealing with mercurial fae moods.

Bayn looked at his phone, a rather useful invention of the humans, he had to admit, and Elise's smiling face flashed up on the screen for a video call. He didn't want to answer. He did, though, because it was Elise.

"Hey, big brother, still alive?" she said before he could utter a word.

"Unfortunately. What's wrong?"

"Why would anything be wrong? Maybe I wanted to say hello and check in on you."

Bayn tapped his fingers against his desk. "If that were the case, you wouldn't be wearing that big know-it-all grin, lil sis."

"I do not have a know-it-all grin!" she argued, her voice high pitched with excitement.

Bayn had played this game with her before and knew when she was holding back. "I give in. What did you find?"

"A relic!" she said triumphantly. "Well, the story of one anyway."

"You practically live in Kian's library. You need to be more specific and also get to the point where it relates to me. I have things to do."

Elise pulled a face. "Oh yeah? Like what? Hot date?"

"Sure, why not." The last thing Bayn was interested in was being around anyone, and Elise knew it.

"The story I found is actually a part of the *Hávamál*, a collection of Norse poetry attributed to Odin. Kian had an older version that had additional content, including a story about Odin receiving a dagger from the Vanir when their war with Asgard was over. The dagger was enchanted for fighting frost giants, melting anything it penetrated, no matter how frozen," Elise explained. She held open a codex to show a drawing of the legendary blade and the brilliant blue stones in the hilt.

"Elise, this is only a story. Such a blade probably doesn't exist," Bayn replied.

"The fae weren't supposed to exist either!" Elise huffed out a breath. "You said you didn't want to look for your mate, that's your choice, but I won't let you just give up and die."

"Why not? It's what I want!" Bayn hadn't raised his voice to Elise before, but her damn excitement, the joy on her face...it took pieces off him. He didn't want to get his hopes up over something that probably didn't exist.

"The curse has disconnected you so deeply from who you really are that you don't even know what you want," Elise snapped, shutting the book. "I know it's a long shot, not only finding the dagger, but that it actually works the way the story says. I don't like the idea of having to stab you with it to see if it will melt your freezing heart. Despite all that, I think the benefits outweigh the risks. Don't you?" She fixed her big blue eyes on him, and Bayn tried not to groan.

"Did you ever stop to think I might not be worth saving, Elise?"

"Do *you* ever stop to think that you are?" she countered. "You're a moody, grumpy asshole, Bayn. Despite that, you are a decent brother, and I know yours would miss you if you did die. I would miss you too."

"Stop trying to guilt-trip me. It won't work."

"If you are too afraid to look because you would have to leave your castle and engage with the world, then that's fine. Stay there. Be miserable," Elise said, lifting her shoulder in a half shrug.

Bayn's hands clenched into fists. "I'm *not* afraid."

"You must be. Afraid to leave your castle, afraid to give the world another chance, afraid to find a way to live—"

"I'm not afraid. I'm tired," Bayn snapped. "I'm sorry that having all my hope stripped away piece by piece for hundreds of years has left me unenthusiastic about looking for lost daggers. You know what? I'll go and find it just to prove you wrong."

"Sure you will. You don't even know where to look."

"Oh, yes? And I suppose you do?"

Elise's know-it-all smile was back again. "No, but I know someone who will."

"Well, send through their details, and I'll go and ask them. Anything to get you off my ass about this." Bayn ran a frustrated hand over his face. "Do you harass Killian like you do me? Because you know he's far more suicidal than I am."

"I would harass him if I could find any useful leads for him." Elise's frown softened. "You are my brothers too, you know. I never had any siblings, and I want to keep you guys around for my sake as well as Kian's."

Bayn laughed. "Kian would cheerfully kill us himself if he could. Don't let him fool you into thinking he's sentimental about us."

"Bayn, he's my mate. I know exactly how he feels about you."

Ah yes, one more reason Bayn never, *ever*, wanted to be mated. Mates could feel each other's emotions, use each other's magic, take each other's strength. He wouldn't wish his feelings and pain onto anyone. It was better that they thought he felt nothing at all.

"If Kian's got any feelings at all, it's because you have infected him with them," he replied. To throw her off, he asked, "Who is this contact of yours? Can they be trusted?"

"Yes, though I won't tell them you are a prince. It might put them off before they even have to deal with your attitude," Elise replied. "They know their stuff, so do your best not to be a total dick to them, okay?"

"I promise to behave, little sister, don't worry," he said with mocking sincerity.

"I'll believe it when I see it," she said. "I am serious, Bayn. If you hurt this contact of mine, I'll get Kian to create a spell where you can only hear the *Frozen* soundtracks in your head for a year."

Bayn grinned back at her. "Ah, and there is my vindictive brother's influence coming out in you."

Elise only laughed evilly. "Good luck, Bayn. You're going to need it." She hung up on him, leaving him cursing under his breath. She knew precisely how to provoke him, and now, he was going to have to find the dagger, or he would never hear the end of it.

Afraid, my ass. Bayn hadn't been capable of fear for a thousand years. Hunting a mythical dagger was an annoyance, nothing more.

Despite what Elise thought, Bayn did venture out into the world. He liked going and listening to heavy metal bands play in Edinburgh at least once a month. No one recognized him as a prince of the fae, certainly not the Winter Prince. Many believed he couldn't leave his castle, and Bayn was happy not to correct them. He liked being just another music struck fae in a crowd.

Bayn was still stewing over being baited by Elise so quickly when his phone buzzed with a message from her.

MARDØLL ANTIKVITETER,
OLD OSLO.

Bayn swore. It appeared he was heading to Norway.

2

Freya was so hungover, she could barely make out the words on her laptop screen. She pushed her long, golden braid over her shoulder and reached for a cup of coffee. She had spent the night with a client, who had purchased a lovely statue of the goddess Frigg from her. He believed in sealing deals with vodka...lots of vodka. She knew that the guy was a gangster of some stamp, even if he was a classy one, so she hadn't risked offending him by not celebrating. She had climbed into bed just as the sun rose in the cold, damp streets of Old Oslo.

If it wasn't for the email from her cousin Elise asking her to meet with a friend of hers, she wouldn't have opened the store today at all. She would be in bed with a bucket.

Get through this one meeting, and then you'll be able to die peacefully. Elise was going to owe her big time for this.

No one had been more surprised than Freya when her baby cousin was announced to the world as the Blood Prince's mate and consort. Elise was always the quiet, studious one, and honestly, the last person on earth that Freya would believe would mess with the fae. She seemed happy, and really, that was all Freya cared about.

Their mothers were sisters, except that Freya's mother had been excellent and Elise's was a total piece of shit. Despite that and the fact Freya's father had been Danish and her family lived in Aarhus, Elise and Freya had always gotten along. Their love of history and mythology had bound them early on. When Elise had gone to study book restoration, Freya had been put to work in her parent's antique store, where her love had been channeled into a more practical application.

Freya had made one remarkable discovery, and the proceeds from the sale had been enough for her to open Mardøll Antiquities in Oslo. She wanted to branch out on her own and get out from under the thumb of her parent's management. They were simultaneously proud of her and still sensitive that she had left them, taking her unique talents with her.

Those abilities had gotten Freya into deep shit eight months ago, but she had refused to reach out to her parents for help. The deal last night would finally put her back on track after months of stress and worry that she would lose the store. With any luck, Elise's friend would be another decent sale.

Freya flicked through her emails, drinking coffee and deleting anything that looked like it would be scammers. Since the fae and now the elves had come out, everyone wanted a magical item of some kind. It didn't matter that genuine artifacts were almost non-existent or that few people knew how to wield them. Everyone with money to burn wanted a piece of the action. Snooty assholes with too much money Freya could handle. It was the shady ones who wished to find weapons that she really had to watch out for.

Like a magical weapon would be much use against the fae, she thought, deleting another request.

The fae had their own for a reason and were much better at using them. They were rare enough that Freya had never had one as a client, but sufficiently dangerous enough that she had paid a ridiculous amount of money to have warded runes tattooed on her body to protect her against glamours and being handled in a way she didn't want to be. She wasn't in any way racist against them, but she was cautious. Freya had learned enough self-defense to protect herself against humans. She saw the runes as the same kind of forward planning. They hurt like an absolute bastard when she got them done but had felt better for it once they were on her.

Freya skimmed over Elise's email again, trying to see if she had mentioned a time to expect her friend. There was nothing. With a tired sigh, Freya made another coffee. Her phone buzzed with a message from her bank, saying that the money from the previous night's sale had cleared, and she breathed a sigh of relief.

No more taking clients this risky. You're out of trouble now, so stay out of it.

That was easier said than done because, with the chime of the door, trouble walked in.

The fae male had to be at least six foot four tall and filled the doorway of Mardøll. Dark sapphire blue eyes scanned the shelves and display cases, taking in the old-world aesthetic. He turned his head, showing the creeping edges of tattoos from under the collar of his black shirt and the silver stud piercings in his pointed ears. Snowflakes were melting like stars in the straight, blue-black hair that reached the middle of his back. Dressed in scuffed black lace-up boots, black jeans, and a leather jacket, Freya knew that the cold mustn't affect him much because he was seriously underdressed for a Scandinavian winter.

He didn't look like her usual customer. He looked like he was there to rob the place.

Freya opened her mouth to greet him, but then his dark eyes landed on her...and narrowed. She wasn't like the women who lost their sense over beautiful fae and elves, and she had never been curious about going to bed with one. Still, this fae's intensity made her pause. She had seen wolves in the wild more than once, and there was one beast in a pack that was always on guard and watched everyone. That was what he reminded her of. He was a wolf dressed up as a man, and her terrified monkey brain knew it.

"Can I help you?" Freya asked, first in Norwegian and then in English, her years of customer service coming to her rescue.

"Apparently," he replied in a deep voice with the soft burr of a celtic brogue.

And he's an asshole to top off my hangover jitters. Two could play at that game, so Freya smiled politely and waited. And waited.

And he just stood there and stared at her. And stared some more.

"Elise thought that you could assist me in finding something," he said, finally giving in but not breaking eye contact.

"Did she?" Freya was going to throttle her baby cousin for not warning her. She was expecting a stuffy academic or a rich kid, the kind of clients Elise had met in her university days and used to send her. Elise lived with the fae these days. Freya should've guessed that her *friend* would be one. Although Kian must've been very secure if he let his mate have a friend who looked like the male in front of her.

"I am searching for a dagger. Did she mention it to you?" he asked, walking toward the polished wooden counter that Freya was determined to keep between them.

"No, she only said she was sending a friend to me. She didn't even tell me your name, Mister—?" Freya let the question hang, and he seemed determined to keep his mouth shut. Something shifted in his eyes, and he gave in.

"Bayn. No mister."

"Freya Havisdottir," she said and held out a hand.

Bayn looked like he would rather cut his hand off than shake hers, so she purposely left it outstretched and slowly raised an eyebrow. It was the eyebrow that got him. He pressed his cool, callused palm to hers, his ringed fingers tightening as he shook her hand.

"It's nice to meet you," she said because she couldn't help making him more uncomfortable.

"If you say so." Bayn let her hand go, pulled out a piece of paper, and tossed it onto the counter. "This is what I am looking for."

Freya unfolded the paper, trying to keep her polite smile in place. As soon as she could see the picture, she forgot all about his bad attitude.

"Where did you get this?" she asked. It looked like a photocopy of a manuscript. The borders were painted in knotwork designs and covered in runes from the Elder Futhark. The picture in the center was of a dagger, jewels in its hilt, and definitely not of Viking make.

"Elise found a story in a book about a dagger gifted to Odin by the Vanir. It was for killing frost giants," Bayn explained.

"I don't suppose she mentioned what the book was called?"

"Does it matter?"

"It could be helpful, especially because it's a story about Odin I've never heard before. Being in the antique business in this country, you can trust I know my Norse myth," Freya replied, tapping her nails on the counter. "I can ask Elise, that's not a problem."

"Then what *is* the problem?" Bayn folded his arms and became a concrete wall of hostility.

You are.

"An unknown object from a rare myth means it will be hard to find, and if it really exists and is in someone's possession, they might not want to part with it."

"That's not a problem. Humans are weak; they all have a price. I'll give them whatever they want."

"And what if they really want a frost giant-slaying dagger?" she murmured and then realized she had said it aloud.

"I will find some other way to convince them," Bayn said, a small, chilling smile on his face. Freya didn't have to use her imagination to know what he meant by that. She had seen that look on men with obsessions before, and it raised every red flag she owned.

"Okay, well, you also have to convince me to take the job on. So factor that in."

His smile warmed up as it grew, and Freya looked back down at the picture without really seeing it. "What do you want, Freya? Name it, and I'll give it to you."

"I'll have to think about it," she said, folding the paper up. "I'd like to keep this or make a copy of it."

"Keep it," Bayn replied. "How long will you need to think about it? I can give you...thirty seconds?"

Freya looked up to see if he was joking. He wasn't. Clearly, someone was used to getting his own way.

"A week," she replied.

"A day."

"Five days."

"Three." Bayn shifted his weight and dropped his arms in a more relaxed position as if to appear less threatening. "If you don't think you can find it, then just say so. If it's too hard for you, I'm happy to go somewhere else."

Freya gave him her sweetest smile. "If it exists, I can find it. My hesitation isn't the dagger. It's you."

"Me? I'm a close friend of Elise's. Surely that's a recommendation of my good character," Bayn replied.

Freya hummed. "In the past, it has been."

"Is it because I'm fae?" Bayn asked, bristling.

"You being fae has nothing to do with it," Freya replied. "It's because you're kind of a prick, and I don't like working with people like that. Especially ones that are willing to do illegal shit to get what they want, which I know you will. Don't bother denying it. I've met men like you before, and you're all the same. I can agree to three days to research and weigh up the risk of working with you, but I don't like your chances."

"I won't deny that I would kill to get what I want, but I'm telling you right now, you've *never* met a man like me, summer." Bayn's ringed hand came down on the counter and slid a white card across to her. "Call me if you decide to stop being a coward."

Freya's temper flared hot as she took the card and dropped it into the small bin next to the counter. "Sure thing."

Bayn's dark eyes sparkled with humor before giving her a low archaic bow and walking out of the store. Freya hurried over to the door, flipped the sign, and locked all the locks...just in case he decided to come back.

3

Bayn had many special abilities and was proud his self-control was amongst his more significant powers. Stepping out into the winter streets of Oslo, he didn't feel the least bit in control of anything.

People gave him curious looks as he walked past them. He made a mental note to dress in warmer clothes to blend in better and put the humans at ease.

Bayn should find a hotel to check into, but he needed to walk off his meeting with the antiques dealer before he did something rash.

Doing rash things was *also* a special ability, and he didn't want to fuck this up. He wanted to prove to Elise that she was wrong about the dagger. Maybe then she'd leave him alone to die in peace. He never should've agreed to this shit in the first place.

"Fucking stupid idea," he muttered, kicking a ball of ice with the toe of his boot. He should've known that a friend of Elise's would be stubborn, but the *attitude* on that woman.

My hesitation isn't the dagger. It's you.

The nerve. He had been tempted to tell her who she addressed in such an impertinent tone. How dare she be so imperious and smug and beautiful at the same time.

Bayn didn't know what he had expected, but it certainly hadn't been a tall blonde with the kind of wide hips a male could lose his head over. Her hair was the color of wheat, her eyes a soft amber-gold to match. She was like looking at summer sunshine. It was offensive.

Dressed in a simple, white button-up shirt and black pants and tie, she had appeared entirely professional, except for those full lips painted a racy red. He already knew they would keep him up at night. She was interested in the dagger, no matter what she said. That professionalism had melted just for a second, and her passion had shone through.

Bayn shook it off and tried to admire the darkening sky, heavy with snow-filled clouds. Magic danced in his veins, the cold air teasing him and silently inviting him to play. Usually, cold and ice made him feel calm. Not tonight.

It was a Saturday night, and he needed a drink, a fuck, or a fight. Preferably all three. He should go and pick up a handful of women in the next three days that looked exactly like her, and then, by the time he went back to her store, Freya and her curves wouldn't entice him in the slightest. This was Scandinavia. There were blondes aplenty.

Bayn shoved his hands into his pockets just as his phone buzzed. For a second, he foolishly wished it would be Freya. He really thought she would cave in on that coward comment.

How did it go? Elise's text said. He almost tossed his phone into traffic.

Fine. Leave me alone, he messaged back.

His sensitive fae hearing picked up a heavy beat from the ground beneath him. That's what he needed. Noise. Lots and lots of noise.

A sturdy black man with silver piercings was standing by a metal door, people waiting in a line to be let in. Bayn kept walking, and the bouncer took one look at the expression on his face and let him pass. Most people did that. They gave him what he wanted or got out of his way.

If only Freya would be as accommodating. Bayn trudged down a steep set of metal stairs and into the thrumming dark gloom.

Bayn was enjoying his bottle of vodka when his phone started burning up with messages again. Elise had taught Kian how to text, and his brother was delighted to be able to harass Bayn whenever he felt like it.

How was the antiques dealer?

I told your mate it went fine, he texted back. *Did they not talk to each other?*

She doesn't believe you, and neither do I.

Antiques dealer is hesitant to take on the job. I'm giving her some time to think about it.

The typing bubble came up and disappeared three times, and Bayn sighed internally.

That was suspiciously generous of you.

Your mate told me to be nice. Bayn downed his drink. *Did Elise tell you anything about her friend?*

Why?

Something doesn't feel right. Can we trust her?

Elise wouldn't do anything to compromise you. She trusts Freya. If you are so concerned about her, maybe keep an eye on her for the next few days if it's going to make you feel better. Just don't be a creepy stalker about it (Elise's words, but I agree).

Bayn considered the idea as he watched a new band play, the music pounding in his bones. Then he went back to his phone and booked a room in the hotel across the street from Mardøll.

∼

Bayn spent the next two days watching Freya as best as he could from his hotel windows.

People visited the shop throughout the day, sometimes bringing Freya coffee and having a chat. Tempting as it was, Bayn refused to return before she sucked up her pride and rang him.

Every morning and evening, Freya came out of the shop in workout gear and ran a two-kilometer lap around Old Oslo. Bayn disapproved of her going out alone, especially when she ran through the icy streets after dark. He *did* approve of the tight yoga pants she liked to run in.

At six o'clock every day, the store lights would go out, and the ones upstairs would go on. Freya wisely kept her curtains closed, except for the second night when Bayn watched her dancing about in her kitchen as she cooked. He was smiling before he could stop and wondered what she was listening to. In the privacy of her apartment, she wore a tank top, and he spotted the protective runes tattooed down her spine. That made him frown. Depending on how strong they were, they would pack a punch if a lesser fae ever touched her. Luckily, he was no lesser fae.

What reason would you have touch her? he asked himself and didn't like it when his brain started to helpfully provide visuals and scenarios.

Bayn hated how much he liked watching her. It was a kind of pleasant torture trying not to think about how he would kill her or what her lips would taste like. If he encased her in ice, he could look at her forever and never have to worry about her unnerving him any more than what she already had.

By day three, Bayn was pacing. He wanted to message Elise and demand that she tell Freya to take on the job. He fantasized about storming across the road and bending the blonde to his will.

Damn, he should've gone and gotten laid. He'd had more than one offer at the club, but Bayn had refused them all. He convinced himself that he wasn't in the mood...and had spent the next two nights having nightmares about Freya's lips, disapproving side-eye glances, and her ass in those damn tight pants.

It's only because she's not interested in you that you're like this.

It was almost nine o'clock at night on the third day when Bayn's phone buzzed on the coffee table with an unknown number.

I'll do the job.

Bayn typed and deleted a variety of responses before settling on a simple, *Thank you, Freya*. He didn't want to antagonize her, at least not over the phone. He thought that would be it, but a minute later, another message came through.

Are you hungry?

4

Freya had spent the first night plagued with lucid dreams about mystical daggers, frost giants, and fae with an air of brutality. Bayn's business card had stayed in the bin where it belonged, and she had only looked at the illustration once. It was too precious to throw out, and Freya was going to find out its origin for her own peace of mind. Oslo was an hour ahead of time than London, so she waited until ten a.m. before calling Elise.

"*Hei kusine*!" Elise answered, sounding bright as a daisy.

"You have some explaining to do," Freya replied.

"Do I? What about this time?"

"Where did you get this illustration of Odin's dagger? Have you been holding out on me?"

"You've met Bayn, how nice." Elise sounded far too pleased and happy about that.

"It wasn't really, and I'll get to him. The picture, Elise. Focus."

"Oh, very well. I found it in Kian's library, in a copy of the *Hávamál*. I didn't remember the story, so I checked the surviving versions, and Kian's one is different because it's longer," Elise explained as Freya's heart did a double leap.

"And you didn't think to share this remarkable discovery with your beloved cousin first? You *know* how I feel about Odin."

Elise definitely knew because she had teased Freya on more than one occasion about her surname being Havisdottir, which translated as Havi's daughter. Havi had been one of Odin's many names, and subsequently, many of her Norse myth loving clients had thought she had picked the surname on purpose. She had used it to her advantage.

Being already interested in the All-Father had been a boon, and now there was only one person in the whole of Scandinavia who probably knew more about Odin than her. And Von would lose his mind over the thought of a longer *Hávamál* being found.

"Freya? Are you still there? Or has your mind wandered off to your happy place?"

"Not a happy place, my hurt place. You've wounded me. You gave this information to some fae with a bad attitude over me? I don't care how hot he is; that's not cool. What is Bayn to you anyway? I thought you had a fae prince already," asked Freya and caught herself. She sounded weirdly jealous.

"I do, and Kian is perfect. Bayn is a close friend of Kian's who has been cursed. I've been looking into a way to break it."

"And you think a dagger for killing frost giants could help?"

"It might," Elise said, uncertainty creeping into her voice.

"What's his curse? Bad attitude? Being too hot when he glares because he can't get his own way?" Freya resented that last one in particular. That glare had been featured prominently in her vodka-soaked dreams.

Elise sounded like she was trying to smother a laugh. "If Bayn wants you to know about his curse, he will tell you himself. Are you going to help him or not?"

"I told him no, but he's given me three days to apparently change my mind." Freya stared at the picture again, her nail tracing the knotwork border. "It's tempting and would be an incredible find. Shame he's such a dick."

"I won't deny he can be, but don't rule him out just yet. Bayn has layers," Elise said. "The curse is difficult to live with, and that affects his attitude. He hasn't been around humans much, and he's isolated himself. He needs help, Freya."

Freya let out a tired sigh. "You're such a bleeding heart. I don't see why he can't find the dagger on his own."

"Because you're the best at what you do, and it will be quicker if you help." There was a low murmur of a male's voice in the background. "Kian said if you work with Bayn, he'll give you his *Hávamál*."

"Oh, now he's just playing dirty."

Elise chuckled. "That's Kian."

Freya frowned at the picture, considering all the possible places such a dagger might be and the complexities of finding it.

"I don't know, cousin. Odin collectors tend to be a bit crazy, and I only just got out of trouble," she said finally.

"That's why you should keep Bayn close. No matter how much of a dick he acts like, he won't let anything happen to you. Trust me on that," Elise replied.

"What if he's the one I'm worried about?"

"He's the last person that will ever hurt you."

I've heard that lie before. Freya's heart did an involuntary clench. She had been hurt by people she cared about a lot in the past year and still hadn't recovered from it.

"I'll have a look through my files and see what I can come up with. I've still got two days left before I decide to do it," Freya said.

"Thank you, cousin. Be patient with Bayn," Elise replied.

After they hung up, Freya reluctantly bent down and took Bayn's card out of the paper bin. There was no name, just a phone number in neat navy print. She ran a thumb over it thoughtfully and then muttered a curse.

"I'm going to need so much more coffee."

Her two days had come and gone. Now Freya was surrounded by papers, printouts, books, pictures, and notes. Her office, which had been clean before, looked like a bomb had gone off in it. She had started with the internet, searching for other versions of the story about the dagger, and she had fallen into a rabbit hole.

The tall wooden card catalog, a replica of the ones that her parents owned, had also been rifled through. Freya had expanded her catalog and added a section of associates, clients, and people of interest. Her ex-boyfriend Leif had teased her about it and then had stolen sections when they broke up.

The whole point of having such vital information as a hard copy was because she didn't trust that her computer wouldn't get hacked by someone obsessive enough to risk it. Leif had simply walked in, broke her heart, and made off with years of work.

Freya still wanted revenge for that, and if she found the dagger and got an ancient copy of the *Hávamál,* it would be a nice 'fuck you' to the guy who had almost bankrupted her on top of everything else. She didn't have what she needed, but she had made a good enough start.

Taking out Bayn's card, she typed his number into her phone and sent him a message. Her stomach grumbled angrily, and without thinking too hard about it, she messaged him, *Are you hungry?*

I could eat, came the lightning-quick response. Freya looked around at the mess of research that had spilled out of her office and onto her dining room table. Bayn would have to get used to it if they were going to work together. She remembered Elise's comment about him being lonely and decided to break the ice.

I'm about to order dumplings. You're welcome to join me if you can get here in the next thirty minutes.

I can be there in ten. I'm in the hotel across the road.

You're kidding me.

Open your curtain.

Freya hurried to her windows facing the street and looked out. Directly across from her was Bayn, his tall body silhouetted by light. He lifted his hand in a half-ass wave.

"Fucking hell." Freya quickly went through the last three days in her mind and hoped that her curtains had been closed all the times she had walked around in her underwear and sleeping shirt.

It was going to be the most convenient place to stay when you agreed to work with me, came a text, like he could see her freaking out from that distance.

Confident of you to think that I would.

I was hopeful.

Flustered, she shut the curtain so he wouldn't see that too. **Food in thirty minutes.**

Freya knew he would arrive at her doorstep on the dot, so she showered and dressed in clean clothes in record time. Sure enough, when she unlocked the door, there he was, dressed all in black and smelling like pine and cinnamon.

"Freya," he said, his Gaelic brogue turning her name to a soft purr.

"Bayn." Freya stared at him a second longer, and then deciding it was still a terrible idea, she let him inside. She did her best not to show how nervous she was as he followed her up the stairs to her apartment. It was ridiculous. She was *never* shy, especially not around men. *Except he's not a man.*

"It seems that you've been busy," he said, looking at the notes on her table as he took off his overcoat. His tight black t-shirt stretched over a muscled chest and shoulders, but it was his arms Freya couldn't stop looking at and not because of the size of his biceps. Both arms were heavily tattooed with navy ink in mesmerizing runes and designs. She had never seen fae tattoos before, and she wanted to know if they meant anything.

"Freya?"

"Sorry, I like tattoos," she said, turning her back to him and going to the kitchen to get some plates. "And yes, I have been busy. I'm a sucker for a mystery, which your dagger most certainly is." Freya cleared a space on the table and put the takeout bags in between them.

"I hope you like dumplings," she said with a smile. She had ordered it specifically because there was no neat way to eat them, and he struck her as someone who didn't like a mess.

"I don't know. I've never eaten them before," Bayn replied, pulling out a chair for her. It was a suspiciously lovely gesture that she didn't expect.

"Then you're in for an experience," Freya said, handing him chopsticks. She thought he would struggle to use them, but he was a master at wielding them.

"What have you learned about my dagger?" he asked, lifting a dumpling. She was wrong about him not being able to eat them neatly as well. *Maybe it's a fae thing.*

"Not as much as I would like, but I've eliminated a lot. That's almost as important," Freya said, trying and failing to eat her dumplings with any class at all. Bayn was watching her struggle with a small, amused expression on his face. She lifted her thumb to lick off a stray bit of soy sauce, and the amusement slipped.

"There is no report anywhere of a dagger claiming to be a gift from the Vanir to Odin. It means two things; one, it's in the ground somewhere, or two, whoever has it isn't dumb enough to advertise it. It would be a serious collector, not someone trying to talk themselves up."

"And both things are bad for us?" Bayn guessed.

"Yes. I've searched as many museum catalogs and archaeological finds as I could, I even reached out to a few academics I know, and all they have heard is rumors."

"Are you feeding me dinner and telling me all this to put me in a good mood when you admit it's impossible to find?" Bayn asked.

"It'll be *hard* to find, not impossible. I'm feeding you dinner because I wanted to," Freya corrected.

"Thank you," Bayn said softly as a strange expression that she couldn't read flickered over his face.

"You're welcome. As I was saying, it's not impossible to find, especially not for me."

"Why not for you? You're just an average human woman."

Freya really didn't like being called 'average' like it was an insult. *Be patient, remember?*

"Didn't Elise tell you? Finding things is kind of my superpower." *Amongst other things.*

"She didn't mention that. Is it magic?"

Freya shook her head. "I don't think so. The best way I can explain it is when I fixate on something, it decides it wants to be found. I find a thread and follow it, and nine out of ten times, the object of my desire presents itself. Since the fae returned and magic with you, I can also sense if an object is magical or not. It's like they give off different vibrations." Freya enjoyed the shocked look on his face before adding, "And I'm not 'average' at anything."

"I'm beginning to see that." Bayn smiled. It wasn't sarcastic or threatening for once. It was blinding, his stern handsomeness ramping up to a whole new level. Like she needed that distraction.

"Trust me, Bayn. I always find what I search for and get what I want."

"I have no doubt. What's our next step?"

Freya noticed the 'our' and tension tightened her muscles. She usually worked alone but was willing to get used to having a partner, if only for this job.

"I've crossed out the academics and the bored rich collectors, so we head for the next best thing; the hopelessly obsessed." Freya leaned over and stole his last dumpling. "And I know just the guy to help us."

5

The club's name was 'Ritual,' and it used to be Freya's go-to watering hole. Runes decorated the doorways along with cut pine boughs and reindeer antlers.

Bayn was leaning against a brick wall, blending into the darkness. With his black clothes and piercings, he would look the part in the club, but the feel of his magic gave him and his hiding spot away.

Freya hadn't mentioned it to Bayn, but it wasn't only magical objects that her radar picked up on. She could feel if someone had power, and even though he kept a tight lid on it, she could feel Bayn's magic lingering around him like an aura. She had almost asked him what he could do with it the night before when his concentration had slipped, and she got a small touch of it. Freya had stopped herself just in time. She needed to have some secrets, and feeling out magical threats was a good one to keep.

"Hey Bayn, what are you doing hiding back there?" she asked. His eyes widened a little like he was surprised she had spotted him. *That's right, you don't know me.*

"Not hiding, watching. I like to know where the exits are if I am going underground. Interesting place to meet. If you wanted to have a drink with me, you should've asked," he said, stepping from the shadows and joining her.

Did he just try and flirt with me?

"In your dreams, fae," Freya said, tossing her hair over one shoulder. She had left it out, and Bayn hadn't stopped looking at it. She tried to pretend she didn't see the non-professional interest in his eyes. She had learned over dumplings and research that Bayn certainly had layers, as Elise warned. One layer was probably capable of setting a woman's panties on fire if she wasn't careful. He was deadly smart and analytical, too, two things she admired.

"My contact is Von Karlsson, the owner of the club. We have been friends for a long time," Freya explained as they headed for the door.

"Freya! My love, I haven't seen you in months. Where have you been hiding?" Johan asked. He was one of the doormen that had been working for Von forever.

"Working, always working," Freya replied, accepting the kiss on the cheek. Bayn cleared his throat behind her. Johan's blue eyes looked him over.

"Who's your friend?"

She waved behind her dismissively. "This is Bayn. Is the boss in?"

"He is and will be happy to see you. He's been missing his favorite girl."

Freya laughed and handed him her coat. He would put it in the staff's cupboard for safekeeping. "They are *all* his favorite girls."

"Better keep a close eye on your date, or Von might steal him from you," Johan added.

"Freya just told me we aren't on a date," said Bayn, sending an unexpected flicker of annoyance through her.

"Then she's going to be busy keeping them off you," Johan said with a big laugh. "Have fun."

"Always." Freya headed down the curving staircase lined with candles and torches in sconces. Heavy metal beats mixed with traditional instruments filled the air, getting louder the further down they went.

Von was obsessed with two things, Odin and metal, and his club reflected both. It was a den that was a fusion of his passions and was like walking through a goth Viking hall. A band was on stage, starting up a runic chant as the drumming got heavier. People were dancing and drinking, giving themselves over to the ritualistic vibe and losing themselves in the music, letting loose occasional wolf howls that got echoed around the club by other patrons.

"This place is amazing," Bayn said, his voice cutting through the noise. His large hand went to Freya's shoulder, moving her out of the way of a guy who wasn't watching where he was going and sloshing mead over his glass.

"Thanks," Freya replied. She loved the black cashmere sweater she was wearing over her leather pants, and trying to get mead out of it would've been a nightmare. That was when she noticed that people were staring at Bayn while instinctively getting out of his way. He didn't seem to notice or care, keeping his eyes fixed on her and safe in a bubble of protection.

He's the last person that will ever hurt you, Elise had told her. For whatever reason, Bayn was watching out for her.

The bartender recognized Freya instantly, passing her two vodka sodas and pointing to the stairs leading to the VIP area. "Von wants to see you."

Freya passed one of the vodkas to Bayn, tapped her glass against his, and had a large mouthful.

"Are you nervous about something?" he asked.

"No. Yes? I haven't seen Von since I broke up with my ex, also a friend of his. It was...messy."

"I see. I'll make sure he's not disrespectful to you," Bayn said with a decisive nod.

"No, that's not—" Freya broke herself off. Bayn was trying to be nice, in his way, so she nodded. "Thank you. Whatever you do, don't mention Kian's copy of the *Hávamál*."

"You don't trust him?"

"Not when it comes to Odin," Freya replied. It would be the kind of item that would easily cause a rift between her and Von, and she didn't know how big the one they already had was.

Freya headed up the twisting black stairs to Von's private VIP area, a ball of knots growing tighter in her stomach. Von was dressed only in a pair of leather pants to better show off his sculpted chest, tattoos, and war paint. His long blond hair was out, the occasional leather-wrapped braid peeking through. Lined with heavy black liner, his blue eyes sparkled with mischievous trouble when they landed on her.

"Odin's daughter finally returns to my hall of decadence," he said, getting out of his fur-covered chair and going to kiss her cheek. "My darling raven, you look beautiful as ever."

"You too, Von," Freya said, hugging him.

"When Johan told me that you were here with a big fae male, I didn't believe him." Von let her go and took in Bayn from head to toe. His smile was utterly delighted by the time he made it to his face. "Well, you've certainly upgraded, that's for sure."

"This is Bayn. He's my...associate," Freya settled on.

"I like your place," Bayn said, offering his hand to Von to shake.

"A true compliment from one of the fae." Von held Bayn's hand long enough for Freya to step between them and wrap an arm around Von's waist.

"Come sit with me. I want to catch up with you," she said, tugging him away. One of Bayn's dark brow's rose behind Von's back, but she ignored him.

"That sounds a lot like you want something, Freya love."

"Only something you're willing to give," she said, sitting on his chair beside him.

"If you want me to be you and the fae's third, you only need to ask, sweet."

Freya laughed. "Stop flirting. It won't work. I wanted to see you, but also, I have a question for you about your favorite subject."

Von tucked her hair over one of her ears, rubbing his thumb against her cheek. "I've missed you. You should have come to me after Leif. I could've helped you."

Freya leaned into his palm. "I was okay on my own. Besides, you were his friend too. I didn't want to put you in that position."

"You didn't think I would choose you over him? You are so wrong. Leif is forging his own path these days and doesn't remember his old friends anymore."

That was news to Freya. If Leif had burned a bridge with someone influential like Von, he must've been confident he wouldn't need him again one day.

"Who is Leif?" Bayn asked. He was standing against the balcony railing with his arms folded, making the tattoos on his biceps flex.

"Freya's old paramour," Von answered.

"He's being polite. Leif is my piece of shit ex-boyfriend and not someone I've come to talk to you about."

Von leaned back in his chair, putting an arm around her shoulders. Bayn caught the gesture, and his expression changed from placid to pissed off and back again. Freya should've told him she didn't need protection from Von. He was affectionate to everyone. He would probably try to get into Bayn's lap if the fae sat down anywhere.

"Okay, Freya, what did you need to ask me?" Von said once they had fresh drinks.

"Have you ever heard of a dagger being gifted to Odin from the Vanir? Specifically, one that would kill frost giants?"

"Oh, an obscure one tonight. I've heard rumors of such a thing, but nothing that could be considered concrete. What interest is it of yours?" asked Von.

"We are going to find it," said Bayn. Freya shot him a warning look. Sure enough, Von's interest went from happy to laser focus.

"Freya, darling, you are holding out on me."

"No, Von, that's not it at all. I didn't want to get you excited about something that might not exist," Freya corrected.

"Who are you hunting it for?" Von asked.

"Me," said Bayn.

"The plot thickens. What need do you have for a giant-killing blade?"

"Maybe I want to kill some giants."

"Don't be coy."

"What does it matter what I need it for?" The corner of Bayn's mouth twitched into a suggestive grin. "If you help us find the dagger, I'll let you touch it."

To Freya's surprise, Von blushed for the first time since she had met him. She didn't blame him.

"Oh, fae, you are dangerous," said Von.

"In many, many ways," Bayn agreed.

Freya nudged Von with her shoulder. "Come on, what are these rumors you've heard?"

"I didn't think there was anything to the story because I haven't encountered it anywhere else. I was in Berlin a few years ago at a Norse myth conference, and there was a professor there called Hans Weber who mentioned a marker stone in Germany that had spoken of a Vanir dagger. Because there was nothing more than that to the story, I filed it away as a maybe and haven't thought of it since," Von explained. He raised his glass back to his lips. "I wouldn't mind knowing how you found out about it."

"I have my contacts like you have yours. Besides, Bayn knew the story, and he's the one who wants it." It wasn't quite a lie. She smiled warmly at him. "Come on, Von, don't you want to know if the rumors are true? What else do you know?"

"Not much, but I could make some calls for you and find out if you don't mind waiting."

"We don't mind," Bayn said.

"That would be great. Thank you, Von-"

"I said I *could* make some calls," Von reiterated.

Freya should've known better. She let out a sigh. "What do you want for it?"

"You know what I want, baby raven." Von waggled his eyebrows, and Freya groaned.

"No, not tonight."

"She's not having sex with you," Bayn interrupted, his voice cold. That only made Von laugh.

"If she was that easy to convince to trade information for sex, I would've taken advantage of it years ago. What I want is something more...musical. You must sing the song for me, Freya, or go home empty-handed." Von looked Bayn over. "Maybe not entirely empty."

"You sing?" Bayn looked surprised, and she tried not to smirk. She liked surprising him, but she hadn't sung properly in months.

"Freya used to sing in the house band. She's excellent, but Leif made her give it up. Too many people were trying to have sex with her."

"That's not entirely true. I got too busy with work to keep up with both."

"Ah, huh. Doesn't matter. I want my song, and then I will give you the information."

"I want a song too," Bayn added unhelpfully.

"I'm out of practice."

"You'll still be amazing. The band will be happy to see you." Von got up and started heading down the stairs.

"You are full of secrets, aren't you?" Bayn held out a hand to help her out of the lounge. Freya hesitated for a moment before putting her hand in his and letting him tug her gently to her feet.

"Does it bother you?" she asked, looking up at him.

"Not even a little bit. I like the idea of learning them all," Bayn replied. They were standing close enough that the air charged between them, and he held her gaze.

"This is a bad idea." Freya didn't know if she was talking about the singing or the spark of desire she was feeling.

"Or a very good one." Bayn's fingers slid from her hand and up the inside of her forearm. "Sing for me."

Heat broke out along Freya's spine as the magic runes on her skin activated. It must have been giving him a warning shock, but Bayn didn't seem to notice or care.

"Okay, but no teasing me if I sound bad. As I said, I'm out of practice," she replied, stepping back from him.

Von had already reached the stage door and made a hurry-up sign at her. Wishing she had drunk more, Freya followed him.

6

Bayn didn't know how he imagined the night going, but it wasn't going to a club to listen to Freya sing. She had stripped off to her lacy tank top, showing off her curvy body and providing skin for Von to paint her arms and chest in runes. She looked like the fierce and beautiful goddess of war and love she was named after.

Bayn stood in the shadows of the stage entrance, happy to stay out of the chaos as the band caught up with Freya and prepped her with equipment. She glowed with happiness as she chatted to them, her nervousness about singing gone.

"You are in for a treat, fae. I know your people love music, and Freya... well, she will make you want to kidnap her and take her into Faerie like your stories say," said Von, coming to stand beside him. His fingers were dancing on his phone as he sent out messages. Bayn hoped a few of them were to get the information they were there for.

"I've never met a human that has tempted me enough to want more than a night with them," Bayn replied because he wanted to keep Von on his side.

The Viking only laughed at him. "And the way you look at her is just professional interest?"

"I don't know what you're implying. I promised her friend that I would keep her safe. That requires watching her."

"If you say so. Her ex would've tried gouging the eyes out of anyone who looked at Freya the way you do."

I'd love to see him try.

"He sounds like a prick. She's better off without him."

"You'll get no argument from me. Freya deserves more than Leif could give her, and I say that as a friend of his. I'm glad you're watching her back. Leif isn't over the fact she left him," Von said.

Bayn picked up the subtle warning he was giving him and nodded. From what he had already gathered about Leif, if he ever came near Freya again, Bayn would happily tear his arms off and beat him with them.

You've barely known her a week. You need to calm down. For the past two days, he had been telling himself that he was only feeling this way because Elise's connection with Freya made him feel obligated to want to protect her. Now he wasn't so sure.

"Show time," said Von. He headed out onto the stage and grabbed the microphone. The crowd cheered and howled until he waved them quiet. "Settle yourselves, my ravens! We have a special guest for you tonight. For those who are regulars, you will remember being blessed by this goddess in the past. With a little bribery, I have convinced her to return to sing my favorite song for me. So put your dirty hands together for Odin's Daughter singing 'Running up that Hill'!"

The crowd went crazy, feet stomping and voices shouting 'Freya! Freya!' as the goddess herself walked out on stage.

"Thanks, everyone... Okay, shut up!" she called, and to Bayn's surprise, they did. The whole fucking club went dead silent as the band started up.

Freya's red mouth opened, and time froze.

Heat raced from Bayn's ears to his lips, down his throat to his chest, curving along the frozen white tentacles of his curse to his heart. A heart that was only beating an average of ten times an hour...and was now starting to pound.

He clutched his fist to his chest, the power and ethereal beauty of Freya's voice stripping him, leaving him raw and hot. She was glowing under the floodlights, the black and gold paint shimmering on her skin, her hair a river of light.

Bayn didn't know the song; it was sad and lovely, full of longing. He knew why it was Von's favorite and why Freya's singing moved them to another place entirely.

The crowd was as mesmerized as he was, all of them staring at her worshipfully. She had an incredible gift, and it made him hate Leif more for making her stop. She loved it. She was the music, and the music was her, and every word of the song was imbued with feeling.

I do want to take her into Faerie and never let her go. The thought should've worried him, but his heart was beating so hard, it drowned it out. *She's magic. She's making it beat again.*

Bayn moved to the backstage steps, out of the shadows. Somehow, Freya sensed him there and gave him a sly wink before turning back toward the crowd, her voice rising louder and higher as the song neared the finale. The crowd went crazy, the spell breaking, and they let their veneration pour over her. She was blushing brightly as she bowed and waved, heading off the stage towards Bayn.

"Are you okay? You are looking a bit dazed," she said, breathlessly. She was a few steps higher than him, so they were eye to eye.

Bayn couldn't think of a single thing to say, so he pulled her up against him and kissed her. Freya's surprised murmur slid over his lips, but she didn't pull away or stop. Bayn smeared the battle paint on her arms as he ran his hands over her. He reached her neck, cradling it so he could tilt her head back and kiss her harder. Her warm tongue searched his lips, and he opened for her, letting her take as much as he did. Her hands were in his hair, moving to stroke the tattoos on his neck.

You have to stop, or you won't ever let her go.

Bayn pulled back slowly. Freya's amber eyes were wide, and her lips were swollen as she released him.

"You are amazing, and none of us deserve you," Bayn said, touching her cheek once before letting her go.

Bayn pushed into the crush of people, needing to get the hell away from Freya before he pulled her through the ice and locked her in his castle forever. He needed as much space between them as possible, or his ancient fae blood would drive him to do something unforgivable. No matter how much they pretended to be civilized, the fae still had to fight the urges to take whatever the fuck they wanted because they had the power to.

Bayn would do what he must to protect Freya...especially from himself.

~

Freya was still standing in a daze when Von caught up with her. Her lips were tingling, her extra senses burning with Bayn's magic. His power had hit her as a series of sensations; midnight darkness and moonlight on snow, the taste of pine, cinnamon and ice, desire and destruction. It had swamped her as her mouth had moved against his, hungry for something only he could give her.

Freya shook herself and pushed that thought away. It was probably a part of his alluring fae magic. That kind of longing was a frightening, obsessive thing, and she was done with those kinds of relationships.

You wouldn't even know what that kind of relationship would be like. Leif was one emotionally fueled disaster after another, and she wouldn't let herself get that lost in a person again.

"Freya? Are you okay?" Von's warm hand touched her shoulder.

"What? Yes."

"What did you do to Bayn? I saw him leaving the club like you had lit a fire under his ass." Von looked at her smeared and ruffled state. "Oh. Well, isn't that interesting. I tried to warn him to prepare himself for you singing, but it looks like his fae weakness for music overwhelmed him."

"And he left in embarrassment. It's fine. What did you find out?" Freya asked, wanting to get what she needed and go home.

"Unfortunately, I've come up with a blank. Don't look at me like that! I'm not going to let you down. I'm just going to need a day or so to dig deeper," Von replied.

"Don't drag your feet. I need this job over and out of the way. Bayn is eager to get it done as soon as possible."

"Are you going to be okay with him?" Von looked genuinely concerned. He had tried to intervene and get her help when Leif had been acting like an asshole. She should have taken him up on the offer and saved herself a lot of heartaches and black eyes.

"Bayn would never hurt me. Not ever," she reassured him. And she wasn't just saying it; she felt the truth of it right down to her soul. Even if he was surly and his magic scarily powerful, Freya felt safe with him. While she had been in his arms only moments before, it was the safest she had felt in months.

"Okay, my darling Freya. I'll let you know as soon as I get some information on the dagger. Please think about starting to do a set for me once a month. I've missed you, Odin's daughter," Von replied, bringing her in for a hug. She kissed both of his cheeks and headed for the exit. She needed a hot bath and a glass of wine to figure out...whatever the hell that kiss had been, and why she felt so terribly lonely now that Bayn was gone.

7

Two days later, Freya still hadn't heard from Bayn, and it was starting to make her twitchy. She shouldn't have cared. It wasn't like she had never been kissed by a random stranger after a gig before. None of them had run off afterward.

And none of them kissed you like that. It still made Freya hot all over just thinking about it. How he tolerated the electric snap of her tattooed runes was a mystery. God damn gorgeous fae. She knew he would be trouble as soon as he walked through the door.

Freya told the voice in her head to shut up and focus on something more productive. She was waiting on Von's leads, so she had started looking for information on the professor he had mentioned, Hans Weber. She tried not to be too judgmental when the name led her to more than one pseudo-archaeology website.

Freya had done everything she could not to get dragged into that crowd. Still, more often than not, it was almost always magical in nature when they produced something. It was the kind of stuff that people had put down as mythical and never bothered to really look for it. At least, before the fae had returned and magic with them. Now digs and searches were popping up everywhere. She had received an invite to help search for Excalibur only a month ago.

Freya picked up her phone and rechecked her messages. It was almost nine p.m., and there was still nothing from Bayn, even though she had sent him an 'Are you okay?' message that morning. Walking to her windows facing the street, she peeked through her curtains.

A tall silhouette was walking around the hotel room she knew to be his. Some of her worries eased, knowing he was still in Oslo. Frustration replaced the fear with lightning speed, so she got a piece of paper from her printer and wrote a message on it in a black felt pen. Bayn happened to be staring out of his window toward her when she stuck it to her glass.

NOW WHO IS THE COWARD?

Freya could just about hear his snarl as Bayn read the message. She shut the curtains on him and walked away.

Half an hour later, Freya was making another cup of tea when there was a knock at her door. She looked through the peephole. Bayn was staring at her through it.

"I can hear you breathing. Open the door, Freya," he said.

"Hmm, maybe I will in two days," she replied, hastily pulling her hair out of its messy bun and trying to smooth it.

"You could, but that means I will have to eat all this Thai food on my own." He held the brown paper bags up for her to see.

Freya's stomach growled. "I could be persuaded if you have a Pad Thai?"

"Of course I have a Pad Thai. Is there any point without one?"

Damn, he's got me there. Freya opened the door but didn't move aside. "Where have you been, Bayn?" she asked. She sounded far more accusatory than what she wanted. Seeing him standing there looking so damn perfect when she had been stressing out the past few days made her want to kick him in the balls.

"Can we talk about it inside and not in your hallway?"

Freya's stomach grumbled again, and his mouth twitched. Bayn offered her the bag of food.

"Smarter than you look, fae," she said, taking it and heading towards the kitchen.

"Did Von come up with any good leads?" Bayn asked, shutting the door behind him.

"You aren't changing the subject that quickly." Freya grabbed bowls from the cupboard and put them down a little too forcefully on the bench.

Bayn was frowning at her. "Are you okay?"

"No, I'm not okay! You kissed me and then just disappeared for days. What the hell? If I had kissed you, then I would at least understand why you would be awkward. If you are embarrassed about it, at least say that—"

"I'm not embarrassed," Bayn said, going from concerned to defensive. "I kissed you because I wanted to. I got caught up in your voice and beauty, and I didn't stop to ask you for permission. I *took* that kiss. I've been quiet for two days because I've been trying to find a way to apologize for taking liberties with you."

Freya's mouth popped open. "Huh." She opened her fridge door, grabbing two beers and letting the cool air calm the warmth trying to creep its way up her chest. She offered him one of the beers. "Don't worry about it. Like you said, it was the heat of the moment, and we had been drinking."

"Despite that, I am sorry. Next time, I'll ask your permission first, or better yet, get you to ask me," he said sincerely.

"And you think there's going to be a next time?"

Bayn lifted the bottle to his smiling mouth. "Oh, yes."

"I'm surprised my rune tattoos didn't shock you," Freya said, trying her best not to be affected by his grin.

"They tickled a bit, but I'm not like other fae," he admitted. He reached into the paper bags and passed her the container of Pad Thai. "Elise told me it's your favorite."

"Of course she did." Freya sat opposite him and tried not to worry about the fact she was wearing her pj's. Bayn didn't seem to notice or care, so she wasn't about to stand on ceremony for him.

"So are you going to tell me what Von said?" he asked once they had bowls full of food.

"He's still digging and is going to let me know what he finds."

"You said you didn't trust him with Odin, didn't you?" Bayn asked.

"Yes, but he also knows I'm his best chance to find it."

"What about Leif? Would he ask him to find it instead?"

Freya toyed with her beer. "Maybe in the past. It sounds like they had a falling out, which doesn't surprise me in the least. Leif doesn't just burn a bridge; he does the town too while he's at it."

"I'm surprised that you dated someone like that. You're too strong-willed. Or do you only save that for me?" Bayn gave her another of his disarming smiles.

"You bring it out in me, that's for sure. To answer your questions, I wasn't always so strong-willed, and I was charmed by Leif from the moment I met him." Freya's phone buzzed, and she glanced at the message. She read it through again, just to be sure, and cursed. "Speak of the devil, and he'll appear." Bayn gave her a curious look, so she said, "Von has gotten us an invite to a party and auction. Apparently, it's run by a recluse collector that loves anything magical."

"What's the problem with that?"

"It's on Tjuvholmen, Thieve's Island. It used to be a prison in the 18th century, but now the whole place is redeveloped and Leif's turf. I haven't gone back there since we broke up." And wouldn't the asshole gloat when she did?

"Is he part of some kind of organized crime?"

"He wasn't when we were together. He has a lot of underworld contacts and friends, though. He bought up what remained of the island and now kind of runs it like an unofficial mayor. He only got the money to do it from selling shit that I found, mostly to dodgy people." Freya ate another couple of quick mouthfuls of noodles, her stress eating already kicking in. "If the party is on the island, he'll know about it. Considering the nature of the party, he'll be there. We need to find another way to get access to this collector."

"Why? If he's going to be there, then it will be the perfect opportunity," Bayn argued.

"I don't want to drag you into my shit, Bayn, that's why! As soon as I step through the door, Leif will see it as me skulking back into his crowd because I couldn't make it on my own. Having you there will be like pouring gasoline on a candle."

"Because he's a jealous, controlling, manipulative asshole who still isn't over the fact that you dumped him?"

"Yes! I mean, no. I don't know. He doesn't like losing. I'm just as likely to try and stab him with something when he starts his bullshit.

That son of a bitch stole whole sections of my life's work when he left, and it still wasn't enough. He's been trying to do me out of clients for the last eight months so that my store will go under, and I'll go back to him. If I turn up on his island, that's exactly what he's going to think I'm doing."

Freya didn't realize she was almost shouting until Bayn's hand covered hers. It was warm and comforting, and it should have made her pull away from him, but she didn't. She liked it when he touched her, no matter how bad of an idea it was.

"He won't ever hurt you again, Freya, I can promise you that." Bayn's long fingers stroked the top of her palm. "If you go to this party, and he's there, don't you think it will be a great 'fuck you' to him? You're not there for his handouts. You're there as a player. His equal, not subject. I'm sure he'll get the message that you have moved on and up from him if you turn up with a handsome, mysterious fae male."

"You have a single friend willing to come on a date with me?" she asked, fluttering her lashes.

"If I did, I'm wise enough never to introduce him to you." Bayn's hand tightened around hers before lifting it and brushing his lips against her knuckles. "Fuck Leif, Freya. If he starts trouble with you, bust his balls like you do mine, and you'll be fine." He let her hand go, and she grabbed her beer and drained it.

"I see what you are doing, Bayn, and I appreciate it, but I'll have to think about it." Freya's voice was cracking as she fought back all the anger and hurt she felt towards Leif. "He really was an asshole in the end." Bayn pushed his half-full beer towards her, and she had a mouthful.

"Want me to kill him?" he asked.

Freya choked on the beer. "Are you serious?"

"Yes. I'll do it if you ask, and it'll never come back to you. After everything I have learned about him, it would be my pleasure to watch the life fade from his eyes," Bayn said, his voice going cold and deadly. Just a whisp of his magic leaked out from behind whatever was hiding it, and Freya could taste iron and ice. It set off every danger alarm Freya had.

"God, Bayn. No. Calm down. Leif is a dick and treated me terribly, but he doesn't deserve to be murdered for it," she replied, and the pressure and magic in the room vanished. "Let's change the subject while I decide whether or not to go to the party. What's the deal with your curse?"

"I see Elise has been gossiping again." Freya waited for him to continue, holding his dark sapphire gaze until he broke. "I'm going to need another beer." Freya grabbed two.

Bayn finished his food off, his eyes far away like he was contemplating how much he could tell her. Freya hoped he wouldn't lie to her. She'd had enough of men doing that.

"I was cursed by a jealous witch. She was in love with my brother, and when she couldn't have him, she burned his world to the ground. I was cursed right along with him." Bayn slowly began to unbutton the black shirt he was wearing, and Freya had the sudden, mad urge to giggle. She knew he would be fit, but damn. With every button undone, she saw more muscle and tattoos. Beautiful, dark, magical tattoos.

"You see this?" Bayn traced the fine white lines that stretched from his right side, across his chest to his heart.

"Yes?" Freya couldn't look away. She wanted to trace those lines, learn what his tattoo's meant, what the magic in them did.

"That's the curse," Bayn continued, his hand dropping away. "Because of my magic, the curse has chosen to slowly freeze my heart. Once this circle is complete, I'm dead."

"No," Freya snarled and shook herself. "I mean, no, it won't kill you because we are going to get the dagger. It's why you're looking for it, right? To stop the curse?"

"In the beginning, it was more about proving Elise wrong. I was ready to die."

"And now?"

Bayn started to button his shirt back up. "Now, I'm intrigued to see what happens. I don't like the idea of stabbing myself with a dagger, but I'm sure you could oblige me if I made you angry enough."

She knew it was a joke, but nausea swept through her guts at the thought of her hurting him. Freya made herself smile her cockiest smile. "I might even enjoy it."

Bayn's eyes heated. "Not a doubt in my mind, summer. You look like you want to stab me every time I see you."

"I do not."

"You really do. It's like you know there's something about me you should disapprove of and can't, so it irritates you. Am I so bad?"

Freya laughed. "No, you're not. Maybe the first time we met, but I'm beginning to see what Elise meant about you."

"And what's that?"

"You have layers. Now I've gotten past the prick layer, you are actually okay."

"Only okay? Hmm. I'll have to work on that."

"Keep bringing me food. That's a sure way to win me over," Freya said. She knew she would probably regret it, but she cleared her throat. "You know, I have a work policy about getting too involved with clients."

"Is that so? Can you be more specific about what 'getting too involved' entails?"

Oh no, not the Bayn flirting layer.

"That smile on your face tells me you know exactly what I'm talking about," she said. The smile got wider.

"Can I put in a complaint to the manager about this policy?"

"Stop it, or I'll stab you right now for practice."

Bayn's hands went up in surrender. "I already told you, Freya Havisdottir, I'm not going to try anything until you ask me to. You should know by now, I'm detail-orientated, so think long and hard about every single thing you want me to do to you before you ask."

Freya brandished her fork at him. "Keep it up, fae."

"I would. All night long."

Freya suddenly wished for his prick side to come back.

"So the curse chose to freeze your heart? Is it because you have an ice affinity that your magic tastes like winter and iron?"

Bayn's sexy smile slipped. "Hiding a few more tricks, summer?"

"Maybe. Am I right?"

"Yes. I have winter magic that can involve ice, amongst other things. The curse twisted it and also because I'm known for being cold-hearted."

Freya could believe it. Even at his most flirtatious, he couldn't hide the predator underneath his skin. His good humor was vanishing, and she really didn't want it to, despite the teasing making her ovaries vibrate dangerously.

"Yeah, me too. I've been called the Ice Queen by men since I got tits. They couldn't handle the rejection," she said flippantly.

Bayn's smile returned as he leaned back in his chair. "Ice Queen isn't an insult to someone with winter magic; it's an invitation to give you a crown."

Freya lifted her beer to tap against his. "I'll drink to that."

8

Bayn stood next to a black limousine outside of Mardøll, waiting for Freya to come down. She had agreed to go to the party, despite Leif, and if the bastard came anywhere near her that night, Bayn might just murder him without her permission. He could make it look like an accident. Freya shouldn't have to worry about him ever again.

Bayn fidgeted with the cuffs of his jacket, straightening them even though they were already in perfect order. He wasn't nervous, he told himself. Something about Freya made every part of him want to be better. He hated it and loved it at the same time.

Bayn had spent the two days hiding from her because he hadn't been able to control the storm of magic inside of him that kissing her had caused. He didn't want to go near her until it settled down, but that damn sign of hers had forced his hand. He wasn't a coward, but he wasn't himself either.

Bayn contemplated texting Kian about the upset in his magic around the antiques dealer. Knowing his brother, the love-struck idiot would have encouraged him to pursue her. Kian had never been like that before he was mated. Now he believed in the transformative power of love. It made Bayn want to punch Kian every time he brought up searching for Bayn's mate.

For the moment, Bayn's magic was contained again. Freya had been determined about her 'policy' and Bayn was going to respect it. At least until they found the dagger, and he was no longer a client. Or she bent that policy of her own accord. Or if—the door to Mardøll opened and Freya stepped out, wiping every thought from Bayn's mind.

He knew it was a formal event and that she would be dressed up, but he couldn't have prepared for the devastating sight of her. His vivid imagination hadn't come close.

Freya had her long, golden hair pinned up and decorated with black and dark blue velvet roses. Her long, black satin dress hugged her curves, and when her skirt flared, it had dark blue silk lining it. He couldn't see the top of the dress in its entirety because she had put on a black fur coat though he couldn't wait for that reveal. Her red smile was wide and delighted by the time he reached her face.

"What do you think, fae?"

I think you're wearing my colors, and I want to hide you away in my castle forever.

"I would tell you, but it breaches your policy," Bayn replied, opening the door to the limo for her.

"You don't look too bad yourself. I picked these colors because I knew you wouldn't deviate from your preferences, and it would make a good impression if we matched." Freya's voice had a slight tremble in it, and he knew the extra effort he had made in choosing the suit had been worth it.

Inside the warm limo, Bayn purposely sat in the chair opposite her. If he was beside her, he'd touch her and wouldn't want to stop. He had tried to pinpoint what it was about her that undid him but failed every time. He couldn't narrow it down.

"You are quiet," Freya said, crossing her legs. The slit in her dress flashed a stretch of soft skin from thigh to ankle, and Bayn groaned inwardly.

"Trying to get my game face on. Do you have a plan?" he asked.

"Not a detailed one. We should go in, see who's there, find the reclusive collector who is running it and ask him about the dagger. Avoid Leif and his cronies if possible. Make contacts for other future jobs." Freya took out a small mirror and checked her hair and make-up.

"You are breathtaking, Freya," Bayn said.

Freya closed the mirror and let out a breath. "Thanks, I'm nervous."

"Don't be. You're a natural, and if Leif is there, he's going to have one more reason to regret ever letting you go."

"You don't have to be this nice to me because I know Elise," she said suddenly.

"Do you think I would bother to be nice unless I truly meant it?" he replied flatly.

"No, I suppose not. Okay, put your prick face on. We are here," Freya said, grabbing her satin clutch.

"Let me get out first, so I can help you. I wouldn't want you slipping on those high heels." Heels that he was already wondering what they would feel like digging into his back as her legs wrapped around him.

Just another item of her clothing to haunt my dreams.

The driveway was bathed in the amber light that spilled from the mansion's high windows. Attendants in uniform greeted the guests who were arriving by boat and car. One moved to help as Bayn stepped out and then backed off instantly. He took Freya's hand to assist her and then wrapped it around his arm.

"Have to keep up appearances, don't we?" he whispered to her.

"I hope you're ready for this. I've been to these kinds of parties before, and they are one of the reasons I've stayed far away from this place," Freya whispered back. Bayn wanted to point out that he was a prince of the fae, and parties were something he could never avoid. These humans had no idea what a real party was.

Inside, another attendant took their coats, and as Freya flashed the black lace back of her dress, Bayn accidentally bit his tongue.

"My eyes are up here," she teased when he caught sight of the deep V showing off the tops of her breasts.

"Fuck, Freya," he muttered, putting her hand back over his arm. "Protecting you tonight is going to be harder than I thought."

Freya only laughed, like she was delighted that he now wanted to gouge his own eyes out so he could think straight again.

"Freya! I haven't seen you in months," a female voice called as soon as they stepped into a hall of partygoers. A tall brunette dripping in diamonds moved towards them.

"Carina, how are you?" Freya greeted, accepting the kisses on the cheek that the other woman gave her.

"Bored out of my skull, but I see you have been busy." Carina gave Bayn a pointed look. "And who is this?"

"Oh, this is Bjørn. He's my new...assistant," Freya replied. She gave him a mischievous grin. "He doesn't talk, which makes him perfect."

"And what does he assist in?" a man asked, joining them.

"Anything I need him to. Bjørn has *many* uses." Freya didn't bother to hide the innuendo. She laughed, high and fake, and the other two joined in.

"I have no doubt, my dear. Leif is going to die when he sees you here," Carina said.

If only. Bayn kept his expression open and polite as they talked. He took note of all the exits, the guards in black suits that didn't hide the guns holstered under their jackets. Everyone looked like they had too much money and not enough taste. No wonder Freya hated going to these parties. She was so real and alive, not like these hungry, shallow people.

"Bjørn, darling, will you go and get me a drink," Freya said, patting his hand. He bowed slightly, and Carina and her companion tittered.

"He bows? How charming. Wherever did you buy him?"

Bayn forced himself to keep walking towards a table covered in champagne glasses that were placed along a white and gold wall. What did she mean 'buy' him?

"My word, a fae! I never thought I would see one of your kind at Leif's party. He's always been vocal about how he feels about you," a bald man said from beside him.

"I don't know who Leif is. I came with my mistress and lover," Bayn replied, picking up two glasses. He knew he shouldn't, but he couldn't resist adding, "Maybe you know her? Freya Havisdottir." The bald man actually paled.

"You came with Freya? God, Leif is going to go mental and kill her for this."

"He can try," said Bayn before going back to Freya. She was alone again, thank the gods.

"Why, thank you, Bjørn," she said, taking the glass and sipping.

"It is my pleasure to serve you, mistress," he purred, slipping his arm around her waist. "Please tell me you are busy making that list of tasks you would like me to assist you with."

"Behave yourself," she whispered.

"You started it. I'm merely taking your lead." They walked casually through the halls and into a small ballroom where people were dancing and drinking.

"This is the public party, the one that will be listed under a charity or some such. The illegal one, dealing with art and artifacts, will be upstairs," Freya told him. Sure enough, they passed a sign asking for donations for an Oslo children's hospital. "Carina said that she hadn't seen any sign of the reclusive dealer but his name is Dieter, no surname, and came from somewhere in Switzerland. He's become a friend of Leif's, and he offered to put this party on to show off to him. Dieter must really be important for Leif to want to spend his own money hosting something like this."

"And Dieter must really want something to come out of hiding."

Freya nodded. "Exactly. Some other deal must be going— Oh, shit, Leif is coming."

Bayn didn't turn to see where she was looking. Instead, his hand went to the small of her back, and he bent his head to her ear. "Remember, you are better than him." He breathed in her summer smell, brushing his lips under her ear and causing her breath to catch.

"Freya, I didn't expect to see you here tonight," a man's voice rang behind Bayn. He slowly turned, not removing his hand from Freya.

Leif looked exactly as Bayn imagined. Ash blonde hair cut stylishly, his pinstripe suit neat, and eyes a washed-out grey. He supposed that women might find him appealing as a human, but he seemed too boring for someone like Freya. No wonder she had gotten rid of him.

"Hello, Leif. I didn't know this was one of your parties," Freya lied in a polite voice, making no move to kiss his cheek. "Von sent me the invitation. He thought there would be some items on sale this evening that would be of interest to me."

"No doubt there will be. It's nice to see that your little store is still open for business."

"You mean after you decided to steal my clients and research? Well, let's say you never knew about *all* the cards I had up my sleeve," Freya said. Bayn hid a smile. She had definitely taken his advice on busting Leif's balls. The man in question looked Bayn over, a flicker of disapproval on his face.

"I see you've branched out in your client base," he said.

"I'm not a client. I'm her assistant and bodyguard," Bayn replied before Freya could.

"It doesn't look like you're an employee unless you've started sleeping with the staff, Freya." She stiffened but then relaxed slightly into Bayn's side.

"Well, the best way to guard a body is to be as close to it as possible. You're hardly in the position to judge, Leif. I'm sure you're still getting all of your *girls* to suck your dick whenever you want."

It was Bayn's turn to stiffen. This stain of a man had actually cheated on her?

"Mistress, the offer I made to you last night is still available should you change your mind," he said, and Freya saw the murder in his eyes. *Please let me kill him.* She smiled and shook her head.

"There will be plenty of time for new sex positions later, Bjørn. We have business to get on with tonight," she said, patting his chest to calm him down.

Leif snorted. "New sex positions? You? What a difference eight months makes."

"It helps to have a partner who can keep up."

"I'm sure shedding a few of those extra pounds you had been carrying has helped out too."

Bayn was going to kill Leif if he didn't stop talking. Freya was tense with anger, but she threw her head back and laughed.

"Oh, Leif, let's not fight anymore. I'm here to have a good time and spend some money. If you don't want me here, ask me to leave. If not, kindly fuck off," she said and took Bayn's hand. "Come, lover, you promised me a dance."

Bayn pushed down all his homicidal feelings and led Freya out amongst the dancers, drawing her close.

"Please tell me you can dance," Freya said, putting her arm on his shoulder.

"What a ridiculous question. I'm fae." Bayn began to move her in a waltz. He looked around at the other dancers. "Usually, the fae's version is a lot more fun than this. Everyone is naked and outside, and it's under a full moon."

"Sounds like it would be a great time, right up until you end up twirling into a blackberry bush with your junk hanging out," replied Freya, making him laugh. He lifted her up and twirled her before putting her back down and not missing a beat to the song. Her amber eyes were glowing with amusement. "You know, I think that's the first time I really heard you laugh."

"Don't get used to it. I've got a frozen heart, remember?" Bayn said.

Freya's hand slipped up to his neck, and he pulled her flush up against him. He wanted to kiss her so bad, it hurt. "Perhaps, you just need to find the right person to help warm it up, fae," she whispered.

"Let me know if you want the job—" Bayn froze, holding her tight. They had twirled right near the ballroom's fireplace, and above it, hanging on a polished ironwood stand were Kian's antlers. The ragged ends from where Vortigern's men had hacked them off had been dipped in gold and were shining with pride.

At that moment, Bayn was back in the mud, his knees stained with the blood of the faelings, ears burning with the screams of his people. He had held Kian's gaze as they had torn the antlers from him, silently promising him revenge for the humiliation.

"What's wrong?" Freya followed his gaze and started as if she had been shocked. "They are fae."

"How do you know?" Bayn asked as he guided her away from the dancers so they wouldn't get crashed into.

"I can feel their magic." Freya paled and took Bayn's hand. "I had no idea they would be here. I've never seen them before, I swear."

"They are Kian's," Bayn muttered. His fury was building like a blizzard in his veins.

"Bayn..." The fear in Freya's voice made him rein himself in again.

She rested a hand on his chest. "Please, we will find a way to get them back, but we can't just rip them off the wall and not expect Leif's men to try and shoot us."

"I could take them."

"I know you could, but the people in this room couldn't. They are here for a children's hospital charity. They aren't ruthless collectors, and they will get caught in the crossfire," Freya said, keeping her voice steady. "Please. Let's go upstairs and get that part over with. When we are out of here, we can figure out a way to get them back without violence."

Bayn nodded, his arms going around her to comfort himself. She was half right. He *would* be coming back for them, but there would most definitely be violence.

9

Freya could feel Bayn's anger as if a thundercloud was walking beside her. What had Leif been trading in that he would so openly display a relic of the fae?

Unless he doesn't know what he's got.

Freya dismissed the thought immediately. Anyone who was remotely magical, or a human who could use magic, would be able to sense the pulse of power coming from the antlers.

No, Leif just didn't care what he had and wanted to show it off. They were only antlers, and no one would look at them twice unless they really knew what they were.

Leif had never shied away from expressing his feelings regarding the return of the fae and the elves. It had been one of the major things they had fought about, but when had he shifted to hating them that much?

Bayn's hand found hers as they ascended a curving staircase. As their palms touched, the thundercloud simmered down, so Freya hung on.

She gave him a sideways glance, trying not to stare and trip on the ridiculous shoes she was wearing.

Fuck, he looked good in a suit. His midnight blue silk shirt was open a few buttons, just enough to show his collar bone and the tattoos that crept up his neck. She didn't have to pretend to be affected by him for the sake of appearances. When Freya had come downstairs that night to see him waiting by the limo, she knew that she was getting a big, bad crush on the big, bad fae.

The fact that Bayn let her take the lead and didn't try and pull any overprotective crap around Leif had made that crush burn a little hotter. He trusted that she could handle herself but let her know he was there if she needed him. And damn, if that wasn't the sexiest thing she had ever seen.

"You are grinning about something," Bayn said as they reached the top of the staircase. His teasing humor seemed to be returning, so Freya was happy to play along and ward off the fury from his eyes.

"Am I? I didn't realize."

"You looked like you were having naughty thoughts about something."

Freya ran the lapel of his jacket between her fingers. "Wouldn't you love to know, *Bjørn*?"

His arm moved around her waist to her hip, the heat of his hand scorching her skin through the satin like a brand. Sapphire eyes roamed over her face to her lips and stayed there.

"If you keep looking at me like that, I'm going to forget that we are pretending," Freya whispered.

One black brow rose. "Who's pretending?"

Run away before you get caught, urged Freya's voice of reason.

"Miss Havisdottir? Are you here for the silent auction?"

Freya looked away from Bayn to where two guards were standing by a gold and cream painted door.

"Yes, thank you," she answered, accepting the glossy brochure the guard handed her. They gave Bayn a slow, calculating once-over. The fae merely smiled in amusement, and both men paled. It made Freya want to know just how badass Bayn was that two well trained, ex-military guards would back down like that. It was like they knew they were rabbits, and a real predator was amongst them. It didn't frighten her half as much as it should have.

"Enjoy the auction," one said, opening the door for them. Freya nodded politely as they moved past them.

"Do you intimidate everyone you meet?" she asked.

"Except for you, apparently."

"It's because Elise would get Kian after you if you hurt me."

Bayn snorted. "Please. I've been able to take Kian in a fight since we were faelings." Freya filed that information away for later because as they stepped through a set of velvet curtains, she was graphically reminded why she hated everything about these parties and the scene Leif was trying to build. The majority of the patrons were rich men, except Clarissa and one other woman, all sitting in booths with velvet couches surrounding a low stage.

Women clad in matching corsets and fishnets were lighting cigars, pouring drinks, and flirting with the clients. A few had brought their own women with them, most half their age. On and above the stage, women were performing an acrobatic burlesque show.

"Welcome to tonight's silent auction. Allow me to show you to a booth...oh, Freya. It's you. I barely recognized you," said Yvonne, one of Leif's oldest employees.

And I barely recognized you without your mouth around Leif's cock.

Freya forced a smile on her face. "Please, lead the way. We are keen to see what Leif has on display tonight." Yvonne's eyes widened as they finally took in Bayn's pointed ears and his hand in Freya's. She turned quickly but couldn't hide the annoyance on her face. For some reason, Yvonne had always been jealous of Freya and her position with Leif. Freya thought she would be pleased or smug that she was finally out of the scene. Evidently, Leif hadn't fallen all over her as soon as Freya had broken up with him.

Their booth was as far away from the stage as possible, which Freya didn't mind in the slightest. She was more interested in the people present than the items up for sale. The booth contained a red velvet chaise and a scattering of floor cushions for any of the whores the patrons would like for the evening.

Bayn helped Freya to the couch before surprising both her and Yvonne by taking one of the floor cushions and leaning his back against the chaise.

"I'll have a vodka martini, thanks Yvonne, hold the spit," Freya said. Bayn held up two fingers, and Yvonne hurried away face burning.

"What's the history there?" he asked.

"I walked in on her blowing Leif in his office the day I broke up with him. It was one of those last straw moments. I suspected he was screwing around, but he had always made out that I was paranoid."

"He's a piece of shit, Freya. Don't regret leaving him for a moment."

"I don't." Freya rested a hand on his shoulder. "Please come and sit beside me. If you stay there, people will think you are my whore."

"We both have our parts to play tonight, summer. If they think I'm just your plaything, they will underestimate me and think you are one of them. They will let their guard down," Bayn replied. He pressed back into her legs, making them widen to accommodate his broad shoulders. He tipped his head back onto her lap and stared up at her. "I can imagine few better places to be than between your thighs, Freya. Don't forget to act like you enjoy me being here."

"Time will tell, I suppose." Freya's hand shook as she stroked his face. Bayn's hard sapphire eyes softened at the touch, so she did it again and a low growl vibrated through him.

"Are you thinking of bending those rules of yours, mistress?"

Freya didn't get a chance to reply as Yvonne appeared again with their drinks and a tablet. "This is for the auction. All bets go through it, and this device is specifically keyed to you."

"Thanks, put them on the table," Freya replied graciously. She had no intention of putting her bank details into anything belonging to Leif. Yvonne's eyes were bugging out of her head as Freya stroked Bayn's dark hair like he was her favorite pet.

"Be careful of Leif, Freya," Yvonne whispered, looking at Bayn again. "His hatred for the fae and anger at you leaving him has only gotten worse. He's dangerous, and his weakness for you only makes him more so."

"Why bother warning me, Yvonne? We were never friends."

"Because coming in here and flaunting your new fae fuck buddy is going to enrage him, and you know better than anyone what happens then."

Freya's eye throbbed in memory of Leif's fists the day she left. Yes. She knew. "Yvonne, you should get out while you can. Be smart."

"I don't have that luxury. Enjoy the auction." She was gone before Freya could press the matter. Yvonne was scared of Leif, and that spoke volumes. She had always been loyal to him and had just risked her own wellbeing by warning her. Freya's eyes went to the cameras in the corners of the ceiling. If Leif was getting more paranoid than usual, there would surely be bugs about the room.

"Are you sure you don't want me to kill—" Bayn began, but Freya quickly leaned forward and put her lips on his, cutting him off. His hands moved to her face, holding her to him. Freya forgot where she was and why kissing him like this was a bad idea. His tongue teased at her lips, and she pulled back.

"I think there are bugs in this room," she whispered very softly, hoping his fae ears picked her up over the music and noise. He nodded, fingers caressing her cheeks. She was fighting not to kiss him again when the dancers finished on stage, and Leif appeared. Bayn made a sound of frustration but dropped his hands.

Leif's grey eyes found them, and Freya purposely ran her hand through Bayn's silky hair. The fae picked up the same game she was playing because he lifted one of her legs and placed it over his shoulder. Freya quickly adjusted her long skirt to make sure she wasn't flashing anyone but left her leg where it was.

"Welcome everyone to tonight's auction. I'd personally like to thank Dieter for sponsoring this event and even contributing a few pieces from his private collection." Leif raised a glass to the woman that Freya didn't recognize. She had a laptop set up with a black screen, but the camera light was on.

"Shit, he's not here," Freya murmured. It wasn't the first time she had seen someone attend an auction as a proxy for someone else, but to not even have his screen turned on? That was odd. It also meant that they had come for nothing.

Leif was talking his usual crowd warm-up, and then girls started to come out, carrying an item at a time to display for consideration. Freya did her best to take note of the other patrons as they began their bidding...and found many were watching them.

"Is it me? Or do we have an audience?" she said, and Bayn chuckled.

"You sound surprised by that. You *are* the most beautiful woman here."

"Yeah, I don't think it's all about me, Bjørn. They probably are as surprised as Yvonne to see a fae here, especially with me. The bitch ex-girlfriend."

"It's good to remind them that they have options if they want to deal with someone other than Leif." Bayn's hand wrapped around her calf, causing goosebumps to streak up the leg she had draped over his shoulder. God, this was such a bad idea. "I'd like to remind you that you have options too."

Bayn turned his head and pressed a kiss to the skin just above her knee. Freya couldn't hide the tremble as he did it again, a little higher, his teeth digging gently into her. Her fingers tightened in his hair as she exhaled a shaky breath. She could feel herself getting wet and wanted to clamp her thighs together. This playing for appearances was getting embarrassingly out of hand. Bayn tipped his head back in her lap again, his smile so smug, she scowled back.

With mounting horror, Freya realized he could probably hear her escalating heartbeat and smell her arousal.

"My, my someone is getting into the spirit of things," he purred.

"I'll have my leg back now," she said, but he held onto it. A throat cleared as a tall man joined them.

"Can I help you?" Freya asked. She had seen him with Dieter's representative.

"My employer would like to know how much it would cost to spend a night with your fae," he said, without any hint of being uncomfortable with the inappropriateness of the proposal.

Freya glanced around the man, and to the woman with the laptop that was feeding the auction to Dieter. She raised her glass to them. Freya's arms went around Bayn's neck like she could physically hide him from the other woman's prying eyes. A growl escaped her lips.

"He's mine, so tell your employer he's not for fucking sale," Freya snarled, so possessively that she shocked herself.

"Understood. No offense meant, Miss Havisdottir. In case you change your mind and ever want to sell him, Dieter pays well for unique pieces." The man passed her a card with a QR code printed on it.

Freya fought the urge not to scrunch up the card and throw it at his head. "I'll keep that in mind." The man nodded courteously and headed back to the table.

"Freya—" Bayn began, but she was already shifting her leg from his shoulder.

"We are done here." Freya got up, straightened her skirt, and headed for the exit. She didn't know why she was so furious. She *knew* what these people were like. They had enough wealth and power that they thought they could buy whatever they wanted. Well, they were going to learn about disappointment.

Freya could feel Bayn behind her all the way down the stairs. She had a quick glance over her shoulder and almost fell. His eyes were burning, face set in an expression that said she wasn't going to escape him as easily as the party.

What the hell had she been thinking bringing him to this place? Exposing him to this horrible part of her past? She wanted to burn the mansion to the ground.

Freya didn't stop to get her coat but headed straight for the valet. By the time she reached the front doors, the limo was already waiting for them. Bayn appeared beside the back door and opened it for her. She brushed his hand aside as she climbed in the warmth of the cabin and scooted across the seat away from the door. Once the door was shut, Freya leaned over her knees, fighting to get her breath steady.

"Take the scenic route back, please," Bayn told the driver before raising the black privacy divider separating them. "Do you want to tell me what that was all about, Freya?"

"How can you even ask me that? That asshole thought he could *buy* you, Bayn!"

"And I'm yours?" he asked.

"Yes! I mean, no. But they don't know that. If I were a man, they wouldn't have ever had the nerve to ask. They were willing to buy you like a slave! Doesn't that bother you?"

"Of course it does, but I'm more interested in your reaction and how much it bothered *you*."

Freya flushed and kicked off her shoes in frustration. "We were playing the part, and I ruined it by being insulted on your behalf. Now they are going to know you are important to me." *And put a target on his back if Leif decides to really go after me.*

"We weren't playing the whole time, Freya, and you know it." Panic raced through her when she saw the look he was giving her. He wasn't hiding his desire for her. He hadn't since they had kissed at Von's club.

Bayn looked like his last shred of control was about to snap, his magic leaking from his hands and leaving frost patterns on the black leather chair. She could feel how much he wanted her as his magic curled around her, leaving the taste of winter air, pine, and cinnamon on her tongue. Freya's hands curled into fists, fighting her own desire that was threatening to overwhelm her.

Bayn's voice had dropped to a growl. "Stop being so damn stubborn and *ask* me, Freya."

Her voice was barely a whisper, her defenses crumbling as she said, "Please kiss me, Bayn." He was suddenly on his knees in front of her again, his face level with hers. His fingers ran down her neck to her shoulders, and he bent his mouth to her ear.

"Kiss you where?" he asked, and her pulse leaped to her throat.

"Anywhere you like, just kiss me," she replied, and Bayn's mouth was on hers. It wasn't like the kiss at the club. That one had been hard and fast. This kiss was possessive...and permanent. Their tongues moved against each other, Freya dragging his bottom lip between her teeth. He met that eagerness head-on, kissing her back with all the heat she had seen inside of him. A fae with winter magic that burned so passionately was a mystery, and it made her want to unravel every one of his complex layers to see what else he was hiding.

Freya grabbed the lapels of his jacket, her legs going around him as she dragged him to her, needing him closer. She gasped, his hands sliding from her shoulders to her breasts, massaging them as his mouth moved to her neck.

Freya pulled his jacket and shirt open and traced her hands over his tattooed skin. The white lines of his curse were cool to touch, but the rest of skin was hot around it. She lowered her mouth to taste the curve of his collar bone, and he shivered under her mouth, murmuring something she didn't understand.

Bayn pulled the front of her dress down, exposing her breasts and making her cry out as he sucked a nipple into his mouth. One hand went to cup her breast, the other sliding up her thigh to her already damp satin panties. She trembled, her thighs shaking as he ran the tip of his finger under the hem.

"Kiss you anywhere I like, Freya?" he asked. Bayn lifted her chin, so she was forced to look into his burning eyes. "I need to hear the magic word."

"Y-yes," she stammered. Bayn's grin was triumphant as he let her go and kissed her. Both of his hands were under her skirt, tugging her panties down her thighs. He kissed her neck and across her chest.

"Relax, summer, let me give you what you asked for," he purred, sliding her legs over his shoulders.

Freya could barely believe what was happening as her hands gripped the seat on either side of her. Despite Leif's stupid fucking barbs, she wasn't boring in bed, but he wasn't as giving as she had been, so she hadn't had a lot of experience with what Bayn was about to do.

Was she really about to...all thoughts left her brain as Bayn's fingers slid through her wet folds. Freya's legs tightened as his warm tongue brushed over her. He made a sound between a growl and a purr as he tasted her again.

"Fuck, Freya," he murmured. His hand grabbed her hip to stop her from sliding in the seat and pressed his mouth back on her. Freya's hands buried in his long hair, gripping it tighter as he sucked on her clit.

The one clear thought she had was that Leif *really* hadn't known what he was doing when he tried to go down on a woman because Bayn made her feel like she was coming apart with pleasure.

She cried out as he pushed two fingers inside her thrusting deep, his wicked mouth not letting up for a moment. She was panting so hard she fought to get air into her lungs. Her body burned with every stroke and touch until her orgasm shook her body so violently, all she could do was hang onto him until it was over.

She was sweating and swearing under her breath as Bayn pressed a line of kisses on the inside of her thigh and pulled her panties up again. He brushed one of her damp curls back from her face, pausing as a pale blue rune glowed to life on his palm.

"What is that?" Freya asked breathlessly. Bayn fisted his hand, pulling it quickly away from her.

"An early warning system, that's all," he said, lifting the straps of her dress back into place. "Nothing to worry about, summer." Bayn took off his jacket and wrapped it around her as the limo pulled up in front of Mardøll.

Freya pulled her shoes back on and clutched the jacket tight. "Are you—would you like to come upstairs?" Getting a head job in the back of the limo was the perfect beginning to a night of what would no doubt be phenomenal sex. Bayn's smile returned as he lifted her hand and kissed her palm.

"Not tonight. I'm known for my patience, Freya, and you are worth waiting for," he said, leaning in and running his lips over her neck. "I'm not some useless man that will only want you for a night. I'm fae. We get possessive over things we want because it's so hard to get our attention, and you definitely have mine. I want you to know exactly what you are getting into and what it means before this goes much further."

"I understand...I think. Good night, Bayn." Freya smirked. "Thanks for the orgasm."

"My pleasure, mistress." Bayn got out of the limo and helped her out. Freya waited until she had her door unlocked before turning back to him. He blew her a kiss, making her shake her head and grin stupidly as she went inside. Freya leaned back against the door.

With sudden cold clarity, she remembered the protective runes tattooed on her back that were meant to ward against fae touching her...and they hadn't worked on Bayn at all.

What the hell was he?

10

Bayn paid the limo driver and crossed the road to his hotel. His heart was racing so hard, he thought he was going to faint. Up in his room, he padded to his windows in time to see Freya in the kitchen, pouring herself a glass of wine and singing to herself.

At least she's not upset about you turning her down. It was the last thing in the world Bayn wanted. In fact, he had planned on taking her upstairs and giving her the gloriously sweaty hard fuck they both needed. That had changed as soon as the rune had appeared on his hand.

Bayn looked at his palm, where the mark was slowly fading. If it was what he thought it was, it would change...everything. He hadn't lied to her; she needed to be ready for something more than a one-night stand if she wanted anything with him.

You have bigger things to worry about tonight.

Bayn grabbed his phone from his pocket and rang Kian. After five rings, his brother answered with an irritated. "What?"

"I'm sorry, am I interrupting something?" Bayn asked. Kian made a frustrated sound, and Elise laughed in the background.

"You are lucky that the something hadn't kicked off yet. What the fuck is the matter? Aren't you meant to be at a party with Freya tonight?"

"I was. I just thought you might like to know I've found your antlers that the kings took." Bayn pulled a black duffel bag out from under the bed and started to arrange a variety of weapons on the cover.

"Tell me everything that happened. You sound like you have murder in your voice," Kian replied. Bayn wasn't the only one that sounded ready to kill things. He recapped Kian on the humans at the party, the antlers, and the mysterious Dieter offering to buy him.

"I'm surprised you didn't put a knife in him," Kian commented.

"I didn't get a chance to. Freya grabbed me and looked ready to do some stabbing of her own." Bayn grinned. No one had ever stepped in like that for him. It made some damaged, sleeping part of himself come alive.

"Freya did what?" There was a scramble as Elise pulled the phone closer.

"She was about ready to shove the guy's business card down his throat. She's quite something when she gets in a rage." She was quite something all the time, but telling Elise that would mean she would start asking questions he wasn't ready to think about yet.

"Freya has all of that hot Viking blood running through her. It makes me happy to hear that you are becoming friends, Bayn. I'm surprised you've managed it."

"I'll have you know I can be rather charming when I want to be, little sister," he said. He kicked off his polished shoes and started unbuttoning his shirt.

"I don't believe it. Kian, is he lying to me?"

"Probably. Bayn, what are you planning?" Kian interrupted.

"You know the answer to that. I'm going to get your fucking antlers back." *And kill anyone that gets in my way.*

"Think it through. We can't have an attack on the place linked back to Freya."

"I know, Kian. I would never do anything to endanger her. I'm going back there for her too. I don't like her shitty ex-boyfriend, and I want to know what fucked up things he's into in case he tries anything on her."

"Be careful of him, Bayn," Elise said. "Freya is one of the toughest women I've ever known, but Leif used to hit her, and the last job he tried to force her to do really scared her. You are there for now, but one day, you'll return to Scotland, and she will be alone and vulnerable."

The hell she will be. Bayn had no intention of letting her be in either state ever again.

"What do you mean he was forcing her to do a job?" he asked, hand tightening on the hilt of his sword.

"You know how she can sense magical objects? Apparently, Leif wanted something, but the owner refused to sell it. He had Freya track it down, and while she's never told me exactly what happened, I think Leif or his men might have beaten the owner until he sold it to them. Or he killed them. She was really freaked out and left him soon after because she didn't want anything to do with it," Elise explained.

"I already offered to kill him, but she said no," Bayn growled. The more he learned about Leif, the more he knew that gutting the fucking weasel would be doing the world a favor.

"You did what?" Kian asked. He sounded like he was smiling all of a sudden, and Bayn didn't like it.

"It doesn't matter. I'm going to go and watch the house, and when it's empty for the night, I'll take a look around. I won't be seen. Freya will be kept out of it, and if Leif ever decides to come after her, I'll rip out his spine." Bayn hung up the phone before Kian could do anything like try and talk him out of it.

Bayn changed out of his suit and into black tactical gear and boots. He filled his pockets with dagger hilts and strips of leather then strapped his sword to his back. Finally, he braided back his long hair and tried to settle the roar of his thoughts. They were all chanting one word; *Freya.*

"No. No. No. This is not happening," Bayn muttered, fists clenching. He needed fresh air and snow to get the smell of Freya out of his nose. He downed a glass of whiskey to wash the taste of her from his mouth. *Gods, her taste.*

Swearing in the old tongue, Bayn pulled on a long overcoat to cover his weapons and headed for the door. If he couldn't fuck, he would kill and hope that it would be enough to calm the raging beast inside of him.

◊

THE PARTY on Thieves Island was still going on an hour later, the fundraising gala only just winding down. Bayn watched the cars pulling up to take drunk and laughing people away. He made a note of their faces and the car's number plates, but none of them had been present at the auction upstairs. He was more interested in downstairs anyway. If Leif was as predictable as Bayn suspected, then he would no doubt have all of his exciting shit in his basement.

When the final guests left and the lights on the first level of the mansion went out, Bayn dropped into the freezing core of his magic and stepped off the side of the building.

The three guards at the mansion's back door fell before they had a chance to draw their weapons. Bayn pocketed their phones and swipe cards. The kitchens were cleaned and empty as he walked through them and into a servant's passageway. The mansion was old enough to have the original halls behind the walls, and Leif was arrogant enough to force the people working for him to use them. He paused by a power box on the wall and opened it. Smiling, he flipped all of the fuses, and the mansion was flooded in darkness.

Bayn opened an entry door on the first level and peered out. Somewhere close were guards with small torches speaking rapidly in Norwegian. Bayn pulled the hilt of a dagger from his pocket and stepped out into the hall. Ice curled around the hilt and fashioned itself into a blade.

The first guard made a gurgling choking sound as the ice dagger sank into his jugular. His companion pulled a gun and started firing, but Bayn was gone, shadows and silent rage. He cut the man down and made for the ballroom.

Kian's antlers shone faintly in the darkness. Bayn fought back the waves of memories and their horror as he pulled them down from their stand. Taking the leather strips from his pockets, he tied the antlers together. *Don't think of the smell of the blood, don't think of the pain...*

"Hold it right there!" Torchlight swung over Bayn. Careful not to show his face, Bayn stood, gripping the antlers in one hand and his ice dagger in the other.

"Drop the antlers, thief, and put your hands up," the guard demanded. Heavy footsteps thundered down the hallways and into the ballroom as more guards rushed in.

"You're surrounded. Do as I say, and we might not kill you."

Bayn started to laugh. It was a sound full of wild storms and magic.

Honestly, the *arrogance* of these humans. The room temperature dropped, the glass of the windows freezing over as Bayn released his power. Men screamed as ice locked them on the floor and pierced their clothes and flesh.

As the blizzard filled the room, Bayn moved through the snow and the shadows, antlers and blade swinging, sending dark blood over the frost left in his wake. He'd had his magic locked up since coming to Oslo, and setting it loose was like taking a deep breath after almost drowning. He paused as he felt another magical signature reach out from underneath him through the storm of his power.

Bayn grabbed a dying man. "What is beneath us?"

"C-cells," the man gasped. "Help. Her."

Bayn shook him. "The doorway! Where is it?"

"Garage-"

Bayn dropped him and stormed through the house. Ice licked up the walls, freezing paintings and sculptures and cracking them to pieces. He kicked open a set of double doors that he'd watched valets coming out of earlier in the evening. Inside was a small foyer with an elevator. Of course Leif had underground parking to keep his clients' privacy.

Bayn went through the swipe cards he had stolen, pressing them one at a time to the panel until it turned green and the elevator doors opened. There were three sub-basements, so Bayn pressed the last one.

Help her.

Bayn pressed the button again. What the fuck was Leif into? When the doors opened, Bayn got his answer. The scent of death and suffering washed over him, and he gripped the bloody antlers tighter. Cells were lining the sub-basement, the walls shining with wards and bars made of iron. They were clean and empty, but no amount of bleach could wash away the horror that coated every inch of them. In a far cell, a woman was curled up on the stone floor. Streaks of blood had soaked through the thin robe she was wearing, and her bare legs were covered in bruises. Bayn gripped the key lock in the door, sending his power into it until it shattered.

"Are you alive?" he asked. The woman shifted her head, and he saw the pointed ears amongst the silver hair. *Elf.*

"I'm not going to hurt you. I'm going to take you back to your people, okay?" he said, unsure if she understood.

"You are fae-kind?" she whispered with a thick accent.

"Yes. I'm Bayn. Can you stand?"

The elf shook her head. "They broke my ankles earlier, and they haven't mended yet. I tried to kick one."

"I would have kicked them too." Bayn tied a loop in the leather holding the antlers together and slid it over the hilt of his sword. Satisfied they were secure enough, he scooped up the elf in his arms. She sighed as he sent healing magic through her. Once she was stable, Bayn froze the cells solid, crushing the wards on the walls and cracking the mansion's foundation.

"You are *that* fae," the elf whispered, eyes wide.

"Yes." Bayn stepped into the elevator and looked at the buttons. He pressed the second level and prayed to the gods that there weren't more cells.

It was full of cars. Beautiful, expensive, one-of-a-kind cars that belonged to Leif and his associates upstairs.

Bayn was tempted to steal one and destroy the rest, but the female elf in his arms needed more than a boost of healing energy. Bayn carried her up the concrete ramp, his power ripping the doors open in a scream of metal. Outside, a winter storm had risen in response to Bayn's unleashed power. An icy gale hid them from view as Bayn created a frozen pool of flawless ice and stepped through it.

Bayn and the elf emerged through a frozen fountain half a block from his hotel. Throwing up a glamour to hide from cameras, Bayn got her upstairs without anyone seeing them.

Bayn placed the elf down on his couch. "Sit here. I'll get you a blanket." He dug about in the cupboards and found spare blankets and pillows. She was staring around the room without really seeing it, so Bayn wrapped the blanket over her and found his phone.

"How did it go?" Kian answered straight away.

"I got your antlers, but we have a problem. I found an elf girl in a cage. Do you have contacts amongst the elves over here? Someone you can call to come and take her to her family? She's going into shock, and she's hurt," Bayn said.

"Give me twenty minutes." Kian hung up, and Bayn went back to the female in the lounge room.

"I will get you to your people, I promise," Bayn assured the elf. He found a bottle of water in the minibar and some kind of crisps and placed them on the table beside her.

"I'm going to get cleaned up. You're safe here." The woman nodded, blinking back tears.

Bayn shut the bedroom door behind him and took off the antlers and sword, placing them on a table.

In the bathroom, he could see why the woman had been staring at him. He was covered in blood sprays and frozen chunks of gore. He stripped off his clothes and had a quick shower to scrub the blood off his skin and out of his hair. He was drying off when he caught his reflection in the mirror again. Bayn swayed, his hands gripping the sink to keep himself upright.

"This can't be happening." He looked again, studying the white tentacles of his curse. The circle that had been forming around his heart had been broken, the skin warm at its center.

Get it together. You don't have time for this freak-out. He pushed away from the counter and went back into his room. He was pulling on a pair of jeans and a shirt when he heard a hard knock on the hotel room door. Grabbing a dagger, he went out into the lounge room and checked on the elf. She was sleeping soundly. Someone knocked again. Bayn looked through the peephole and thanked the gods for Kian. He opened the door to the two angry warriors. They were dressed in matching black suits, but there was no hiding the death in their eyes. One was an elf, and the other was...something else.

"Thank you for coming. I'm Bayn," he greeted, letting them in.

"I am Arne, and this is Torsten," the tall elf with black hair replied. He nodded to Torsten, who moved to examine the female on the couch.

"We have been looking for Yrsa for over a month. Torsten is Úlfhéðnar, and even he couldn't find her," Arne said. Bayn was impressed. He had never met one of the wolf shifters before. In the old days, they were Odin's berserkers, and looking at the sheer size of Torsten, Bayn could believe it.

"How did you find her, fae?" Torsten growled. Bayn fixed himself a whiskey, pouring one for each warrior.

"Here, you are going to need it," said Bayn, pushing the glasses towards them. Careful of Yrsa sleeping, Bayn told them what he had found in Leif's mansion. Arne and Torsten shared angry glances, words passing silently between them.

"You already knew about this?" Bayn guessed.

"Not exactly. We've been hearing reports about creatures going missing, and Yrsa is the fifth elf. We thought that they might have been exploring the world more openly now that the humans know about us," Arne replied.

"But you were looking for Yrsa?"

"Yrsa is a friend. I knew she wouldn't have left Norway without telling me," answered Torsten. Hate flared in his silver eyes. "I'm going to gut these fucking monsters."

"Leif could have only been holding her. If you attack him, we might not find out who is actually dealing in slaves." Bayn thought about the woman with the laptop at the auction and the male assistant who had passed Freya a card if she wanted to sell Bayn.

"I've got an idea who could be behind it, but I'm going to need a few weeks to get to the bottom of it."

Arne nodded. "We owe you a debt for finding Yrsa, so we promise not to attack this human until your investigation is complete. I only ask that you share your information with us, and if it comes to a fight, you call us so we can wet our blades in their blood."

Bayn grinned and held out his hand. "It's a deal."

"I think I like you, fae," Arne said as they gripped each other's forearms. "Happy hunting."

After they had gone, Bayn took his drink to the windows and stared across the street at Freya's building. His worry for her was spiking. Leif was clearly into darker shit than she knew about, which made him even more dangerous. He was going to have to tell her everything for her own safety.

Bayn rubbed at the newly warmed skin over his heart. It hadn't been like that before the party, and the horrible truth he had been pushing away all night forced itself to the forefront of his mind.

Mate.

With that one word, Fate burned his world. He would be damned if he'd let it destroy Freya's. He had nothing left of his wretched heart to offer a mate, let alone a woman burning with life like Freya. She had left Leif because he had frightened her. If she really knew what Bayn was—*who* he was—she would run in the opposite direction. His whole body clenched in fear and anguish at the thought of never seeing her again.

In that blinding second, Bayn knew he was irrevocably and undeniably fucked.

11

Freya woke the following day with a grin on her face. It was the best she had slept in months despite that shit show of a party. She looked at the pillow beside her and allowed herself to feel a twinge of regret that Bayn hadn't come upstairs the previous night.

I want you to know exactly what you are getting into and what it means before this goes much further... Bayn's words came back to her, causing goosebumps to rise on her arms. It had been good of him to warn her. But would she really consider dating a fae? Elise had done more than that. She had mated with one and was happier than Freya had ever seen her. Was wanting to date her what he had even been asking her? She had no idea and had been too dazed out with post-orgasm endorphins to get clarification.

With a groan, Freya dragged herself out of bed and fell into her morning routine. She was too lazy to brave the freezing, stormy day for her run, so she did yoga instead and had a hot shower.

Freya fought the urge to text Bayn, even though she checked her messages far more than she should. What would she even say that wouldn't sound awkward?

"God, you are so bad at men," she muttered to herself. So she did the thing she was good at and worked. She made a new card for Dieter in her catalog, jotting down all the information she knew about him and his associates. Her blood boiled as she looked at the card Dieter's assistant had given her in case she wanted to sell Bayn. As if he was just another pretty trinket to mount on a wall. Even if she *did* own Bayn, she wouldn't ever let him go.

Will you even listen to how crazy you sound right now? You barely know him.

Freya messaged Von to ask him what he knew about Dieter and did a fruitless Google search. The sun was going down when she grabbed her phone to message Bayn but chickened out at the last second. She was about to put her phone down again when Elise rang.

"Hey cousin, what's up?" Freya answered, opening a beer.

"Have you seen Bayn today?" Elise asked, her voice hitching with concern.

"No. He hasn't even messaged me. Why?"

Elise swore. "He had a rough night last night, and I'm worried."

"What are you talking about a rough night? We went to a party, and we...um..." Freya stopped herself.

"You *what*, Freya?" Elise had a distinct tone of disapproval that she usually only brought out when Freya had done something terrible, like getting tattoos when drunk.

"Nothing?"

"Bull shit. What happened?"

"We might have hooked up a bit," Freya mumbled. "But it certainly wasn't something that would constitute a rough night." Steamy and sexy maybe, but not rough.

"He really hasn't talked to you today? His night didn't end with you, Freya. God, he is the worst. Can you go and check on him? He's not answering my calls or Kian's, and I'm worried. He shouldn't be alone after what he did."

"What the fuck did he do?" asked Freya, dread settling in her stomach. Elise hesitated so long, Freya had to check that they hadn't been cut off.

"He can tell you when you go and see him. Or was it awkward after you hooked up?"

Freya huffed out a breath and tried not to squirm. She was a grown woman, damn it, she could talk about men.

"It wasn't awkward. It was hot, right up to the point a mark glowed on his hand, and he got a little intense and bailed out on taking it further. He kind of implied fae don't do one-night stands, so unless I want something more serious, it's not going to happen. Probably for the best, right, cousin?" Freya said in a long rush.

"What kind of glowing mark? Maybe like an odd sort of rune?" asked Elise.

"Yeah, how did you know?"

"No reason. Just a fae thing, I'm sure."

"You don't sound very convincing right now. Is this something I should be worried about? Because I like him, Elise, but I'm not ready to have my heart broken again." Freya drained her beer. "You know what? This is a dumb conversation. I don't know him. Not having sex with him is a good thing, and I should forget all about it."

"No, you shouldn't. If Bayn's warning you about it, it means he's already gone on you and is trying to do the right thing. Look, don't worry about it now. Bigger things are going on. Go and see him and get the details from last night. Then call me because I'm pretty sure Kian held back on the interesting bits."

Freya's dread curled tighter in her stomach. "Bayn's not hurt, is he?"

"Kian didn't say, and he's not worried. I'm the one that's stressing. Bayn usually takes my calls even when I've pissed him off. I know he's in room number 302, but I don't want to get the hotel staff to bother him unless it's an emergency," Elise explained.

Freya's phone buzzed with a message against her ear, and she quickly checked it. It was from Von, and it was enough for fear to dump down her spine.

Leif's place was attacked last night. Someone with ice magic. If you are involved, don't tell me.

"Freya? You still there?" Elise asked.

"I have to go. I'll let you know if I see Bayn," Freya replied and hung up. "Fuck. Fuck. *Fuck!*"

Freya changed into warm gear, trying not to think about what Leif would do to whoever had attacked his mansion. She locked up, double-checking the alarms, and stepped out into the blizzard.

Looking around at the empty streets, she kept her keys between her fingers as she hurried across to the hotel that Bayn was staying at. If Leif suspected her involvement in the attack, it wouldn't be beneath him to have her place watched or to send some of his thugs to question her.

Freya strode through the cozy foyer of the hotel, ignoring the probing look from the receptionist. She was trudging snow everywhere and was too angry to feel bad about it. In the elevator, she took one look at her snow soaked appearance and cringed. She flicked her braid behind her and squared her shoulders. How dare Bayn worry Elise and now her?

You could be wrong, and he could've had nothing to do with the fight at Leif's mansion.

Freya banged on the door before she chickened out. "Bayn? Open the goddamn door!" Voices murmured inside. Oh god, what if he was with another woman and she had just— Bayn opened the door and folded his arms.

"Good evening, Freya." Bayn was glaring at her, so she frowned right back.

"Please tell me you had nothing to do with the attack on Leif last night because if you did, I swear—"

A voice cleared behind Bayn, and a stunningly handsome man stepped around him. Freya's eyes took in the gorgeous black-haired male and focused on his ears. The points weren't as sharp as fae ears. Light Elf. What was one of the Ljósálfar doing with Bayn?

"Thank you for sharing what the elves have been investigating, Arne," Bayn said.

Arne looked between Freya and Bayn. "Good luck with *that*, my prince." Arne smirked at Freya on his way past, and she fought the urge to kick him in his perfect ass.

"Come in, Freya. I'm not having this conversation in a hallway," Bayn said. Freya relented and followed him inside. She pulled off her soaked jacket and boots and sat down on the black velvet couch. Bayn placed a glass of whiskey down in front of her and took a seat a safe distance away. He looked tired, long hair still mussed from sleep and clothes wrinkled like he had dressed in a hurry.

Damn fucking sexy.

Freya gave her hormones a mental slap. She spotted the pair of antlers propped up against a wall on the other side of the room, and a sinking feeling filled her stomach.

"What the fuck did he mean by 'prince'?" she demanded. "Who *are* you?"

Bayn's eyes glowed with power as frost curled in patterns over his arms. "I am the Winter Prince."

12

"I am the Winter Prince."

Those words of confirmation rattled through Freya, and she was forced to reassess everything that had happened since the moment she met him.

Freya wanted to hurl her glass at Bayn's head even though she didn't know what she was so angry about. She drained the whiskey instead.

"No wonder Elise was so vague about how she knew you. Kian is your brother, which is why you lost it when you saw the antlers. I am going to *kill* my cousin for this."

It was Bayn's turn to swear. "Elise is your cousin through blood?"

"Of course she is. Wait, she didn't tell you that either?"

Bayn shook his head, and if possible, he looked even more pissed off.

"I thought you a recluse who never left Scotland."

"I do when I need to hunt mythical daggers with beautiful women."

Freya snorted. Being a prince surely explained where his arrogant streak came from. "Don't expect me to kneel, even if you are royalty."

Bayn gave her a look that should've been made illegal on the spot. "There's only one reason I would want you to kneel before me, and it wouldn't be because I'm a prince."

Freya only rolled her eyes and got up to get the bottle of whiskey from the minibar. Bayn didn't take his eyes off her, a lazy smile spreading over his face.

"You were worried about me tonight, weren't you? That's why you came charging over like an angry Valkyrie," he said, looking absurdly pleased about it.

"No, Elise sent me over. Now that I'm here, please explain why you would choose to attack Leif instead of having sex with me." Freya wanted to stuff something into her mouth, but once she saw his confused expression, she couldn't stop. "I would've rocked your world. I do have that list you asked for, and it's a shame you won't find out what was on it. Especially number fifteen. You would've seen the face of God with that one. Now you're never going to know."

Bayn's sapphire eyes danced with amusement. "Oh, my darling Freya, you know that's a lie."

"I don't think it is because clearly, you're more interested in starting gang wars than having mind-blowing sex." Freya sat back down and got comfortable. "Who is Arne?"

"He's an elf warrior." Bayn ran a hand over his face, his frustration palpable. "I don't want to involve you in this shit, Freya."

"It's too late for that. As soon as you walked through my door, I was involved."

"You won't understand. You're never going to accept me once you know what I'm capable of!" Bayn shouted.

Freya flinched at his tone. After Leif, she was terrible around the shouting kind of anger. Bayn didn't seem angry at her, though, but himself.

The Winter Prince.

Freya knew the stories. *Everyone* knew about the fae prince who had built a castle of ice and claimed the north of Scotland. While Kian had become the fae representative to the world, hated and loved in turn, there was nothing but speculation when it came to his brothers.

Elise had said that Kian's youngest brother had been the hardest to convince not to take his revenge out on the humans. And that if they fucked up the treaty, he would happily ice the world over. Freya couldn't fathom that kind of power.

And yet, Elise had sent Bayn right to her door. She hadn't told her about him...but neither had he.

"Why didn't you tell me you were a prince?" she asked softly.

"Because I didn't want you looking at me like you are now." Bayn's hand was gripping his whiskey glass so tightly, Freya thought it would crack.

"Bayn, look at me." He fixed her with those cold sapphire eyes that didn't hold an ounce of warmth. She wouldn't back down just because he wanted her to. "I don't care that you are a prince. I care that you are lying to me by not telling me everything that is happening. Why did you attack Leif, and how does it involve the elves?"

Bayn drained his whiskey. Freya pushed the bottle towards him, and he refilled both of their glasses.

"You have no idea what seeing those antlers meant tonight...what it triggered," he began and cut himself off like he wasn't sure where to start. She folded her arms.

With a sigh, Bayn gave in and told her about what had happened after he had dropped her off. With every revelation, Freya was more shocked and upset. That he took on all of Leif's bloodthirsty thugs on his own was terrifying.

"Are you hurt?" Freya asked.

"That's all you have to say after I told you I wounded and probably killed a bunch of your ex-boyfriend's employees?"

Bayn had a point, but it didn't stop her from looking over him for any signs of wounds.

"Leif only hires bastards for his guards. Ex-cons, men who have been kicked out of the army, that sort of crowd. You are my—my friend." Freya didn't know how else to describe him.

Bayn's expression melted just a little. "I am fine, Freya, which is more than I can say for Yrsa."

"Leif is trafficking elves," she croaked, struggling to say it out loud.

"And other creatures. I have to ask if you knew about it."

"Of course I didn't! How can you even think that?"

"Because it's better that I ask you than Arne. The elves are pissed because this is their fifth person that has gone missing. They are out for blood. You were Leif's girl, and that's enough for them to put you in a suspect pile," Bayn argued. "This isn't about finding the dagger anymore. We have to find and stop this ring of traffickers."

"You have to believe me, Bayn. I would never have been a part of anything like this."

"Then what made you leave him? You must have known something was going on."

Freya curled her knees up to her chest. "I knew he hated the fae and elves, that he thought they were going to become a threat. I really didn't think he would get involved in trafficking." Bayn got up and brought her a bottle of water. She took his hand and held onto him. "Do you really think I could be involved in something so horrific?"

Bayn sat down beside her, his fingers gently closing around hers. "No, but I had to ask. I'll protect you from Leif, and the elves are smart enough not to come near anyone under my protection."

Freya didn't dare look at him. "And I am?"

Bayn cupped her cheek with his warm hand. "Most definitely. You have to tell me what you know about his operation because the elves are holding back out of respect for me. It won't hold them for long. Stop trying to protect this piece of shit."

"I'm not trying to protect him but *me*! When I left, he said if I told anyone what had happened, he would kill me too." She had spent the last eight months holding back her fear, trying to get her life back on track, and fighting the nightmares.

"He's never going to lay a finger on you again, summer. His days are numbered," Bayn promised. His arm went around her, and she leaned back into him, drawing on his warmth. Her head dropped to his shoulder, feeling like the groove was made for her.

"There was a collector who told Leif he didn't have an amulet that Leif wanted for one of his mafia guys. The problem with dealing with those men is that if you take on a job, you have to follow through no matter what," Freya began, her old frustrations coming to the surface. "I told Leif not to take it. Begged him. At the beginning of our relationship, he used to listen to my gut instincts. Then he got greedy and stopped caring. This collector pretended he didn't have the amulet, but Leif wouldn't believe him. I got woken up in the middle of the night and stuffed into a car by some of Leif's men. We ended up in a lakeside mansion out in Kolbotn.

"Leif was there and had strapped the owner to a chair. Someone had beaten the shit out of him. I tried to talk some sense into Leif, but he... He pulled a gun on me and made me use my ability to search the mansion. I found the amulet hidden in the frame of a painting, and Leif put two bullets in the collector."

Freya swiped away a tear from her cheek, not wanting the horror of that night to overwhelm her.

"The next day, I packed my things and left. Leif tried to stop me, but I threatened him that if he didn't let me walk away, the file I had created on him would go straight to the police. My bluff was good enough that he let me go with two black eyes and a promise if I ever told anyone what had happened, he would kill me. I went to my parent's place in Denmark for a few weeks to let things in Oslo calm down. When I got home, Leif had gone through Mardøll and stolen a bunch of things. I changed the locks and alarms, and even though it hurt me financially, I let him get away with it. He's left me alone since, and I've done everything I could to stay out of his world and not cross paths with him."

"And I made you go back in. Gods, Freya, I'm sorry," Bayn said, his arm pulling her closer.

"Don't be. If we hadn't, you would never have found Yrsa." Freya shifted so she could look at him. "Please tell me there is no way they can track the attack back to you."

"I destroyed all the cameras I could and blew out all the lights. In saying that, they will know that a fae or an elf attacked them because of the magic involved." Bayn showed her a file on his phone. "Arne sent me this. It's all the information they have on the disappearances. None of us think Leif is in charge, only a tool, but the way Dieter's assistants reacted to us has put them high on my shit list. They weren't shy about offering to buy me, which means they had done it more than once."

Freya pushed her hands into her hair. "Oh God, they think that I would be the kind of person who would *buy* a fae?"

"It might work in our favor if they do. We can use it as a way to get closer to them," Bayn said. "It's going to get dangerous, Freya, so if you want out, now is the time."

Freya glared at him. "You think I'm a coward who's just going to walk away and let you do this on your own?"

"That's not what I meant."

"I don't care what you meant. I'm not letting you do this alone. I should've stopped Leif eight months ago, then those elves might never have been taken." Freya rested her palm on his chest. "I'm not going anywhere. We are going to find out who is doing this, and stop them."

"This won't be some soft human justice, Freya. The fae and elves take out their revenge in blood. I've been responsible for giving out this kind of punishment for centuries. It's not a side of me that you are going to like or want to see."

Freya knew that Bayn was telling her the truth, that he was a warrior down to his bones and would shed blood if he needed to. Unlike Leif, she knew he wouldn't be the type to get off on it, and that made all the difference. He seemed to genuinely care that her opinion of him would change, which surprised her.

"It doesn't matter, I want Leif and people like him stopped permanently. I'm not some fragile flower, Bayn. I've seen the dirty parts of the world, and I will see this through."

Freya summoned her courage and hoped she wasn't about to make a huge mistake. Her grip on his shirt tightened as she looked up into his eyes. "And I want to know *all* of you, even the dark and ugly bits. I don't know how to explain it, and honestly, I really should know better, but I feel like you will be one of the most important people I ever meet. I'm not going to walk away from you without a fight, so don't make me."

Bayn's expression darkened even further. "Freya, I don't deserve that."

"Probably. You said you won't do casual with me. Well, I won't even consider serious based on half-truths and hidden bullshit. I don't want any more lies, Bayn." Before he could argue more, Freya leaned forward and kissed him lightly on the lips. "But if you take the risk and don't push me away, I promise number fifteen will really be worth it."

Bayn's serious expression cracked, and he laughed loudly. "Why do you have to be so infuriating and beautiful at the same time?"

"I have many special talents."

"Don't you know that I'm trying to keep away from you for your own good?"

"Hmm, never really been one to let other people decide what's good for me." Freya was about to kiss his smiling mouth again when her phone started ringing with an unknown number. "Hello?"

"It's Von. Leif is sending guys to collect you from Mardøll. Get the fuck out of there, now!"

13

Bayn was up in a heartbeat and by the windows overlooking Freya's store. Within thirty seconds, two black cars pulled up in front of it, and six men got out. Freya joined him, her hand taking his again in fear.

"You are going to stay here and let me handle this," he said.

Freya's eyes went wide. "What are you going to do?"

Bayn didn't know what answer to give her that wouldn't scare her away. "I'm going to make sure they know you are protected by someone scarier than Leif."

Freya opened her mouth to protest, but Bayn kissed her. Her soft lips gave under his, and the rage that had been churning inside of him all day finally calmed down. "Please, Freya, don't fight me on this. I can't let anything happen to you."

Freya nodded. "Okay, I'll stay, but be careful."

Bayn only laughed. "Look how cute you are, thinking those thugs even stand a chance against me."

"Fine. Go get shot, see if I care. Just make sure you don't trash my place in the process," she said, shoving him back from her.

Bayn grabbed two of his dagger hilts from the bedroom, Freya's mouth popping open as he created blades of ice. "Do I get a kiss before I go?"

"You might get one if you come back alive," Freya replied, pulling a chair up to the window so she could watch.

"And they say I'm the one with a cold heart."

"Just as long as your dick is hot, I don't care," Freya said, and damn if he didn't want to climb over the couch and prove it was.

"Keep thinking about my dick. I'll be back soon."

Bayn stepped out onto the balcony and let the cold air calm him down. He shot Freya a goodbye grin as he stepped off the side and landed three stories down on the icy pavement.

The first of Leif's men stationed outside of the door saw Bayn only when his fist was driving him to the pavement.

So much for a lookout. He found a small bomb rigged to Freya's door, but the contraption was inactive. He treaded up the stairs on cat soft feet and found three men in her office.

"Enjoying yourselves?" Bayn asked casually. All three men pulled guns on him. "Maybe you can tell me what you're looking for, and I can help?"

"Fucking fae." The man closest to him went to spit and found his face gripped tight. Bayn shoved him into the wall, and the man hit the ground.

"Would either of you like to tell me why you are placing a bomb in my lady's apartment?"

"She's Leif's lady, asshole, and the bomb was for you," said the younger of the two remaining men. Bayn only laughed at them.

"You pathetic humans really don't get it. Freya *is* my lady, and Leif isn't the one you should be afraid of." Ice whipped out of Bayn's hands, freezing their guns and forcing them to drop them. The smarter of the two held up his hands in surrender.

"I'm not going to kill you because Freya asked me not to make a mess of her apartment. But you are going to take a message back to Leif. Tell him if he ever comes near Freya or this building again, I will destroy everything he loves starting with his small dick that he feels the need to wave about where it's not wanted. Understand?"

"Yes," both men said through gritted teeth.

Bayn nudged the unconscious man on the ground with the toe of his boot. "Take that with you." He escorted them out, burning with the need to rip them apart.

After they had gone, he sent magic through the apartment and the store, making sure they hadn't planted any other bombs. That they thought such a ridiculous device could stop a fae told him just how much they underestimated him. He gathered up the half completed device at the door and encased the parts in ice so he could dispose of everything safely later. Satisfied everything was in order, he went back to the hotel.

Freya was pacing when he came in, her face visibly relaxing as soon as he walked through the door. Maybe he should have let one of them get a punch in so she could have fussed over him.

"Still alive?" she said, shutting away her concern.

"Don't sound so disappointed. Your ex continues to be mediocre." Bayn went into his bedroom and started to put his gear back into his duffle bag. "He tried to plant bombs to take me out. I found his men going through your office too."

"Did you kill any of them?" she asked from his doorway.

"No. I knocked a few about, but I sent them back to their master with a warning. Next time they try this shit, I *will* kill them." Bayn grabbed his toiletries from the bathroom and zipped up his bag.

Freya shifted nervously. "You're leaving?"

"I'm not going far." Bayn slung his bag over one shoulder. "I'm your new flatmate."

"What? No! I didn't agree to that," Freya said, putting her hands on her hips.

"Too bad. It's happening. Staying with you is the only way to ensure that you're protected, not only from Leif, but also from whoever he is working for. I embarrassed him tonight, so he'll regroup and find another way to get at me. I've known men like him before. With any luck, he will go to whoever he is working for and flush them out for us." Bayn grabbed what was left of the bottle of whiskey. "Don't worry, I'll be a good faeling and stay in the guest room."

Freya's eyes narrowed. "I don't like this, even though I know you're right. If you overstep and become an overbearing asshole, I'll tell Elise, then Kian can deal with you."

Bayn tried not to laugh in her face. He had been able to kick Kian's ass for centuries. He gave her a grave nod. "Yes, Freya. I understand, Freya. I'll be good, Freya." She only muttered something in Norwegian under her breath and walked away.

That's my mate, laying down the law. Bayn couldn't believe how adorable she was when she was bossy, her tight pants made her storming off an even better experience.

"Stop looking at my ass, too," Freya threw over her shoulder and opened the hotel room door.

"I wouldn't dare do that. I'm a prince, remember?" Bayn said, grinning behind her back all the way to her apartment.

Freya checked her office first, cursing impressively in three different languages when she saw the mess.

"What do you think those assholes were looking for?" Bayn asked. Freya was going through the small drawers of the wooden cabinet and checking the cards.

"Who knows? Leif took a third of my research last time he stole from me. It all looks to be here still." Freya let out a relieved breath. "Thank you for stopping them. I don't think I could've started again after last time. It's too disheartening."

"I told you I would protect you, and I meant it. That includes your assets."

Freya sat down in her swivel chair, her professional face suddenly back up. "Why, Bayn? You barely know me."

"I keep my promises. Besides, you're the first person I've liked in five hundred years," he replied with what he hoped was a nonchalant shrug.

Freya's severe mouth quirked. "Very well. Let me show you to your room."

～

BAYN DIDN'T CARE how late it was. As soon as Freya had gone to bed, he whipped out his phone and video called Kian. His brother was slow to respond, as always.

"What's wrong now? Have you learned anything more from the elves?" Kian answered. He was wide awake, which meant he was probably working and not spending time with Elise.

"Oh, I did learn something. It's about your mate and how she likes to lie to people," Bayn snapped. He should've known it wasn't only about the dagger.

"Be careful how you talk about my mate, little brother." Kian's eyes flared with golden power.

"Were you in on this too? Was this whole thing a set up?" Bayn was fighting to keep his voice down. He didn't want Freya to think that he was angry at her.

"What are you talking about?"

"Freya is Elise's cousin by blood! She didn't even tell Freya that I was the Winter Prince. This whole god damn thing has been a set up because Elise doesn't want me to die in peace."

Kian's head whipped about, looking at something behind him. "Is this true?"

Elise appeared on screen, fire in her eyes. "First of all, asshole, I didn't tell you that she was my cousin because I didn't want you to doubt her professional capacity. Second of all, I didn't tell her you were the Winter Prince because she wouldn't have taken you as a client. I don't know what about this has your panties in a knot when I was only trying to help your big, dumb—"

"I'm angry because I think she's my fucking mate!" Bayn interrupted. He had kept it together all day, but now the sheer terror of the truth was ripping him apart. Kian dropped the glass of wine he was holding, but Elise...Elise looked sheepish. "I suppose you knew that too, *sister*."

"I wasn't a hundred percent certain, but she told me you two had hooked up, and when a rune appeared, you freaked out. I wasn't sure if it was a rune like when I was with Kian."

Bayn was going to be sick. "You didn't tell Freya what it meant, did you?"

"No! Like I said, I wasn't sure if it was the same thing, so I dodged the question."

Bayn slumped down on the bed, his chest hurting from his heart beating so hard. Kian moved Elise gently out of the way and kissed her forehead. "Let me talk to him alone, my love."

"Bayn, you have to believe me. I didn't even consider that she could be your mate," Elise said before leaving the room.

"Little brother, breathe," Kian commanded. He had been saying those words to Bayn since he was a faeling, so he automatically did, and the tightness in his chest eased. "Now, are you sure she is your mate?"

"My heart is beating again, and I'm not talking metaphorically." Bayn pulled off his shirt and showed Kian the curse lines. "I also feel like murdering everyone who has ever harmed her, her fucked up ex-boyfriend first." Bayn told Kian about the bombs and the attempted kidnapping.

"I'm honestly surprised he's still breathing."

"I can't leave Freya alone. It's going to bring out his boss, but when we have them, I'm going to kill that fucker," Bayn swore. He pushed his hands through his hair. "What am I going to do, Kian? I can't mate this woman and bind her to me. She's a good person, and alive and wonderful. I'm a mean old bastard that deserves to die. I don't want to fuck up her life."

Kian's golden eyes filled with compassion. "She's definitely your mate. Maybe you need to discuss it with her and see how she feels about it? Wait until you've dealt with this trafficking ring first, then *talk* to her. Elise will fill her in on any details if the idea frightens her."

"Of course it's going to frighten her! I've been the family assassin since I could wield a blade. She has no idea about the blood on my hands. The shit I've done."

"Elise accepted me, and you know I belong in the darkest circle of hell right along with you."

"The mating bond won't give her a choice but to accept me."

Kian shook his head. "No, you're wrong there. Elise had a choice, even after we had sex. I've been keeping a record of the changes and effects that the mating bond has had on us both, and there is a pattern."

"That is just weird."

"No, it's not. We have no real information about mates, only stories. I want to be able to help others like my blockheaded brothers, so they have an easier time of it than I did," Kian replied. He looked down his nose at him. "Something that's going to assist you now."

Bayn rolled his eyes. "Okay, dazzle me with your observations, great scholar."

"The runes are a sign, a way to recognize that you've found a mate. We also instantly felt connected to each other, even though we hated each other. The bond grew fast between us because we exchanged blood, but I believe that was specific only to Elise and me because of the curse. She got my speed early on. It was triggered by her need to protect me," explained Kian.

"When we had sex for the first time, the runes appeared everywhere on the both of us. It's like a magical marking that strengthens a bond. The actual mating bond didn't become unbreakable until we verbalized that we accepted the mating."

"So what you're saying is I can have sex with her and not get mated unless we say 'I accept you as my mate'?"

Kian pinched the bridge of his nose. "Of course your mind would only think about the sex."

"Has Elise shown you a picture of her beloved cousin? It's kind of hard not to think about sex when she's around," Bayn argued. In fact, he couldn't remember a time when he had thought about sex more. It was embarrassing.

Kian frowned, his magic flashing around him again. "Don't fuck around with her, Bayn. Whether you want to take her as a mate or not, she is Elise's family, and you need to respect that. Freya isn't some one night stand you can fuck and leave."

Bayn groaned in frustration. "Beira's tits, don't I know it. Stop thinking the worst of me, will you? I knew from the moment I saw her I could only have something serious with her. I even did the princely thing and told her that out right after she invited me to fuck her senseless. I turned her down, Kian, for both our sakes."

"Bet you regretted doing that," Kian said with a sideways grin.

"*So* much." Bayn choked out a laugh. "But my resolve still stands. She has to want more from me than just a fuck because I don't think I could be with her and have her walk away afterward. She's not fae, she could do it, and I would lose my fucking mind. What's left of it anyway."

Kian laughed with him, and it felt like it was for the first time in centuries. "Would mating Freya really be so bad? You seem almost happy."

"No, Kian, it wouldn't be bad for me. I worry it would be for her, though, and you know what it's like...their happiness has to come first no matter how much it fucks you up," Bayn said.

"I understand, but you don't know that you won't make a good mate to her. Deal with this trafficking disaster, talk to her, and let Freya decide for herself whether she wants you," Kian replied. Because he couldn't help himself he added, "Though gods be with her if she does. Good luck, baby brother."

"Thanks, I'm going to need it."

14

Freya didn't know how she was going to sleep that night. Leif had tried to kidnap her and blow up her store; he was trafficking elves like they were trinkets, and that was before she got to Bayn.

Bayn, the fucking Winter Prince, who was determined to protect her.

No one had tried to protect her before. She had always been one to fight her own battles, from schoolyard bullies to the cluster fuck of a relationship with Leif. Her father had always been supportive of her being able to stand up for herself. It wasn't like she couldn't take care of herself, but Bayn looking out for her felt...nice. She was also smart enough to know this was one fight she wouldn't win on her own. She could barely fathom that she was in it at all.

Fucking bombs in my building. Who the hell was Leif working for that he felt secure enough to risk that kind of retaliation? If he didn't know that Bayn was the one that attacked him, then she had to assume Leif was acting like this because he was jealous she had been with a fae. He clearly didn't know Freya at all if he thought kidnapping her and killing her lover was the way to win her back.

But Bayn's not your lover, she reminded herself. Was he? He was three doors over, and his presence filled her apartment like it was almost too small to contain him. Instead of suffocating her, it was reassuring.

Freya had a knee jerk reaction to him coming and staying with her, but seeing the mess Leif's asshole men had made of her place made her feel better about Bayn staying with her.

Except for now, when she was trying to sleep, imagining him in her guest bed, his big, muscled body stretched out and naked on her favorite quilt. Freya put a pillow over her head and groaned.

Bayn's muffled voice carried through the walls, and she sat up, listening. Who was he talking to now? She cringed, hating the sting of jealousy. She heard him say 'Kian,' and she fell back onto her mattress with a relieved sigh. Then she went back to groaning into the pillow.

Pathetic.

∽

FREYA WOKE hours later so cold that she couldn't feel her toes. She turned on the lamp on her bedside table to figure out why her heating had turned off. The whole of her roof and bedroom wall was covered in frost, the tang of Bayn's magic in the air.

"What the hell?" Freya got out of bed and stumbled sleepily down the hall. "Bayn?" Covering her hand with her shirt sleeve, she opened the frosted door to the guest room. Snowflakes as big as her hand hung suspended in the air, frost covered the walls, and in the center of the bed, Bayn was sweating and clawing at the sheets, caught in a night terror.

"Shit," Freya muttered. How did one wake a fae without getting smacked?

"Bayn! Wake up!" she called, her breath pluming in the frigid air. He didn't stir, just twisted in the blanket. Freya put out a hand and pushed the suspended snowflakes out of her way.

"Bayn? Wake up, you're having a nightmare," she said, and with a shaking hand, she touched his shoulder. Pain streaked through her mind the instant she was sucked into his dream.

Blood and small bodies were scattered across the ground. Kian was screaming while Killian was pulling him out of a burning house. Bayn drove his sword through the guts of a human warrior, dodging the spear of another before freezing him solid.

Killian was fighting as warriors held him down and beat him bloody. He refused to reveal his wings for them to hack off like they had done to Kian's antlers.

The curse burned through Bayn, sucking him into Faerie, into a land they would have to fight to keep.

Then years passed, an eternity of cold darkness, of assassinating anyone that would threaten his brothers and their people again.

Bayn was on a throne of ice, slowly freezing and vanishing bit by bit to become a part of the throne too.

"No!" Freya screamed. She ran to the throne, took his face in her hands, kissed his frozen lips. "Wake up, Bayn!"

Freya gasped as the magic let her go. Bayn's dark eyes snapped open, saw her hovering over him, and he attacked, lifting her up and pinning her to the bed with a feral growl.

"Bayn! Snap out of it!" she shouted in his snarling face. Recognition spread through his eyes as the nightmares finally released their grip.

"Freya?" he whispered, hand touching her cheek. "Fuck, Freya, did I hurt you? What are you doing in here?" He looked about the room, saw the state of it, and shrank back from her.

"I'm fine. Are you okay?" she asked, sitting up.

Bayn made a small move with his hand, and the frost and giant snowflakes disappeared. He started shaking, tears spilling down his cheeks as he wrapped his arms around himself.

"Hey, you're all right," Freya tried to soothe him. She couldn't stand to see him confused with sleep and distressed.

"None of this is all right! I could've hurt you."

"But you didn't." She reached out for him, tugging him back to bed. "Come here."

Bayn let himself be led, and she pulled him down and gently into her arms. He rested his head in the groove of her shoulder, his arm going around her waist and hanging onto her like she was his lifeline. He was still shaking, so she stroked his dark hair over and over.

"Just breathe, Bayn. You're okay. It was only a nightmare," she whispered. But she knew that it wasn't. She had talked to Elise, not to mention saw Kian's broadcast about the humans slaughtering the fae. Seeing the living hell in Bayn's mind and how it still haunted him made her want to kill every bastard who hurt him and made him become a killer just to survive.

"Freya, I'm so sorry," he murmured.

"Don't be. We are both okay."

Softly, she began to sing him a lullaby in Danish that her grandmother used to soothe her with. Bayn pulled her up against his hard body and slowly melted into her as the terror lessened.

Freya put her arms around him and swore that she would never, ever, let him vanish away like he had in the dream.

~

THE NEXT MORNING, Freya woke tucked up in her own bed and with her phone buzzing insistently on her bedside table. Her hand fumbled for it, and she answered it with a grunt.

"Cousin, what have you been up to?" Elise asked.

"Just waking up, so not much at all. Thanks for telling me Bayn is the Winter Prince, you asshole." Freya rolled over into a more comfortable position. *He put you back in your own bed.* She didn't know why she felt disappointed by that.

"I didn't tell you because I knew you wouldn't take on a job with him. Bayn is intimidating enough without his title on top of it."

Freya grunted. "Bayn likes to think he's intimidating."

"Kian said that he's moved in with you. If he starts to get pushy, don't put up with it. He's the biggest prick out of all the princes, and they are *all* pricks."

"Bayn's okay. I'm glad he's here. Leif has clearly lost his mind."

There was a long pause before Elise whispered, "Is Bayn in bed with you right now?"

"What? No! Why would you think that?"

"Because you were saying nice things about him, I assumed he was there. We are talking about the same Bayn, right?"

"Tall, hot, tattooed, has an ass so fine that you want to sink your teeth into it?" Freya rattled off.

"Jesus Christ, you have a crush on him," Elise gasped.

"My ovaries still work, so naturally I do."

"Where is he now? I'm worried he's going to overhear you."

Freya sat up and strained her ears. There was a clang of pans, a whir of the espresso machine, and a deep voice humming something.

"Sounds like Bayn's making breakfast." Freya yawned, feeling like she needed another two hours of sleep. "He better be making enough for two."

"Bayn. The Winter Prince. Is. Making. Breakfast."

"Are you going to repeat everything I say now?"

Elise let out a giggle. "If only you knew how strange and hilarious this all is."

"Says the woman who mated the first fae she met."

"They can't mate with just anyone. I was lucky that fate pushed us together." Elise always sounded a bit dreamy when she talked about Kian, which had made Freya want to gag. Right up until Bayn had kissed her at Von's club. Then it all made sense.

"Is there a reason for this call, Elise?"

"Nope. Just wanted to check in and make sure that Bayn wasn't driving you crazy and that you weren't freaked out by everything that happened last night," Elise replied.

"You know me, cousin. I tend to roll with everything while it's happening and have my breakdown later when it's all over. Bayn and I will get to the bottom of everything, and then I'll find some cabin in the woods to have my freak-out."

"Bayn does have a nice castle that you could go to for some rest and relaxation."

"Elise, if I didn't know better, I would think that you set this entire thing up with the dagger just to hook us up. You do have the *Hávamál,* don't you? That wasn't something fake."

Elise groaned dramatically. "What is it with you and Bayn thinking that I would do such a thing! He's dying, Freya! That's kind of a priority right now, not seeing if he would date my cousin. The *Hávamál* is real.

The dagger, I hope, is real, and you still need to find it to save him because he doesn't seem to be open to the only other thing that could."

"And what would that be?" asked Freya. If they really couldn't find the dagger, she wouldn't stop until she found an answer. The vision of him freezing into a part of a gruesome throne rose up in her mind. No way was she going to let that happen.

"The prince's curses can be broken if they find their mates. Bayn has always been against the idea, so I wouldn't worry about it," Elise said vaguely. She had a weird hitch in her voice that Freya couldn't interpret, so she ignored it.

"Well, if we can't find the dagger, maybe I can help him find his mate?" As soon as she said it, Freya regretted it. The thought of finding another woman, his soul mate, and then letting him go to be with her... She knew she wasn't that good of a person.

"Hmm, maybe, but you'll have better luck with the dagger," Elise replied. "You had better go before your breakfast gets cold."

"True. Thank you for checking in on me, but I'm fine. Bayn is fine too. I'll let you know if anything happens."

Freya went into her en-suite, brushed her teeth, and got the snarls out of her hair. She needed coffee before she went through the whole process of showering and getting ready to open the store. With another yawn that cracked her jaw, she went to see what Bayn had been doing.

Freya took one look at Bayn at her espresso machine and discovered a kink she didn't know she had. His tight black t-shirt clung to his muscled back, his biceps flexing as he frothed milk in a silver jug.

"How would you like your coffee?" he asked over one shoulder. His eyes skimmed over her flannel PJs and sleepy shirt with 'Wake me and die' on it, and he grinned. Refusing to give in to the urge to run back to her bedroom and change, Freya sat down on one of the bar stools at the counter.

"Hot and sweet," she replied as unbothered as possible. She opened one of the white paper bags. "You went to the bakery?"

"Yes, I saw there was nothing in your kitchen to eat, so I thought I'd better go grab some supplies," Bayn said, placing a latte down in front of her. "I wanted to say thank you for last night. Breakfast seemed like a good start."

"Wise male," Freya replied, half of the apple danish already in her mouth.

Bayn put a plate of scrambled eggs and toasted sourdough next to her coffee. "Try and eat something proper with all that sugar." Freya stuck her tongue out at him but still picked up her fork.

"I'll start going through all of Arne's files today and see if I can find something the elves overlooked." Bayn sat down beside her with his own breakfast. He put his knife and fork down. "Look, Freya, about last night. I haven't had a night terror like that in a very long time. There's been no damage done to the apartment, and I've put up wards all around my room, so if it happens again, the magic won't leave that space. I didn't mean to frighten you or—"

"Bayn, it's fine. Really. I get nightmares, too, all the time, in fact. And if you keep making me breakfast every time you have one, you're welcome to frost up my guest room whenever you like," Freya said, trying to make him smile.

"I could've hurt you. You really should be more afraid of me."

Freya laughed and took another pasty. "I'll pass. You might be a badass and all, but you can save it to scare everyone else."

Bayn was giving her a look that was a mixture of helplessness, want, and frustration. "I really hope that never changes."

Freya was growing hot all over, so she looked back at her half-empty plate. "You can set up at the spare desk downstairs if you want. I'll see what I can find out on Dieter and hopefully track down a contact number for the guy who was talking to Von about the dagger."

"Good idea. I don't want to be too far away from you in case Leif is stupid enough to come by again. You know it actually pains me not to go and put a dagger in his throat," Bayn said, becoming the stern fae prince once more. Freya slid off her chair and placed her plate in the dishwasher. She grabbed her coffee and stood on tiptoes to kiss his cheek.

"Thanks for breakfast."

Bayn grabbed the laces of her pajama pants and pulled her back towards him. He bent his head and pressed a silky soft kiss to her lips. His tongue lightly brushed hers before pulling back.

"Thanks for waking me up last night," he purred, releasing her.

Freya sipped her coffee, winked, and then walked as calmly as she could back to her bedroom. Once there was a door between them, she let out a shaky breath and wiped her sweaty hands on her pants.

Odin's beard. She didn't know how she was going to handle a whole day with him after that.

15

Bayn sat in a back corner of the store, using an elegant antique desk as his work station.

"You break it, you buy it," Freya warned playfully before taking up her spot at the counter. She was wearing a black high-waisted skirt and a red silk top, her long hair pinned in a tousled updo. Freya was gorgeous in a way that made Bayn regret agreeing to work downstairs. She was so distracting that he had been staring at the same file on his laptop for twenty minutes without seeing it.

A customer came in, and Freya went to greet them, taking her out of sight long enough for Bayn to breathe properly.

That's your mate, who looks like summer and smells like a dream. He still couldn't get over it, but there was no denying it.

Last night had proved it to him on a level that he couldn't imagine. Freya had woken him up from a hellish night terror, something his brothers had never been able to do. She had appeared right in his nightmare, demanded that he wake up, and he had. Then she stayed with him until he slept once more.

Bayn thought that he had dreamed the whole thing when he woke, but he found Freya still snuggled in his arms. He was at peace for the first time since he was cursed. It had spooked him enough that he had carried her back to her own bed so he didn't wake her when he freaked the fuck out.

Gods, she smelled so good, *felt* so good with her soft curves pressing into him. Bayn groaned inwardly.

Freya laughed and said something to her customer in Norwegian. He was a tall, well-dressed man with a pleasant smile that he aimed right at Freya as she wrapped a vase he was buying.

Don't snap him in half. Don't snap him in half. Don't snap him in half.

As if sensing death lurked around nearby, the man looked up, spotted Bayn, and quickly swiped his credit card, his smile gone. Once he had retreated from the store, Freya turned on Bayn, folding her arms and cocking her hip to one side.

"Did you just glare at my nice customer?" she demanded.

"What customer? The one that was drooling all over you?"

"He wasn't drooling! He was just telling me about his collection." Freya's whiskey eyes flashed with anger. "You scared him away."

"I didn't say a word to him," Bayn said innocently.

"You were wearing your murder face."

"That *is* my normal face."

Freya muttered something under her breath. She turned around and leaned against the counter to start filling in a book, giving Bayn an excellent view of her ass in that tight skirt.

"What was that?" Bayn asked.

Freya didn't bother to turn around to answer him, her pen scratching angrily. "I said you're not my boyfriend. You didn't even want to have sex with me, remember? You didn't want me, so you don't have the right to be jealous every time I talk to another man."

Bayn was behind her in the blink of an eye, his body moving of its own accord. Freya stilled instinctively, her hand clutching her pen tighter. Bayn placed his hands on the counter on either side of her.

"You're wrong about that. I said I'd protect you, that includes against creepers. As for your other accusation, do you honestly believe I didn't want to give you a screaming fuck the other night?" he whispered in her ear. "Is that what has you so angry? Are you still pent up and frustrated, baby?"

"I'm angry that you think you have some kind of right to scare customers away from me," Freya replied, her voice trembling slightly. "And I've never screamed during sex."

"That's because you've never had sex with me. I wouldn't even need to use my dick, and I'd get you screaming my name."

"Are you going to use your personality? Because I feel like I could scream at you right now," Freya said, even as she angled her hips slightly against him. Bayn slid one hand down her hip, over the sloping curve of her ass, pulling her up against the already painful erection straining against his jeans.

"You can feel how much I want you."

"You didn't even want to wake up in the same bed as me this morning," Freya whispered. He could hear the hurt in her voice now, the sound driving nails into his gut.

"I keep walking away from you because if I'm inside you just once, I won't ever want to walk away from you. I'm trying to give you a choice, no matter how hard it is. Even if it goes against every fae instinct I have."

Bayn's hand moved down her thigh again, needing to touch her and soothe her hurt feelings, to let her know how much he wanted her. Freya rested her head back against his shoulder.

"You drive me insane," Freya admitted. With a soft sigh, she leaned further into his touch. "Maybe you need to assure me that you aren't going to turn into an angry possessive asshole in the long term. I won't do that again, no matter how right you feel."

"I'm not a shitty human who won't recognize the treasure that he's got. I'll make sure that you know how perfect you are, how safe and cared for every moment." Bayn's hand slipped under the hem of her skirt, his fingers stroking her soft skin. "I won't need to be a possessive asshole because if you are mine, you won't ever want another male's hands on you."

"And you think your touch is going to be worth giving up all others?" Freya asked. Bayn saw her mouth twitch, and he realized what she was doing.

"Are you purposely trying to stir me up? Because that's a dangerous game to play," he growled, grip tightening on her thigh.

"I have no idea what you mean," Freya said, long lashes fluttering.

Bayn pressed a kiss to the back of her neck, his teeth pressing in when she made a small helpless sound of desire. Bayn flicked his spare hand out, his magic bolting the store door. They were shielded from people looking into the windows, but he wasn't about to risk getting interrupted.

"If you wanted my hands on you, you only needed to ask, Freya." Bayn stroked higher, Freya's skirt hitching up and exposing her thigh. He found the hem of her panties and ran one fingertip along it.

"I-I want your hands on me, Bayn," Freya stammered.

"Thank the gods." Bayn tugged her skirt up to her waist so he could see her ass and the red satin panties she was wearing. He hummed in approval. "You're matching almost like you planned this."

"I don't know what you're talking about," Freya said, her legs shaking as he bent her over the counter. He gently moved the sides of her panties up to better show the curves of her luscious ass as he palmed it. He shifted his boot against her red high heel, making her widen her legs for him.

Bayn tried to drown out the roaring in his head, demanding that he shove his dick inside of her. Instead, he put his hand underneath her from behind and cupped her.

Freya murmured something in Norwegian and pressed her bare ass up against his jeans. He moved her panties to the side and curled his fingers underneath, finding her sweet folds already wet for him. Freya gasped, hands gripping the edge of the counter. She went to rise up, but he lay his body over hers, pinning her down tight.

"When you finally give in to me, I'm going to fuck you just like this," Bayn growled in her ear, pressing two fingers inside of her. His hips moved against hers as he started to thrust in and out of her. "Can you imagine how good it's going to feel, Freya? I'm going to fill every inch of you and make you writhe in pleasure."

"Fuck, Bayn." Freya reached back and grabbed his ass hard. Her hips moved, pushing back with every stroke.

"Tell me what you need, baby," he begged.

"Harder," she cried. Bayn slipped in another finger, and she made a sound of pleasure so guttural, he almost came in his jeans. His hand was drenched in her wet heat, and still, she pushed. He grabbed her ass with his other hand, gripping her tight as he thrust faster.

Freya's whole body shuddered under him, and she screamed his name as she came hard on his hand. It was the best fucking sound he had ever heard. Bayn eased up from her so he wasn't crushing her. He removed his hand from her panties, giving the soaked satin a pat.

"Didn't I tell you that you'd scream for me?" he whispered, licking the curve of her ear. "And so quickly too." He didn't get a chance to gloat as Freya turned on him and shoved him up against the wall. She kissed him hard and breathless before lowering herself down to her knees.

"Freya," was all he managed to say before her hands had undone his belt and jeans.

Bayn's heart was pounding dangerously fast as her cool hand pulled his dick free. He was sure he was about to die, but he still took some pleasure in seeing her eyes widen as she stared at him. Her red lips lifted into a wicked smile that made him momentarily fearful, then she wrapped those lips around the end of his dick.

Bayn couldn't breathe as her tongue stroked along him and her fingers tightened around his shaft. Freya moved her free hand up under his shirt, humming as she touched his abs. Bayn felt that hum straight down his dick, and he had to grip the wall to keep himself upright. He swore in the old tongue as she stared up at him with the fucking hottest eyes and sucked harder.

Any sense of control Bayn thought he had over the situation vanished as her nails dug into his chest, and she pulled her mouth free, her hand sliding the wetness further along him.

"Let's see who screams the loudest, shall we?" she said, desire thickening her voice. She moved forward, taking him in her mouth again, sucking so hard, light spots danced in front of his eyes.

"*Fuck.*" Bayn stroked her cheek with trembling fingers, but she wasn't about to let up. Her hand moved from his abs to his lower back, dragging her nails sharply down to his ass. He couldn't handle the sweet torture any longer, and he began to pump his hips slowly so he wouldn't hurt her. Freya responded by taking him deeper, pulling his hips towards her until he was fucking her perfect mouth.

Holy fucking gods, he didn't deserve this even as he thanked any deity who would listen. Freya moaned, and his control shattered. His head dropped back against the wall, and he shouted her name, coming harder than he had in his life. He was shaking as she swallowed him down and released him with a final slow suck.

With a naughty smile, Freya tucked him back into his jeans and zipped them up. She gave his dick a pat and said condescendingly, "Didn't I tell you that you'd scream for me?"

Bayn's legs couldn't hold him up as he sank to the floor beside her, dragging her into his lap. He whispered her name like it was a prayer, scattering soft kisses all over her face. She pressed her breasts against his chest as she slid up his body and kissed the tip of his pointed ear.

"Best lunch break ever," she said, and they both started laughing, Bayn holding her to him and never wanting to let go.

∼

Freya couldn't stop grinning when she re-opened the store twenty minutes later. She had to redo her hair and fix her makeup, but it had been worth it. God, had it been worth it, even if her hands had glowed with blue runes for ten minutes afterward.

Freya wanted to ask Bayn about them, she was sure they were similar to the ones that appeared on him in the limo the first time they had hooked up. It seemed to throw out his mood that night, and she wasn't about to ruin the good vibes that were now buzzing between them.

Freya was also determined not to look at Bayn for the rest of the day because she wouldn't be able to stop giggling.

Be cool, Freya. You can always ask him about the runes over dinner tonight. She was too busy trying to act like she hadn't enjoyed a mind-blowing orgasm. She would never be able to look at her work counter the same way again.

The bell chimed, and all of her post-coital feel goods vanished. Dieter's assistant, who had offered to buy Bayn, was standing beside a set of glass shelves. He was admiring a collection of miniature Russian ikons from the 14th century with an interested smile. She felt Bayn's attention go on high alert, feeling him moving behind her without needing to look.

"Hello again," Freya greeted politely, moving out from behind the counter but keeping a safe distance from him.

"Miss Havisdottir, what a charming store you have," he said.

"Thank you. Are you looking for something in particular that I can help you with?"

The man's eyes flicked over her right shoulder to Bayn, and every one of her nerves burned with angry fire. Freya casually shifted her posture, blocking him from view.

"Dieter has asked me to extend you an invite to another of his gatherings tonight at his mansion in Trondheim. He was disappointed to see you and your companion leave so suddenly at the last auction. I do hope it wasn't something I said?"

Freya forced a dazzling smile. "Not at all. I just can't stand Leif. He's my ex-boyfriend for a reason."

"Ah, Leif. Terrible misfortune he had later that evening."

"Let me guess, he broke a nail? Someone told him he wasn't pretty?" Freya replied playfully. The assistant laughed.

"You are amusing, Freya. I like that. Unfortunately, Leif was robbed and is rather out of sorts about it."

Well, if you lie down with dogs, you're bound to get up with fleas. Freya shook her head sympathetically. "Poor Leif, I do hope he can bounce back."

"Undoubtedly, he will. Men like him always do." The assistant pulled out another card and handed it to her. It was made of the same stock and design, except this one had a street address. Her extra sense about magical items flared to life as soon as she touched it. Her skin crawled, but she didn't dare fling it away from her. "I do hope you can make it tonight, despite the short notice."

"I wouldn't miss it. I have money I didn't spend at Leif's auction, so here's hoping something catches my fancy," Freya said brightly.

"Save your money, my dear. This is a networking event for like-minded people. A good place to make some contacts for someone like you." The assistant gave Bayn another long look before smiling coldly at Freya. "I hope to see you both there." Freya watched the man leave and then dropped the card to the carpet, before she started to dry heave.

"Freya? What is it?" Bayn was beside her in an instant, his hand on her back.

"There's something magical infused in that card. Don't touch it, I-I think it's meant for you."

"It's okay, let me have a look." Bayn crouched down beside the white square. His magic rose, and Freya's nausea was washed away with the smell of winter air, pine, and cinnamon. Dark green runes appeared on the card, their ink rising from the white surface.

"Compulsion spell, and a rather good one at that," Bayn said. He took a photo of it on his phone before sketching in the air above it. A sigil made of frost appeared over the runes, and they melted away. "It should be fine to touch now."

"Let me." Freya took a pair of white gloves from a desk drawer and picked it up. "Son of bitch, mother fucking think I'm going to sell you—"

Bayn was trying not to laugh. "Someone is triggered."

"That bastard wants you."

"And you're not going to let him have me?"

"Absolutely not!" Freya snapped and then scowled at him. "Shut up, Bayn."

They placed the card in a small wooden box, and Freya searched the address on her phone. It was a property on the edge of the Skarvan og Roltdalen National Park.

"What do you think? Trap?" she asked, showing Bayn the location.

He nodded. "Most likely."

"But we are still going?"

"I don't like taking you into a fight, but they are expecting both of us," Bayn said, passing the phone back.

"That's right. You better be ready to take my orders, *Bjørn*."

Bayn's sapphire eyes shone with a deviousness that delighted her. He bowed low, taking her hand and kissing her knuckles. "Your wish is my command, mistress."

16

Freya found a neglected black satin dress in the back of her wardrobe and was surprised it still fit her properly. It would be snowing in the north, so she paired off the dress with some sheer tights and stylish, but warm knee-high boots. It would have to do last minute. Something told Freya that it was intentional to see how desperate she was. Deiter hadn't done his research if he thought he could throw her off so easily.

When Freya had asked Bayn how they were going to get to Trondheim, a seven-hour drive away, he had smiled and said he'd take care of it. It would have to be by helicopter this late; the party was meant to start in less than an hour.

Freya thought of her last limo drive with him and had to drop the shoulders of her coat to cool down. She wondered if it was a part of his fae magic that made her so hot and bothered. She contemplated asking Elise but knew her cousin would want details that she was too private to share.

Freya touched up her lipstick and went to find out if Bayn was ready to leave yet. He was sitting at her breakfast counter, a glass of whiskey frozen halfway to his lips. He looked at her like she had hung the moon and handed him stardust. Freya suddenly wanted to keep him looking at her like that forever. It made her feel like a queen that could conquer anything. Heat raced up her back, but she kept her smile casual.

"Are you ready to go?" she asked.

"Huh? Yes?" Bayn was dressed in another suit that showed off his broad shoulders. He had the top half of his hair tied back, making his face even more severely handsome.

"Are you sure?" Freya took his drink from his hand and drained it.

Bayn brushed his fingers lightly against her cheek. "You know, I have fought in many wars, slayed monsters, faced horrors you can't even imagine. None of them frighten me like you do."

Freya leaned into his touch, her heart swelling dangerously. "If you keep talking like that, we won't get to Trondheim at all, and we will miss our chance to investigate Dieter's house."

Bayn let out a pained sound and moved his hand away. Runes were glowing along his skin, but this time when he saw them, he only smiled a little helplessly.

"Are you ever going to tell me what they mean?" asked Freya, taking his hand and twining her fingers with his.

"When the problem with the trafficking is dealt with, then yes, I will." Bayn kissed her forehead, making her eyes burn from the sudden tenderness. "Let's go."

Bayn led her out into her back garden, where a pool of perfectly clear ice had formed on the courtyard stones.

"I'm confused," Freya said.

"Hold onto me," Bayn instructed, pulling her close and into the warmth under his overcoat. Freya pressed her hands along his back as Bayn tightened his grip. "Don't scream."

"Why would I—" Freya said and screamed as Bayn stepped through the ice. Freya held onto him as they were pulled through a blurred world of grey and blue and black. Just when she thought she would hurl, they were dragged upwards again, and they popped out on the ice at the edge of a lake.

Freya drew in a massive, frightened breath into her burning lungs before smacking Bayn's chest.

"You could have warned me!" she shouted. Bayn pulled her close again, his whole body shaking with laughter.

"I'm sorry, I didn't want to warn you in case you refused to try it." Bayn rubbed her back. "You were safe. I had you."

"If you ruined my hair, I'm going to kill you," Freya sniffed, pulling back from him. He looked her over and adjusted a curl over her neck, fingers lingering on her skin.

"Perfect, as always," he assured her.

"Stop sucking up."

"No."

Freya ignored him, turning to look behind her and up at the glowing mansion. It had been built right by the lakeside, with glass walls along the front to admire the view. She could already see the glittering party-goers moving about with drinks in their hands.

"Shall we, mistress?" Bayn offered her his arm. Freya took it and tried not to smile. He lifted her off the ice and onto a wooden deck so she didn't have to slog through the snow in her nice boots. It was the kind of thoughtful gesture, like making her breakfast, that made Freya's heart soften in ways she didn't know were healthy for her. She had always been so independent that to have someone be considerate of her messed with her head.

Well, he is ancient. Maybe it's a fae manners thing? Even as she thought about it, she knew it was wrong. Bayn didn't do anything he didn't want to, even social niceties.

"What's the matter? You have the strangest look on your face just now," he said.

"It's nothing," Freya replied automatically and then stopped walking. "Just promise when we stop the traffickers, and you have the dagger that you won't disappear on me?"

Bayn's concerned frown lifted in surprise. "You don't want me to? I thought you wanted your life to go back to normal."

Freya shook her head. "Maybe I could live without the bombs in my apartment, but I don't want you to go back to Scotland and never talk to me again. I...like you."

"I promise I won't disappear back to Scotland." Bayn kissed the top of her head. "I like you too."

Freya smiled, a pressure in a chest releasing. "Good. Now, let's go charm everyone we meet, *Bjørn*."

"You will have to do the charming because I don't talk, remember?"

Freya reached up and pinched his cheek. "That's right, you just focus on looking pretty."

Bayn gave her a look that promised retribution, but they were interrupted by a guard.

"What are you two doing down here?" he demanded.

"Just taking in the beautiful sights," Freya replied and passed him the card that Dieter's assistant had given her that day.

"My apologies, madame, please come this way. We are due for another temperature drop in the next hour. We wouldn't want you to freeze," the guard replied with an apologetic smile. Bayn's arm tightened fractionally, making Freya's grin widen.

"Such a gentleman. Please, lead the way," she said sweetly.

Inside of the mansion was filled with treasures. Expensive art hung on the walls, contrasting with the ancient manuscripts on the bookshelves. Music was being played through invisible speakers, and everywhere she looked, people were drinking, laughing, kissing, or conspiring. She kept her expression neutrally pleasant and indifferent as eyes lingered on Bayn like he was one of the evening's entertainments.

Don't lose that Viking temper of yours, Freya. She had to keep reminding herself that it was why they had been invited. She had never been so overprotective of Leif or any of her other ex-boyfriends, but as soon as someone looked at Bayn, she wanted to snarl at them like a beast.

What the hell is the matter with you? You're not even a couple. You're working together. But no matter how much she told herself that, her feelings of possessiveness were only getting worse.

∼

AN HOUR and many tedious conversations later, Freya retreated to a women's powder room. She had collected a handful of business cards that she would give over to Arne and the elves so they could investigate them. 'Like-minded' people, Dieter's assistant said. It turned out what they were all obsessed with was the fae and the power the magical creatures had...and how they could acquire it. Bringing Bayn amongst them was a mistake. They all desperately wanted to paw at him like he was an exotic pet...

Freya went to the sinks and scrubbed at her hands to try and get the sensation of other people touching them off of her. A small choked sound of someone trying to muffle their cries came from behind one of the cubicle doors.

"Hello?" Freya dried her hands and tapped on the door. "Are you okay?"

"Yes, I'm fine."

"Doesn't sound like it."

The door opened to reveal a beautiful woman in a golden dress. Her silky black hair was tied up in braids and threaded with gold. Freya's attention snagged on her ears that curved into delicate points.

"You're an elf?" she asked. The woman gave her a stern look.

"I'm not for sale."

"Oh god, no. That's not why I ask." Freya scanned the room and under the cubicles to make sure they were alone. "Are you here against your will?"

"What do you think?" The woman held out her wrist where a thick iron ring sat. It was ugly and out of place next to her other stunning jewelry. Freya touched it to inspect the runes, and a wave of nausea hit her so hard, she recoiled. "Who are you?"

"My name is Freya. I'm here to find out who is responsible for trafficking magical beings. Do you know Arne?"

The woman lowered herself onto one of the couches in the room. "Arne Steelsinger?"

"Um, I don't know his last name. Tall, black hair, warrior, handsome as hell?"

"That's him. He's a legend amongst the elves. How do you know him?"

"I met him through my fae friend, Bayn. He rescued an elf called Yrsa in Oslo and got her back to your people," Freya explained.

The woman clutched at her chest. "Yrsa is alive."

"Yes, and safe. The same way I'd like you to be."

"My name is Estrid, and there is no escaping this thing." She shook the runic bracelet at her.

"Arne or Bayn will find a way." Freya took photos of the bracelet and one of Estrid. "Who did this to you?"

"The one called Dieter. He sent me here tonight as another of his acquisitions, to show the others what he can provide to them."

"Is Dieter here?"

Estrid shook her head. "He doesn't ever leave his house. I'm not sure where it is. They always cover my head. I know it's in the northern islands."

"Okay, I'm going to message Arne and see what we can do about the cuff. We will get you out, I promise." Freya sent the photos through to Bayn with instructions. "Now, we better leave these bathrooms before someone comes looking for you." Freya helped Estrid tidy her makeup, which had smeared from her crying.

Shaking with anger, Freya tried to get a grip on herself as she returned to the party. Bayn was at the bar, already waiting with a cocktail for her.

"Interesting trip to the bathroom?" Bayn said softly. He stroked her forearm. "Freya, you need to take a breath. Your face is red with fury, and you look ready to burn this house to the ground. People will notice."

"Kiss me," she said. Bayn didn't hesitate, he just gave her a deep kiss with zero fucks if they had an audience. Freya's hand rested on his chest, and she let his strength and warmth steady her.

"Better?" he asked.

"Yes, at least now, if I'm flushed, people will think it's because I'm overcome with desire."

Bayn raised a dark brow. "And you're not?"

"Well, maybe a bit," she admitted and had a mouthful of her cold cocktail. "Did you forward the messages to Arne?"

"Yes, he's dispatching a team that will be here in an hour to extract Estrid and get rid of that infernal charm off her wrist. I would like to know how a human like Dieter knows such magic."

As if saying his name summoned the devil, the assistant that Freya had started to fantasize about strangling, arrived at the bar with a welcoming smile.

"Freya, you came. I'm so pleased you also brought your handsome companion," he said. Freya tapped Bayn on the chest.

"Don't leave home without him. He's the best accessory I have ever had," she replied with a sly smile.

"I don't doubt it. Dieter has asked for an audience. If you would follow me," the assistant said, not really asking at all.

"It would be my pleasure. I didn't know he was here," Freya replied. She took Bayn's hand and hung onto it with a death grip.

The assistant led them up a curved flight of stairs and into a room with no windows, its walls painted black. The only piece of furniture was a small black table with a laptop open on it.

"And this is where I leave you," the assistant said with a bow. As soon as he left the room, the laptop screen turned on, and they got their first look at the illusive Dieter. It was absolutely no surprise to Freya that he was a middle-aged white man with a stylish haircut and unremarkable features.

"Freya Havisdottir, I have heard so much about you," Dieter said. His accent was softly German with the faintest Norwegian lilt. His hazel eyes looked at Bayn. "Ah, and your companion. Bjørn, wasn't it?" Bayn only nodded. Dieter chuckled unpleasantly.

"I wouldn't believe everything that Leif tells you, Dieter. I assume he's your source?" Freya asked, moving in front of Bayn. He rested his hand on her back to steady her.

"Leif is an ambitious man and is very upset that you broke into his mansion and stole his things." Dieter held up a photo of Bayn entering the back doors. "You got all the cameras inside, but not out, my friend."

"He stole from me first, and I did warn him that I would get my revenge eventually," Freya said, keeping her voice calm. "You know how it is. Reputation is everything."

"Indeed. Before Bjørn scared away Leif's men, they took a photo of your desk too. Can you tell me what interest you have in this object?" Dieter held up another photo of her illustration of Odin's dagger.

Fuck fuck fuck.

Freya shrugged. "I'm looking for it. I have an obsession with Odin. My name is Havisdottir, after all."

"And this page? Where is it from?"

"I have my sources. Why do you care?"

Dieter smiled and held a dagger out to the camera. *The* dagger.

"Shut the fuck up. Where did you find it?" asked Freya, trying to put all of her terror out as excitement.

"I have my sources too."

"Did Professor Hans Weber find it for you?"

Dieter's brows rose. "My, my, you did do your research. It doesn't matter how or where I found the dagger, only that I did. Now, how badly do you want it?"

"Why? Are you interested in selling it?"

"If the price is right. And no, I don't need any more money. Money is common and easy to acquire. I'm only interested in the rare and divine." Freya knew what was coming, and it still filled her with blinding anger. "I want your fae."

"Bjørn? Why? I'm sure that a man such as you has acquired his own fae. Your assistant seems very open with offering to buy anyone he sees," Freya said, and Bayn rubbed her back again as if telling her to calm down.

"True, but I want him. He has a skill set that my other slaves do not. I was impressed with the state that he left Leif's mansion in. Quite spectacular. I have many uses for a male like that." Dieter twirled the dagger in his hands before sheathing it again. "That's the deal I offer."

"I'll have to think about it. Bjørn is very helpful to me, so his loss will be great. I have to weigh up if Odin's dagger will be worth it," said Freya, thoughtfully.

"I understand." Dieter looked at his watch. "Although, I do advise you don't take too long. Leif has sent bounty hunters after you, and they are closing in. I'd hate for you to miss out on this deal and lose your fae too." The screen went dark, and Freya snapped it shut.

"How close do you think those hunters are?" she asked, unplugging the laptop. Bayn cocked his head, listening.

"They are downstairs, searching the party. I can hear the murmurs of the guests." Bayn had gone from charming arm candy to a cold-blooded killer in seconds. He pulled a dagger hilt from his pocket, a blade of ice forming on it. He turned and kissed Freya once, quick and hard. "Stay close to me."

"I will," she promised, clutching the laptop to her chest.

Bayn cracked open the door, struck one guard in the throat, dodged a blow from another, and stabbed him in the armpit. Freya didn't look at the blood, just stepped around it and kept focused on Bayn's back. Heavy, booted feet were coming up the stairs, and Freya reached for the back of Bayn's coat.

"We can't go down, so we go out," he whispered. He tried the nearest door, but it was locked. With a powerful kick, he broke the door down and pulled her into a bedroom as bullets flew past their heads.

Bayn's power burst out of him, smashing out the glass doors leading to a balcony. Without a second to argue, he scooped Freya up and jumped off the side. They landed in deep snow, and Bayn pushed through it to get into the shelter of the trees.

Freya spotted men with torches running around cars. "They are coming from the left side of the house." Bayn put her back on her feet and took her hand.

"Don't let go. Don't let them separate us. We just need to get somewhere safe and I'll portal us out," he said, and they began running. Bayn never let her fall, and Freya didn't know how he could see a damn thing. Whizzing sounds streaked past her head, and Bayn yanked her behind a tall pine.

"Stay!" he commanded, letting her go. Magic charged the air between them, and Bayn started throwing ice daggers into the darkness as quickly as they formed in his hands. He was so focused on what was in front that he didn't see the man coming up from his right-hand side.

No! Freya scrambled, dumping the laptop, and raced toward him. She had done knife disarms so many times in her self-defense class that her muscle memory overrode her fear. She knocked the man's knife arm to the side, took the knife in a quick move, and drove it into his neck with a shout. Bayn whipped around, slicing the man open with his blade as he fell. Freya was panting, staring at the blood on her hands.

"No time to go into shock, Freya!" Bayn grabbed the laptop off the snow with one hand and threw her over his shoulder with the other. Freya hung onto his back as he cleared the trees and ran out onto the frozen lake. Bullets flew past them, one striking at their feet.

Freya screamed as the ice cracked underneath them. Bayn shouted something as they hit the freezing water, and she was sucked into a world of pain and darkness.

17

Freya's body was screaming like acid was being poured over her skin. The roaring darkness suddenly ended, and she fell through the air, Bayn catching her before she smashed onto the polished floor of a throne room.

Bayn started shouting something in the language of the fae, giving orders as he held Freya close and all but ran through the halls.

"You're going to be okay. We just need to get you heated up," he said, trying to reassure her. Her hands clung feebly at his clothes, and Freya saw the blood still on them.

"I k-killed—" she tried to say through chattering teeth.

"He would've killed you and me if you hadn't. It was self-defense," Bayn replied. The air was getting warmer as they passed through a large bedroom the size of her apartment and through another wooden door.

Blessed heat curled over her skin as he placed her down next to a steaming, sunken pool.

"I'm going to help you strip and get you into the sauna to get your body temp back up," he said, and gripping the back of the coat, he tore the frozen fabric in half. He took it off, carefully making sure her skin wasn't stuck to it. "You weren't in the water very long, but you're so fucking human, Freya."

Bayn sounded more unstable by the second, his hands shaking as he helped her stand and get out of the rest of her clothes. Wrapping a thick towel around her, he carried her into a hot sauna room, placed her down on one of the pine benches, and put another towel over her.

"I'll be right back. I'm going to get a healing elixir and some water." He kissed her frozen cheek and disappeared.

You killed someone to save him, a small voice whispered in her mind. In that second, Freya hadn't thought about the law or morality. It was with pure, feral instinct when she drove the knife into the man who was going to hurt Bayn.

Freya's body started to pound as it thawed, sharp pains shooting through her. With numb hands, she did her best to rub the cramps out of her legs.

The sauna door opened, and Bayn came in with a towel slung low around his waist. Freya momentarily forgot the pain in her body as she stared at the tattoos covering his arms and chest.

Bayn offered her a glass vial with a pale pink liquid inside. "Here, drink this. It will help." He popped the cork off and passed it to her. Freya managed to keep her grip on it as she tipped it into her mouth. It tasted of rose creams and sunshine as it went down. Her lips started to tingle, and her throat and chest warmed. Whatever it was, it worked quickly. Bayn took the empty vial and passed her a bottle of water.

"Thanks," she said hoarsely.

"You don't ever have to thank me for trying to save your life, Freya. You wouldn't have been in that horrible place if it wasn't for me. That knife wouldn't have hurt me either. The magic in my tattoos would have protected me. They are wards. Never do that again. My heart can't take it."

Freya nodded, too shaken up to answer him. Bayn went out and came back with a dish of water and cloths. He washed the blood from her hands and wiped the remains of the make-up from her face with the same tenderness that made Freya's emotional walls collapse. Tears clogged her throat, but she swallowed them down.

"Where are we?" she asked.

"At my castle in Scotland. As soon as we hit the water, I panicked and took us to the only place I can guarantee your safety," Bayn replied, putting the bowl and cloths aside. "Are you ready for more heat?"

Freya nodded, and he ladled some water on the hot stones. Steam filled the air, and Freya leaned back against the wall with a sigh.

"It's been a long time since I had a decent sauna. Crap circumstances, but a decent end to the night," she tried to joke. Bayn's intense frown eased a little.

"Your sense of humor is coming back. That healing potion must be working," he replied. "Our phones and the laptop are waterlogged, but I have people that can restore them. I hope Arne and the elves razed that fucking mansion to the ground. You know, sending bounty hunters after us was a declaration of war, Freya. If they had come after me alone, maybe I would have handled it differently. But they shot at you, and I won't ever forgive that." His voice was filling with rage again, so Freya grabbed his hand.

"Look at me. I'm okay."

"You could've *died,* Freya," Bayn growled.

"You're not going to get rid of me that easily, Winter Prince," she huffed.

"Stop joking about this! If anything happened to you, I'd lose my goddamn mind."

"Why? You barely know me!"

Bayn's sapphire eyes filled with cold fire. "That's bullshit. You know me in your very bones, like I know you, summer. You're lying to yourself if you say otherwise. There's a reason you killed that man tonight, and why you're so vicious whenever anyone tries to buy me. We belong to each other. It's as simple as that."

"You seem very sure," Freya said, folding her arms. A deep pulsing ache was spreading through her chest as his words settled inside of her. After everything that had happened with Leif, she had promised herself, never again. Never again would she let a man have any power over her heart. And yet, here she was.

"I've been sure of it since the moment I heard you sing. I'm just waiting patiently for you to catch up."

Freya thought about being bent over her counter, and she grinned. "Not that patient."

Bayn shook his head. "You're still making jokes? Infuriating woman."

"It's why you love me," Freya quipped automatically. Bayn's expression shifted to the kind of helplessness that she sometimes glimpsed when he thought she wasn't looking. For the first time, she realized what that look meant. Oh. *Oh.*

"Are you feeling warm yet?" Bayn asked, changing the subject and looking away from her.

"Yes." In fact, Freya was starting to burn up, but it wasn't just from the sauna.

It's not only you feeling things. That's a good thing. It was, and yet it freaked the holy hell out of her. If she struggled to have a half-decent relationship with a man, how much more complicated would one be with a fae male?

To distract herself, Freya pulled what remained of her hairpins out, unraveled her damp hair, and finger-combed it to get out the worst of the snarls.

"I want to know if Arne got Estrid out. That cuff she was wearing, I had the same reaction to it that I had to the business card," she said.

Bayn poured another ladle full of water on the sauna stones. "It was most likely created by the same practitioner. Maybe Deiter has someone on his payroll capable of such magic."

"Or it's Dieter himself. Like all the other people at his house tonight, he's obsessed with magical creatures and their relics. Maybe he's trying to teach himself magic. Now that it's returned, there's no reason why humans can't start using it too with the proper instruction." Freya turned so he could see her back. "These runic tattoos were done by a human. Although I'm tempted to get my money back because they don't seem to work."

"They work, Freya, just not on me," said Bayn, tracing the lines of one of the runes with his finger. "I can feel the magic in them."

"And why don't they work on you again?"

Bayn shrugged. "Probably because I'm too strong for them, or the magic recognizes that I'm not a threat to you... and that you want me to touch you."

Freya rolled her eyes. "Did you get all those big muscles from carrying your ego around?"

"You noticed my big muscles?" Bayn gave her a shit-eating grin, and she flushed.

"Kind of hard not to when you are flashing them about." Sweat was finally starting to bead on her skin, so Freya grabbed one of the spare cloths and wiped her face. Her hands were shaking like they knew she was about to go past the point of no return.

Bayn leaned back on the wall, putting his arms behind his head and making his tattooed biceps flex. He sighed. "So much for gratitude."

"Oh, you want gratitude, do you? After making me almost freeze to death while we somehow traveled *through* the ice and popped out thousands of kilometers from my home?" Freya didn't understand why she was picking a fight with him, but she could not stop now that she had started.

"You can't go home until we send people to make sure it's safe. Leif wants to kill us if those bounty hunters were anything to judge by."

"Leif only wants to kill me because you attacked him!" Freya pointed out.

"Is that so? I'm pretty sure it was a matter of time before he came after you. Even Von said that he hadn't gotten over the fact you had left him. Now that he's got some power, I'm sure Leif would've eventually gotten one of those runic cuffs around your wrist too."

Freya hadn't thought of that. Leif would have done it, not to keep her because he loved her, but out of spite. She was going to be sick.

"Look at me." Bayn lifted her chin. "He's never going to touch you again, Freya. I will kill him if he tries."

"Why are you so protective of me?"

"Because you snarled at Dieter's assistant when he tried to buy me. Because you said afterward that I'm yours." Bayn ran his thumb over her bottom lip. "You're mine too, summer. Don't ever forget that."

Freya couldn't hold back anymore. She leaned up and kissed him. Bayn's strong hands moved down her shoulders, pulling her closer. Freya climbed into his lap, her arms going around his neck as she lost herself in the deepening kiss. She pulled back from him, trying to catch her breath.

Pushing Bayn's tousled dark hair from his face, Freya whispered, "Yeah, I'm falling in love with you too."

Every muscle in him seemed to lock up, and she suddenly wished she could take the confession back.

"You're in shock. You saw what I am tonight when I cut down those men in the woods. You can't mean that," he said, words quick and disjointed.

Freya took his face in her hands and did her best to push down her sudden anger. "Don't you dare try and tell me I don't know my own mind. It's okay if you don't feel the same, but I got shot at tonight, and I'm likely to get shot at again until Dieter is stopped. So I'm saying it now, *way* too early, because I don't want to die without you knowing."

Bayn frowned as he took in her reasoning. "I just ruined the moment, didn't I?"

"Yeah, you really did."

"Say it again, so I'm ready for it."

Freya shook her head. "Nope. I'm only going to say it once, and now you'll have to wait until after Dieter is dealt with to hear it again because I feel embarrassed."

"Why? I've told you from the first time I was with you that I wanted more from you than a good, hard fuck. You didn't see me being embarrassed about starting to fall in love with you, which happened the moment you dropped my card in the bin."

Freya laughed. She couldn't help it. He was so damn gorgeous when he was sincere. "Then why did you question it when I said I was starting to feel the same?"

"Because I'm not worthy of it, no matter how much I want it."

"Bayn? Shut up and deal with it," Freya said stubbornly. He opened his mouth to argue again, so she untucked the edge of her towel and let it fall down to her waist. "Oh no, would you look at that? My towel fell off."

Bayn's gaze dropped to her breasts, eyes turning feral with desire. "Freya, I'm trying to be a good male here."

"I know. It's one of the reasons I want you, for more than a night, for something serious. If you want it too." She wished she could be more articulate, but the way he was staring at her, with that mixture of longing and helplessness, it was undoing all her confidence.

Bayn's smile turned wolfish, and he bent down to kiss the side of her neck. "Is this what I think it is? Are you finally giving into me?"

"I don't like to think of it as giving in, but a mutual consent to fuck until we choose to stop," Freya replied. She began to lift her towel back up. "But if you're not interested—"

"Must you always try and stir me up?" he asked, placing his hand on the towel to stop it going any higher. She was about to hit him with another smart ass reply when he put his hand on her breast and gently squeezed. Bayn kissed her, and her hands slid into his hair.

"Finally," he said against her lips, pulling her tight up against him. "Finally, I have you."

Freya thought she was going to combust as Bayn's mouth made a path along her collar bone and over the curve of her breast. *Finally* was about right.

Freya had wanted Bayn's sinful lips on her again since the night of the first auction. She hung onto his shoulders as he gently bent her back, keeping one arm around her so she didn't fall, and he got better access to both breasts.

"I promise that you won't ever regret this. Regret me," he murmured as lips and tongue tasted her.

"I better not." Freya moved her hands between them so she could untuck his towel. God, he was beautiful everywhere, and if she wasn't so horny, she might have been intimidated. *Might* have.

Freya traced her nails along the curving patterns of his tattoos. "These are amazing. I haven't stopped thinking about them."

"I like knowing you've been thinking about me." His hand skimmed down to pull away her own towel. Bayn made a satisfied growly sound in the back of his throat.

"Have you been thinking about me too?" Freya couldn't resist asking because he was still staring at her, mesmerized like he had never seen a naked woman before.

"Every bit of you has been on my mind. Constantly. Painfully." Bayn stroked between her thighs, making her rise up on her knees and grab onto his shoulders. He toyed with her clit, applying the slightest pressure, knowing precisely what made her gasp. He kissed her, pulling that gasp right out of her mouth.

"Let me know if you get too hot."

"Isn't that the point?" Freya asked, slightly dazed.

Bayn bit her lip playfully. "I meant the sauna. If you're going to pass out tonight, it's going to be from coming so hard you blackout, not from dehydration."

Freya half laughed, half groaned as he slipped a finger inside of her. He was already hard beneath her, so she stroked him, taking her time to touch him. She was going to explode if she didn't get him inside of her.

Bayn cursed softly as he watched her touch herself and slick him down with her own wetness.

"Ride me," he begged, lifting her by the hips. "I want to see you, every second." Freya guided him inside of her, gently moving up and then a little further down to allow her body to adjust to the size of him.

Bayn let out a sound between a whimper and a growl, and it almost undid her. She grabbed his hair, pulling him back to her mouth as she fitted him all the way.

"Holy fucking gods," Bayn murmured, his breathing heavy, hands tightening on her hips. "You feel so fucking good."

Freya pressed her forehead to his. "You do too." Then she began to move, getting lost in the sensation of him and her own pleasure.

For the first time, she let go and took what she wanted, setting the pace until they were both sweating and panting.

Freya groaned as he scooped water up in his hand and let it trickle slowly down her back, cooling her as she rode him harder. The orgasm she had been chasing hit her swiftly, and her nails dug deep into Bayn's sweating chest as wet, aching heat raced through her.

"You're so beautiful when you come," Bayn said, his arms clenching around her. In a smooth move, he twisted her back onto the wide wooden bench.

Freya locked her trembling legs around his hips as he took over and plunged back inside of her. She stared at his powerful muscles flexing with every shift and thrust inside of her. She could've come again from that sight alone.

"My perfect, pain in the ass fae love," she whispered.

Freya's skin lit up with indigo runes making her gasp in awe. Bayn groaned as they danced from her to him, and suddenly they were both glowing and coming together. Bayn kissed her until their pulses calmed, whispering in fae every time they came up for air. Freya hung onto him, scared that if she let him go, she would fall.

"I need to get you out of this heat," Bayn said, gently sliding off her.

"You're going to have to carry me. My body is incapable of moving," Freya panted, struggling to get her breath back. Bayn chuckled a thoroughly satisfied male sound and scooped her up in his arms. He carried her through the sauna door and lowered her into the pool, Freya's skin steaming as the water cooled her down.

"Looks like my servants are earning their keep," Bayn commented as he found the water bottles and cold beer that had been set out for them.

Freya took the chilled beer he offered her. "They earned a raise."

"They are brownies. They don't want money, only the chance to be useful."

Bayn got into the water beside her and positioned her back against his chest, so her head rested on his shoulder. They sipped their beers in comfortable silence, Freya too exhausted to form words.

"What's with the runes, Bayn?" she asked finally.

"It's nothing to be worried about. Just a fae way of saying you're perfect for me in every way," he replied, a touch flippantly. "Something I already knew."

Freya frowned. "So it's like a compatibility magic?"

"Exactly."

"Well, considering you just fucked my brains to mush, I'd say it's spot on."

"As you did mine." Bayn laughed loudly and kissed her. "You know, I've laughed more in the past few weeks with you than I ever had in my life? Believe it or not, I'm known as the surly prince."

"I can't help that I'm naturally hilarious." Freya turned her head to kiss his shoulder. "And I *can* believe you are the surly prince. I've seen your glower. I'm sure it's been used to terrify men and fae alike over the centuries."

Bayn looked savage again as he said, "Oh, summer, if only you knew."

18

Bayn stood at the end of his bed, watching Freya sleep. She was naked and wrapped in furs, her golden hair in bright tangled waves against the pillows. She was so beautiful that his chest hurt looking at her.

The curse's white lines had left his heart and now only came to the middle of his torso. Freya was healing it, healing *him*, just by being around him. The mating bond was growing between them, clawing at him and urging him to make her his forever. After last night, it was a loud, maddening chant in his head.

I'm falling in love with you too. Freya's words were still shattering him. He hadn't expected it, even as he wished for it. The runes that had danced on their skin only hours before felt like hope, not a death sentence.

You can do this. He could be the mate she needed. The mate she deserved. Part of that was keeping her safe from the god's damned assholes who had shot at her.

Bayn took one last look before shutting the bedroom door behind him. He took out his new phone and rang Killian. On the seventh ring, the infuriating bastard finally answered.

"What?" Killian asked, sounding like he had his face in a pillow.

"Wake up, asshole. We have a problem."

Killian muttered a series of elaborate and ancient curses. Bayn went out onto a balcony and took in the calming winter landscape below, letting his eldest brother drag himself out of bed.

"Okay, I'm upright, and coffee is on. What's the problem now?" Killian asked.

"I got attacked last night by bounty hunters."

Killian sniggered. "Who did you piss off this time, baby boy?"

"The ex-boyfriend of my mate," Bayn replied.

"What mate? You have a mate? When did this happen? Why wasn't I told?"

"Because you never answer your fucking phone. I'm surprised Elise hasn't called you to gloat. It's her cousin Freya. Elise sent me to her to search for a dagger..." Bayn let the whole story tumble out, needing Killian to understand that bounty hunters were bad for everyone, not just him.

"I suppose the only real question I have is: why the fuck didn't Elise introduce me to her cousin before you? Surely, she likes me better than you. Is the cousin hot?" Killian asked. The snarl was out of Bayn's throat before he could control it. "Ohh, very tough. Hang on, Kian is trying to get in on this call. Your phone have a camera?"

"Yes, but why—" Bayn didn't get a chance to turn it off before his brothers' faces appeared on the screen. Killian started laughing.

"Look at you with a sex glow. Your mate must be exhausted," he teased.

"Try not to be too jealous," Bayn replied. He had a glow?

"You have told Freya she is your mate then?" Kian interrupted.

"I'm getting to it. Haven't had the time with fucking people trying to shoot her. We have fae bounty hunters working again. Not good for any of us."

Kian frowned. "Fae bounty hunters. What was that family called that almost assassinated you, Killian?"

"Ironwood. My thigh still hurts where they shot me with a crossbow bolt. Half an inch to the right, and they would've got my pride," Killian complained.

"What did you do to them again?" Bayn asked.

"I was so impressed I let the assassin go and told them better luck next time. I'm sure if they are still around, they've forgotten about it. Wait, you don't think they're still operational, do you? They were based here in Ireland, and they never had their fae population banished like England did."

Kian shook his head. "No, surely not. It's just the last time we had to deal with bounty hunters, that's all. And you getting shot was hilarious." He looked at Bayn. "Do you need our help? The elves sent me a message to say that Freya's store is clear, but they didn't get to the house in Trondheim in time to save their female. I'll message them to let them know about the hunters too."

"Freya might be able to give us more on what Estrid said about Dieter's other house," Bayn said thoughtfully.

"Well, go and get her. I want to meet her," Killian insisted, running his hand through his thick black hair to neaten it. He flashed his lady killer smile.

"She's sleeping, and I'm not going to wake her just to inflict you on her. She went through a traumatic experience last night."

"If your fucking is bad enough to be classified as a trauma, you're doing it wrong, baby brother."

"Fuck off, Killian. I was talking about her getting shot at and stabbing someone for the first time," Bayn growled. He ran a frustrated hand over his face. "I'm going. Kian, please message the elves. Killian, try not to get yourself killed for being a raging asshole."

"There it is, the little icicle I know and love," Killian replied. Bayn hung up on the both of them. Gods, they were exhausting.

Bayn knew he would have to take Freya back to Norway, but for now, he was going to take the day and curl back up with her. He opened the bedroom door, but Freya was gone.

"Freya?" Bayn checked the bathroom, but she wasn't there either.

Where did she go? He cleared his mind and closed his eyes. It was his castle, and he could find anything in it. He placed a hand on the wall and sent a silent command to find her. The answer came back, and he started running.

Fuck, fuck, please don't let her see it. But he was too late. The door to the lower halls was open. He found Freya standing in front of the throne of ice, surrounded by his enemies' frozen bodies.

∼

FREYA HAD WOKEN ALONE, every part of her pleasantly exhausted except for her stomach that was demanding food. She found some of Bayn's clothes in a dresser and stole a shirt and a pair of pajama pants with a drawstring she could use to keep them up. Wrapping herself in a coat, she went exploring.

Freya had imagined the Winter Prince's castle to be made entirely of snow. In reality, only the columns and ceiling were made of blue glacier ice, designs carved across them. The rest was dark, polished wood. It wasn't cold, but nothing was melting.

She touched an ice pillar and felt something tug inside her like when she could sense a magical object. She closed her eyes and tried to touch whatever was calling out to her. The ice stopped feeling cold. It felt...alive. Freya stepped back in surprise. Was Bayn's magic inside of it that kept it from melting? She would have to ask him.

Freya kept moving down to the next floor and paused by a door laced with ice patterns.

Where have I seen this? It felt familiar like she had been there before. Freya pushed open the door and went inside.

Bayn's nightmare that she had been sucked into flashed through her mind as she looked at the fae, men, and creatures that were frozen statues around the hall. Covering her mouth with her hand, Freya stepped around them, drawn to the dais where a throne of ice sat.

"No, no, it was a nightmare..." she murmured. It was the exact throne that Bayn had been disappearing into.

You will never have him, she told it silently, backing away from it. Even if Freya had to find his damn mate to break the curse, she would do it. She wouldn't let him be consumed by the curse, destined to be another frozen male in the hall of the dead.

Freya turned, and Bayn was standing amongst the dead, a look of despair on his face.

"What is this place?" she asked, her breath fogging out in front of her.

"This is a room that hasn't been used in a long time," Bayn said. She wished he would take her hand, but he refused to move a step closer. His walls that had come crashing down over the last few days were back up, locking her out.

"These are my enemies. I have always been the family's executioner and assassin. This room was used to intimidate anyone who even dreamt about crossing us. Faerie is a harsh, cruel place, and when we were locked into lands that weren't our own, we subdued it, conquered it, made it safe for our people that were caught up in the curse with us."

"You killed all these people?" Freya couldn't fathom it, the burden of being an executioner.

"Yes. And many more." Bayn crossed his arms, his shoulders going back.

"Bayn..." Freya began, but he didn't give her a chance to speak.

"I'm taking you home. Arne has assured us that your store is safe, and you don't belong in this place."

Freya worked hard to keep the hurt from her face. She wanted to tell him about the nightmare, that she wouldn't let him disappear into the throne. One look at his face, and she knew he wasn't in the mood to listen to anything she had to say. She nodded and followed him into the next set of rooms.

A frozen pool stood in the middle of another hall, and Bayn stopped in front of it. Instead of pulling her close, like he always had, Bayn gripped her by the shoulders, and they stepped through the ice.

Freya shut her eyes tight, cold and darkness whipping around her. Then Bayn gave her jacket a hard tug, and they emerged in her courtyard in Oslo.

Freya leaned over her knees, fighting to keep herself upright as her mind and body tried to sync up with each other.

"Stay here, I'll do a check inside," Bayn said, using magic to open her doors.

Freya didn't know why he was so angry. She knew he wasn't some angel, that he was a warrior and a prince, with all the blood on his hands that came with it. She needed to talk to him, assure him that it didn't matter...

Bayn reappeared and opened the door for her. "Everything is clear. Nothing has been touched since yesterday."

"Thanks," Freya said. She went to touch him, but he stepped back from her.

"I need to go and talk to Arne. What do you remember Estrid saying about Dieter's other house?"

"She didn't know where it was, only that it was on an island in the north."

Bayn gave her a stern look. "Don't leave, not even for a run. I want to make sure there's no one watching from other buildings."

"Bayn, don't go. We need to talk—"

"No, we don't. I need to make sure no one is going to put a fucking bullet in you. Keep the curtains closed, and don't argue with me just this once, Freya." Bayn was out of her back gate and gone before she could stop him.

19

Freya spent the rest of the day pacing the store and the apartment, making food to stress eat and wondering when Bayn would come back. She tried to distract herself by checking emails, doing her business bookkeeping, and making a list of all the small islands in the north where Dieter might be hiding.

Freya didn't have a phone, otherwise, she would have called Elise for advice on dealing with fae male mood swings.

Mixed in with her worry about where Bayn was hiding was a wave of growing anger that he would just walk away without talking to her. *He* was the one determined not to have sex until she was sure she wanted to be serious, then she was, and now he was backing out as fast as possible. *Not going to happen.*

Freya was trying to watch the news when Bayn finally did come back. It was almost nine o'clock, and she was past the point of worry.

"Here, have something to eat," Bayn said, putting some bags down on the table. He looked as pissed off as ever.

"Don't use that fucking tone with me," snapped Freya, getting to her feet. "You might be a prince, but I'm not one of your subjects."

Bayn shrugged. "Fine. Don't eat."

"What is your problem? Why are you so fucking angry at me?" Freya closed in on him, not knowing if she wanted to kiss him or hit him.

"I'm not angry with you."

"I thought sex would lighten you up, not make you grumpier. What changed since last night? You are okay with fucking me, but not with talking afterward?" Freya asked, getting in his face. "Is it because I saw your hall of the dead? You think I'm some naive girl who didn't know what you were when I spread my thighs?"

"You think you're so tough? I saw your face when I found you in there. You were horrified and disgusted. You can't pretend that you weren't," Bayn replied.

"Not with you! The night I woke you from the nightmare, I saw what you were dreaming." Freya charged on, not giving him a second to interrupt her.

"You were disappearing into that throne bit by bit. I didn't know it was a real place! I saw the throne and panicked because I was trapped in the nightmare again, losing you bit by bit. *That's* the horror you saw on my face, not at what you've done to protect your brothers and your people. I could never understand what you went through or judge you for carrying out the law of the fae."

Bayn looked like he had been kicked in the guts. The walls behind his eyes came down, and Freya glimpsed the worry and torment inside of them. She couldn't handle it. She crashed into him, wrapping her arms tight around his waist.

Freya was shaking, afraid he would disappear again and never come back. She was desperate and panicking like she never had before, stress tears starting to fall before she could stop them.

"I'll get the dagger off Dieter, and if that doesn't work, I'll find your mate for you. I don't care, I'm not going to let your curse freeze you."

"Fuck, Freya. Don't cry," Bayn begged, and it only made her cry more. Swearing under his breath, Bayn picked her up and carried her over to the couch. He wiped the tears off her cheeks.

"I'm sorry, I upset you. I assumed you were disgusted with me, so I was trying to give you some space."

Freya pushed back from him. "You should've stayed and talked to me and not been a big fae asshole. Where were you all day?"

"On the roof mostly." Bayn gave her an embarrassed look. "I was setting wards over the building so nothing can get in or out without our permission. I met with Arne at the cafe across the street to keep an eye on you at the same time. He did the food delivery and brought you a new phone too. It's in the bag. I wasn't going to leave you alone. I couldn't."

Freya hugged him, resting her face against his neck. "Promise me you won't storm off like that again and leave me to worry about you. I'm too young to get grey hairs, Bayn."

"I'm sorry. I really thought you wouldn't want me anywhere near you."

"I'm not an idiot. I know you're not like other men. I don't care who you were when you were the executioner. I care who you are now. You *made* me care, so don't be a dick and lock me out now that I do."

"I promise I won't." Bayn tilted her face up and kissed her. "Did you really mean what you said about finding my mate if it means breaking my curse?"

Jealousy stabbed at Freya at the thought of another woman's hands on him. "If I have no other choice, I will. I might have to kill her after she breaks your curse, but I'll try not to if she makes you happy."

Bayn ran his fingers through her hair. "I have to tell you something —" Freya shifted back as Bayn's pocket started vibrating. "Wait, I have to answer this." He pulled out his phone and put it on speaker. "Arne, what did you find out?"

"We looked at the magic on the cuff that Freya took a photo of, and we recreated it to get a feel of its signature," the elf said. "To give you the abbreviated version, we used it to track the magic to Soroya. It's an island in the north. We've sent in a team to raid it."

Bayn's grip tightened a little. "Let me know what you find, and don't forget the dagger is ours."

"I'll call you in an hour," Arne replied, hanging up.

"That's good news. Hopefully, Estrid is okay after last night."

Bayn gave her arms a rub. "Come on, let's eat before our Pad Thai gets cold."

"You bought me Pad Thai?"

"And dumplings."

Freya shifted off him, fighting a smile. "Wow, you really were going to suck up, weren't you?"

"I was going to try, but then you gave me attitude and put me on the defensive," Bayn replied.

"You shouldn't have used your arrogant prince tone with me." Freya dug about in the bags, pulling out the dumplings.

"I shouldn't have done a lot of things today." Bayn got beers out of the fridge and cutlery from the drawers. It was a weirdly domestic moment that made Freya's heart flutter.

Freya thought about the conversation Arne had interrupted and decided not to bring it up again that night. She had only just cleared the air with Bayn and didn't want to have to talk about his mate that was still out there somewhere.

Arne would find Odin's dagger with any luck, and Freya wouldn't have to worry about Bayn's mate ever again.

An hour later, Freya was contemplating taking Bayn to bed for sweaty makeup sex when his phone started ringing again.

"Arne, how was the raid?" Bayn asked.

"Good and very bad. Estrid and two other elves were found hiding in the forest," Arne answered, his phone service crackling.

"And Dieter?"

"Dead. He had been dead for a few hours before we got there, and the house he was in had been cleared out. Estrid and the others escaped through a bathroom window as soon as Dieter died, and the magic in the cuffs broke. Bayn, I think you need to come and see this place before we burn it to the ground."

Bayn went still, eyes going cold. "Why? What is it?"

"They left a message for you," Arne said. "And it was written in Dieter's blood."

∽

DIETER'S HOUSE on the island of Soroya was another modern and stylish Scandinavian mansion with ocean views and a forest around it. Bayn had wanted to make Freya stay behind in Oslo, but his own need to protect her wouldn't let him risk not having her with him.

Damn mating bond. He knew it wasn't only that. Bayn was in love with her, and it scared him. He wasn't going to relax until he knew that Leif and the bounty hunters were in the ground.

Bayn could sense that Freya was still upset about their argument that day, and he wanted to punch himself in the face for making her cry. He had never been affected by the tears of anyone before. Seeing hers had shredded him from the inside out.

Dressed in proper winter gear this time, Freya had taken the trip through the ice a lot better. Bayn kept her gloved hand tight in his as they cleared the forest and found Arne waiting for them. He looked angry enough that his glare alone could've set the mansion on fire.

"Thanks for coming." Arne slanted a glance in Freya's direction. "You might want to stay here, Miss Havisdottir."

Freya's whiskey eyes narrowed. "I might not, Arne Steelsinger." Arne looked to Bayn, who only shrugged.

"If she wants to go, I'm not going to be the one to stop her," Bayn said. It was the right thing to say because Freya gave him a look so charged with desire that Arne cleared his throat.

"This way. Watch your step. There is debris and blood everywhere," the elf warned.

The back door of the mansion had been smashed in, so Bayn helped Freya around the broken bits of timber and up a set of stairs. The first level was a kitchen and dining area. The bookshelves had been emptied, the pictures on the walls taken, and furniture smashed. It was like a group of rampaging children had gone through it, leaving destruction behind. They went up to the second floor, following a trail of blood that stopped at the feet of a dead man.

"One of Dieter's bodyguards, we are assuming," said Arne. Freya looked away from it, keeping her eyes fixed on the half-open door in front of them. Blood sprays stained the white door, two bullet holes piercing it.

Bayn stepped into the office first, lifting Freya up over the pool of blood soaking the carpet. Dieter was sitting in a plush leather chair behind a black desk, a slit from his throat to his groin. Freya looked from the dead dealer to the message scrawled along the glass wall overlooking the sea.

Havi's dagger, for Havi's daughter.

"Fucking Leif," Freya ground out between clenched teeth. Bayn opened his mouth, but she held up a hand. "If you say 'You should've let me kill him,' I swear I will throw you off that balcony." Bayn shut his mouth again.

"There is nothing left of value. Dieter must have been expecting him because the security alarms were disarmed, and the bodyguards around the place didn't have their weapons drawn," Arne said. "They must have kicked out the back door to take out some larger item that needed the space."

"Where is Estrid? Is she okay?" Freya asked, looking away from the gory message.

"She and two of the other missing elves are on their way back home with Torsted. I had to give him something to do before he tore this place apart with his bare hands. Úlfhéðnar can be unpredictable in a rage, and I knew you would want to see this." Arne crossed his arms and looked at Freya. "This Leif, you know him best. What do you think his next move will be?"

"He's an arrogant cock face, so I'm assuming he will send us a message on where to meet for the exchange. It will be ridiculous however he gets it to us because that's his style," Freya said irritably.

Arne fought back a smile. "Did you just call him a cock face?"

"I said what I said." Freya frowned at Dieter's desk, her head dropping to one side.

"What's wrong?" Bayn asked.

"Something isn't right about this desk." Freya stepped on the clean patches of carpet to get a closer look. "It's antique. That's no surprise. How many drawers can you see on the other side?" Bayn went to stand next to Dieter's body to count them.

"Three. Why?"

"Because on this side there are four panels, not three, which means..." Freya took a letter opener from the desk, shoved it into the middle panel's join, and wedged it. With a sharp pop, the wood came off, and Freya laughed. "Leif is such an idiot." She pulled out a thick leather journal with a grimace. "I can feel Dieter's gross magic all over it."

Arne picked up a decorative pillow from the small couch and pulled its case off. "Here, put it in this, so you don't have to touch it."

"You take it, it's of no use to me, but you might be able to track other spells in it and find your last elf," Freya said, handing him the book.

Arne nodded. "Thank you, Freya. Now, if you two are done, I'd like to burn this house to the ground."

The three of them joined another two elf warriors outside. It was snowing, the cold sea air calling out to Bayn and whispering to him to unleash his magic. This wasn't a night for his power. The two elves held up their hands, performing graceful movements in the air. Heat roared out of them, and within seconds, Dieter's mansion was burning.

"We need to stop Leif before anyone else gets hurt. If he's confident enough to kill his own boss, then I hate to see what he's capable of," Freya said, the orange and red flames reflecting in her angry eyes.

"We will get him, Freya. I promise," Bayn replied, tucking her under his arm. And there was no way in hell Bayn was going to let the worm live.

20

Freya woke late the next day, Bayn's warm body wrapped around her. She had thought she wouldn't be able to sleep at all after yesterday's emotions and dead bodies. As soon as Bayn had gotten in beside her, the tension had left her. He had kissed her softly, and she had fallen into a deep slumber.

Now that Freya was awake, all she could think about was what the hell Leif thought he was playing at, trying to trade her for Odin's dagger. She thought he would want Bayn and revenge for wrecking his house, not her.

"It has to be a trap," Freya murmured.

"Of course it is," Bayn said, pressing his lips against her shoulder.

"So we change the deal and get him off guard."

"What are you thinking?"

"Nothing formed yet. I need coffee for my brain to work." Freya went to move, but Bayn put his leg over her, pinning her in place.

"I don't want to get up yet," he grumbled. His hand moved under her shirt and rested on her warm stomach.

"I suppose there's nowhere we have to be today," she said, shifting her hips back with a grin. Bayn's hand stroked lower, slipping under the hem of her pajama pants.

"That's right. The only place you need to be is here with me," he whispered in her ear. Goosebumps rose on her neck as his lips kissed her skin. Bayn's long fingers cupped and teased her, Freya leaning back into him to grind against his erection. Bayn flipped her slowly onto her stomach and pulled her hips up. Pressing a kiss to her lower back, he tugged her pants down and off.

"I have been thinking about this since I had you bent over that counter," Bayn said, pulling her singlet off so he could run his palms over her breasts to her ass.

"Me too." Freya bit her lip as his grip on her tightened, and he pushed the tip of his dick inside of her. Bayn kissed her bare shoulders and back, Freya gasping as he filled her with each slow, hard slide. Her skin was burning with the strange runes again, but she didn't care. Nothing mattered at that moment but the pressure building in her core and Bayn's strong body above hers.

Freya cried out into the pillows beneath her as she came swift and hot. Bayn murmured sweet fae nothings in her ear as he shifted positions. Stars broke through her vision until Bayn found his own release and was left shaking above her.

"Fuck, Freya," he panted as he shifted out of her and collapsed on the bed. "Let's never fight again because I don't want to go a day without being inside you."

"Has anyone told you that you have a filthy mouth for a prince?" she said, turning to kiss him.

"You've never worried about my filthy mouth before." Bayn smiled his wolf smile. "Especially when it's between your thighs."

"And I'm never going to," she said with a throaty chuckle and kissed him again.

FREYA WAS STARING SHAMELESSLY at Bayn's ass while he made her coffee on the espresso machine. She decided that she could handle mornings if they came with sex and coffee, in that order. The doorbell downstairs rang, and she slid off her stool.

"I'll get it."

"Don't open the door if you don't know them," Bayn said.

"I won't. It's probably just my mail," Freya assured him and went downstairs. She looked through the peephole, but the snowy street was empty. "Weird." Freya opened the door and found a bright pink box tied in a red ribbon. "Bayn!" He was beside her in seconds, crouching down to inspect the package. His magic crackled around him as he touched the lid.

"No bomb and no magical tampering," he assured her and picked the box up. "Do you have another boyfriend I don't know about, summer?"

"God no. You've seen what my taste in men is like." Bayn gave her an unamused look, so she quickly amended. "I mean past taste in men, my love."

"Thank you," he said, carrying the box upstairs and placing it on the breakfast counter. Freya cut the ribbon and lifted the lid. She grimaced and stepped away from it.

"Didn't I tell you Leif would be ridiculous when he sent his next message?" she complained. Inside was a dead raven, its chest split open and body cavity stuffed with red rose petals.

"And this means something to you?" asked Bayn. He was staring at the bird with so much rage in his eyes that Freya squeezed his hand.

"Raven's Perch. He bought some land a few years ago, north of here, near the lake at Bogstad. The day he showed it to me, he gave me red roses and kept talking about the house he was going to build there for us," she explained. Trying not to be too grossed out, Freya lifted the dead raven and found a message scribbled on the box: *Today. 5pm.*

"I've got an idea," Freya said, fishing out her phone from the pocket of her robe and finding Von's number. It was midday, so she tried calling him.

"Freya! Thank Odin, you're okay," he answered on the first ring. "Leif has lost his fucking mind."

"Yeah, I know. He just sent me a dead raven."

"What the fuck?"

"Don't get me started. I need you to get a message to him for me. Tell him that I'm offering him a new deal," Freya said, looking up at Bayn. "Tell him that if he forgives me and lifts the bounty on me, I'll give him the fae, and he can keep the dagger."

Von made an exasperated sound. "Freya, come on. Don't do this. The man is unhinged and needs to be stopped, not aggravated more. He almost chopped one of my fingers off last night because I beat him at cards."

"Von, please do this for me. I can stop him. I have big strong friends who are going to help me. Just do your part, and I'll give you a very special Odin related gift," Freya replied.

"If you die, I'll never forgive you," Von huffed. "You keep that brawny fae with you at all times."

Freya fluttered her lashes at Bayn. "I promise I won't let him out of my sight for a second." Von swore under his breath and hung up on her.

"What are you up to, summer? I thought you had forgiven me, and now you're going to trade me?" Bayn asked.

"I would never! You're far too good in bed for me to want to do that. I want Leif feeling super confident, though, and if he thinks I'm crawling back to get his forgiveness, he might let me get close enough."

"To do what?"

Freya let him see all the hurt and anger inside of her as she muttered, "Stop him once and for all."

∼

ARNE TURNED up thirty minutes later with the biggest damn Viking Freya had ever seen. He was taller than Bayn, with braided blonde hair, a trimmed beard, and eyes as grey as storm clouds.

"Freya, this is Torsten," Arne said by way of introduction.

The Úlfhéðnar. Von was going to lose his shit when Freya told him that Odin's sacred berserkers were still getting around.

"Nice to meet you. I've made pancakes if you're hungry," Freya greeted him.

"Tor's always hungry."

"Let me help," Torsten said in a deep voice, following Freya to the kitchen. Bayn and Arne stood in the lounge room, looking at the raven in the box and muttering together.

"They are plotting," Freya commented.

"Arne can't help it. He's a spymaster. I swear his mother was knocked up by Loki himself." Torsten helped carry plates and cutlery to the dining table, and Bayn made more coffee for everyone.

"You really think Leif is going to let you walk right up to him after everything he's done to you?" asked Arne as they ate.

"He will if he thinks I'm scared of him, and I'm super apologetic. I might have to kiss him to let him know I'm on his side," Freya said.

Bayn muttered, "Then I will really have to kill him."

"We need to interrogate him first," Torsten reminded him. "What can you tell us about the land he wants to meet on, Freya?"

The property in Bogstad had been bought before Freya realized just how fucked up Leif was. She described the small stretch of trees hiding the main property from the road and the part of the lake that fringed it.

"We can hide some of our people in there, keep an eye on the exchange and come in as backup if needed," Arne said as he finished the last of the pancakes. He looked at Bayn. "That is if you don't turn it into a desolate crater of ice because you lost your temper."

"No promises." Bayn leaned back in his chair. "I still don't like how much danger it's putting Freya in."

Torsten grunted. "I wouldn't want my mate anywhere near this either, but she's the best way to get our female back."

Freya went still. Her whole body was on fire, and blood roared in her ears. "What did you just say?"

Torsten gave them all a confused smile; Arne looked embarrassed, and Bayn had paled.

"Would you look at the time? We had best be going. Thank you for the pancakes, Freya," Arne said, hustling a frowning Torsten out of the apartment. Freya's hands clenched into fists, unable to look at Bayn, unable to think straight enough to form a sentence.

"Freya—"

She held up a finger. "No." She got out of her chair and headed for the bedroom.

"We need to talk about this," Bayn said, but Freya shut the door on him. Black started to stain her vision, and she lowered herself to the carpet and put her head between her knees.

How can I be his mate? It wasn't possible. Elise said he didn't want a mate, was that why he didn't tell her?

Bayn broke the lock on the bedroom door and came in. "Yeah, we are talking about this now before your mind makes up its own wrong conclusions," he said, sitting down on the floor beside her.

"Did you know when you came to Oslo?"

"No, and neither did Elise. It really was about finding the dagger. I didn't know you were her blood cousin either. It means you are from the same line of kings, Hengist and Horsa, who were responsible for my curse. Only a mate from their bloodline can break it."

Elise had told Freya about them having the king's blood from way back, but she had forgotten all about it. "But you figured out that I was your mate?"

"I did, the night of the first auction we went to when the runes appeared on my skin. Kian filled me in on what else to look for."

Freya's chest ached. "The auction? And you never said anything."

"I didn't want to scare you off, and we had bigger things to worry about."

"Elise said you don't want a mate."

"I didn't, even if it meant breaking my curse."

Freya flinched, curling further in on herself. "You would rather die than be my mate?"

"That's not what I said. I didn't tell you, not because I don't want you as a mate. It's because you deserve better than to be joined with me forever," Bayn said, his voice breaking. Freya glanced up from her knees. He looked more upset than she had ever seen him.

"You don't think I would want you? That's ridiculous," she said.

"No, it's not." Bayn's expression hardened. "Do you know why I call you summer? It's because you're golden and vibrant and full of life. I am the Winter Prince. I couldn't bind you to me. I wouldn't be able to handle it if I destroyed your light bit by bit."

"If you really think that's true, why have you been sleeping with me instead of shoving me away? Is it the mating bond forcing you?"

"It's got nothing to do with the damn mating bond. I can't stay away from you because I'm in love with you!" Bayn exclaimed.

"You are?"

"Gods, yes. Being around you feels like I can breathe for the first time in my life. You make me want a future. I haven't said it sooner because I'm not a nice man, Freya. You need someone better than what I am."

"Thanks, but I'm pretty sure I can make that decision for myself," Freya replied, her heart doing backflips. "The fae believe mates are chosen by fate or destiny, whatever you want to call it, right?"

Bayn nodded miserably.

"Then did you ever stop to think that I was your mate for a reason? No, you're not a *nice* man, but you're a good one. Do you really think I could tolerate a *nice* man? This mate's thing isn't just about you, you arrogant ass. I have already told you that I'm not some delicate flower who can't handle what you are. I'm a goddamn Viking." Freya leaned back against her bed with a huff. "Is it already a done thing? Are we mated?"

Bayn shook his head. "No. According to Kian, it's not unbreakable until we verbally say that we accept each other as our mates and mean it. When that happens, you might get some of my abilities, like Elise did with Kian." Bayn placed a hand on her knee. "I'm never going to force you into being my mate, Freya."

"But you wouldn't hate it if I were?" she asked.

Bayn smiled. "No, I wouldn't hate it. I might not think I'm good enough for you, but I would do everything I could to be a good mate to you."

"I should think so," Freya sniffed. Bayn shook his head at her and pulled her into his lap. The idea of being his mate was unnerving, but she was already in love with him, so how much more terrifying could it be?

"I was going to tell you last night, you know. I held off because I didn't want to give you something else to worry about. I wanted this shit with Leif to be over and have the perfect moment." Bayn kissed the top of her head. "Bloody Torsten, ruining my big plans."

Freya laughed. "What a jerk."

"You're not freaking out and trying to kill me, so can I assume you are okay?"

Freya raised a brow at him. "I'm pissed you didn't tell me earlier, but I understand why you didn't. I'm thrilled I'm not going to have to find some other woman to be your mate."

"Me too. You are the fierce Viking goddess I've always dreamed of."

Freya took a steady breath. "You are really going to leave the decision to mate up to me, aren't you?"

Bayn nodded. "You can take as long as you want. I'm not going anywhere. If we get the dagger tonight, and it works on breaking my curse, then you don't ever have to decide."

He was doing his best to sound like he would be okay with that, but Freya knew better. She could feel his sadness at the thought, so she put her arms around his neck.

"Maybe you need to start thinking about all the ways you can convince me that mating you will be the best thing that ever happened to me," she said and kissed him. Bayn's arms tightened around her, and he let out a frustrated growl.

"I will, but we don't have time to start now." Bayn kissed her forehead. "We have to get ready to go, and we need to come up with a way for it to look like I'm your prisoner."

Freya laughed evilly. "How do you feel about chains?"

Bayn considered the question for a long moment. "All depends, can we keep them afterward?"

Freya rolled her eyes. "And you think we aren't compatible mates."

21

Bayn shifted in the cold silver chains, imagining all the things he would do with them once Leif was dealt with.

"Stop smiling like you're having a good time, or you're going to spoil the deception," Freya chastised him.

She drove them to Bogstad in her black SUV. In her black overcoat, leather pants, and black sweater, she was stunning. He wanted to rub his face all over the soft fabric, then drag her into the backseat...he stopped himself, grumbling in frustration.

"I can't help it. A beautiful woman has chained me up, and now I'm at her mercy," he replied.

Freya tugged on the end of his braid. "You're always going to be at my mercy even without the chains, lover."

"Stop flirting with me, or I'll make you pull this car over and fuck me."

Freya waggled her eyebrows at him. "Maybe on the way home. It's the first time I've seen your hair braided back, and it's doing it for me."

"We are going into a fight. That's why it's braided. You know what kind of warriors don't tie their hair back before a fight? The fucking dead kind."

Freya put her indicator on, and her smile vanished. "This is it. Put your scary warrior face on."

Bayn spotted Leif and a group of guards standing at the edge of the frozen lake. His hands itched to wrap around the man's throat and watch the life drain from his eyes.

"Deep breaths," Freya said.

Bayn didn't know if she was talking to herself or to him. She got out of the car and opened his door. Bayn brushed his fingers over the back of her palm to reassure her. Her face remained locked down as she took the chain lead and waited for him to get out of the car. The ice and snow crunched under their boots, Bayn clamping his magic down so he wouldn't hear its call.

"Freya, darling, I never thought you would have it in you," Leif said by way of greeting.

"You know me, I always liked to surprise you." Freya bit her bottom lip and looked at her feet. "I want this bad blood between us gone, Leif. Oslo is too small to have us fighting. This fae attacked your place without my knowledge, so you can have him to punish however you wish."

"A generous gift." Leif nodded at his men, who took Bayn's chain and brought him forward. Leif punched him in the ribs, a weak hit, but Bayn still groaned and went to his knees. Leif yanked at the chains, inspecting the runes that they had scratched into them.

"Freya, you've been holding out on me. I had no idea you were capable of magic like this."

"My cousin married one of the fae princes. It's come with perks," Freya said. Leif cupped her cheek, and she curved her face into it.

"You were always so resourceful. We are meant to be together, Freya, surely you can see that now. I fucked up thinking you weren't strong enough, that you wouldn't be a good business partner."

"And I fucked up not believing that you could rule Norway like you always wanted. Can we start over? I think we can make it work."

Bayn's vision burned red as Leif kissed her. Freya's hands went in his hair, yanking him closer and making him believe how much she wanted him. Bayn was going to be sick. He went to move, but the guard behind him shoved him back down.

Don't kill them all, not yet. Not until Freya is done.

"I have missed that," Leif chuckled.

"Me too, baby. Did you really find Odin's dagger?" Freya asked, wide-eyed.

Leif nodded and held out a hand to one of his men. They passed over the dagger, and Leif unsheathed it. Ancient, powerful magic sang from the blade, but only Freya paused. The other humans couldn't hear it at all.

"Show me," she said, reaching excitedly for it. Leif nodded, and Freya was grabbed from behind by one of his men and dragged a few meters back from him. "Hey! What the hell, Leif?"

"Nothing personal, darling. I just need to do one thing first, just so I know that you're beginning fresh with me," Leif replied. He turned to Bayn. "You touched my woman, fae, and you destroyed my house. Consider this an eye for an eye." And he drove the dagger into Bayn's chest.

"No, no, no!" Freya screamed, thrashing against the men holding her. The magic in the blade burned through Bayn as he fell to the frozen ground, amber blood seeping out of him. Leif was saying something he didn't catch. He could only stare at Freya's furious face.

"Winter Prince!" she shouted at the top of her lungs. "I accept you as my mate! Bayn, do you hear me? I accept you as my mate!"

"I accept you too, Freya," he mumbled into the snow and mud. The bond he'd been fighting inside of him clicked into place, and power rushed through it.

The world turned white as Freya unleashed an unnatural scream of primal rage. Magic burst out of her, the ice from the lake cracked, and icy spears shot out, piercing two men and dragging them under the water.

"You had magic this whole time? You lying, fucking bitch," Leif snarled, pulling out a gun.

Bayn broke the chains around him, yanked the knife from his chest, and threw it at Leif. The man screamed as the blade pierced through his forearm and the gun slipped from his fingers.

"You dare stick a blade into my mate?" Freya demanded in a distant, furious voice.

"Your eyes—" Leif gasped. Freya snarled, and sharp points of ice pierced through Leif's boots. His scream was high-pitched and terrified as he tumbled back and was impaled on spikes through his thighs and shoulders.

"You stuck a blade into my mate." Freya grabbed the hilt of Odin's dagger and, with a vicious tug, ripped it free from Leif's arm. She placed the bloody tip of the blade on his cheek, just under his eye. "An eye for an eye, right, Leif?" Freya slashed the blade across his eye, and Leif screamed and screamed. Bayn dragged himself upright, tugged Freya away from the bleeding man, and pulled her to his chest, wrapping his arms around her shoulders.

"Enough, summer, enough now. I'm okay," he murmured.

"Bayn." Freya's body softened, and she leaned into him. "How are you alive?"

"Look." Bayn pulled his shirt up so she could see the healing wound on the very edge of his tattoos. "The blade got it right on the side of my body wards. It wasn't fatal. It just knocked the air out of me."

Freya looked around at the dead, still bleeding men that the ice had torn apart then back to him. One of her eyes was golden, and now the other was the blue of glacier ice. "I t-think I got some of your power."

Bayn let out a soft laugh. "Yes, my mate, I believe you did." He kissed her and could taste the ice and storms in her veins. The winter tempests that had always calmed him were now trapped inside of her, and he knew that he would be home wherever she was.

"Is it safe to come out?" Arne called, a sword resting casually on his shoulder. He let out a long whistle. "Remind me to never piss off your mate, Winter Prince."

"Did you leave any alive?" Torsten asked, appearing through the trees.

"Only this piece of shit." Freya pointed at Leif, who had passed out. Torsten smacked him hard across the face, jolting him awake.

"Where is the elf you have taken?" Arne demanded.

"Door. Well," Leif groaned through bloody lips.

"You cliché, piece of shit," Freya muttered. She waved at them. "This way."

Bayn followed his mate through a row of birch trees where a stone well had been covered with rotting planks. Torsten lifted the cover off, and inside was a set of stairs. The smell of old blood, earth, and suffering met Bayn's nose, and he took Freya's hand.

"You don't need to go down there," he said, looking at Torsten.

"I'll check, my lady. He might have set traps."

Freya huffed out a breath. "Okay, but only because you called me, my lady."

"Well, you are a princess now," the wolf berserker said.

Freya gave Bayn an appalled look. "Tell me it's not true."

Bayn tried to not laugh. "You did accept me as your mate."

"Only because I thought you were dying!" she argued.

"Do you two always fight this much?" Arne asked. Torsten appeared through the dim light, an elf woman slung over his shoulder.

"She lives but is hurt," he said, carrying her out. "You should see the weapons they have down there."

Freya hugged herself. "I've seen enough for one day."

"This is the last elf that was missing?" Bayn asked Arne. The warrior nodded. "Good. Mind if I borrow your sword for a moment?"

"Not at all." Arne gave him the blade. Bayn left Freya with them, walked back to Leif, and hacked his head from his body in one satisfying stroke.

22

When Elise arrived unannounced at Mardøll the following day, Freya was torn between being overjoyed to see her and pissed off that she wouldn't be able to spend all day in bed with Bayn. She needed to sleep for a week after using magic for the first time yesterday, and she wanted time to study the dagger that was now on her bedside table.

"Oh my god, you mated him," Elise said. She was bundled up in a heavy coat and beanie, a massive grin on her face.

"I did. Come in and get out of the snow," Freya replied, pulling her cousin in for a hug. "What are you doing here?"

"A good question." Bayn was standing at the top of the stairs with only a pair of pajama pants on, glaring at Elise with righteous fury.

"Big brother! Your curse is lifted!" Elise hurried up the stairs and wrapped him in a hug, utterly impervious to his pout. "I'm so glad that you're okay and that Freya hasn't killed you yet."

Bayn sighed, looking pleadingly at Freya over the top of Elise's head. "I'll go find a shirt."

"No need," both women said at the same time and then burst into giggles.

"Where is Kian? Surely he didn't let you come on your own."

"He's in the hotel across the street. He thought you would be pissed off to see us, but no growly fae was going to stop me from seeing my cousin," Elise said, letting him go. She smiled up at him, a big glowing smile. "Isn't that right?"

Bayn actually squirmed under her intensity. "No." He mumbled something in fae as he walked away.

"Don't you call me that, you dick," Elise said to his retreating back. "And if you had answered your phone, I wouldn't have had to resort to *Frozen* music and turning up on your doorstep to get your attention!"

"So *that's* the reason I've had 'Into the Unknown' stuck in my head all day." Freya threw one of the decorative pillows from the couch at her. "Asshole!"

"I didn't know he had mated you," Elise replied, shrugging off her coat and sitting down on the couch beside her.

"As a matter of fact, she mated me," Bayn corrected.

"It was a life-or-death situation! I thought it would help."

"You keep telling yourself that, summer," Bayn growled, sapphire eyes glowing with magic. Freya quickly turned to make coffee when her doorbell rang again. "I'll get it."

"Is that true?" Elise asked.

"Sorry! Can't hear you over the machine!"

Freya didn't regret mating Bayn; it just had happened a lot quicker than she anticipated. Leif stabbing Bayn replayed in her mind, and she almost dropped the cup she was holding. Her hands shook, and she gripped the counter to steady herself.

He is fine. You are fine. The crackle of magic was dancing on her fingertips, her left eye throbbing in response. It was silently begging her to unleash it, calling out to Bayn's power to play. Freya took some steady breaths, and the roaring of winter winds calmed. A warm hand touched her shoulder, bringing her back to herself.

"Kian's here, but I'm happy to kick them out if you need me to," Bayn whispered.

"I'm fine," Freya assured him. She turned with a bright smile on her face. Kian was standing in the middle of her lounge room, looking around with a curious smile. Freya's mouth popped open at the sight of his amazing antlers. Seeing them mounted on a wall was nothing like seeing them in the flesh. He was terrifying and magnificent at the same time. She could hear his magic, like battle drums in her head. Elise was smiling up at him with adoring eyes, as if the Scourge of London was the only man in the world. Freya shook her head.

"Please tell me we don't look that pathetic together," Freya told Bayn.

"No one can look that pathetic." Bayn put an arm around her waist and led her over. "Freya, this is Kian."

Kian smiled. "Bayn's mate, you poor girl."

"I can handle it. What brings you two here to Oslo?" Freya asked. Elise dug about in her satchel bag and passed her a book.

"The *Hávamál*, as promised," Kian said. Freya's fingertips tingled as she stroked the cover.

"Thank you, it's beautiful."

"You're welcome. Arne would like us to go and view the weapons cache too. I thought you and Elise could catch up at the same time." Kian looked at Bayn and grinned. "You don't have a problem with that, do you, little brother? There could be other fae relics there."

"I don't like the idea of leaving, Freya—"

"From Arne's account of yesterday's events, Freya can handle herself just fine." Freya tried not to snigger at how the brothers glared at each other, a silent battle of wills.

"I'll be fine, Bayn. Go with your brother and have fun."

"Yeah, Bayn. We need to talk girl stuff," Elise added.

"You're outvoted. Get your coat, baby brother. It's cold out there," Kian said his sharp grin widening.

"Fuck off, Kian," Bayn snapped but grabbed his overcoat anyway. "Let's go." Bayn took Freya's face and gave her a sound kiss that made all kinds of delightful promises for later.

"Behave yourselves," Kian said and hustled Bayn downstairs.

Elise made Freya sit on the couch and slung her feet over Freya's lap like she used to when they were kids. "Okay, the big ears are gone. Tell me what's been going on."

There was no arguing with Elise when she was determined, so Freya got comfortable and told her everything since Bayn had appeared in her store, and her life had imploded.

"God, that's a lot, cousin," Elise said when she was finished. She raised a dark brow. "Drinks?"

"All the drinks," Freya agreed. "I know the best place."

Freya got changed quickly and tucked the *Hávamál* safely in her bag. She opened the door to leave and yelped in surprise. A towering fae was standing outside in the snow staring at her.

Where Freya heard battle drums from Kian's magic, this fae's magic whispered silky, dark things done behind closed doors. He was taller than Bayn and Kian, his black hair hanging in waves to the center of his chest, with one streak of silver shining at his temple. Emerald eyes glowed in his golden-brown face, and his smile was perverse enough to make Freya's face burn as he looked her up and down.

"Well, well, so the rumor is true," he purred in a deep voice that was like warm honey in her ears. Freya was shoved unceremoniously aside as Elise barged past and threw herself at the fae with an ecstatic, "Kill!"

The massive fae smiled fondly at her. "Baby sister, I had a feeling you would be here."

"The boys are off looking at weapons, so we are going to get a drink."

"Then my timing is perfect. I'd rather drink with two beautiful women than deal with my brothers any day."

"Kill, this is Freya. Bayn's mate. Play nice, or he'll rip your head off," Elise said.

"I always play nice. Freya, a pleasure to meet you. I am Killian." He bowed gracefully.

"The Night Prince," she replied, eyes widening.

Killian raised a dark brow. "The one and only."

"Please tell me no one else is going to appear in the dark. I don't know how many more imposing gorgeous fae I can handle," Freya said, with a saucy smile.

Killian returned it with an extra dose of sass. "Oh, my dear, you are going to be wasted on my brother."

∼

RITUAL WAS IN LOUD, fine form as the three of them descended into its dark belly. Freya's senses exploded, heightened by mating with Bayn, and she could've gotten lost in the thrumming of drums and pounding of feet. She led them to a booth overlooking the dance floor that she had called ahead and reserved.

"Now *this* is my kind of place," Killian said.

"Bayn likes it too," Freya replied. "So what's your curse about?"

"Freya!" Elise hissed.

"What? I'm family now. I want to know."

Killian held up his hands that were still in their tight black leather gloves. "My curse is a poisoned touch. Literally."

Freya looked at the fae that all but radiated sex and shook her head. "Fucking hell, first drink is on me."

Killian laughed. "Thank you, sister."

"I've been looking for something that can help break Killian's curse, too, like I thought the dagger would work for Bayn, but nothing has been useful yet," Elise explained. She was frowning like she was personally offended by that fact.

"Finding things is my superpower, so I'll help. What happens when you touch someone?" Freya asked.

Their drinks arrived, and Killian drained his and ordered another round.

"Black lines of poison spread from the place of contact, and they are dead within minutes," he said, with a mockingly sad smile. "I haven't touched anyone in centuries. You have no idea how horny I am."

"You poor dear." Elise patted his gloved hand. "You know, I used to think you were the Voldemort of the fae because no one would ever talk about you, but I think they stopped because the curse made you boring."

"Woman, please, if I'm going to be *any* pop culture villain, it's going to be Kylo Ren because no matter how bad I get, women still want to fuck me," Killian corrected her. "And if you must know, the fae don't talk about me because I started a rumor when I was young that if they spoke my name, it was giving me permission to invade their dreams and corrupt them with their darkest desires."

"And did you?"

Killian thought about it. "Not if they were ugly."

Freya was still laughing when Von appeared at their table. She was up in a heartbeat, wrapping him in a hug.

"Odin's daughter, I'm so happy to see you in one piece." Von cupped her face and tipped her chin up. "Wow, you really are his daughter now. One normal eye, one magical. I'm so jealous, I could die."

"Don't be too jealous, I have a present for you."

Von's eyes went straight to Killian. "I accept." The Night Prince only laughed, and Von turned bright red.

"Unfortunately, Killian isn't it." Freya dug in her bag and offered him the book. "For saving my life and helping us, I give you a complete copy of the original *Hávamál*. Promise me you'll make me a digital copy, though, because I'm dying to read it."

Von's eyes welled up with tears as he took the book reverently and opened the front cover. "Oh, Freya."

"Should I tell him that Odin was a total dick?" Killian asked with a raised brow.

"I already know. That was half of his appeal," Von laughed, not realizing that Killian was so old he could've been speaking from personal experience.

Freya didn't dare ask; there was only so many shocks she could take in one night. She was reaching for her drink when the cold snap of Bayn's magic whipped at her senses. With unnerving accuracy, she found him instantly in the crowd below. Kian was with him, his antlers glamoured away so he didn't cause a riot. Bayn's face was promising death, so Freya gave him a little finger wave. Killian choked on his drink.

"Maybe I was wrong, and you're going to be the best thing that has ever happened to the sour little icicle," he said with a deep laugh.

Kian slid into the booth beside Elise. "You were supposed to stay at the apartment."

"Were we? I don't remember agreeing to that," she said, cuddling into his side.

"They have been completely safe. I've been with them the whole time," Killian added, giving Bayn a shit-stirring smile. "Your mate is delightful."

Bayn folded his arms. "She is. I'm surprised you left Ireland."

"I wasn't going to, but I had to see that you were really mated for myself. Congratulations, baby brother." Killian raised a glass to him. "May she bang the frown permanently from your face."

"*Skal!*" Freya shouted, tapping her glass against his before draining it.

Killian grinned at Bayn, who looked ready to punch him in the face. "Now, tell me, ladies, do you have any other cousins hiding anywhere?"

23

It was another hour before Freya took pity on Bayn, and they slipped into the crowd and out of the club. Bayn fought every instinct he had not to magic her away to Scotland where his meddling brothers wouldn't be able to interrupt them.

Bayn took Freya's hand, and she beamed up at him. He would never get used to how she smiled at him like she was always happy to see him. They walked in comfortable silence all the way back to the store.

"The cold isn't bothering you?" he asked her.

Freya held out her hand to catch snowflakes. "No, it doesn't feel the same. The winter feels..."

"Alive," Bayn said, and she nodded.

"Exactly. Does it worry you that I have some of your magic?"

"No, it makes you that one bit more perfect for me." As they stepped into the privacy of her back garden, Bayn pulled her into his embrace. "I know the mating happened sooner than you wanted, but please tell me you don't regret it."

Freya placed a warm palm on his cheek. "Bayn...*of course* I don't. I was teasing before when I said it was because I thought you were dying. I mean, it was, but I don't regret making you mine. Not even for a second."

Bayn's knees almost buckled with relief. His heart was bursting with love as he gripped her tighter to him. "We didn't get a chance to talk about it properly before Elise arrived, and I needed to hear it—" Freya kissed his fears away.

"You're mine, Winter Prince, now and always, and God help whoever tries to get between us again," Freya growled.

Bayn's dick hardened at the sound of that possessive growl. "Those fae traits are coming out already."

"That's right, you better remember that you were the one silly enough to mate a Viking, and our tempers run hot."

"Don't I know it."

"Tell me about Edinburgh," Freya said quickly.

"Why?"

"All of the horrible business with Leif has soured Oslo for me, so I thought I would check out real estate in Edinburgh. See if they need a decent antique store." Freya sounded casual about it, but Bayn knew otherwise. She was going to move her store for him. He tried to stop from pouncing on her with joy.

"Well, if you are going to come and live in Scotland with me in a castle, I have a present for you." He held out his hands and concentrated. His magic circled his fingertips, and fine filaments of ice wove together to create a crown. Freya's face shone with delight as he placed it on her golden hair. "Didn't I say you deserved a crown, Ice Princess?" Freya climbed up into his arms and wrapped her legs tightly around his waist.

"Take me upstairs, Winter Prince. I believe it's time for number fifteen on my list," she said with a wicked smile. Bayn gave her a deep, silky kiss that had her thighs tightening around him.

"I'll get the chains."

EPILOGUE

With the return of the fae to England, magic returned to the world of the humans. We thought that the danger had passed as the peace treaties held, and threats like the events in Oslo continued to be neutralized.

No one, neither humans nor magical beings, could have predicted that the biggest threat to their survival wasn't one another. Other angry and vicious beings were prowling restlessly around the gates of the human world.

The return of the fae and the surge of magic had sent echoes through Faerie itself, all the way to the brutal lands of Tir Na Nog.

The fae's wrath was meant to be the start of a greater war and a release of the ancient horde.

The phantom queen, the goddess of war and fate and doom, had waited for thousands of years for her prophecy to be fulfilled. Blood mist, battle drums, and raven wings would have heralded her return, and the humans who had abandoned her would know she was not the female who would tolerate being put aside.

Now, with the promise of her own revenge against the humans slipping through her clawed fingers, the Morrigan turns her black eyes to Ireland.

Only one prince remained useful. An unholy terror in his prime that all feared and wanted. Whom the Morrigan herself had once spent a night with, filled with ecstasy. He would be useful, or he would break beneath her blades and boots.

The world didn't know the worst was yet to come, and make no mistake, the Morrigan would demand fealty in blood.

Wings of the Night Prince

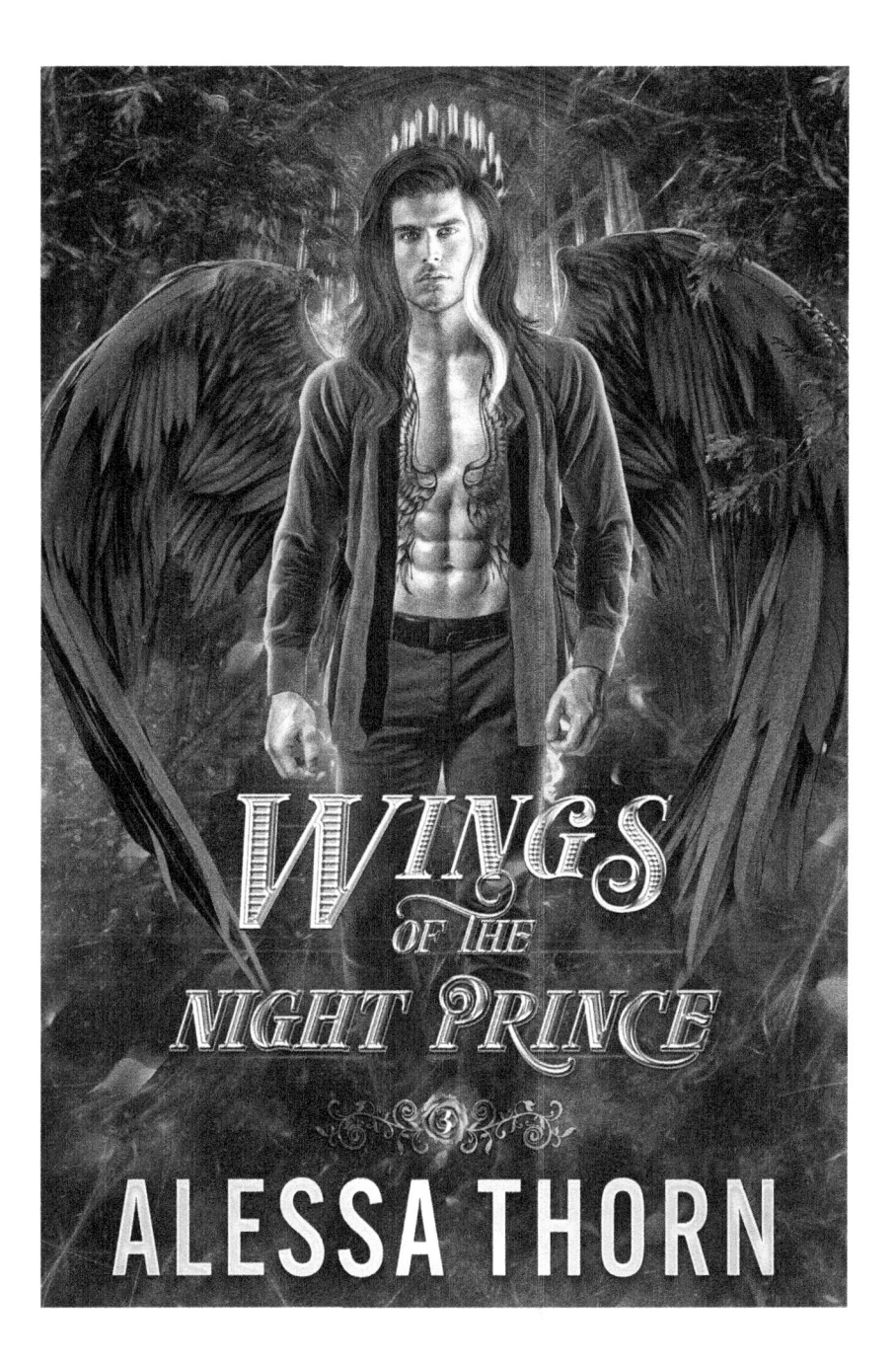

ALESSA THORN

PROLOGUE

No one holds a grudge like a goddess. A goddess mostly forgotten by the humans that once worshipped her takes that kind of insult personally. Mankind was about to get reminded why Morrigan was feared and revered by its ancestors.

It wasn't the first time the goddess of war and fury had tried to break out of Tir Na Nog and back into the world of man. Last time, a fae king and his wife had used their combined power to keep her out. They died in the effort because such magic always had a price and took payment in blood.

But like all spells, time had a way of weakening them if they weren't strengthened and renewed.

Morrigan thought she could manipulate the king's three sons into setting her loose. She only came close with one: Killian, the Night Prince. All the prophecies, including her own, saw that only he could be the one to stand by her side and cast the world into darkness.

Morrigan might not have been able to set her feet in the world of man, but she had those loyal to her who could.

So, while the world remained distracted by the magic that had returned to it, and the growing acceptance of fae kind, Morrigan's crows got to work.

They had not forgotten their goddess and were more than happy to unleash hell on the world that had.

1

Killian sat in a dark booth in one of his favorite pubs in Dublin's Temple Bar district. It was packed, but no one tried to slide onto the leather seats beside him. In fact, unless they were fae or had magic, they wouldn't have noticed the booth at all.

Only the waitresses seemed to be able to find it, so despite his better judgment, Killian had become known as a regular.

They all thought that he was one of the many fae that had appeared after the treaty, and no one had gotten close enough to learn the truth of his identity.

The Night Prince.

Killian used to crave the attention and delight in being an object of unattainable desire.

To survive, he and his brothers had taken on the roles that had suited them most. Kian was the diplomat and general; Bayn was executioner and assassin, and Killian was the whore or torturer depending on what the occasion called for.

He had played his role well, reveled in it, earning a reputation that induced fear and desire throughout three worlds. Then the curse happened, and he hadn't been touched by another being for fifteen hundred years.

It was little wonder why he drank.

Killian didn't know how many pints deep he was in. The music was good enough that he just tilted his head back and let it wash over him. His phone buzzed in his pocket. He fished it out and almost choked on his Guinness.

Freya had sent him a selfie of her in front of a sleeping Bayn. She had put his hair in high pigtails and was giving the camera a thumbs up with a wide shit-eating smile. Only Freya would risk the wrath of the Winter Prince with such shenanigans.

That wild streak of mischief made Killian love her to pieces. He loved both of his brother's mates. Their warmth and affection had brought them all joy. His brothers had found worth in living again, and had finally begun to heal their bloody pasts.

Killian had never been jealous of his brothers until then. He had always been the one who secretly wanted a mate, unlike them, and yet, he was being denied her by Fate.

Even in his years of playing the whore, he had always searched for her. *His promised one.* He could remember his parents and the bond they shared. They weren't mates as far as he knew, but they were powerful and inseparable. He had always wanted that for himself, and had never found it.

At least you can die knowing your brothers will be taken care of.

Killian sent Freya a photo of him raising his almost empty glass to her in appreciation of a prank well done. He was still grinning when a fae slipped into the booth beside him.

"Is this seat taken?" the female asked with a wide smile. "You looked a bit miserable over here by yourself, so I thought I'd buy you a drink."

"Awfully bold of you," Killian replied.

She only shrugged. "Is it? I thought it was just me trying to be friendly." The waitress turned up with a fresh pint for him.

She's trying to be nice. Don't be a dick.

"Thank you. Sorry, I have a lot on my mind." It wasn't a lie. The curse was twisting around inside of him, eating away at the last bit of him. He carefully kept its progress hidden from his brothers and Freya and Elise because they would all have loud opinions and feelings on the matter.

Unless his mate somehow magically fell into his lap, Killian would die, and he was strangely at peace with that.

"What brings you to Ireland?" Killian asked, realizing he had been silent for too long. The fae female's accent wasn't Irish, though she wasn't someone he recognized from Kian's people.

"I wanted to connect with some of my family here. See if any of them remain," she said and raised her glass. "To the fae, may we never disappear again."

"*Slainte*." Killian raised his fresh Guinness to hers and tapped his glass. He drained half the pint before setting it down. He didn't want to be rude, but he was too moody for company. The room swayed, the band and people blurring around him.

"Wow, that shit works fast," a new voice said. Killian couldn't make out the male's face, only the ears that marked him as fae.

"Our queen wouldn't give us something that wouldn't work."

"You...idiots," Killian slurred just as a black hood was shoved over his head, and his world went dark.

2

Three years later, Killian still had trouble believing that he had been so fucking stupid. Stuck in the bowels of a castle dungeon, with no alcohol whatsoever, had given him plenty of time to think and go over every mistake he had made in his two thousand years of life.

One of the biggest was not telling the fae female to fuck off the night she sat in his booth.

Killian stretched his arms as best he could, shaking them in their hexed chains as he tried to relieve the pain in his shoulders. He thought the curse would've killed him by now, but no such luck.

"Wake up, asshole," a guard snapped, throwing a small rock at him. Killian opened his emerald eyes just as a tray of slop was pushed through a slot. Killian got to his feet and strode lazily to the bars of his cage like he had all the time in the world.

He drank down the water with a sigh and lifted the bowl to inspect for anything too suspicious. After he stopped eating in his first month there, his jailer had made sure his food remained unsullied. That didn't mean it tasted any better.

"Eat up. You have an audience with the boss today." The guard sneered. 'Audience' usually meant 'torture session,' and it was better his body had some nourishment before he was subjected to whatever was coming next.

The guard was still laughing when Killian's hand shot between the bars and flicked him hard on the nose. The guard battered his hand away and swore. He paled right before he started to scream, and black lines of poison spread across his face. Killian calmly sipped his porridge as blood spurted out of the guard's nose, then eyes, then mouth as he collapsed onto the filthy floors.

When Killian was finished, he placed the cup and bowl back where the slot was, and went to the niche in the stone wall that he liked to lean against. He smiled as the shouting started, the guard's companions dragging the body away and cursing him.

"Don't blame me. He was the one that got too close," Killian said, giving them a shrug.

"I'm looking forward to seeing you scream today," another guard spat.

Killian sighed. "I'm ready when she is."

∼

THE GUARDS that came for him next time were all high fae and weren't so easy to fuck with. They were more valuable servants than the lesser fae, so they dressed accordingly. Protective armor shielded their bodies, leaving no patch of skin revealed. Only their lifeless eyes could be seen through the slots of their visors.

"That time of the week already, boys?" Killian asked cheerfully as they fixed an iron collar around his neck. Wooden sticks were slotted into the collar to steer him without getting within his reach, and they marched him out of the cell and through the dank dungeons.

Killian wasn't particularly keen on torture, but anything was better than the endless days of boredom. Even pain could become a novelty when life was tedious enough. He only needed to hold out until the curse killed him.

The guards shoved and pulled him up a steep flight of stone stairs. With each step, grey light began to filter through the darkness. Killian took a deep breath of the rain-soaked air as he was led in the middle of a small arena. A dais was erected in the center of it, and sitting on the stone rings around them, the dread horde screamed and chanted.

Killian knew that most of the horde couldn't come out in daylight, especially the three generals, but what he saw was enough to strengthen his resolve to never give in to Morrigan.

Creatures of nightmare were howling and roaring. Dark power had twisted them into beasts of war, with fangs and horns and horrid insect bodies. He could make out the ones that could have been high fae at some point. They had all sold whatever counted as a soul to the woman that sat on the black and silver throne.

"Kneel," the nearest guard hissed.

"Not in this lifetime," Killian replied. Two synchronized spears drilled through his thighs, and he fell to his knees. Amber blood soaked the mud underneath him, the spears tearing at his flesh as they were ripped free. Killian ground his teeth together, swallowing down the scream that would only excite his audience.

Silk rubbed against leather as Morrigan lifted her goblet for an attendant to refill.

"Killian, my love, must we do this dance again?" she asked, her voice softly coaxing.

"If you wanted to dance, you should've told your fuck boys not to take out my knees," he replied, raising his head.

Morrigan was a gorgeous horror. Black hair hung in perfect battle braids, red eyes were lined with black, and full lips were painted like crimson petals. The goddess of battle and prophecy had used her servants to snatch him from Ireland and take him to her dark castle in Tir Na Nog. There he had stayed, her plaything and punching bag.

A sword sat across her lap, waiting for its mistress to finally take Killian's head.

If only she would. Morrigan needed him for her plans to work, so as much as she wanted to kill him, she couldn't. And didn't she hate that?

A tingle swept down Killian's spine, and his eyes slid from Morrigan to a figure in the crowd. The woman was dressed in the servants' drab, grey clothes, pale face dirty and...wrong. Her face flickered for a split second, revealing brown skin and dark eyes before the glamor readjusted itself. How the horde around her didn't sniff out the magic was beyond him. Whatever game she was playing, Killian wasn't about to call her out.

Another blow connected with his cheek, rattling him. Morrigan had asked him something, and he had completely ignored her.

"How long must we do this?" Morrigan asked. She came to stand in front of him.

Killian spat out a mouthful of blood at her boots. "I don't know, how long has it been?"

"Three years. No one is coming to save you, Killian, because no one wants you." Morrigan's gloved hand brushed against his cheek. "No one except me. We were made for each other, and you know it."

"I know you need me to undo my parent's spell that's keeping you locked out of the human world, but that's about it. You're not capable of anything more."

"There was a time I remember when you yearned for me." Morrigan's red eyes glowed, and her heady dark power curled around him. Long ago, the feel of it made him burn for her, and she had used it to toy with him. Only once did he ever get her into bed, and her plans to release her horde had come spilling from her lips.

Morrigan had thought Killian was in her thrall, and a part of him was. The bigger part of him wanted to know what she was planning, so he could always stop her. That was the only way he could honor his parent's sacrifice.

Sex always helped loosen the tongue, and Killian had used it to get secrets from people for centuries. The goddess was no different. There had been few beings ever game enough to take her to bed, and she was furious that when she got Killian back, she couldn't touch him without the curse killing her.

Even after not getting laid for fifteen hundred years, Killian saw it as a blessing. Morrigan would have found all new fucked up ways to torture him if she could actually use his body against him.

"I was faking it, babe. I'm sorry," Killian said, giving her a sad smile. "You have to learn to move on, Morrigan. I'm never going to love you."

"Love is of no use to me. I want your fealty," the goddess spat. "If Aoife hadn't been so weak for your brother, I would have been free fifteen hundred years ago. Instead, she used what I gave her to banish him because of her ridiculous feelings."

"Ah, so it was you all along." Killian had wondered where the human sorceress had gotten the spells and power to cast them all out of Britain. That Morrigan was whispering in her ear from across the worlds made the final piece of the puzzle fit together.

"Aoife's betrayal doesn't matter, Killian. The spell holding me is almost broken by time. In less than a month, I will free my horde into the human world. I want you by my side when I do it. Release your wings and plunge the world into glorious darkness." Morrigan stroked his hair. "Be the dark king that you are intended to be. Take your place by my side and seize your destiny."

Killian would be lying if he said he wasn't tempted. But then Freya's goofy photos and Elise's bright wit moved through his mind. The way his brothers were with them, the way they smiled at their loves. It was enough for Killian to want to protect the world they lived in.

"Sorry, Morrigan, I'd be a terrible king."

Fury burned in her eyes, and Morrigan screeched a high-pitched battle cry. Her dark power clenched in anger around him, and Killian finally screamed in agony. The horde went crazy, chanting for his blood and pain.

Through the rage and helplessness, Killian caught the eye of the drab servant again. She was the only being there that wasn't cheering. She was looking at Morrigan with death in her eyes, not adoration.

Brave lass.

Killian managed to shoot her a wink, her flickering dual faces the last thing he saw before the pain grew too much, and he embraced oblivion.

3

Bron Ironwood had grown up listening to stories of the Night Prince. Sitting on her grandmother's knee, she had been told all about his wings that trailed darkness and stars whenever he flew across the sky, of how he was responsible for all dreams and nightmares, and how he could destroy a woman's reputation just by smiling at her.

Grandmother Cara had told her about their great ancestor, Fergus Ironwood, who had once shot the Night Prince in his thigh in a failed assassination attempt. The Night Prince had made a dreadful promise to Fergus as he had tossed him from the castle steps. When he returned to the human world, he would kill all the Ironwoods.

For all her life, Bron had dreamed of the prince in that castle of onyx and moonlight, with his soft sable wings and burning emerald eyes. Then, five years ago, the princes had returned to England, and the dreams had stopped.

That was when she knew she was finally going to get her chance to kill him.

When the bounty had come through to find the missing Night Prince, it had gone to her as her right as the eldest Ironwood. It was her duty to protect the family above all other oaths, and the Ironwoods had never forgotten the prince's promise to kill them all.

The only problem was that their mysterious client had demanded the prince be delivered to him alive so he could have the pleasure of killing the bastard himself.

It wasn't ideal, but as long as the Night Prince ended up dead, Bron would have to be satisfied. They needed the bounty money to keep their ancestral manor more than Bron needed the honor of killing a fae prince.

"You have to do this for the good of the family," her mother, Kenna, had said when Bron had bitched about it. If it wasn't for her baby sister needing to be taken care of, Kenna would've been the one to take the contract. Having five daughters hadn't stopped Kenna Ironwood from hunting. Nothing ever would.

Grimacing at the thought of home, Bron chewed on a heel of old bread. For all the stories of the magic of fae food, they really couldn't cook for shit. It was gritty and sat too heavy in her guts, but anything was better than the rations she had lived off for weeks.

It had been three months since she had taken the contract to hunt the prince down, leading her through Faerie and to the very edges of Tir Na Nog.

Oh grandma, if only you could see me now.

Bron straightened the shabby servant's dress she had stolen a week ago and tried to mentally prepare for what came next. She had thought that she would feel more excited when she got to this point. She was the first Ironwood that infiltrated Morrigan's keep. If she made it back alive, her name would become a family legend.

She *had* been excited...right up until that afternoon when she had watched Morrigan torture the Night Prince.

The bread in her stomach churned. He wasn't what she had thought he would be. He didn't have wings, which she was kind of disappointed by. Morrigan wouldn't make a mistake like stealing the wrong fae prince, but Bron had her doubts that he was *the* Night Prince.

Then she had seen his eyes. Piercing emerald green that had cut straight through her glamour. He had known she was hiding behind one straight away, unlike every other fae in the castle. When the torture had really started, he had still found the energy to wink at her as if to say, 'I see you, imposter.'

That wink and his pain had struck something deep inside of her, but it hadn't weakened her resolve. Bron hadn't dragged her ass all the way through three worlds to walk away without her prize or die trying.

Ironwoods died; that was a lesson that had been ingrained into her since birth. But Ironwoods always died fighting, and that was the important bit.

"Here, girl, the guards are too drunk to feed the beast tonight," the cook said, shoving a tray towards Bron. From what she could tell, the female was some kind of a faun, with curved horns and hooved feet.

"Yes, mistress." Bron nodded obediently, keeping her eyes downcast. She mentally had to move up her plan a few days, but that wasn't bad. Morrigan's castle was a dangerous place, and the longer she lingered, the sooner someone would realize that she shouldn't be there.

Bron picked up the tray and made her way carefully through the kitchens and towards the halls. There were usually guards on every twist and turn to the dungeons, but they must have been partying hard because the halls were empty.

Thank the saints and stars for bloody miracles. She sent the grateful prayer upward. There would be fewer throats for her to slit and bodies to hide, which was only a bonus. Bron set her face in grim determination and moved down to the rows of cells.

Darkness had a different feel in Morrigan's castle. It was bitter cold and had claws that would trace against skin, inciting a relentless terror and anticipation for when they finally attacked. The protective wards and glamours around Bron made it only just tolerable. Unfortunately, they did nothing for her sense of smell.

The cells on either side of her stank of blood and shit and unwashed terror sweats. She made a point of not lingering anywhere or looking too hard at whatever horrors the prisoners were subjected to.

Eyes on the prize, Ironwood.

When Bron could go no deeper, she found the very last cell. An oily lamp on the black stone wall barely gave off a glow. She gripped the tray tighter, forcing her eyes to adjust as they searched the cells. A slightly darker shadow was lounging in the back corner.

"Are you alive?" Bron whispered, lowering the tray to the slot by the door. A deep, silken chuckle echoed back through the darkness, making the hair on the back of her neck stand on end.

"Unfortunately." Two glowing emerald eyes opened, and she felt them slide over her like a touch. "Those are some impressive glamours you have. I'm surprised someone hasn't sniffed them out yet."

Bron didn't reply, couldn't think straight as the shadows moved. The Night Prince was suddenly standing on the other side of the bars. The fae were all bigger than humans, but God, he was massive.

"I have a proposition for you," she said, finding her voice.

"You've come to the wrong prisoner, beautiful. I'm not that kind of boy."

"Not that kind of proposition. I'll get you out of this cell if you surrender yourself into my custody."

"Sounds like a good way to get yourself killed. Don't risk it. I'd hate to see what Morrigan will do to you when we get caught. I'm not worth it, trust me."

Bron stiffened. It had been a long time since she had her abilities doubted. "Your concern for my safety is noted but misplaced, fae. I have a way out of the castle too."

The Night Prince looked her over again, his gaze sharpening. "What's the catch?"

"You will become my prisoner and make a vow to not harm me. I will take you back to Ireland, where you will be turned over to my employer. Whatever he has planned for you can't be worse than this," Bron replied, straightening her shoulders.

"Color me intrigued. Fine. If you can get me out of here, I'll go with you," he said challengingly.

"I need you to do something for me first." Bron looked him dead in the eye. "Turn around and pull down your pants." His answering chuckle was filthier than the floor she was standing on.

"I thought you said it wasn't that kind of proposition."

Bron didn't blink. "It's not. This deal is only for the Night Prince, and I need irrevocable proof that you are him."

He raised a single black brow. "And showing you my ass will do that?"

"I'm not interested in your ass, but the scar on your thigh." Bron folded her arms. "Hurry up. You're wasting time."

The Night Prince's smile turned sly as he turned and dropped his dirty jeans. Bron looked at his golden-brown skin and perfectly muscled ass with as much clinical coolness as she could muster. On his left thigh, as the family legend promised, was a scar from a crossbow bolt.

"Looking is free, but touching will cost you," the prince said with a wink over his shoulder.

"I've seen all that I care to." Bron searched underneath her skirts and found a pair of silver manacles in the side pocket of her cargo pants. She pushed them through the bars at him, the cell's wards snapping at her skin. "Put those on."

The Night Prince did as he was told, wincing as the magic kicked in. "Well, aren't these nasty."

"They will keep you being a good boy." Bron pulled off the dress and unwrapped the scarf from around her head. She straightened her long-sleeved thermal and made sure all of her weapons were in the correct place.

"I'll take that oath from you now," she said, unsheathing a dagger and cutting the pad of her thumb.

The Night Prince's eyes glittered with malice as he bit his own. "I, Killian the Night Prince, promise not to bring harm to this charming Ironwood that's going to spring me from this hell hole."

"How did you know I am an Ironwood?" Bron demanded.

"Only an Ironwood would want to see the scar where their ancestor got a lucky shot in." The Night Prince stuck his bleeding thumb through the bars.

"I accept your promise and oath, Killian," Bron replied and pressed her thumb to his. The malice on his face turned to confusion as he stared at their thumbs touching. Bron felt the magic in the oath curl up her arm and settle inside of her like a warm tendril of power. She removed her thumb.

"Excellent. Now, let's get you out of there." Bron didn't have time to read into Killian's expression or wonder why the fae prince lifted his cut thumb to his lips and sucked their combined blood from it. Pulling out a pair of lock picks, she got to work on the cell door.

These cells were a combination of metal and magic, but Morrigan didn't plan for an Ironwood being bold enough to bust one open. Especially an Ironwood with a sister who was a genius at hacking into other people's magic.

Bron pulled out a small patch of woven metal and tossed it at the invisible wards, just as the lock popped. The wards lit up as they short-circuited and vanished. Bron moved a careful distance from the door.

"Let's go, prince."

4

Killian was still staring at his thumb when the cell door swung open. A silver chain spooled from one of his manacles before flicking up to join the other.

"A chain? Really?" he complained. The Ironwood only turned on her heel and walked away.

"If you can prove that you're trustworthy, I'll get rid of the chain."

"You know these cuffs have enough magic in them that you could send me screaming to the ground whenever you liked?"

"I know."

"So what's the use of a chain?"

"What's the use of arguing with me about it? The guards will only stay at their revels for so long."

She had her dagger out, carefully checking around corners. Killian wandered after her, the muscles in his legs twinging from the healing spear wounds. He was still a little dazed from the magic of the bargain she'd extracted from him, and the fact he had just touched another being for the first time in fifteen hundred years without killing them.

She would've done her research on him, but no one knew about his curse except his brothers, their mates, Morrigan, and a few of her guards.

He was surprised that the Ironwood hadn't gleaned that information from the castle.

"You know, no one has ever escaped Morrigan's prison before," Killian said, catching up to her.

A cocky smile that was pure Ironwood arrogance flashed across her face, making her glamour shudder. "No one has ever had me helping them."

Killian had to admit, he was intrigued to see what her escape plan was. He grinned. He definitely wasn't bored anymore.

The Ironwood dropped, dodging a spear that came out of nowhere. A guard let out a shout and charged at her, but she used his momentum to flip over him with graceful ease that came with hours of practice and drove her dagger into his throat. She didn't even stop to see if he was dead before she kept walking.

"Hurry up!" she hissed, her Irish brogue getting stronger the more impatient she became. Killian picked his jaw up off the floor, stepped around the blood pooling on the dirty stones, and hurried after her. He wanted to see what she would do next.

"Give me a hand, will you?" she whispered from a dark alcove stacked with barrels and wooden boxes. Killian grabbed one end of the box she was lifting and shifted it. Underneath was a wooden trap door.

"How did you know this was hiding here?" he asked.

"This is where I came in, and I've spent the last week getting shit stored here to hide it from eyesight." Killian would save his praise for later. He grabbed the metal ring and lifted the trap door up. He gagged as a foul smell hit him full in the face.

"It's the sewers," he choked.

"It is. Get your ass down that ladder, prince."

"Why me?"

"Because I need something to chase off the rats. And let's face it, you're already dirty." She waved her bloody dagger blade at him. "Off you go."

"Unbelievable," he muttered. Making sure his chain would be long enough, Killian held onto the rotting ladder and climbed down into the fetid darkness. The Ironwood followed him, pulling the trap door closed. There was a flash of violet magic, and it sealed shut.

Killian waited for her, his hands itching to reach out and lift her down. He didn't risk it. Maybe their thumbs touching hadn't affected her because of the bargaining magic to do her no harm?

The Ironwood produced a small flashlight from one of the many pockets of her pants. She reached up until she found a stone niche and pulled down a dusty backpack.

"It smells bad, but this part of the sewer is dry at least. Enjoy it. It won't be nice for long," she said, slinging the pack on. She straightened her shoulders, and the glamour she was wearing melted away with a glow of the same violet light. Bit by bit, Killian got his first proper look at his rescuer. Sandy brown hair bled out to a dark auburn braid, her pale skin turned brown, and washed-out blue eyes went dark.

"You don't look like the last Ironwood I met. The accent is the same. Are you from a better-looking branch of the family?" Killian asked.

"None of your business."

"Why the glamour anyway?"

The Ironwood straightened the dagger sheaths on her forearms. "I've found that as a boring-looking white girl, I can get in just about anywhere. Let's get a head start before the goddess realizes her prize pet has been stolen."

"I think it's time for a proper introduction. I'm Killian, though some people call me Kill," he said, smiling at her. She didn't smile back. There was, indeed, a first time for everything.

"Yes, I know."

"Do you have a first name, Ironwood?"

Dark eyes filled with annoyance. "Miss."

Killian laughed, strangely relieved it wasn't a 'Mrs. Ironwood,' and his reaction seemed to piss her off more. "Lead the way then, *Miss* Ironwood."

"Keep up and watch your head. Tree roots and rocks are sticking out everywhere," she said, moving past him and down the tunnel. The tip of her long braid brushed against his hand, and Killian fought the tremble that shot up his arm. That was twice he had been touched in one day.

It was only her hair. Maybe it has to be skin to skin.

Despite Killian being the family spy, he had done everything he could to avoid dark, dank tunnels under castles. He was a creature of the sky, or he used to be when his wings worked. Being underground set his teeth on edge. It was one of the many reasons why Morrigan had dumped him as deep as she could.

"How much longer do we have to trudge through these sewers?" he asked.

"We've only been down here twenty minutes," the Ironwood said, padding in front of him.

"I don't like it."

"Well, I don't like traveling companions who don't know how to stop talking." They reached an intersection of four tunnels, and she swung her torchlight up at the bricks. On the edge of a stone, higher than the stain of the waterline, was a mark in chalk. "This way."

Killian wanted to tell her that he was genuinely impressed that she had come through Morrigan's basement, but she was prickly enough that anything he said would probably provoke her.

"You must be the oldest Ironwood, yes? Are your people still matrilineal?" he asked instead.

"Why do you care?" came the response. The Ironwood carefully stepped around a pile of rotting bones. Her nose didn't even wrinkle at the smell that had him gagging.

"Just trying to pass the time. Get to know my new traveling companion—"

The Ironwood moved so quickly, Killian didn't have time to step back. She grabbed him by the front of his shirt, slammed him up against the slimy stone wall, pressed a dagger to his throat with one hand, and clamped the other over his mouth.

"Shut. Up," she whispered, teeth gritted.

She looked up, and Killian spotted another trap door entrance. He could make out voices on the other side. He didn't care about the voices. His biggest problem in that second was the small, calloused palm over his bare face. Sensation and emotion batted him as his eyes fluttered close against his will. Under the funk of the sewer, he could smell her faint lilac and rose perfume. He wanted to shove her away for fear of infecting her and pull her closer at the same time.

It's okay. She's not dying. It's okay.

The voices above them vanished, and the Ironwood stepped back.

Killian's eyes opened and locked on her dark ones. They were full of annoyance and anger. Her breath hitched as she held on a fraction longer, expression shifting to confusion.

"Listen, prince. I'm not your traveling companion. I'm your fucking keeper. You don't need to know anything about my life story, and I don't care about yours. I just need to get you back to Ireland so I can get paid. Keep your mouth shut because I swear if you get us caught, I will gut you before Morrigan can," she hissed in his face.

Killian frowned as dark shadows moved behind her. He grabbed one of her daggers from her thigh sheath and threw it.

She dropped her hand quickly and spun around as a rat the size of a labrador screeched and died, her dagger buried in its eye.

"Understood, Ironwood. I'll just keep watching your back, shall I?" Killian asked. He was still shaking from having a woman pressed up against him for the first time in centuries. She ignored him, pulling her dagger from the dead rat and flicking blood and eye slime from the blade.

"We have another hour on foot before we get to the end of these sewers if the guards don't catch us first. Can you run on your damaged legs?"

Killian nodded. "They are fine. Just make sure you don't trip in your haste and make me fall too."

"I won't trip." She sheathed her clean dagger and kept the other ready in her hand. "This way."

Killian rubbed his thumb over his bottom lip, trying to get rid of the sensation of her off his mouth.

Why can an Ironwood touch me and no one else? What magic have they gained? Killian shook himself and jogged after her. They would have time before they reached Ireland for him to pull out all of her secrets, one by one. He grinned in the darkness. He hadn't had a decent challenge in years.

5

Bron didn't have to check that the prince was still following her. Killian gave off an aura that thrummed with enough power that her hackles were constantly up. If only she was as aware of her enemies as she was of him. She should have heard that damn rat coming up behind her. It was only a few feet from her when Killian took it down.

So fucking embarrassing. It could have killed her, all because she got stunned as soon as she touched him.

Bron had been dreaming of him since she was a girl, and it was surreal to have him in the flesh in front of her.

Touching him had been something else.

It had triggered every one of her internal alarms. She was pissed at him, and at the same time, she wanted to press her nose to his neck and breathe him in. It was confusing and infuriating because he'd been a prisoner and smelt like one. He was her family's enemy, and saving her from one damn rat wouldn't change that.

Fucking fae. Bron knew they were built to seduce, and they had used it as a weapon against humans forever. If the stories were to be believed, he was the worst of the lot.

Killian managed to keep his mouth shut since the incident with the rat, thank God. He would bring Morrigan's entire army down on them with his constant chatting.

Making friends again, Bronagh? Imogen's voice mocked in the back of her head. Her sister only called her by her full name when she wanted to piss her off. Which was all the time. When she got home, Imogen was going to owe her the nicest bottle of whiskey. She just needed to get the prince back to Ireland without getting caught or killed.

"Arawan's balls, how much further?" Killian complained. Bron turned, ready to snap at him, and spotted the sweat shining against his golden skin, the tenseness around his eyes.

"Are you hurt?" she asked. *Why do you care?*

"No, I'm...claustrophobic." It looked like it actually pained him to admit it.

"Seriously? I saw you defy and be tortured by bloody Morrigan, and you're worried about a dirty sewer?" Bron might not like him, but she would never, ever forget the sound of his screams for as long as she lived.

"I was tortured where I could see the sky," he said like it explained everything.

"Can you take some deep breaths?"

Killian grimaced. "I could, but this air is disgusting enough to catch hepatitis just by breathing it."

Bron pulled out her watch from one pocket. "By my calculations, we have about fifteen minutes before we reach an exit in the forest. You've held it together this long. You'll be fine."

"What if I'm not? Will you hold my hand to get me through it?"

Bron shook her head. "No. I'll just make you walk ahead of me, and every time you slow your pace, I'll prod you with my dagger."

Killian clicked his tongue. "Fucking Ironwood down to your bones."

Bron focused on the dark tunnel, hiding her small smile. She had a different father to her other siblings and had always been self-conscious about it. She made up for it by being the toughest, most Ironwood of them all. As the oldest, they were all her responsibility, and to keep them safe, she would give the prince over to be killed without batting an eye.

Three more turns, and Bron got her first lungful of clean smelling air. She slowed her pace, listening for any guards that may have been waiting at the sewer entrance. She had done her best to hide it with branches and other collected brush from the forest floor, but not all of Morrigan's soldiers would be fooled by that.

"It's not yet dawn," Killian whispered and then pushed past her, running to get out. Bron swore and raced after him. If he walked into a trap, she would murder him.

Killian had torn back her carefully placed branches at the entrance, and Bron froze as she stepped between them. The fae prince was staring up at the night sky, breathing deeply, with eyes silvered with unshed tears. Even filthy, he was mesmerizing in the moonlight. The shadows seemed to caress him as he held his hands out as if to embrace all the stars at once. His attention shifted to the castle in the distance, lights still burning along its battlements, and his outstretched hands moved to stick his middle fingers up at Morrigan.

Bron cleared her throat. "That's enough. We need to get going before dawn arrives. I've hidden some supplies by a stream not far from here."

"Lead the way." Killian gave her a wide, open smile.

"You shouldn't be so happy. I'm leading you to your death, you know that, right?"

"Maybe, maybe not. I don't suppose you know who it is that wants me dead?"

Every Ironwood since Fergus.

"My mother takes care of those details. My duty is to get you there."

"So you *are* still matrilineal."

Bron scowled at him and pulled the folded-up map from her pocket. She had been drawing it since stepping into Faerie. It wasn't constantly shifting like the stories said, but it was easy to get lost in a place that you couldn't Google. Bron had hidden caches of supplies all along her journey home, mostly to mark out decent camping spots, and it would make the trip go quicker.

She had taken three months to track the prince down because she had to work as a human in Faerie, but now she had him, she could make the journey to the nearest gateway and back to the human world in a week.

Bron slanted a glance at the fae walking beside her. A week would be a long time without killing him. It had taken less than an hour to pull a knife on him.

Think of the money. How Kenna will stop stressing about not having the funds to fix the manor and pay for David's medical treatment.

Her mother and stepfather were a good team in keeping five daughters and two cousins in line, but that many mouths to feed, clothe, and train wasn't cheap.

She straightened her shoulders. She could handle a week. She didn't think about the myriad of things that could delay them, including Morrigan's soldiers.

Dawn was staining the sky pink and gold by the time Bron found the stream she was looking for. She crouched down by the oak where she had buried gear and dug about its roots until she found the handles of the plastic bag and pulled it free.

"Here, I got you some clean clothes and a bar of soap," Bron said, tossing the bag at him. "We need to make sure no one recognizes you, and it would help if you didn't look and smell like a prisoner."

"You thought of everything, didn't you, Ironwood?" Killian mocked. He toed off his boots that were still stained with his blood.

"I had to. The client was very specific that you had to be in proper order by the time we got you back." Bron pointed to the stream. "Hurry up. We need to maintain our head start if we are going to outrun the soldiers."

"Gods, you're bossy." Killian pulled his shirt up and over his long, matted hair and tossed it to the ground. Bron kept her face blank as she got an eyeful of lean, golden muscle. He had Celtic knotwork wings tattooed on his chest and stomach, and her eyes lingered on the dark hair scattered over it and down to the fly of his jeans.

Killian noticed her watching and smirked, turning around as he undid his pants. Bron noted the lack of wings with a fresh twinge of disappointment that they were only a story. In their place were ragged, vicious scars that looked like someone had slashed into him with a dagger.

"I'm going to get shy if you keep staring at me like that, Ironwood," Killian said over his shoulder.

"I need to make sure you aren't going to run off."

He shook the chain of his cuffs at her. "Not possible. I can feel the magic in these. I wouldn't get very far before the paralysis would kick in. I'm not just a pretty face, you know."

"I never said you were," Bron said.

Killian replied by dropping his jeans and stepping into the water. Bron looked away, digging about in her bag for her stash of protein bars. After a week of the food given to servants, the vegan chocolate protein bar was a sweet, delightful luxury. She picked up Killian's blood splattered shirt, cut it into strips, and scattered them around the glade. It wasn't much, but it might be enough to confuse Morrigan's dogs that would be out to track them.

"Will you come and help me wash my hair?" Killian called with a mischievous smile.

"Sure," Bron replied, and his smile changed to delight. He turned his back to her to give her better access to the tangled raven hair that hung to his waist.

"This is very nice of you," he purred.

"No problem at all." Bron gathered his hair at his shoulders into a ponytail, put her dagger blade underneath it, and sliced it off. Killian let out a small shriek of horror as she tossed the length of filthy hair into the water beside him. "Happy to help, prince. Now hurry the fuck up."

Bron took a not-so-secret delight in the shock on his face.

"Are you this mean to everyone, or do I just bring it out in you?" he asked, stepping out of the water.

"You're not special enough to bring anything out in me, prince." Bron dried the water from her dagger and slid it back into her thigh sheath. It wasn't entirely true. She knew her natural tendency to avoid people meant that she was often mistaken as mean or sullen. Killian just set her off far too quickly, and the more he flirted with her, the meaner she became.

"You cut my hair," he snarled through the clean shirt he was pulling over his head.

"Your worry about your looks over your life says a lot about you."

"I feel shorn."

Killian ran his hand through his dark locks self-consciously. He didn't look bad with the shorter hair, and now all the dirt was out of it, Bron could see the gleam of a silver streak over one pointed ear.

"It'll grow back." Bron tossed a protein bar at him. "Peace offering. You can eat while we walk."

"Do you boss your boyfriend around this much?" Killian asked, pulling his boots back on.

"I don't have one."

"I can see why," he murmured under his breath.

Bron's temper frayed. "Like I care what you think. I'm sorry I don't fawn all over you, prince, like you obviously believe I should. I'm sorry, I want to get out of Morrigan's lands before she flays me."

"I won't ever let Morrigan lay a hand on you," Killian said, his voice suddenly cold with promise. Bron's anger fizzled out under the intensity of his stern expression. She turned away from him and grabbed her backpack.

"Let's get moving."

6

In the light of day, two things became abundantly clear to Killian. The first was that the Ironwood was irritated by his very existence; the second was that none of his legendary charms worked on her.

It was just his fucked-up luck that the only woman he had been able to touch in fifteen hundred years seemed to hate him with an intensity he didn't understand.

Killian had been following her silently all day, and she seemed pretty content to keep to herself. Killian had been equally content to watch her curved ass in her tight cargo pants as he tried to figure out who would want to kill him.

Surely, the list had to be smaller than it had once been. Time had taken care of the ones he could remember. One thing that hadn't changed with time was how militant the Ironwoods still were.

He went over everything he had seen and heard since the Ironwood had sprung him from his cell. Something was driving her, and he didn't think it was all about the money. Killian was a professional when it came to secrets, could just about smell them, and not knowing hers was already niggling at him.

Killian was glad to be out of the cell, despite the company and possible death sentence. He'd been hooded for his trip to Morrigan's castle and was surprised that the lands around him were wild and beautiful. He started humming softly, determined to maintain his growing good mood as the sun began to set.

Killian was free and wasn't going to let the goddess take him alive again. He needed to get back to Ireland and talk to his brothers, warn them that their parent's magic blocking Morrigan from the human lands was weakening. He might be about to die, whether by the Ironwood's client or by the curse, but he wanted his brothers and their mates to be safe from the goddess's wrath before he went.

Maybe the client who wanted him dead would let him have some dying requests? His list was the same as it had always been; see his brothers, have a really good drink, get fucked into oblivion. The last one had been wishful thinking until... He looked at the Ironwood's swinging, dark auburn braid.

His ears pricked up at the faint whooshing sound that drifted out from the trees. He knew that sou—

Killian leaped, tackling the Ironwood to the forest floor as four throwing daggers sailed overhead.

The bounty hunter moved one arm around Killian, the sleeve of her jacket riding up as she shot two small bolts from a device on her wrist. Someone screamed, and four fae appeared through the trees in hunting leathers, the fifth dead on the ground with a bolt through his neck.

"Great shot," Killian said appreciatively. The Ironwood managed a grin.

"Thanks."

"Grab the girl. She can touch the prince without his curse killing her," the dark-haired fae demanded. "Morrigan will want to question her."

"Like fuck you're taking her," Killian snarled and rolled up to his feet. The Ironwood was straight up behind him, sliding into a fighting stance. She placed the hilt of the dagger into his palm.

"Don't make me regret this," she whispered. The chain binding his manacles disappeared.

The four fae hunters attacked, and Killian released three years' worth of rage and frustration.

Killian dodged the blade of a short sword, drove his dagger up into the fae's arm, and yanked him forward. He slammed his hand down on the male's face, and the curse tore through him. He screamed in terror, clawing at his skin, and Killian turned to the next.

An arrow struck his shoulder and he yanked it free, before he drove it into the hunter's eye. Killian grabbed him around the throat and hurled him at his companion sparring with the Ironwood. They hit the ground in a cursing tumble, and the Ironwood slit their throats before they could rise again. Her chest was heaving, flecks of amber blood smeared on her face. She looked at the male who had died from Killian's curse.

"You did that just by touching him?" she asked.

"Yes."

Her face clouded with confusion. "I've touched you more than once, and that never happened."

Killian let out a bitter laugh. "I am aware."

"Why, though?"

"No idea. I only know that you're the first person to touch me in over a thousand years and not die." Her dark eyes went wide, and Killian could see the information she knew about him rearranging itself in her head.

"But why me?"

"I don't know, and we don't have time to find out." Killian offered her the dagger back. She shook her head.

"Keep it. More will be coming," she said, just as a howl echoed through the trees.

"We are losing daylight, so be careful where you tread," Killian replied, pointing at the trail through the trees.

"Try and keep up, old man," the Ironwood said with a spark of teasing fire he hadn't seen in her before. Maybe the killing had put her in a good mood. Killian snapped his teeth at her.

"Run, Ironwood."

And run, they did. She was swift as a deer, and even with his Fae strength, he had to fight to keep up with her. His imprisonment had taken a bigger toll than he realized if a human was outrunning him. He lost sight of her around a bend, and a large splash and a scream of alarm had him sprinting for her. He slid to a stop before he toppled into the marshy swamp water after her.

"Help me, I can't get out!" she squeaked in panic, water and mud up to her waist. Killian strode to the bank, laughing his ass off.

"Oh, Ironwood. You're in a tight spot, aren't you?" he said, leaning against a tree.

"Are you going to help me or not?" she squirmed, thrashing her arms. She sank lower, the filthy water reaching her chest. "Our bargain said you wouldn't hurt me!"

"I'm not hurting you, Ironwood. I don't have to do anything, just watch you drown. That is if the serpents don't get you first." He pointed to a far bank where the reeds were shivering, alive with water serpents. Genuine fear flashed over her face, and she thrashed.

"Don't do that. It excites them." Killian was enjoying her distress far too much. "You fearlessly went into Morrigan's castle, and it's water serpents you're worried about?"

"I'm Irish! We don't do snakes!" She seemed to struggle internally for a second, but another rustle in the reeds had her screaming. "I'll make another bargain with you!"

"For my freedom?" he asked.

"No. It's not in my power to give you that. Pick something else." She looked like she was about to start weeping as the water rippled around her.

Killian counted a few moments in his long life where his conscience had gotten the better of him and he'd done the noble thing, but this wasn't going to be one of them.

"I will save you if you give me a night with you," he said, the words coming out of his mouth before he could consider them. She stopped thrashing.

"What do you mean by that exactly?" she asked, tone icy.

"Exactly what you're thinking, beautiful. I haven't felt the touch of a woman in fifteen hundred years. You're going to hand me over to be killed. I want one last night with a woman before I meet my end, and you're the only one that can touch me without dying from my curse."

Killian's heart was thrumming dangerously at his audacity to ask an Ironwood such a thing. She gave him a look more venomous than the snakes circling around her. Dogs started baying nearby, catching on their scent.

"Better decide quick, Ironwood, or I'm going to leave you there."

The fear was back in her eyes, fighting against the anger. "Fine! I will spend a fucking night with you if you pull me from this water."

Killian was going to cut his fingers, but the bargain screamed through his veins, and he hissed as a black wing appeared on his wrist. The Ironwood cursed foully as the same mark appeared on hers.

"Fuck you, Killian," she snarled.

He chuckled deeply. "You're definitely going to, Ironwood."

His amusement vanished as three of Morrigan's war hounds appeared on the trail behind them. They were the size of miniature ponies, all fang, muscle, and hate. The Ironwood screamed and stabbed out at the water, the serpents finally going for her. As soon as he turned, the hounds would attack, but when she screamed again, something snapped inside of him.

Heat raced up Killian's spine as magic tore open his back, and his wings snapped out. A hound leaped for him, and he launched himself upward, his wings catching him on the wind for a silent second before he dived. The Ironwood stuck her hands out of the mire, and he grabbed her, heaving her out with a mighty flap of his wings, and pulled her free.

"Hang on!" he shouted, and she wrapped muddy legs over his hips, her arms going around his neck. He held her slippery body close as he sailed over the treetops of the forest. She was shivering with fear and cold, clinging to him with all her strength.

"B-Bronagh," she said against his throat, her chest heaving in shock. "But I prefer Bron."

Killian pulled her closer into the warmth of his body. "Nice to meet you, Bron."

∼

"I THOUGHT you didn't have wings," Bron said sometime later.

Killian figured there was enough distance between them and the hounds, so he was trying to find a decent place to rest for the night.

"Of course I have wings. I just don't leave them out for everyone to see," Killian replied. It wasn't a lie, but the truth was a little more complicated. He had hidden his wings centuries ago, and no matter how hard he tried, he couldn't get them to reappear. He imagined that it was the final stage of the curse. They were aching from fatigue and disuse, but they were out and had saved them.

"There," Bron said, pointing. "I'm sure I camped there while I was tracking you." Her nails dug into his shoulder as he swooped down and landed. He fought not to collapse as he set her on her feet.

"I hate you," Bron said, "But thank you for saving me."

"There is something I have to tell you, Bron. A confession."

A dark brow rose. "Oh? And what's that."

"You smell really bad," Killian said. He was still grinning when she scooped drying slime from her clothes and swiped it down his face.

"Likewise, dick." Then she started laughing, a big full laugh that lit up her grim face.

"Look at that. You can smile after all."

"Go and be useful somewhere else, Killian." She dumped her dirty pack on the ground. "I have a swamp to get off me." She peeled off her long-sleeved thermal shirt, and Killian's mouth watered.

"I'll go and do a quick soar, make sure there's nothing nasty around." He shot into the sky, wings protesting with every flap.

The cold night cooled his sudden desire, the delight of flying again finally taking over. Under the light of the moon, he checked over his wings for damage. His chest ached as he saw that their once rich black feathers were now a dull washed-out grey.

At least they are back.

The manacles around his wrists began to burn with a warning that he was getting too far away from his keeper.

A fucking Ironwood that he had made a bargain with—somehow—without blood. He had always been the one to strike deals, unlike his brothers, and was a master at getting what he wanted. Maybe he still had enough of her blood in his veins from the first bargain that it had just accepted another one? He had never dared have a double deal with anyone.

Killian studied the wing on his wrist. It was different from the others that had ever appeared there, its design a complex twist of knotwork. Usually, they were a plain black wing that disappeared once the deal was done.

"Mysterious, beautiful Ironwood," he growled, his mind providing an unhelpful image of the bare brown midriff he had seen earlier. He had never had to make a bargain for sex before and was a little horrified how low he had fallen.

"No undoing it now," he told the stars, and when his manacles burned again, he turned and headed back to camp.

7

Bron knew that she didn't have much time before Killian returned, so she sketched warding sigils around their camp and went looking for her soap.

Wiping the slime off her hands, she opened the straps of her pack and prayed that the waterproof guarantee was as good as it was advertised. The bottom layer of shirts was damp, but the rest of the rations had stayed clear of the swamp water.

Finding the soap and using her torch for light, she knelt on the sandy soil of the stream and dunked her head into the water. The creek was freezing, but at least, it was clean.

With her hair and chest washed, she stripped off her sports bra and put on a clean one. She wasn't shy. She had been on enough boot camps with real soldiers and jobs with other bounty hunters over the years that she wasn't a prude. But it was a tactical no-no to get into a river naked and hope that nothing attacked. She stripped off her boots and pants last and washed the mud off her legs.

When Bron was finally clean, she lit a small fire to dry out her boots and soaked clothes. Feeling calm and in control again, she studied the tattoo on her wrist.

It was a twisting knotwork wing that proclaimed to the world that she was dumb enough to make a bargain with the Night Prince.

Of all the stupid mistakes you've made, this is the worst.

It didn't matter that logically Bron knew she couldn't have gotten out of the swamp without help or that between snakes and Morrigan's hounds, she would have been dead or worse. She had failed and would now have to spend a night with Killian before she got back to Dublin.

There was no way in all the hells that she would have the mark of shame on her skin when she stepped through the doors of the Ironwood Manor. Kenna would kill her, and that was before her sisters kicked her ass.

Bron was gnawing on another protein bar and studying her map when Killian landed by the creek.

"We should be okay for the night. I couldn't see anything that will give us any trouble," he said, pulling off his shirt. It was stained with mud from Bron, clinging to him like a baby bear. God, it was embarrassing.

Killian's wings folded in behind him as he knelt and washed his shirt in the stream. Bron had a powerful urge to touch the feathers and see if they were as soft as they looked.

"Why aren't they black?" she blurted out before she could stop herself.

"It's a part of my curse," Killian said, his biceps flexing as he wrung his shirt out. He was sickeningly handsome, but all the fae were. He was washing the mud smear off his face when he flashed her a smile over his shoulder. "Why are you so interested in my wings?"

"I'm not," Bron replied, looking back at her map.

Killian hummed but didn't push it. He flicked the last of the water from his shirt and hung it over a tree branch to dry. "What do you have there?"

"A map I drew of Faerie. Just trying to figure out where we are," she said, not looking up.

"If it helps, I saw a river and a mountain range," Killian offered, sitting down on the other side of the fire.

"That does help. Um, thanks."

"Not a problem... Bron," he said, holding his hands out to the flames.

She passed him one of the protein bars and tried to ignore how her name sounded on his tongue.

Bron found the mountain range on her map, her fingers tracing the river. If they followed the stream they were camped beside, it would lead to the river where she could hire or steal a boat. A day sailing without any attacks, and they would make it to the mountains. She had crossed them on her way to the castle and spent an uncomfortably cold night in a cave there. They hadn't gotten as far off course as she feared, so that was something to be thankful for.

"Do you know what my brothers have been up to?" Killian asked.

"No idea. They are alive, and the peace still holds. Prince Kian has been keeping your kind under control," Bron replied. "At least when I crossed over into Faerie, that was the case. It took months to track you down."

"Really? I'm sure my brothers are searching for me, if only so they can yell at me for being dumb enough to get kidnapped. Makes me wonder why they couldn't find me, but you could," Killian said, his eyes studying her again like she was hiding something.

"That's easy. I'm the best at what I do." Bron said it without any arrogance. She *was* the best bounty hunter in Ireland. It was why Kenna had assigned the job to her and her alone.

"I don't doubt it. If you're good enough to have a workable map of Faerie and the edges of Tir Na Nog, you're more than good," Killian commented. He wasn't teasing or flirting with her. He sounded genuinely impressed. "Also, the fact that you managed to stay alive and undetected as a human in Morrigan's castle is next level."

"I have a sister that is excellent at glamours and magic. It's her wards that you can feel around the glade. I couldn't have gotten this far without her." Bron tried not to feel like she was betraying Charlotte by offering up the information.

Killian grinned with sin and promise. "Before you think it, no matter how good she is, you're not going to be able to break that bargain, Ironwood."

Bron *hadn't* thought about it, but the fact he took away that hope before she did really pissed her off.

Killian pretended to be oblivious to her scowl and lay back on the grass to look up at the sky. He started humming softly under his breath again, the same song he had been humming all damn day.

Bron turned her back to the fire, using one arm as a pillow and putting the other over her head, trying to block out the song and drown out her own humiliation of now being bound to a damn fae.

∼

No matter how tired Bron was, she couldn't relax enough to go to sleep. Killian was snoozing across the dying fire, a small smile on his face like he needed to mock the world even in his sleep. He had made a blood vow not to harm her, but that didn't mean she was going to let her guard down. Not with his ancient promise to kill all the Ironwoods ringing in her ears, and certainly not after the swamp.

Bron placed more wood on the fire, scratching idly at the tattoo on her wrist. Maybe she would be able to sleep if she didn't hear her mother's accusing voice in her head, berating her for being scared of snakes.

"Shut up," she muttered under her breath before lying down again.

Bron must've dozed at some point because she woke with sunlight pouring into the glade and the smell of cooking fish in the air. She cracked open a tired eye.

Killian was still shirtless, his jeans rolled up, and he was standing in the stream. His wings were out at strange angles, and it took a second for Bron to figure out what he was doing.

The sun caught the silver on the talons at the top of his wings, sending light across the water to attract fish. As quick as lightning, Killian snatched one out of the water and tossed it up on the bank. He saw that she was awake and straightened.

"Morning, Ironwood. Are you hungry?" he asked, walking out of the water.

"Yes. Are you sure these fish aren't poisonous?"

"Positive. I'll eat it first if you don't trust me," Killian replied. He had taken one of her daggers while she was asleep and used it to gut the fish. He used a green stick of pine as a skewer and positioned it over the fire to cook.

"I never thought a prince would be so...outdoorsy," Bron admitted. He looked like he had done it more than once.

"I used to take off when looking after my brothers got too much. Bad habit, I suppose. You know what it's like being the eldest," he replied.

"How do you know I'm the eldest?"

"I'm observant. You are classic eldest sibling material. It's probably why you're so bossy. Let me guess? Four siblings?" Killian passed her a cooked fish, and Bron nodded. "Better you than me. I am terrible as the eldest. Kian took on all the responsibility of that as soon as he was old enough. Thank the gods."

"And you were happy to let him do it?"

"Of course I was. I kept them alive and safe after my parents died. I did my bit. If you met Kian, you would know what I mean. I wanted to make him king." Killian frowned like he had said too much and didn't like it.

Bron pretended not to notice and took a bite of fish. It was hot, and her stomach unclenched as real food filled it.

"This is surprisingly good," she said.

"Anything is better than protein bars."

Bron shrugged. "They do the job."

"They might, but they taste like ass." Killian pulled on his boots. "Where to next, babysitter?"

KILLIAN HUMMED the song for the first hour of walking until Bron told him to stop it, and he started singing instead. It wasn't loud enough to get attention, but it was relentless. The songs were a mixture of bawdy tavern songs, modern pop tunes, and Irish classics.

God have mercy.

It didn't matter that he had made her breakfast or was trying to be friendly with her. She was going to kill the bastard before she got him back to Ireland. Either that, or he would bring Morrigan's hunters down on them.

"Will you stop?" Bron said irritably. "We are about to hit the river, and I don't want you drawing attention."

Killian sighed. "You are seriously uptight, you know that, right?"

"Yes, I do, and I don't care. I know you're excited to be out of jail, but I'd prefer not to be caught because you can't stop singing like some kind of demented Disney princess."

Killian held up his hands in surrender, his infuriating grin back. She had never met someone who could get under her skin so quickly. She thought her little sisters were annoying, but the Night Prince was about to take first prize.

They reached a tree line of weeping willows, and the river opened up before them.

"I've never been to this part of Tir Na Nog before. I had no idea how pretty it was," Killian said, his eyes moved to Morrigan's castle in the distance. "That's probably why I stayed away."

Bron was careful as she walked along the riverbank, too afraid of accidentally stepping on a snake. She hated being scared of anything, but the swamp had instilled a fresh terror inside her.

I'm never leaving Ireland again.

The snakes distracted her from the other thing that her brain was fighting not to think about; Morrigan's threats of releasing her horde. The entire arena had heard her threatening Killian before she tortured him, and if whatever was keeping her from the human world was weakening...she needed to talk to her mother and put the word out to the other hunters.

"There's a boat," Killian said, pulling her out of her own troubled thoughts. It was a broken wooden rowboat, half-hidden by the reeds.

"Very funny. We need something that can actually float." Not to mention carry his bulky weight.

Killian clicked his tongue and reached out to sketch a rune mark on the rotting wood. Emerald green magic swirled around the boat, pulling it from the reeds. The damage to the small hull repaired itself, and it floated out onto the river.

"How can you even use magic with the cuffs on?" Bron demanded before she could check herself.

"These are very cleverly made," Killian commented. He shook the silver bands around his wrists. "But not quite strong enough to deal with my level of magic."

Arrogant ass.

"If they don't affect you, why don't you just take them off?" Bron asked, pulling the boat over and dumping her pack in it.

"I thought about it, but I'm rather intrigued to find out who wants to kill me. I'm at a loss to think who I could've pissed off so much."

"I've known you for two days, and I want to kill you. I'm sure the list is bigger than you think."

"You are such a charmer."

Killian held the boat steady and offered her a hand to step in. She reluctantly took it. Wobbling precariously, she managed to get in and take a seat. She went to take her hand back, but he hung on and pressed his lips to the wing on her wrist. Heat burst up her arm and across her cheeks as horrible, unexpected desire shot through her veins.

"That's the other reason I'm not going anywhere, Ironwood." He let her hand go and climbed into the boat before casually lounging against the curve of the hull. He gave her a lazy, knowing smile like he knew exactly what the kiss had sparked in her.

"You and I have a deal, Bronagh Ironwood, and I'm not leaving your side until I get a chance to turn your frown upside down."

8

Killian had been traveling with Bron for hours, and there had been no sign of the girl that had smeared mud on his face. The hunter had locked herself up again so tightly that it gave Killian a headache just looking at her.

At least the day was nice on the river, his magic coasting them along so they wouldn't have to row. He was tired of running and having his blisters break and heal, then break and heal some more. And the Ironwood wasn't about to slow their pace for a second. A part of Killian wanted Morrigan's soldiers to catch up with them so he could release some of the rage and frustration he had been bottling up for the last three years.

Killian made sure that he sent out a low-grade 'fuck off' beacon as they traveled. If snakes bothered Bron, he didn't want her to see what was lurking in the river underneath them. She didn't notice the magic either, despite the glamours and wards she used.

Bron was a riddle, and it was starting to bother him. That and the fact that she blushed a little every time he flirted with her, which she seemed to loathe, had all his attention.

Killian had never met anyone that would barely look at him unless they were angry. And Bron seemed to be mad at him all the time.

Bron used the time in the boat to take out her whetstone and began to methodically sharpen the many weapons she had hidden about her person and backpack.

"What do you do for fun?"

Bron didn't look up from her stone. "You're looking at it."

"So you live up to your name," Killian shook his head in despair. Bronagh meant sadness, and it was a cruel name to slap on a child.

"I'm not sad because I don't feel the need to fill every moment with noise, unlike you."

"I have three years of only getting to talk to Morrigan, so I'm sorry if I'm bored and want to know more about my rescuer," Killian said, trailing his fingers in the cool water beside the boat.

"You want to talk? Why don't you tell me about how the hell you got mixed up with the goddess of war?" There was a spark of challenge in her dark eyes that Killian hadn't seen all day.

That's it. Come play with me, Ironwood.

"It's not as exciting a story as you might think," Killian began, propping his long legs up on the side of the boat. "My parents were responsible for the spell that's keeping Morrigan locked on her lands."

"Why did they do that? I thought the fae revered the goddess."

"They found out about her plans to release the dread horde. What you saw lingering about the castle is *nothing* compared to what's locked in the caverns. They are controlled by her three generals, and they are the worst of them all." Bron started sharpening her blade again, but she was listening.

"If they ever got released, it would be pure carnage. Morrigan took it really personally when the humans started to worship other gods, the Christian one especially. She wanted to release the horde to teach the non-believers a lesson. That's what she still wants."

"And you factor into her plans how exactly? I saw Morrigan rip the throat out of a servant who didn't get out of her way quick enough, but she kept you alive for years," she said, the dagger flicking over her knuckles.

"You don't think it could be because of my charming personality?" he couldn't resist asking.

Bron didn't even blink. "You have one of those?"

"It works on everyone except for you."

That, of all things, made the side of her mouth kick up in an almost smile.

"Morrigan once tried to use me to break my parent's spell. I wanted to know what her plans were, so I pretended to return her affections. When I learned that she was going to release her generals and the horde, and that she wanted me to rule with her, I got my ass out of her reach as quickly as possible. She took the rejection poorly," Killian continued.

"She used Aoife, the sorceress, to do her will, but Aoife was pining for Kian, and when he turned her down, she used Morrigan's power to curse us all. Morrigan was foiled again. Then she got her servants still in Ireland to snatch me, but my curse is powerful enough that she couldn't touch me. Otherwise, I doubt my torture sessions would have been so mild."

"That was mild?" Bron couldn't hide the horror in her voice. The mangled scars on Killian's back throbbed with memory.

"Yes, that was mild. She knows the spell holding her is weakening. Torturing me was just something to do to pass the time. I'm not an important part of her plan anymore." Killian sat up and leaned his arms on his knees.

"I know you need to hand me over when we get to Ireland. I can see that your family duty will always come first. I only ask that you send a message to my brothers somehow, telling them about Morrigan's spell weakening. If she gets out, Bron... You have no idea the horror she'll unleash. What you saw in her castle is nothing compared to what the horde is capable of. My brothers will be needed to stop her generals from tearing the world apart."

For one second, Killian glimpsed the conflict inside of her as it tried to override the training that would've made all the fae out to be monsters.

"I will talk to my mother about it," Bron said finally. It wasn't a straight 'no,' so Killian took it as a win. He gave her the peace and quiet she wanted for the next few hours as they passed tiny villages and other fishermen.

The mountain range he had spotted the previous night was now looming in front of them, casting the river into shadows.

"Can you row us to the bank there?" Bron asked, pointing to a rocky shoreline.

"Sure thing." Killian tugged on the magic controlling the boat and beached them. Bron climbed out first, not waiting for him to help her.

It is probably a good thing.

The more Killian touched her, the more he wanted to. He didn't know if it was her or the novelty of being touched again, but it was intoxicating. He could still taste her skin on his lips from that one small kiss to her wrist, her lilac and woman scent in his nose.

She could glare at him all she wanted. He had seen that flash of heat on her cheeks when he had done it. She hadn't driven one of her daggers into him either.

You're thinking about seducing an Ironwood. Gods, how desperate are you?

Once they had their gear out of the boat, Killian removed his magic from it, and the craft rotted before their eyes.

"Magic," Bron whispered with a shake of her head.

"Where to, navigator?" Killian asked cheerfully. The sun would set soon, and they had hopefully put enough distance between them and Morrigan's hunters to have a decent night's sleep.

"There are caves all along the mountain trail. If we can find one that isn't occupied, it will be a good spot to spend the night. A day of hard hiking tomorrow will get us through the passes," Bron said. She gave him the smallest of smiles. "Thanks for using your magic on the boat. We've cut at least a day of traveling."

"Hurray, I'm a day closer to dying," Killian replied and instantly regretted it. The smile vanished from her face. She turned away from him, slung on her pack, and walked away.

Killian ran his hands through his hair. "Fuck."

9

Bron kept her eyes on the twisting trail ahead. It was only three feet wide and wandered like a goat track through boulders of jagged stone. One slip, and she would slice herself to pieces. The danger of the trail kept her focused on it and not on the prince at her back. They were almost at the caves, and then she would be able to get some space from him.

A small kernel of guilt was beginning to form in the back of her mind, and she hated it.

You are an Ironwood. You are a hunter. You don't befriend your prey. You kill it. Kenna's cold voice kept reminding her.

There were things about the job Bron was starting to question. Like who was the client? Kenna hadn't bothered to tell her. Why did they want Killian? To kill him. What had he done to deserve it? None of our fucking business.

Two days, and he's already in your head. Weak child.

Bron told the voice to fuck off just as her foot hit a patch of loose gravel, and she slipped backward. There was a sickening moment of nothingness as she fell, shutting her eyes to brace for the pain she was about to be in.

Strong arms caught her, stopping the fall and the thousand cuts it would have earned her.

"Almost ate the rocks," Killian said, setting her back on her feet.

"Let me go," she snapped. She wiggled out of his grasp and fixed the straps on her pack.

"I was only trying to help."

"Well, don't, okay?" Her face was burning hot with sweat and rage.

"What is your fucking problem, Ironwood?" Killian growled, the charming prince vanishing into something lethal and furious. *That* was the prince she had been expecting in the jail cell. "What did I ever do to earn such hostility from you?"

"How can you ask me that? You know why I can't trust you! You can act as nice as you like, and I'm still not going to buy into it for a second." She looked him over, a snarl on her lips.

"Don't think the Ironwoods have forgotten your vow to wipe us out. I might not like the idea of handing you over to be killed, but I'm going to do it because as soon as you're dead, my baby sisters will be safe."

Killian reared back from her like she had slapped him. "What vow? I never made *any* vow to hurt Ironwoods. In fact, the only times I encountered one of your family members, I was getting shot in the ass or fucking tortured!" he shouted, his voice bouncing off the stones around them.

"The first time, I let Fergus go instead of killing him. And the second time, when I *would* have killed him because he killed my people, he stood back and laughed as fucking Vortigern carved up my back. He was *still* laughing when I got my ass thrown into Faerie for fifteen hundred years." He was panting, so furious Bron could barely hold his gaze.

"No. No, you're lying," Bron said, shaking her head. "After Fergus shot you in the leg, you let him go and said that you were going to make sure the entire Ironwood bloodline died at your hands."

Killian laughed cruelly as he closed in on her. Her back hit one of the jagged boulders, and her hand went to her dagger.

"I've been back in the human world for years. Don't you think I would've come for you? I can tell you right now, Bronagh Ironwood, I follow through on my vows, and all the bounty hunters in the world wouldn't have stopped me from getting my revenge."

"No. I don't believe you," she said stubbornly. Bron had been told about the Night Prince wanting to kill them since she was in diapers. There was no way it was bullshit.

"You've been lied to, and I'm going to prove it." Killian slapped his hand on her shoulder, and she was suddenly thrown into a memory that wasn't her own.

Bron was standing in an opulent bed chamber lit with candles. The four-poster was hung with midnight blue velvet, and the ceiling glowed with shifting constellations.

Killian stepped out of a bathing chamber, a towel around his waist and black wings dripping on the floor. He walked to a side table and was pouring wine when the bedroom window behind him opened. A night breeze shifted the curtains to reveal a red-haired man dressed in black leather.

Killian whipped around as the hunter shot a bolt from his crossbow. He snarled as it hit his thigh, magic whipping out of him to knock the weapon out of the hunter's hand, the second streak of power driving the man to the ground. With a hiss, Killian ripped out the bolt and tossed it to the floor. Amber blood poured down his leg as he grabbed the hunter by the back of the jacket and dragged him out of the bed chamber.

"You know, you're the closest an assassin has ever come to killing me. Well done, Mister..."

"Fuck you," the hunter growled. Killian's emerald magic wrapped around the hunter's head, forcing him to reveal his identity. "Fergus Ironwood."

"Mister Ironwood, that wasn't so hard, was it?" Killian pulled Fergus along like he weighed nothing, down a curved sweeping staircase. Black doors opened to reveal a forest and endless night sky. Killian tossed the man outside and dusted off his hands. "Better luck next time, Ironwood." Then the black doors shut on Fergus's furious face.

Bron ran, trying to get away from the memory, and fell into another one.

The world went up in flames around her, fae screaming as their dwellings burned. Killian charged in, cutting down humans with his sword. The small bodies of the slain faelings littered the ground. He couldn't look at them, couldn't acknowledge that horror, until every last one of the bastards who did it were dead.

The memory shifted again to a crowd of humans cheering, Fergus Iron-

wood in the front with the king's banner on his chest. His clothes and weapons were covered in the amber blood of the faelings.

"Give us your wings, and this can all be over," a torturer snarled in Killian's face. Vortigern stood watching, his golden crown glowing in the firelight.

"Never," Killian spat. He screamed as Fergus and the soldiers cheered on the man wielding the hot dagger on Killian's back, slicing the flesh away to try and find the wings they wanted as trophies. Bron started screaming with him as she fell to the bloody ground and reached for him...

∼

BRON JERKED out of the memory, weeping and thrashing. She sat up, daggers in her hands and ready to kill whoever tried to hurt Killian next. The prince was nowhere to be seen. She touched the silver cuff on her wrist, the magic in it telling her he was still close.

Bron sat up and wiped her sweating brow. She was in a cave beside a small fire. Emerald runes were sketched on the grey stone walls around her.

Wards to protect me as I slept.

Bron put down the daggers and drank deep from the canteen of water Killian had placed beside her.

What the hell happened?

Fergus had lied, that's what. Bron fought back the tears at the thought of all the Ironwoods since him living in fear of a fae prince...who had let him go after a failed assassination. Cara Ironwood would have been horrified to learn one of the family stories was total bullshit.

Bron's stomach grumbled, and she reached for the mug of soup that sat on a stone kept warm by the fire. Killian had gone through her pack of rations and made her dinner. She had a mouthful, too hungry to feel embarrassed that he'd touched her things.

"You're awake." The shadows at the cave's mouth moved, and Killian came back to sit by the fire.

"I'm..." Bron began and stopped, words failing her.

"Does your family really believe that I want to kill them all?" he asked.

Bron nodded. "All of us were told that as children. I've dreamed of you coming to get revenge since I was four years old. My sister Moira is seven, and she already sleeps with a knife in case you try and attack her in her dreams."

"I would *never* harm a child," he hissed.

"I know," she replied. He studied her face and muttered something that sounded like a curse.

"You saw the memory of the slaughter, didn't you?"

Bron nodded. She would never forget the horror and despair on his face, the monster that had come out of him to avenge the babies. She put the soup down, her appetite disappearing.

"I didn't mean to show you so much. The magic had other ideas." Killian poked at the fire with a stick. "I'd make another deal so you'd know for sure that I'd never harm an Ironwood, but you make my magic too unpredictable to trust it. Besides, I don't think you would be able to handle two nights with me, let alone one."

He wasn't joking when he said it, though the gleam in his eye turned dark with something she couldn't identify.

"I'm sorry that Fergus sat back and cheered as they hurt you," she said softly, swallowing hard.

"I'm sorry you believed I meant you and your family harm." Killian sighed, looking ancient and ageless at the same time. He nodded at the sleeping bag he'd laid her out on. "Go back to sleep, Bronagh Ironwood. I'll watch over you."

Bron finished her soup and lay back down. She needed sleep, but she was scared about the nightmare fuel his memories had now given her. Killian started to hum softly, the same song he had for days.

"What is that song?" she asked, using her arm as a pillow.

"It's a lullaby my mother used to sing. When she died, I used to sing it to my brothers to soothe them. They were so small when she died, I kind of took over as a parent. I didn't want them to forget the song, or her, so I got into the habit of humming the lullaby to them to keep that part of her alive." Killian shrugged. "I hum it once a day, so I don't forget it either."

It was a raw and personal answer, so Bron summoned her courage and said, "I wish I remembered my father."

"He died?" Killian guessed.

"Before I was born. You asked when we met if I came from a different branch of the Ironwoods. It's sort of true. My mother, Kenna, was sent to Egypt to help with a hunt. They thought it was some kind of demon possession. My father was Egyptian and ran the crew. They got close and hooked up. The next day, he died in a fight with the demon, and my mother returned to Ireland heartbroken with a belly full of arms and legs."

Bron stared up at the rocks above her. "I don't even have a picture of him, but I must look like him because I don't look like Kenna. All my sisters do. They are *pure* Ironwood."

Bron hated the bitterness in her voice and the fact that she had spent thirty years trying to get rid of it. "My mother called me Bronagh because I was a sad baby. Not crying, but always sad. My grandmother told me that it was because Kenna was grieving for my father when she was pregnant with me."

Something in the prince's face softened at her confession. "Your sisters might look like Ironwoods, but you're a pure hunter. And I'm not just saying that. You broke into Morrigan's castle in fucking Tir Na Nog. I don't see any other Ironwood's—or any other sane person—doing that," Killian replied. "You did that to get me out of jail. A fae you believed promised to kill your family. I'd say you have the biggest balls I've ever seen if you weren't so beautiful."

Bron couldn't stop the husky laugh that came out of her. She didn't laugh very often, and it sounded strangely disused. She risked looking sideways.

Killian was smiling at her, his golden skin glowing in the firelight. His wings curved out to stop some of the heat from escaping through the cave mouth. Even in ill-fitting, dirty clothes and haggard from prison and escaping it, the Night Prince was...gorgeous. She was woman enough to acknowledge it. He caught her staring, and his smile vanished.

"Go to sleep. You never know what tomorrow is going to look like," he said, focusing back on the fire.

Bron pulled the sleeping bag over her and shut her eyes. She was asleep in minutes, the sound of Killian's lullaby filling her ears.

10

Killian wanted to scream at the night sky in sheer frustration. He looked across the fire at the hunter who had finally drifted off to sleep. He wanted to go back in time and kill Fergus when he had the chance. Bron thought he was going to kill her baby sisters... No wonder she had hated him on sight.

Killian was her monster under the bed, and the Ironwoods' whole reason for being was to kill monsters.

"Fucking hell," he muttered, running a hand over his face. The truth that he didn't want to harm them didn't matter. She would hand him over to their client because that's what she had been hired to do.

Maybe the asshole would want some kind of glorious fight to the death? Killian knew his chances of walking away from that were high.

Making sure Bron was really asleep, Killian crept outside and tried to use his magic to send a message to Kian. He sketched runes, cleared his mind, and poured magic into it. The cuffs on his arms burned and burned until he had to stop.

"You bastards couldn't have given up looking for me so quickly," he told the night sky. He knew that Elise and Freya wouldn't have, that's for sure. Maybe Bron would warm up to him enough that she would let him make one last phone call before he got his head taken off.

Inside the cave, Bron made a sound of distress. Killian raced back in, ready to kill whatever was attacking her, but there was only her, twisting in the sleeping bag.

"Shit." Killian knelt down beside her and untangled her. If she had night terrors, it was because of him. He hadn't wanted her to see the slaughter, only the night of the assassination attempt. When she had come around, she hadn't looked at him in pity, only...regret.

Feeling guilty for putting horrors in her head, Killian took her hand and sent some of his dream magic into her.

～

Killian stood in his castle in Faerie, the last place he thought he would be. His wings were black and gleaming in the firelight. Why the hell was the Ironwood dreaming about his wings?

A door opened, and he turned, his breath catching. Bron walked toward him, dressed in a gauzy black gown that revealed her pale brown breasts. Her dark auburn hair was out in loose waves, and black eyes glittered with trouble as she looked him over.

"You had better get dressed, or you'll start a riot," she commented, her burgundy painted lips lifting in a smile. "Not that I mind." She put her arm around him from behind and kissed him right in between his wings. Killian trembled at the touch, at the intimacy and familiarity of it. She ran her cheek over the soft feathers.

"I'm dreaming," he said, unable to turn as sensation flooded him. Bron laughed softly.

"Are you? I know you would like to get out of seeing your brothers and their guests, but it's not going to happen. I've put on a dress and everything."

Killian stilled as Bron slipped a hand down the front of his black pants. Her small hand rubbed his dick, making it hard in seconds. "Hmm, maybe they can wait a little longer. What's the point of wearing a dress if you're not going to fuck me in it?"

～

KILLIAN PULLED himself out of the dream so quickly, he fell backward onto the cave floor. He scrambled away from Bron, trying to escape her and the dream. His dick was rock hard and throbbing in his jeans, and he was sweating all over. Bron was smiling a little, sleeping peacefully again.

"What in the seven hells?" Killian cursed. He got to his feet and all but ran out into the cold night. He thought she was having nightmares, not sex dreams. Killian paused...sex dreams about him.

"Well, isn't that interesting?" He laughed softly. The Ironwood might have hated him, but she also desired him. Killian grinned.

Where was that side of her hiding? And what could he do to bring it out?

Something cold and wet hit his cheek, and Killian held out his hands to let the snow fall on them. Even snow was welcome weather after the prison cell. It would be hell to get through in the morning, and Bron didn't have the benefits of magic to keep her warm.

Suddenly worried about how much cold a human body could take, Killian adjusted the runes on the cave wall to hold in all the heat they could before putting some more wood on the fire.

～

BRON WOKE the next day to a grey and silver world. Her eyes focused, and she realized that above her were...feathers.

She didn't dare move quickly, but she tilted her head to find Killian beside her. He wasn't touching her. There was a respectful distance between them, but one massive wing was over her, shielding her from the cave.

The Night Prince is trying to keep me warm. Bron remembered the vivid dream from the night before, and she was glad he wasn't awake to witness her shame.

You had a sex dream about your mortal enemy. But he wasn't anymore, was he?

Bron stared at his sleeping face. Unlike other fae she had seen, Killian had fine lines around his eyes and a silver streak in his hair. How old was he to even have those small signs of age? It added character to a face that would have been too pretty without them.

His inky eyelashes were so long they brushed his skin, and his mouth—Bron looked away and back up at the wing above her. Her body was hot, skin too tight under her clothes, the tattoo on her wrist throbbing insistently.

In her dreams, Killian's wings had always been black, but the silver-grey was equally lovely. Her fingers moved on their own accord as she reached up and lightly touched them.

Killian didn't stir, so she did it again, stroking their silky softness. Bron bit back a gasp as something glittered amongst the feathers. Tiny pinpricks of light started to glow where her fingers had been.

He really does have stars in his wings.

Bron was about to touch them when he finally stirred, and she quickly stuffed her hand back under her sleeping bag.

One sleepy emerald eye opened. "Hey. How long have you been awake?"

"Ten seconds?" Bron lied. She raised a brow at his wing.

"You were shivering in your sleep. You're warm now, aren't you?" Killian smiled, and her toes may have curled just a little.

"Yes? I mean, thank you."

"Did you sleep okay?" he asked. A graphic visual danced in her mind of sliding her hands in his pants, and something throbbed low and insistent in her core.

"Yep. Time to get up." Bron shoved her sleeping bag down and ignored Killian's smirk as he lifted his wing away. She gasped as freezing air rushed over her.

"It's been snowing since midnight," Killian said, rolling onto his back and stretching like a lazy cat.

"Just because hiking this path isn't going to suck enough," Bron complained.

"Don't worry, Ironwood. I won't let you fall," Killian purred, fluttering those long, long lashes.

Saints have mercy. She needed to get outside so she could dunk her head in the snow.

Killian had put her jacket over her as well in the night. She quickly shoved her arms into the sleeves and zipped it up tight. It was considerate of him, but Bron refused to read too much into his gesture as she found her gloves.

With as much calm as she could muster, Bron got to aching legs and went outside to see how bad the snowfall was. The cold bit into her, but it was sharp enough to cut away the lingering sleep and foggy desire in her brain.

It was just a stupid dream. It didn't mean anything.

Bron wanted to smack herself in the face for being so ridiculous. He revealed a few crumbs of his past, and suddenly, she didn't hate him? Not that she had hated him before, but it had been easier not to like him. Bron still had no choice but to hand him over for the good of the family.

Get back to Ireland and worry about it then.

Bron took out her map from one of her side pockets. If they made it out of the range that day, there was still another two days of traveling before they reached the gateway to Ireland she had come through. The path could still be seen through the snow, so hopefully, it wouldn't hinder her too much.

When Bron finally went back to the cave, Killian had packed up her gear and had put out the fire.

"You are being suspiciously nice," she said as she braided her hair again.

"Consider it an apology for throwing you into the hellscape of my memories yesterday. Also, I'll have you know, I'm very nice to the people I like," Killian replied.

"You don't like me, though."

"Don't I?" Killian folded his arms.

"I'm selling you off. There's nothing to like there," Bron pointed out.

"True, but when you relax for five seconds, you're okay. For an Ironwood."

Bron smiled and continued to tie her hair. "That's a low bar, and you know it."

"Perhaps it's a challenge to lift that bar higher." Killian grabbed her pack and put it over his shoulder. "I know you can't resist a challenge."

Bron headed for the trail. "How do you know that?"

"You are pissing off a goddess of war. Call it a hunch," Killian replied. Her smile widened when she thought he couldn't see it.

Despite the snow, they kept a good pace through the passes. Bron was careful not to get too lost in her thoughts and worry about what would happen when they got back to Ireland. She needed to convince Kenna that Killian had never made the vow to hurt the Ironwoods.

And then what? She's not going to back out of the contract, and you know it.

Killian could offer to pay out the contract, and Kenna wouldn't do it. It wasn't only about the money, but the Ironwood reputation.

"You are glaring so hard, the sun is scared to come out," Killian commented. "Dare I ask what's wrong?" He didn't look bothered by the cold despite not wearing a jacket, and Bron figured magic was involved somewhere.

"Just thinking about how I'm going to tell my family that their nemesis isn't one after all."

"I'm sure they can find another one if they try hard enough." Killian bumped her gently with his shoulder. "Does this mean you don't see me as the enemy anymore?"

"I didn't say that. Only that you're not the Ironwood nemesis," Bron replied, trying hard not to laugh.

"Don't worry, Bronagh, I know you're still going to hand me over." Killian leaned down to whisper in her ear. "Even if you like me more than you're willing to admit."

"Keep telling yourself that, prince," she replied, unable to keep the hitch out of her voice. His answering laugh seemed to slide straight down her spine, reminding her too much of the sex dream she was trying desperately not to think about.

"You—" Bron bit off her words as a foul smell reached her nose. She knew that smell from her time as a servant. She grabbed Killian and pulled him down as a spear hit the rocks above him. No, not a spear. It looked like some kind of insect stinger. One of the horde creatures scuttled over the ridge above them.

"Fuck, they have found us," Killian muttered. Bron was already pulling out a throwing dagger. He grabbed her by the forearm. "They aren't going to do any good at this range. Its outer shell is too strong."

"So what do we do?"

"Run because there is never just one."

Bron didn't argue with him, just followed his lead. The path started to curve downwards, and Bron's stomach lurched as scarab creatures the size of cows moved up the cliffs on the right side of them.

"Kill—"

"Don't look at them! Just keep going." Killian grabbed her hand to steady her descent down icy stone stairs, and she held on tight.

"Do you have a plan?" she asked breathlessly.

"I do, but you're not going to like it."

High pitched buzzing started to echo around the stones above them, and Bron risked looking back. Behind them, the horde creatures covered the stone cliffs, clogging the path back, which meant...

"Killian, they are coming up the other side to pen us in!" Bron shouted just as black shells and horns appeared on the path.

"And now comes the part you're going to hate." Before Bron could ask, Killian threw her over his shoulder and leaped off the side of the cliff.

11

Killian held tight to Bron as the world dropped around them in a blur of silver and grey. She was screaming over the roar of the wind, but he didn't bother to tell her to stop.

His wings snapped out and caught them, Bron's scream stopping abruptly as she slipped. Killian gripped the back of her belt, and she curled her legs around him.

"I hate you so much," she half sobbed.

"Better the drop than that," Killian replied, pointing at the twisting path beneath them, which surged with creatures. "I knew we had gotten away from them too easily." He had hoped that Morrigan would deem it a waste for her horde to have a searching party. His shitty luck had struck again.

"C-can we outfly them?" Bron asked, her teeth chattering.

Killian murmured under his breath, and his magic enclosed her in a shield to keep her warm. His power was growing again, now that he was out of Morrigan's wards and influence. Even the cuffs were a weakening hindrance.

"Not for long, but we might not have to. We've crossed into Faerie. I can feel it in my magic," Killian said as he flew lower to get the feel of their location. The drop had taken hours off their journey, and there was an expanse of forest in the distance.

"You say that like it's going to be a good thing. Faerie is just as dangerous as Tir Na Nog."

"True, but I've traveled all over it when I was exiled here. It will make knowing where to hide easier." Killian adjusted his grip on her, and he tried not to think about her soft, warm body pressed up tight against him.

"Will Morrigan be able to send creatures through the borders?" Bron asked.

"Of course she can. She might show a little restraint because she will want the rulers left in Faerie as allies, but we aren't going to be safe until we cross back to the human world," Killian replied. He didn't point out that meant *her* safety and not his.

"The gate I came through is still a few days away," she said, moving her mouth next to his ear so he could hear her over the wind.

"I might be able to find one closer than that. My brothers and I tried to find all the gateways we could so we could test them. The spell that kept us out was too strong. That doesn't mean they won't work now."

"But how do you know where it will take us?" Bron asked, her breath warm against his neck. Killian tried his best to focus on flying and not the soft lilac warmth that he wanted to nuzzle into.

"I don't. Faerie gates are tethered to Ireland, Scotland, Britain, and Wales. It doesn't matter where we pop out because we can get back to Ireland easily enough."

Except if they came through the Stonehenge portal and right into Kian's territory. And then what would he do with the little Ironwood in his arms? His mind started to provide unhelpful suggestions and positions.

"Will you still come back? Or will you fight me about it? Because I really don't want to have to activate those cuffs, prince," Bron said.

"Are you forgetting our bargain so quickly?" Killian whispered in her ear.

"Are *you* forgetting that I'm going to hand you over to my client, and I won't be tied to any bargain if you're dead?"

Killian laughed, and she stiffened in his arms. "And you're so certain that your client is going to be *able* to kill me? Many have tried and failed before. You never know, Ironwood. Maybe the promise of a night with you is something that's going to make my life worth living again."

Bron pinched the skin under his wing, making him yelp. "I changed my mind, drop me. I'm ready to die."

"Not a chance." Killian tightened his grip as he laughed. "And to think, I used to make whole courts beg for the slightest touch."

"Hmm, sounds like another rumor to me," Bron teased.

So she's capable of flirting after all. Killian wondered just how long it would be before she realized. It was keeping her mind off the horrors of the horde almost getting them, so he was happy to keep it up as long as possible.

"You didn't ask where they wanted me to put that slightest touch," he said, and her cheeks heated.

"It's because I don't care."

"You keep telling yourself that. No, really, do it. It will make it all the sweeter when I prove how wrong you are."

Bron leaned back a little so she could look up at him. "Has anyone told you that you're kind of insufferable?"

"Not recently."

"Allow me to be the first—you are insufferable."

"And *you* are beautiful when you're trying to be mean," he countered. She only rolled her dark eyes at him. "Keep it up, Ironwood. I find your hostility so hot."

"You have mental issues," she said, smiling as she shook her head.

"You would too if you hadn't been touched in as long as me."

A playful light danced in her eyes. "I forgot about that. Are you sure you're going to be able to keep up with *me* for a night? You are probably going to have a panic attack as soon as you see a pair of tits."

"If you're really concerned about not being satisfied, you could always give me some practice peeks just to be sure," Killian replied.

Gods, he hoped she wasn't right about that. He *was* practically a virgin again. He remembered the low-cut dress in the dream the night before, and his goddamn mouth watered.

"Hey! Focus on the flying, prince," Bron chastised, and he realized his eyes had dropped to her chest.

"You started it," he said, dragging his attention back to the forest that was now underneath them.

Bron pulled herself back up against him, like pressing her breasts up against him was going to help him stop thinking about them. Her face moved to rest between his shoulder and neck, and he tried not to notice how nice it felt. He really needed to find a place to set them down for his own fraying sanity.

Killian flew down across the treetops, and ancient power pulsed out to him. He stopped, hovering mid-air, listening.

"What's wrong?" Bron whispered, sensing the alertness in him.

"I think my shitty luck is about to change," he replied and flew slowly, following the power he had felt. "Hold on, we are going to land."

Bron tightened her grip as they dropped through the thick canopy of trees and landed beside a twisted oak. Killian carefully set her down, keeping his hand under her elbow as she swayed.

"My legs went numb," she complained, leaning over to rub feeling back into them.

"Need a hand?" he couldn't resist asking.

Bron flipped him off. "Just go and find what has your knickers in a knot."

"You should know I'm not wearing any," he said, trying to pick up the magic again.

"Me neither," Bron replied, and he tripped over a tree root and only just managed to stay upright. "That was too easy, prince."

"Oh, I'm going to make you pay for..." Killian stopped dead.

The trees and rocks around them were heavy with so much moss, he almost walked past the standing stone. He brushed aside some of the moss and leaf litter to reveal a carved triskelion. Power thrummed under his hand, and the curving twists of the carving lit up with golden light.

"What is it?" Bron asked, coming to stand beside him.

"I think it's a gate. Gods, it's old, though." Killian made his way to the next stone, activating it. "Come and give me a hand, muscles. This one is out of alignment." Bron dropped her pack and moved to help him.

"How can you tell?" she asked as the stone scraped against the forest floor. It trembled underneath their hands as it slid into place.

"That's how." Killian ignited the triskelion before moving to the next stone. When the last one was activated, the stone circle thrummed with power. Ancient runes covered the rocks, and Bron whispered a prayer under her breath.

"I've never seen one like this before," she said.

"Don't look a gift gate in the mouth," Killian replied, dusting off his hands.

"You...you don't want to try going through it?" Bron asked. She looked uncharacteristically uneasy.

"Don't worry, Ironwood, I'll protect you." Killian grabbed her pack and took her hand. "Honestly, where is your sense of adventure?"

Bron opened her mouth to argue when a roar shook the trees. It wasn't the sound of a natural enemy.

"Looks like Morrigan is risking sending the horde," Killian said. A creature that could have once been a bear charged through the clearing and let out another howl. Bron was frozen in fear and shock, her dagger shaking in her hand.

"Nope, not today, Bron."

Killian pulled on her hand, dragging her into the golden light of the portal. Bron turned and grabbed onto him as the world dropped away.

Killian didn't know how long they were pulled through the worlds, but his lungs were burning when the portal spat them out. They hit wet grass, and Bron landed hard on Killian's chest. She pitched forward onto her hands and knees and vomited all over the ground.

"Breathe, Bron. You're okay," Killian wheezed as he righted himself. The sun had set, the sky still faintly pink. They were in the middle of a graveyard, the ruins of a church beside them. "Where are we?"

Bron spat and sat back against a gravestone. She took in the church and let out a weak laugh.

"We are at Templecorran," she said. Her smile slipped as she leaned back over and vomited again.

"No more portal travel for you." Killian searched her pack and gave her the bottle of water. "Now what?"

Bron took a deep drink and struggled to her feet. "Now, we find somewhere that has bloody hot water and a phone line."

12

It took Bron forty minutes of walking to find a cliffside pub with a payphone. She had been in Faerie for long enough that she was strangely out of sync with the human world's technology and changes.

Seeing people and not having to worry about them attacking her was also something she would have to readjust to.

"It's good to be back," Killian sighed, tilting his head to let the salty mist fall on his face. His wings had disappeared again, and Bron tried to ignore the strange pang of sadness in her chest.

"And in record time, too." Bron bit her bottom lip. "I'm worried that finding that gateway was too convenient."

Killian brushed a damp black lock from his face. "Sometimes Fate throws you a bone. If we hadn't been flying over it, I don't think we would have found it at all. It called out to me, Bron. That's a sign from the gods. Don't question every good thing that happens to you," he said.

"Maybe."

Bron still didn't like it. She stepped into the tiny phone booth and lifted the handset. Her fingers hovered over the numbers, knowing she should call the Ironwood manor and let them know that she was back.

Hell, Imogen would probably jump in a car and drive up from Dublin tonight if she knew Bron was there.

Bron dialed the number and let it ring. Killian was leaning against the booth door, the silver cuff on his wrist not hiding the tattoo that matched her own. How was she going to explain the same wing on her? Or her sudden empathy for the enemy? Or that underneath her constant annoyance with him, she might actually like him. Just a little.

Bron turned back to the phone and hung up. She dialed for a local cab company instead.

"You didn't call the family," Killian commented as they waited for the cab to turn up.

"I want one good night's sleep before I go back to the chaos of them," Bron admitted, surprising herself. Killian nodded in understanding.

"I'm looking forward to a hot shower. I haven't been properly clean in...years."

"I've noticed," Bron replied, wrinkling her nose.

"You are no summer bloom either, Ironwood," Killian leaned against the phone box, looking her over with a wicked grin. "I can still smell the swamp on you."

"Then stop sniffing at me, fae," Bron replied and waved down their cab.

It was a twenty-minute drive to Belfast, and even though the back seat smelled of sickly-sweet air refresher and unwashed bodies, she sank back into the seats with a sigh.

"You two giving up on hiking the cliffs?" the driver asked.

"Aye, turns out the princess here doesn't find sharing a tent as romantic as I do," Killian replied, and Bron scowled at him as the driver chuckled.

"This from the man that was missing his hairdryer," Bron said.

The cabbie tsked. "Probably best you're going back to the city by the sounds of things. You two married?"

"Recently engaged," Killian piped up. "She comes across a lot meaner than what she is, don't worry. I knew she was the one from the first time she glared at me."

"That's lovely to hear. Not enough people getting married these days." The driver shook his head. "It's nice to see a traditional couple."

"Well, she's not, but I said, 'No, Bronagh, my love, we must wait until our union is official in front of God before we consummate our love.' I've been saving myself for the right girl," Killian continued, and Bron almost choked on the bullshit in the air.

I am actually going to stab him, she thought as he continued to spin a story of their great romance to an intrigued cab driver.

By the time they got to Belfast, Bron was ready to drown them both in the Lagan.

Bron paid the cabbie with her credit card and got out of there as quickly as she could. Killian, of course, accepted the driver's blessing on their happy marriage and got out grinning like a fiend.

"The bullshit that spews out of your mouth never ceases to surprise me, prince," Bron said.

"Now, my love, is that any way to talk to your fiancé?" Killian replied.

Bron ignored him as they stopped in a clothing store for fresh gear and headed to the nearest hotel.

"Shall you be needing two beds?" the receptionist asked, looking up under her long lashes at Killian.

"Oh no, one bed. Bron and I are on our honeymoon," he said, putting an arm around her shoulders and kissing her forehead. "You better make it a king-sized bed...with a very sturdy frame."

The receptionist blushed a vivid crimson. "We can absolutely do that. Would you like the room with the spa? It is available."

"What are the chances? That would be perfect. She gives the best back rubs and —"

Bron elbowed him. "Now, really, sweetheart, this poor lady doesn't need to know any more," she said through gritted teeth. She could barely look at the woman as she accepted the plastic key card and headed for the elevator.

"I can't wait to have a bath," Killian said happily.

"I might just drown you in it." He still hadn't moved his arm from around her shoulders, and she pretended not to notice.

"Come now, it's just a bit of fun. You are allowed to have some occasionally," Killian replied. The elevator door opened with a chime.

"I get the first shower!" he said, rushing in the room as soon as Bron opened the door. She couldn't fight him over it because he had already kicked off his boots and dropped his shirt on the carpet. He paused by the bathroom door and flashed her a coy look. "You want to come?"

"Don't use all the hot water." Bron tossed his bag of new clothes at him. "I'll order us some dinner."

"And whiskey!" he called as the door closed behind him.

An hour later, Bron had finished the beef and Guinness pie with mash and veggies she had ordered and had poured herself another glass of red wine. She was too dirty to sit on any of the white furniture, so she had sat in front of the fireplace and let glorious warmth soak into her bones.

Killian came out of the bathroom with a cloud of steam. Thankfully, he wasn't naked but wrapped in one of the thick towel robes the hotel provided. His wet hair was combed back, and he looked... Bron quickly glanced away and got to her feet.

"That water better still be hot," she said, gathering up the clean clothes she had purchased. "Food is under the cloche. I've warded the door and phone, so God help you if you try to escape."

Killian stretched out on the bed with the bottle of whiskey. "You know I'm not going anywhere. Go and enjoy your bath, Bron. Relax a bit. Morrigan can't reach us here." He lifted the bottle to her. "You won."

"Yeah, I guess I did," Bron replied. So why didn't she feel as thrilled about it as she should have been?

13

Bron was relieved that Killian hadn't left the bathroom a total mess even though he had scrawled, 'Looking good, Ironwood' on the misted mirror. She shook her head and ran her hand through it.

Bron didn't relax until she was standing under the shower and letting the hot water soak into her. She looked at the color of the water coming off her in disgust. She really hadn't had a decent bath since crossing into Faerie over a month ago.

Bron used a whole bottle of the hotel's shampoo as she washed her hair three times. Letting the conditioner sit in her tangled ends, she shaved her legs and armpits before scrubbing her skin until it turned red.

The tattoo on her wrist caught her eye again, and she traced a finger over it. What if she told her family it was stamped on all the servants when they went into Morrigan's service? She was sure Killian would back her up.

The only problem, really, was her sister Charlotte. She was highly sensitive to magic and would *know* it was Killian's power. Bron couldn't risk that Charlotte wouldn't tell Kenna under pressure.

What if she covered the tattoo with shirts or makeup? A chunky watch? She would only need to keep up the charade until their client came and cut off Killian's head. A sharp pain sliced through her from the pit of her stomach to her chest.

"It's just indigestion from eating too quickly," she whispered, getting out of the shower. She dried off before wrapping the other robe around her. Her brown skin was flushed, and she had lost more weight than she liked while she had been traveling.

A few regular meals will fix that, she thought as she brushed her teeth.

Bron took her time blow-drying her mahogany hair that reached the center of her back and then spent minutes running her hands through it to feel the silky, luxurious feeling of clean hair. She was never going to complain about washing it ever again.

Bron reached for the bag containing her clean underwear and pajamas and dropped her hand. She looked at the wing on her wrist again and blew out a long breath. Her cheeks were already flushed, but somehow, the blood in her body heated even more.

You can do this. You're a goddam Ironwood. It's not like you've never had sex before...and he's not your dreaded enemy.

Bron smoothed her hair back, straightened the tie of her robe, and opened the bathroom door. Killian was reading a magazine in bed, his towel and robe on the floor, but a sheet over his lower half.

Dear God, he is gorgeous. Bron almost lost her nerve as she stared at the muscle, the tattooed wings, and broad shoulders. Killian glanced up, his green eyes darkening as he looked her over.

"I've never seen your hair out," he said, his fingers clenching on the magazine cover. "It's a beautiful color."

Bron fidgeted with the tie of her robe. "We need to go back to Dublin tomorrow," she said in a quick rush. "And I can't have this mark of your bargain on me. So we are doing this tonight." Before she could back out of it, Bron untied her robe and let it drop to the carpet.

Killian's eyes went as wide as saucers. "Ah. Ironwood. Look, about the bargain, I didn't mean it had to be fulfilled straight away. I was hoping to clear up the mess with whoever wants me dead, and then I could call that bargain in sometime after... I mean, when you wanted it... Can you put your robe back on? I can't focus."

"I'm sorry. No. I can't step under my family wards with this thing on my wrist." Bron put her hands on her hips. "Are you trying to tell me after your nonstop flirting that you don't *want* to have sex?" She knew she had a good body thanks to the hours of training, so she didn't see what he could object to.

Killian shook himself and dragged his focus back on her eyes. "Of course I want to have sex, but—"

"Then we are doing this," Bron repeated. She climbed on top of him, and his wings popped out. "I was wondering where they had gone." Killian's hands were clenched by his sides as he stared up at her.

"Are you okay? You're not going to have a panic attack, are you?" Bron asked.

"I...no. I haven't been touched skin to skin for so long, it's overwhelming."

Bron had never seen him without the cocky confidence, so now that she did, she couldn't stop the mischief that rose up in her. She ran her fingers down his chest, and he trembled.

"I might have to have sex with you, but no kissing on the mouth, are we clear?" Bron said, her nails digging into him. Killian's face flashed with disappointment, but he nodded.

"Fine, but it's my bargain, and I'm going to touch you everywhere and take my time doing it." Killian sat up, running his fingers down her spine, and her confidence faltered. "And I'm not even going to attempt to have sex with you when you're this wound up."

His fingers moved back up her skin, finding all the knots she had from weeks of sleeping on the hard ground. Bron bit back a groan, her eyes closing as he massaged softly. This close, she could smell the alluring scent of his skin like sandalwood, belladonna flowers, and something intensely masculine. The urge to burrow her nose into him grew with every inhale.

Killian's breath brushed against her ear, voice like pure sin as he said, "I've never met someone so reluctant to have sex with me, but you should know I'll make it good for you because I'm not a selfish lover. And before you ask, I won't ever tell anyone this happened."

"Thank you," Bron whispered. "I'd really hate to kill you for being a loudmouth."

Killian laughed softly. "You're so violent." Bracing his hands on her back, he rolled her off him and face down on the bed. "First things first, I'm going to get those knots out of your back. No wonder you're so tense all the time."

"It's where I hold my rage," she joked.

"Then they definitely need to come out."

It wasn't what she was expecting when she dropped her robe, but Bron wasn't going to ever turn down a massage. His fingers traced over the tattoo in between her shoulder blades. "Now, this must have a story."

Bron slid her head onto a pillow. "It's the eye of Thoth. My father had one in the exact same spot. I got it done one day when I felt particularly disconnected and wanted to feel like I belonged to someone, even if it was a dead man. It's not only that; the eye of Thoth is a symbol of protection. That can't hurt in my line of work."

"It also symbolizes sex and magic," Killian said.

"Of course you know that."

Killian's warm lips pressed to the tattoo, and Bron shivered. She forgot her nerves at being naked in front of him as Killian's strong hands moved over her bunched-up shoulders. She groaned again when he worked on a particularly tight knot.

"God damn, Bron, I'm starting to understand why you're so grumpy all time. I should've offered to rub you down the first night we met."

She smiled against the pillow. "I probably would've cut your fingers off if you tried."

"Can I tell you something with all sincerity?" Killian asked by her ear.

"Sure?"

"Of all the bodies out there that Fate could've let me touch without hurting, I'm glad she chose yours." Killian's hands moved down to her hips. "Every part of you is so strong and powerful."

Bron smiled into the pillow. "Thanks. I've been training my entire life." Killian moved down the sides of her hips, and the feathers of one of his wings trailed the back of her leg in a sensual sweep. Bron tensed but forced herself to relax again.

"Can I ask why you got wings tattooed on your chest?" she asked, trying to distract herself.

"It's a spell. When Vortigern tried to carve my wings out of me, I had to use all my energy to keep them hidden. Once I had healed, I got Bayn to help me do the spell work to hide them whenever I needed to. He has some that work like body armor," Killian explained, his hands moved down the aching muscle of her thigh. "I bet you thought it was out of vanity."

Bron smiled over her shoulder at him. "You are the vain type. You almost burst into tears when I cut your hair."

"I was in shock. Still am a little," he said, running a hand through his hair self-consciously, the muscles in his arms flexing.

"It suits you shorter," Bron replied, turning back to the pillow. Killian started on the foot of her other leg. He was careful of her blisters as he worked up her ankles to her calves.

"Feeling more relaxed yet?" he asked.

"Hmm, I could go to sleep right now."

His grip tightened on her thigh. "Don't you even think about it. You were the one that dropped the robe and gave up sleep for the night." Bron shivered at the promise in his words. She should have been feeling far more disgusted or angry or reluctant, but she wasn't. She put aside all the Ironwood bullshit on what she *should* do, and for once, just let herself be Bron.

The palm of Killian's hand reached the top of her thigh and paused.

"Last chance to change your mind."

Bron didn't have to look at him to know he was serious. He had been careful not to get too close to specific areas with the massage like he expected her to back out.

"I'm not going to, prince," Bron said, anticipation curling pleasantly in her belly. "Or are you too afraid?"

Killian's warm chest pressed into her back as he leaned down over her. "I'm not afraid. I just don't go where I don't have permission to be."

Bron didn't turn her head to face him, knowing if she saw those brilliant emerald eyes, she might lose her nerve.

"You have permission," she whispered, and to her surprise, her voice didn't tremble once.

"Thank you, Bronagh," Killian replied, kissing her shoulder. He went back to the massage, but this time, when he reached her lower back, his hands moved to the curve of her ass.

"Gods, even your butt has knots in it," he teased.

Bron didn't laugh. Her attention was too focused on his long fingers moving against her. Warm pressure was starting to build between her thighs the more he touched her. She tilted her hips up as he worked on them, and a soft growl echoed through his chest. She could feel the burn of his gaze on her like a phantom touch.

Killian moved to her inner thighs, working in slow circles higher and higher, touching her everywhere but where she was aching to be touched. The dream she had about him came back to her, making her anticipation amp up.

Bron bit the pillow as he finally cupped her at the junction of her thighs and held his hand there. He whispered something under his breath and moved his palm in a slow circle.

In response, Bron lifted her hips higher to give him better access. Killian took the cue, his hand exploring her gently and finding just how wet she already was. She didn't risk looking at him as he stilled.

"Well, what do you know? You do like me after all," he purred.

"Don't gloat, or I'll roll over and go to sleep," Bron replied. His fingers clamped firmly on her.

"Oh no, you're not going anywhere. Tonight, you belong to me." Killian stroked her, spreading her wetness up to her clit and making her breath catch. His other hand continued to move down her back like he was soothing her even as he explored and teased.

Blood was racing to Bron's head, her core pounding until she was panting against the pillow. Killian slid a finger into her, and she cried out.

"So tight," he murmured, kissing her back. "Relax for me, love." He began to gently thrust his finger in and out. Bron was burning up. She pushed back against him, finding his rhythm, and he slid another finger into her.

"God, Killian, I think I'm—" her words broke off into an articulate cry as his other hand found her throbbing clit, and she was coming hard, her body breaking apart.

In her haze, she knew there was at least one story about the Night Prince that was true.

14

Killian was murmuring curses in old fae, his voice full of awe as Bron trembled on the bed. The sight of her wet and destroyed under his hand was tearing at something inside of him.

He wanted to put his mouth on her, taste that shining wetness, fuck her with his tongue. He held back, knowing there was an intimacy in it that she might not be ready for. He moved his hand out of her and put his fingers to his mouth, needing to know what she tasted like. His dick instantly went so hard it pounded painfully.

Fucking heaven, that's what she tasted like.

Bron pushed her damp hair from her face and gave him a shy smile that cut him to the quick. "Don't stop now, prince. You are doing so well." She was teasing to hide whatever she was feeling, so Killian grinned.

"I can't believe you're so surprised," he said as she turned away. He moved behind her, widening her sweet brown thighs. Gods, the sight of her like this would be seared into his mind forever. Whatever plan he had vanished.

"I can't wait any longer. I need to be inside you," Killian said, voice breaking. He grabbed onto her hips and dragged her up against him. He slid his dick slowly through her wetness, using it to slick him down and tease her clit.

Killian prayed that he could control himself and not blow like a faeling as soon as he was inside her. He should have had more than one frustrated wank in the shower. He had no idea she would step out and drop her robe. His heart had stopped at the sight.

Slowly, Killian pressed the tip of his dick into her soft entrance. Fuck, she was so tight and hot. He gritted his teeth against the urge to force his way into her.

Bron made an encouraging sound and pressed back, pushing him a little further. The sight of her on his dick made Killian's heart pound, and he pulled out a little before thrusting in more.

"You're killing me," Bron complained.

"I'm not going to hurt you, not ever," Killian said, softly kissing her shoulder and pressing forward until he was all the way in. Bron's back arched as she rose up onto her elbows.

"Fuck," she whispered as her body adjusted to him.

"Are you okay?" he asked, stroking her hair, momentarily worried.

"Yes, it's just...been a while."

Killian ran his hand underneath her and clasped one of her soft breasts. "Not as long as me." He felt like he was dreaming as he started to thrust slowly in and out of her, the sensation of her robbing him of breath and thought. Bron synced with his rhythm, trying to make him go faster.

"You're not hurting me, Killian," she tried to reassure him. The next time he pulled out of her, she moved quick as a snake and used his surprise to flip him on his back.

"If you want something done," she said with a devilish smile. She touched the silver cuff on her wrists, and his manacles locked together above his head. He tried to move, but they fused to one of the metal posts of the bed head.

Killian laughed. "I'm loving these surprises tonight."

"You were taking too long." Bron straddled him and slowly guided him back inside of her. Killian strained against the magic in the bonds, the urge to take her breasts in his mouth overwhelming him. She seemed to like the control, so he relaxed and let her lead.

"I apologize for being a gentleman," he gasped as she began to ride him, hard and deep.

"I don't need you to be a gentleman. I need to be fucked," Bron replied, pushing her long hair back. Her hips rolled in a slow circle, and his back bowed, arms straining. Her hands went to his chest, short nails gripping onto him as she did it again.

"You're undoing me," Killian gasped. Bron's wicked smile was back as she leaned down and kissed his chest, her tongue stroking over one nipple.

"Don't have that panic attack on me just yet, prince," she said huskily. Bron picked up her pace, fucking him with an intensity that shocked him.

Killian couldn't look away as her skin shone with sweat, sleek muscles rippling with control, face flushing with growing pleasure. Bron leaned forward and stroked the curve of his wings, and Killian cried out. Her eyes went wide with realization, and she did it again with a little more pressure.

"Bronagh, stop, or I'm going to come," he begged. He never let any lovers touch his wings, hated *anyone* touching them. She did it, and it felt so damn good he was going to lose his fucking mind.

"Not before me, you're not," she growled, thighs clamping around him. She picked up her pace again until she was breathing heavily, her pleasure breaking through her. She didn't stop as she took his wings near his shoulders and squeezed. She pressed her sweaty forehead against his.

"Now, Killian," she gasped. Killian's magic snapped the bonds holding his cuffs, and he sat up, his arms going around her. One hand rested around her throat, the other on her hip, pinning and pulling her down tight on him as he came hard, her name on his lips. Magic roared through him, and emerald green fae runes exploded all over their skin. Bron was shaking in his arms as she leaned back a little.

"Gods, I should've known," he whispered. Killian didn't know whether he wanted to laugh or sob or fuck her again.

"W-what are they?" Bron asked, trying to catch her breath.

"Nothing, love. They won't hurt you," he assured her. *Only me.*

"Okay," she said, resting her forehead against his shoulder. "So at least some of the rumors about you are true."

That did make Killian laugh. "Good to know I didn't disappoint, Ironwood."

Bron slid off his lap, and he took the opportunity to watch her naked rune-covered body head for the shower. *His runes.* Fucking, fuck, fuck.

"Are you coming?" Bron asked.

Killian got out of bed on shaky legs. He wasn't going to turn down an invitation like that. Especially because he would only have this one night with her.

Killian stepped into the warm shower behind her and ran his hands over her wet curves.

He pulled her gently up against him, her body lining up perfectly with his, and his heart broke a little further.

I finally found you, and it's too late.

∽

Bron's heart was beating too hard, her body thrumming and hypersensitive. Killian was better in real life than the dream. She was glad her back was to him so he couldn't see the goofy grin on her face. Bron had never lost control like that, had never taken charge, and he had let her.

What the hell has come over you? She didn't know and didn't care. She might have to hand him over tomorrow, but tonight was stolen, and it was hers.

It really was a shame he was going to die. The pain in Bron's chest was back, but as Killian's arms came around her, it went away, and she leaned back into him.

"I didn't think you would be the type to enjoy a post-coital cuddle," she said, stroking his muscular forearms.

"There's a lot about me that would surprise you," Killian replied, his fingers gliding down her stomach.

"These runes are a surprise. Do they mean anything?" Bron studied the fading magic on her hands and arms.

"Nothing to be worried about." He sounded a little sad, but before she could ask him about it, she noticed the wing on her wrist was still there.

"Hey, isn't this meant to be gone?"

Killian's hand went around her wrist, bringing it to his mouth and nibbling it. "The bargain is for a *night*, love, not a fuck."

The hand on her belly drifted down between her legs. Bron took a shaky breath as she leaned back into him and found his dick hard against her lower back. He dropped her wrist and clasped one of her breasts.

"Kill—" she groaned.

Killian spun her around and lifted her up, pressing her against the cold tiles, Bron's legs locking around him. His eyes were glowing with magic and lust as he pinned her wrists above her head and slid his dick back into her.

Bron made an inarticulate sound as he filled her. He was so huge that she had to catch her breath, thighs tightening. Killian's smile would have made a nun break her vows in a heartbeat.

"Being inside you feels like the best kind of damnation," he said, going to kiss her but stopping at the last second, his lips going to her neck instead. Bron tried to move her arms. She wanted to grip his shoulders, touch those silky wings, but he held her firm.

"Revenge is sweet," he said and lowered his mouth to kiss and suck on her nipple. Bron cried out as his teeth scraped over her, her hips moving more urgently against him.

"Gods, you're magic," Killian groaned, letting her hands go so he could grip her hips tight and pound harder into her. Bron hung onto his powerful shoulders, her teeth sinking into his golden skin to muffle her scream as lights exploded through her.

She was shaking, and if it wasn't for Killian holding her, she was sure she would be on the floor. Killian lowered her slowly back to her feet, his eyes wide as he gently stroked her face as if he was memorizing it.

"I think you're going to have to carry me to bed," Bron said with a shaky laugh.

"Here I was hoping you'd carry me," Killian replied. He turned the shower off and toweled her down. It was oddly nice, Bron had to admit. She took the other towel and started to gently pat at his wings. He stilled, uncertain, but then gave her a nod, turning around to give her better access.

Like she had in the dream, Bron kissed in between them, where they joined his back. She kissed the scars beside them, and unexpected tears filled her eyes. She blinked them away rapidly before he turned and picked her up.

"I was joking about carrying me to bed," Bron said, her arms going around his neck. She almost kissed him but held off. If she kissed him now, she wasn't sure what would happen, only that it would mean more to her than him.

"There's something you need to know about me, Bronagh." Killian laid her down softly and brought the blanket up over them.

"And what's that?" she asked, rolling on her side to face him.

Killian's wing came up to shelter her, and he pulled her up against him, dragging her leg over his waist.

"I'm definitely a post-coital cuddler."

Bron laughed softly into his chest. "Yeah, me too. Sing the song, Killian." His lips pressed a kiss to the top of her head, and he started humming the faerie lullaby, sending her straight into a dreamless sleep.

15

Killian woke the following day to Bron already dressed and ready to leave.

"We need to hit the road, prince," she said.

"Good morning to you too," he yawned. He anticipated that she might be weird about the sex the next day, but it was like it had never happened. "What's wrong?"

"Nothing. I talked to my mother. She's expecting us, so we need to go." Bron showed him her wrist. "The mark is gone."

Killian's was too, but little did she know that they were now tied closer than any bargain.

Get out of this jam and then tell her.

"Congrats. Now you won't have to be embarrassed about being scared of snakes, especially mine," Killian said, getting out of bed without bothering to cover himself up.

"Today is going to be hard enough, Killian. Don't make it worse." Bron's calm, icy face had slipped to want and despair before she looked away from him.

So she's feeling the mating bond too.

Killian hid his surprise. "I won't. I'm actually looking forward to meeting all of the formidable Ironwoods."

"That makes one of us. I don't know how I'm going to convince them Fergus lied to everyone about your vow."

"I'd check with the family chronicle if you have one. Fergus was buddies with the king. I'm sure he wanted to boast about it somewhere."

Killian dragged on his jeans and boots. He searched for his shirt when he noticed the scattering of raven black feathers along the bottom of his right wing.

Gods, she's started to lift the curse. He wanted to grab Bron and spin her about in happy circles. He couldn't. Not yet.

"Okay, love, take one last look at these wings before I hide them," he said, giving her a cheeky smile. She didn't look amused. "I'll even let you touch them."

"I wouldn't want to give you a hard-on that you can't use," she replied, deadpan.

"Look at you pretending they don't turn you on." Killian turned away from her and summoned the magic that hid them away, leaving only his scars. He pulled on his shirt and headed for the bathroom before he kissed her and risked a dagger in the ribs.

It was a tense drive from Belfast to Dublin. With every mile, Bron seemed to grow more and more anxious. It made Killian want to know what the hell her mother had said to her that had upset her so badly.

Tamper down that protective instinct, idiot.

Killian didn't push her. Bron looked so caught up in her own head, he didn't want to provoke her. Instead, he turned the radio on and let the world pass by him.

"I honestly never thought I would see Ireland again," he commented. "I was lucky you came to save me when you did, Ironwood."

"Saving is a matter of perspective," she replied, her eyes not leaving the road.

"Any death is better than what Morrigan had planned for me. So yeah, you did save me from that." Bron paled, her hands gripping the steering wheel. "Don't look so glum. You're going to make me think you're going to miss me."

"Ha. You wish, prince. I might actually get five minutes of peace and quiet," she retorted.

"You say that, but when you're alone at night, thinking of the best sex of your life, there I'll be, pride of place in your spank bank," Killian teased. He regretted it almost instantly because it got him thinking of her touching herself over him.

"You'd be lucky to make an appearance in the Top 10," Bron replied.

"Now you're just being hurtful." Killian risked running one of her curls between his fingers. "And you're lying."

"Cut it out," Bron said, without any venom, and batted his hand away.

All teasing stopped as soon as they reached the outskirts of Dublin. They pulled up in front of a wrought-iron gate in Castleknock. Bron typed a code in the keypad, and it swung open. Killian let out a low whistle as they drove through parklands.

"The Ironwoods have certainly moved up in the world," he said as a grey stone mansion came into view.

"Looks great, but it's a fucker to maintain," Bron replied. She looked like she was going to throw up, not like someone pleased to be home.

"If you take these cuffs off, I promise to take you away from it all," Killian offered and she knew that he meant it.

"Maybe in another lifetime, I would've said yes to that, prince," Bron said, pulling up and getting out of the rental car.

A pair of huge black German Shepherds were suddenly racing out of the trees towards them. Bron smiled and bent down to pat and croon at the beasts.

"Don't bite too much off him, okay?" she told them as the dogs circled Killian.

"I won't tell you animals like the fae and they won't attack me," Killian said, holding his hands out for the dogs to sniff.

"Baron! Duchess! Heel!" A sharp voice commanded, and even Killian straightened to attention. A woman with greying auburn hair and a pale blue gaze, penetrating enough to cut, was standing in the door of the mansion. She must have been in her early fifties, but she still looked strong and fit enough to take on the toughest of monsters.

"Hello, mother," Bron said and kissed her cheek.

"Nice to see you back and successful."

"Lady Kenna Ironwood, it's a pleasure to meet you at last," Killian said and bowed. "I can see where Bronagh gets her impressive glare from."

"Indeed." Kenna nodded at Bron. "Go on. I can take him from here."

Bron didn't even turn to give him a parting glance as she disappeared inside. Killian internalized the sharp disappointment and pain that hit him in the guts, the tinge of panic of having her out of his sight.

Stupid mating bond.

"This way," Kenna said, letting out a low whistle to the dogs so they positioned themselves on either side of him. Killian followed her through the main entranceway. It had high ceilings and a grand stone staircase that split on the first floor and disappeared to different sides of the house.

The place had to have been a castle at some point, and Killian wondered if Vortigern had gifted it to them. Banners of the black and white Ironwood insignia of crossed arrows over an ax hung from high windows. Large oil paintings of hunting scenes decorated the walls. All that was missing was the customary suits of armor and bearskin rugs.

A low murmur of feminine voices tittered overhead, and he glanced up to see two more Ironwoods looking down on him.

"You're a big un, aren't you?" a high voice said, and Killian found himself staring down at a girl of about seven years old. She had another German Shepherd at her side, a tiny dagger in her belt, and a lollipop sticking jauntily out of her mouth.

"Aye."

"Not big enough to stop my sister, though," she replied with a smug little smile. Killian tried not to laugh.

"She's pretty tough, but I still had to help her out of a swamp when she slipped into one," he said.

Her tiny chin lifted. "Don't lie. Bron doesn't need any help ever. Especially not from a big, dumb fae."

"I don't lie. There were snakes—"

"Moira! Stop talking to him and get back to your training," Kenna snapped, reappearing to see what was holding him up.

"Big snakes," Killian whispered, shooting the little girl a wink on his way past.

"I'd thank you not to talk to my children," Kenna said as she opened a door with an iron key.

"She talked to me first," Killian replied.

He followed her down a stone staircase to a dungeon. She opened the door of a cell. It had a decent bed with clean linen and a small bathroom, which surprised him most of all.

"This seems like the nicest cell I've ever been in," Killian commented as he stepped inside, and she locked the door behind him.

"I was instructed to keep you comfortable."

"Ah, yes, the mysterious client. Don't suppose you could tell me who he or she is?"

Kenna looked uncertain for a split second and then covered it. "No. But I can tell you that we are both going to have the pleasure of meeting them tomorrow morning. Someone will feed you later." Kenna looked him over. "Where did Bron find you anyway?"

"The dungeon of Morrigan's castle. She's rather impressive, your daughter," Killian said. Because he didn't know if he would get another chance to speak with the matriarch, he added, "I never made a vow to hurt your family, Kenna Ironwood, and I promise I never will."

"It hardly matters, fae. Business is business, and you're going to be dead tomorrow," Kenna replied and disappeared out of the dungeons. Killian was starting to understand what had killed Bron's mood.

16

Bron managed to get to her wing of the house and kick off her boots before a deep sob wracked her body.

You did it. You made it back. She hadn't allowed herself to feel it until she stepped through the doors of the manor. A part of her had left knowing that her chances of returning were next to nothing. She had succeeded in getting the Night Prince back to Ireland, and instead of victory, she only felt a growing sense of dread.

Bron had woken that morning, curled in the arms of her contract, if not her enemy, and it felt like the most peaceful and natural thing in the world. Now that peaceful feeling was gone like it had only been a dream.

"God damn, looks like I owe you a fifty," a voice said from her bedroom door.

"And a bottle of whiskey, and not that cheap shit you like to drink," Bron said, turning to face Imogen.

Her fair hair was currently streaked in a rainbow of pastel blues, purples, and pinks. She was wearing her usual uniform of shredded jeans, boots, and a t-shirt of some band Bron had never heard of. Warm brown eyes looked her over.

"You've lost weight, skinny bitch."

Bron shrugged. "That's okay, sis, you've found it." They both glared at each other, and then Imogen was in her arms, squeezing her so tight she could've cracked a rib.

"I missed you, big sis," Imogen said, not letting go. "I was starting to worry you were dead."

"Ye, of little faith," a calm voice commented, and Charlotte joined the hug. "I didn't doubt you for a second."

"Shh, she's lying. We all thought you were dead," Imogen said as they broke apart.

"Where's Layla?" Bron asked. Her third-youngest sister was missing.

"On a hunt with Lachlan and Ciara in Germany. They should be back in a few days," Charlotte said as she detangled a brown curl from her glasses. "Please tell me my glamours worked."

"Did they work?" Bron huffed dramatically. "I walked around Morrigan's castle for a week without anyone noticing."

"Fuck. Off." Imogen shoved her. "You did *not* go into Tir Na Nog."

"Had to. That's where Kill—the Night Prince—was being held. I'll tell you all about it over dinner. I only want to tell it once if I can help it. The cousins and Layla can get it when they return home."

"Fair enough, but can I be the first to say... God damn, is that fae hot. We just saw Mom bring him through." Imogen fanned herself. "I don't care if he does want to kill us."

"I had to stop her from whistling at him. It was disgusting," Charlotte added, her nose screwed up.

Bron cleared her throat. "He doesn't actually want to kill us. The so-called vow he made to Fergus was bullshit."

"And how would you know?" Imogen asked, a fair brow rising.

"He showed me the memory of it." Bron rubbed at her face. "Look, can we talk about this later? I need a few hours of sleep before dinner. It was hard getting back—"

"Catch me!" Moira shouted as she launched herself up into Bron's arms.

"Hey, grub," Bron laughed, squeezing her wriggling baby sister. King, her dog, was hot on her heels and nudged at Bron's hand for a pat.

"Why did you fall in the swamp?" Moira demanded, pulling a blue lollipop out of her mouth.

"How did...fucking Killian," Bron groaned.

"Oh, *Killian*, is it?" Imogen winked at Charlotte.

"Try and act your twenty-seven years of age for the love of God," Charlotte sighed.

"He told me that you fell into a swamp, and there were big snakes, and he had to get you out, and I told him that he was a big dumb fae," Moira declared in one long breath.

Maybe I should have taken Killian up on the offer to run away, Bron thought as her sisters all began to talk at once. She was about to start yelling at them when their father came through the door in his electric wheelchair.

David was in his fifties with hazel eyes and had the same dark brown hair as Charlotte. He had received a knife to his spine during a banshee hunt five years ago, but nothing stopped him from organizing their training and co-ordinating their missions.

"All right, back off and give Bronagh some space, you animals," he commanded, giving her an apologetic smile. "You know what they are like on a sugar rush."

"It's good to see you, David," Bron replied. She had been three years old when he had married Kenna, but she couldn't remember a time when she had called him Father or Dad. He had been introduced to her as David, and that's what he had remained.

"Kenna wants you all down at dinner at six. Imogen? I'm still waiting on your report from the selkie sightings. Charlotte, that alchemy experiment you're doing is stinking out of the lab, and Moira, *you* were due for knife practice ten minutes ago," he instructed, and they all hustled out.

"Thanks," Bron said, sitting down on the edge of her bed. "I haven't really talked to anyone else in a month."

"I figured as much. It's good to have you back. Kenna might actually get a decent night's sleep."

"Even with a fae in the basement?" Bron said with a laugh.

"It's only for a night. I'm sure she will be fine," David replied. Bron's stomach dropped, and her mouth went bone dry.

"What do you mean a night?"

David's smile widened. "Kenna got confirmation that the client will be here to collect him tomorrow."

"Collect him," Bron repeated slowly. "You mean kill him."

"What they do with him after delivery is none of our business and shouldn't be a concern of yours," David said. He was pragmatic about such things, like all hunters. "You've done exceptionally well, Bron. Take some rest, and then come down to celebrate."

Bron put on a fake smile and nodded. "Sounds good." She waited until he had gone before she shut her door and locked it. Only then did she let the irrational panic take over her.

"Get yourself together," she hissed. She pulled off her shirt, which somehow smelled of sandalwood and belladonna just from sharing a car ride with Killian.

Bron changed into a pair of old sweats and went into her bathroom. She looked as upset as she felt, her eyes hollow.

It was ridiculous for her to be this worried about Killian. She knew how annoying he could be. It was no surprise that someone would want to kill him. But only a night? She thought a few days at least, so she could...what? Try and prove that Fergus had lied? It didn't matter. This wasn't about Killian and the Ironwoods. It was about him and whoever he pissed off.

No concern of yours, like David said.

Bron splashed her face with cold water and pulled her hair up in a ponytail. On impulse, she had left it down that day. She had caught Killian staring at it more than once, and for some reason, she had kind of liked it. She tried not to think about him fisting it in his hand the night before as he made her body sing and heart pound.

Bron splashed her face with more water and shoved the memory in a box in her mind. They had a bargain. It was only sex. It didn't mean anything to him other than convenience.

It didn't mean anything to you either, she reminded herself. It was a good fuck that she had long been overdue for, and that was all there was to it.

And there I'll be, pride of place in your spank bank, Killian purred through her mind.

"Not today, Satan," she muttered, drying her face roughly.

Pushing down every unpleasant feeling, Bron shoved open another door and stepped into her training area.

Downstairs, a whole hall was dedicated to their practice, as well as places around the estate grounds for shooting, but this space was hers alone. Bron had wanted to move out of the estate when she turned twenty, and this had been the compromise.

Her training room looked exactly the way she had left it. The entire floor was covered in cushioned mats, battered boxing bags hanging down one end, and her collection of swords and sabers down the other. The solid oak posts that held up the roof were nicked from blades and dinted from fighting sticks. This place had been her sanctuary when the world was too loud or when she had to work the frustration out of her limbs and the rage out of her heart.

Bron lay down on the mats and stared at the roof. "Home," she whispered, the word ringing hollow inside her chest.

~

DINNER WAS its usual rambunctious affair of daily updates. Bron was overwhelmed with so much noise and people but did her best to hide it. She sat beside Imogen, pushing food around her plate even though she loved lamb stew.

"Are you okay, Bron?" Kenna asked from the head of the table.

"Fine, just tired." She toyed with her glass of wine. "I thought I should probably feed Killian."

"Sarah already did it," Kenna replied, referring to the cook that had been with the Ironwood estate since Bron could remember.

"Oh, okay. Good."

"He smells nice," Moira piped up beside her.

"Yeah, he does," Bron agreed and drained her wine. "Now eat your vegetables and stop giving them to King." The dog at her side looked lovingly at his young charge.

"And how would you know what the prince smells like?" Imogen asked in a teasing tone.

Bron rolled her eyes at her. "I had to travel with the annoying bastard, that's how." She let out a loud yawn and got up. "Sorry, guys, I'm going to have to call it a night. I'm wrecked."

"You get a pass because it's your first night back," Kenna said with a nod. She was strict about the family eating together until everyone was finished, whether they liked it or not.

Bron headed up the staircase that led to the upper floors, pausing only once to stare at the door that went to the cellars and the dungeon.

He's totally fine. You know exactly where he is.

Bron changed into flannel pajamas that felt almost too light after sleeping for over a month fully clothed and armed. She climbed into bed and retrieved a thick, old tome that she had taken from the library before dinner.

The Ironwood family crest was stamped into the scratched-up leather cover. How Killian knew that they had a family chronicle was beyond her. They didn't only have one, but a whole shelf full of them. Hunters tended to have a lot of children to make up for the fact so many used to die....still died.

The chronicle in Bron's lap was the first one in the set. Fergus lying about his encounter with Killian was like a scratch on the roof of her mouth, irrationally annoying.

She flicked through the pages, searching names and estimating dates because the books had been collated from original scraps and scrolls in the seventeenth century. In any other circumstance, she would have asked Charlotte for help. No one knew the estate library better, but she didn't want to explain why she wanted more information. Imogen was already sniffing about like she knew that something had happened between Bron and Killian.

"There you are, you bastard," Bron tapped Fergus Ironwood's name before reading the short paragraph underneath it.

Was a friend and loyal subject to King Vortigern and his court. For his efforts in the Fae War, he was given the king's niece's hand in marriage.

"Fae War my ass," Bron muttered. She had seen that so-called 'war' in Killian's memories. It had been a massacre of innocents. How much more of the chronicles were total bullshit?

Bron shut the book and turned off her light. She only needed to get through tonight, and then tomorrow, when Killian was gone, everything could go back to normal. She rubbed at her chest, hating the clogged emotion sitting there. She had never felt like she was doing anything wrong when she had completed contracts before.

You never had sex with any of them either.

Bron turned onto her side and held one of her pillows close to her. Everything felt too soft. She had slept fine the previous night in the plush hotel bed. Parts of her body pulsed to remind her exactly *why* she had been too exhausted to stay awake.

When they had arrived that day, Bron had known Kenna was watching too carefully. She couldn't have said anything to Killian without her mother suspecting something. If Kenna had thought Bron was under some kind of glamour or influence, she would be in a cell right beside him. Tomorrow would be no different.

Bron wouldn't even get a chance to say goodbye before he got handed over to whatever horrible fate their client wanted to inflict on him.

Bron tried to shut out the memory of his screams as Morrigan had tortured him. Bitter saliva filled her mouth, and she sat up, feeling like she was going to vomit. She took a long drink of water and got out of bed.

The house was dark and silent as Bron crept downstairs. She double-checked David's study, but all was quiet. She might have been disorientated dealing with her family members, but her muscle memory knew the house well enough to avoid the floorboards that creaked. She took a deep breath and opened the door to the dungeons.

Bron made it halfway down the stairs before she heard Killian humming. No lights were burning, but she knew the way from years of playing hide and seek with her sisters. She made it to his cell and could just see his large body outlined on the pale linen of his bed.

"Do I detect a little mouse?" Killian said, and Bron could hear the smile in his voice.

"I wanted to see if you were awake," she replied, feeling like an idiot.

"Can't sleep?"

"No, I think I got used to being on edge that I'm having trouble unwinding. That, and I looked up Fergus in the library tonight." Bron fished her lock picks out of her pocket. "You want company? I can leave if you need to sleep."

"I doubt I'll be sleeping much tonight, Ironwood. Come on in if you dare."

Knowing she would probably be murdered if she was caught, Bron picked the lock to the cell and stepped inside, carefully locking it behind her.

"I'm blown away that you can do that in the dark," Killian said. "Tell me what you learned about your illustrious ancestor that has you so upset." Bron leaned against the cell door, wondering what the hell she was doing.

"Apparently, he stayed good friends with Vortigern after they had you banished," she said before edging closer to the bed. Her eyes had adjusted to the darkness, and she could see more of where he was lying on his side, a wing resting over him and on the cover beside him.

"That doesn't surprise me. Fergus was a climber," Killian said.

"He climbed high enough that he married one of the king's nieces." Bron heard his breathing hitch. "You didn't know?"

"No, it makes sense, though." Killian let out a sigh that sounded precisely how she felt. "Why are you really here, Bron? Have you come to spring me?"

"No. I can't, even if I wanted to." Bron hugged her arms around herself, hating that she couldn't think straight when it came to him. She couldn't even explain to herself why she was there, let alone him.

"I guess I wanted to see you in case I didn't get the chance tomorrow. You've met Kenna. She's not the kind that would understand why I wanted to say goodbye. We saved each other's lives in Faerie, and it didn't feel right not talking to you one last time."

"It's okay that we became friends, Bron. You don't have to beat yourself up about it," Killian said.

Bron huffed out a laugh. "I wouldn't go as far as friends, but I got used to having you around, I suppose. Stressful situation and all that. I'm pretty sure that I can't sleep right now because it's so quiet. No one is singing to annoy me, and no one is trying to kill me."

"Anyone would think you wouldn't like your life to go back to normal."

"I thought I did, but they are louder than even you," Bron replied, risking another step closer. "Are you worried about tomorrow?"

"No. Death has been dogging my steps for years. I thought I was ready for it."

"And you're not sure now?"

"What can I say? You reminded me how fun life can be."

Bron was glad it was dark so he couldn't see the smile on her face. "Fun isn't something that's used to describe me. Are you sure it's not because you finally got laid?"

Killian laughed, a warm, soft sound in the darkness. "It's not just about the sex, though it was...well, you were there."

Yes. Yes, she was.

"But," he continued, "it was also fun to hang out with you. You're not half bad company when you stop being so defensive. Maybe you should let that side out more often and let people in occasionally."

"Maybe I need to hang around with more annoying fae princes," Bron replied.

"Now, now, don't be too hasty. This one isn't in the ground yet, and I call dibs until I am."

"It's not a competition."

"It absolutely is. You're mine until I'm dead," he said, suddenly serious.

Bron rubbed at her arms to stop the goosebumps his tone caused. She should leave, *needed* to go—

"You're shivering."

"It's cold down here," Bron said quickly. The large wing on the bed lifted up, a silent invitation. Bron's heart stuttered, but she still climbed in beside him.

"Gods, you're freezing," Killian murmured, his arm coming around her. He was a furnace as she wriggled into his side. His wing came down over her like a warm blanket.

"You tell anyone about this, and I'll kill you," Bron said into his chest. His laughter rumbled under her ear.

"Your secret is safe with me, love," Killian whispered, the arm around her stroking her back gently. Bron breathed in his sandalwood scent, and she melted into him further, her body finally relaxing for the first time all day.

"Kill?"

"Yes, Bron."

"Sing the damn lullaby."

17

Killian woke alone in his cell, the smell of his mate still on his sheets and clothes. Bron had turned up last night, and his heart had been beating so loud, he was surprised she didn't hear it.

Despite being back in her ancestral home and having her disapproving mother reminding her that he was her enemy, Bron had still come to him. He had spent the rest of the night watching her sleep and trying hard not to kiss her soft lips or wake her and tell her that she belonged to him. He could imagine how well she would take that.

Killian was washing his face in the small basin when Kenna arrived in the dungeon. He couldn't see much of Bron in her face. She had taken so strongly after her father, but that glare... The glare was spot on.

"Come, prince, you're due to be collected," she said briskly. She was dressed in black cargo pants like the ones Bron favored, daggers in her belt and a holster with two sleek black guns within easy reach.

Killian stretched his long body with a yawn. "Good. I'm getting tired of being a prisoner. No offense to your hospitality, my lady, but I'm quite sick of being stuck in small spaces."

Kenna made a small gesture, and a chain appeared on his silver cuffs. He spotted the silver cuff on her own wrist and wondered if Bron had passed it over without a fuss. He didn't mind the manacles when they were attached to her.

"I don't know if your lovely daughter has told you, but Morrigan is planning to bring her horde into the human world. You have to prepare yourself for that, Lady Ironwood. Protect your daughters—"

"Bronagh mentioned it." Kenna opened the cell door. "And my daughters are capable of protecting themselves against whatever comes at them."

"Don't be proud. Bron saw a tiny part of the horror of the horde. You can hate my kind all you like, but you must take this threat seriously," Killian said, his protectiveness a roar in his mind. "Keep Bron away from Morrigan because if I die today, nothing will be standing in the goddess's way."

Kenna's blue eyes narrowed. "What is my daughter to you that you'd be concerned about her safety?"

"She saved me from Morrigan and pissed her off in the process. You really think Morrigan doesn't want revenge on the one person that managed to infiltrate her prison and steal her prize?" Killian took a deep breath. "Just watch out for her."

"I always do, prince." Kenna nodded at the stairs, and he knew that he wouldn't get much more out of her. She followed him up the stone stairs and out into the main entrance hall.

At least Killian would finally know who put the bounty on him and hopefully talk or fight his way out of it. Kenna might not believe Morrigan was a threat to Bron, but he did, and if he was going to die, he wasn't going to make it easy on them.

The Ironwood sisters were standing on the stairs, and Killian gave them a lazy grin. They all were beautiful, fierce as shit, and armed to the teeth. Even little Moira was dressed in matching cargo gear, her dagger at her side, and looked downright adorable. Bron had her arms folded, her face cold even if her eyes were full of conflict.

Hello, love. He didn't say it, even though the words were on the tip of his tongue. He gave her a cocky wink, trying to reassure her that he had this under control, and she didn't need to look so worried. Bron's eyes went heavenward, lips twitching.

That's my girl.

"Well, this all seems ominous, doesn't it?" Killian commented, hating the silence.

"I've just buzzed their car in," a man said, coming through in a wheelchair.

The stepfather. Killian could see the likeness in the sisters' faces. Bron's comment about them being 'pure Ironwoods' hit a little different. She was the odd one out because she didn't look like Kenna or David. No wonder she felt like she didn't belong.

That's because she belongs with me.

Killian shifted his gaze, trying to focus and get his head in the game. As soon as the Ironwoods removed the cuffs, his magic would return, and he would unleash fucking hell on—

The heavy wooden doors opened, and Killian's heart skipped as two stunning women stepped through them and closed in on him.

"You son of a bitch," Elise said, smacking him hard across the face with her gloved hand.

"Do you know how worried I have been?" Freya's hand came up and smacked the other cheek. Then they were both hugging him on either side, careful not to touch his exposed hands.

"You know these women?" Bron's voice was icy cold, fury palpable in her dark eyes as she looked them over.

Killian's grin widened, delighted that the mating bond was messing with her. "Yeah, I know them. How are my favorite girls?"

"Not alone in their anger at you," Kian said as he and Bayn walked in. Kian was dressed in an immaculate suit with a deep red shirt, the tips of his black antlers painted in gold. Bayn looked his usual thuggish self in boots, jeans, and a leather jacket. Both stared at him with expressions that said they were going to kick his ass as soon as they were in private.

"I don't think I've been happier to see you assholes in my entire life," Killian replied honestly. Kian ignored that comment as he turned his imperious expression onto the Ironwoods.

"Kenna, it is a pleasure to meet you in person at last," Kian said, giving her an elegant bow.

"The princes are our fucking mysterious client! Are you kidding me?" Bron exploded. "I risked my life to go into Tir Na Nog for his damn brothers!"

"Don't sound so pissy, love. We had a good time, didn't we?" Killian asked, enjoying the show more and more. All of the Ironwoods were shocked, and Killian wanted to bask in it as long as possible.

"You will have to forgive us for the deception," Kian continued as if Bron's outburst hadn't happened. "I didn't think you would work for us if you knew the truth, and you *are* the best bounty hunters in the business."

"But I've worked for you for years," Kenna stammered, a little dazed.

"Well, I *am* responsible for the judgment of all the fae as a part of the treaty. You have been, and I hope you will continue to be, a valuable asset in helping me in that endeavor." Kian turned an utterly disapproving glance at Killian. "We knew that only someone with your skills would be able to find my brother. You were in Tir Na Nog?"

"Morrigan's castle," Killian replied, and both of his brothers flinched.

"Then I'd say that has earned you a bonus," Kian said to Kenna. "Can one of you please remove those cuffs from my brother? It has been a long few years, and I would like to take him home."

Bron stepped forward before Kenna could, and Elise and Freya let him go. Killian's smile grew wider as he held out his hands to her. "Don't look so glum, Ironwood."

"I'm just disappointed they aren't going to cut your head off," she said, her finger stroking against one wrist as she removed the first cuff.

"We still might." Bayn grunted as Freya elbowed him.

Once Bron removed the other cuff, she took a step back from him. Magic surged up through Killian, and his wings tore out of his back. He shook himself, running a hand over the top of one wing just because Bron was watching. "That's better. Shall we go?"

"After you, *brother*," Kian said through his teeth. He was staring wide-eyed at Killian's wings and the scattering of black feathers. *He knows.*

"Yeah, yeah, I'm coming." Killian turned back to Bron, took her hand, and bowed deeply. "It's been a pleasure, Bronagh Ironwood. If you ever have need of me, I'm sure you'll know how to find me." He kissed her knuckles, tucking a small feather into her hand as he did so. He let her go, taking one last glance at her confused face and turned back to his brothers. "Come on, family, I have a strong urge to drink."

18

Killian was afforded enough time to have a shower and get changed into new black jeans and a black shirt before his brothers and their mates threatened to turn on him like rabid dogs.

His apartment in Usher's Quay was still the same as it had been three years ago. Elise had organized it to be cleaned and aired out once a month, so it wasn't a total mess. It was an eerie feeling to be back, but at least Morrigan's dogs hadn't found it.

"Pizza is here!" Freya called through his bedroom door. "Hurry up, or I'll start without you."

Killian opened the door. "No need to shout."

"I haven't even begun to shout." Freya squinted at him. "Who the fuck cut your hair?"

"Bron did it with a knife when I pissed her off."

Freya laughed. "It looks like it. I'll fix it after we eat."

"Bron. The woman you can touch without hurting. That woman?" Elise said from where she was perched on the end of one of his barstools.

"Subtle as a brick you are, sis," Killian replied, getting a piece of pizza from a box.

"The Ironwood is your mate, Kill. How the fuck did that happen?" Bayn asked.

"And how did she get you out of Tir Na Nog?" Kian added, passing Killian a beer. Tears almost came to his eyes as he had the first mouthful. Gods, he had missed beer.

"Alright, everyone get food and get comfortable. I'm only going through this once," Killian said, loading up a plate and collapsing into an armchair. He told them about Morrigan's cronies taking him from the bar, his years in Tir Na Nog, the barrier holding her back that was slowly weakening. Things only got better when Bron arrived to get him out, how they had run to get to Faerie and took the ancient portal back to Ireland.

"And how did you find out that she was your mate?" Freya asked. Killian tried to think of the best way to put it.

"He fucked her. Gods, you seduced an Ironwood," Bayn said.

Killian glared at him. "She seduced me, actually." He filled them in on discovering that he could touch her and the impulsive bargain he had made. Elise started smacking him.

"You tricked a woman into having sex with you? You utter bastard!" she said, adding an extra smack for good luck.

"It wasn't like that! I wasn't going to call it in until I could take her on a date, maybe court her a bit. She got back to Ireland and dropped her robe and demanded it had to happen before we got back to Dublin. What was I going to do? Turn her down?" Killian said, trying to defend himself.

"You wanted to date her before you knew she was your mate?" Kian asked, his lips ticking up into an annoying smile.

"Yeah. I did. I mean, I do. I like her."

"She wanted to watch us cut your head off," Freya pointed out.

"She was only teasing. She was trying to make sure she stayed cool in front of her family." Killian picked at the label on his beer. "I'm sorry I worried you all."

"I'm just glad you're back so I can focus on more important things," Kian said.

"The main thing to focus on is finding out what the fuck Morrigan is planning. She's going to be here by the next full moon. I can feel it in my bones," Killian replied, getting up to pace. "We need to get some warriors posted at all the gates, find out which ones have been active or something. We need to warn the humans."

"Oh shit, Kian, he's going full mother hen mode," Bayn commented. Killian whirled on him, and Bayn put his hands up in surrender. "I didn't mean you're wrong, but I haven't seen you this excitable about anything in years."

"Morrigan is going to target my fucking mate first when she gets here. What the hell am I meant to do? Sit around with my dick in my hands and wait for it to happen?" Killian snapped.

"No, we need to prepare. You are correct there, Kill." Kian was using his calm tone on him, which pissed him off even more. "We will need the Ironwoods on board here in Ireland and any other hunters they are friends with."

"Let's hope Kenna is still willing to play with us because you embarrassed her today," Killian said. He had loved every second of it, but he was sure it would have consequences.

"You think your mate could convince her? She was in Morrigan's castle. She knows what's coming," Freya asked.

"I know Bron already tried to warn them. She'll go against Kenna if it means protecting her sisters."

"You need to tell her that she's your mate," Elise said softly, her big blue eyes squishy with feeling.

"I know, but I'm not going to do anything about it just yet. Now isn't the time. She needs some space to figure out stuff on her own. And you can all stay the fuck out of it," Killian added because they all looked about to argue with him. "Bron will be an ally, whether she's mated to me or not."

"We can ask Arne and Torsten to come over. They are always keen for a fight," Bayn said.

"The more, the merrier." Kian rubbed at his temple. "Please tell me you still have Father's sword."

"Of course I do. It's under my bed," Killian assured him.

"Put some wards on it and make sure you can get it wherever you are. It's the only weapon that we have that can hurt Morrigan."

"I know. Trust me, if she comes through a portal to Ireland, she's going to get reacquainted with it quickly," Killian replied, darkness curling inside of him.

"Gods, I haven't seen that look in your eye for centuries." Kian cursed. "Just keep your temper under control, Kill. We need to stop Morrigan, not wipe out Ireland because you're stressed about protecting your unclaimed mate."

"Where are you lot staying?" Killian asked, the word 'unclaimed' ringing in his head.

"At a hotel a block away. We need to make some calls, see if we can get warriors at the portals around Britain, just as a start," Kian said, rising to his feet.

Elise pulled on her gloves and took Killian's face in her hands. "You ever disappear on us like that again, and I *will* kill you."

"Don't worry, sis, I have no intention of getting caught again."

"I'm going to check out what antiques I can get while I'm in Dublin, but we will be close by if you need us," Freya said, punching him in the arm.

"What are you going to do while we hustle the allies?" Bayn asked.

Killian grinned, sharp and violent. "I am going to hunt down the fuckers who are working for Morrigan. I want every one of her eyes blinded as quickly as possible. Especially those bastards who got to me at the bar that night."

Kian raised a brow. "Try and keep a few for questioning."

"Don't tell me how to do my job, baby brother. I'm the family torturer, aren't I?" Killian snapped. He didn't think he would ever have to take up that particular mantle again. To save Bron, he'd commit just about any atrocity. He ran a hand over his face.

"Try and talk to your fucking mate. I don't need you going crazier on us," Kian growled.

"I missed you guys too," Killian said brightly, opening his front door. "Now, kindly get the fuck out."

Elise poked him on her way out. "Don't be an ass, big brother. There is a new phone in a bag on the kitchen bench. Use it."

Once they were finally gone, Killian warded his apartment up against anyone that wasn't them. He pulled the edge of his dark green quilt back on his bed and stuck an arm underneath it, searching. His magic pulsed as his fingers found the hilt of a sword and pulled it free.

As the eldest, he had inherited their father's sword. Like Killian, he had been the one with wings and an affinity with the night.

Killian pulled the blade free and felt the weight of its magic settle on him. It was an ancient blade, made of a matte black metal no one knew the name of. Three moonstones were inlaid into the blade near the hilt, each one of them throbbing with power. When wielded against creatures made of dark magic, the moonstones glowed with pure light and power.

Killian sheathed it and went to find his coat. He had hunting to do.

19

Five days later, the Ironwood house was still reeling that they had been working for the Blood Prince for years. It had been outed in front of the whole family, so Kenna couldn't hide it, and she had lost her temper more than once since over that fact.

"Money is money," Kenna had finally snapped at them. "Hunting creatures preying on humans has always been our foundation, and if we are doing it for Prince Kian, at least it's sanctioned by the human laws."

Bron had known better than to push her mother on the subject. Nothing had changed, and yet everything had. She had been so worked up at the thought of Killian being killed that seeing his brothers had filled her with equal parts relief and rage.

If you ever have need of me, I'm sure you'll know how to find me. Bron had thought a lot about that statement. The truth was she didn't *need* Killian, but she kind of...missed him.

Trying to fall back into her everyday life and routine was making her itch. Nothing felt right anymore. It was like being around Killian for a week had rearranged important shit inside of her. He had gotten under her skin in ways she couldn't imagine or articulate.

Bron had caught herself singing his mother's lullaby every time she was feeling bored or anxious, and she had even hummed it while putting Moira to bed the previous night.

"That's a new song," her far too clever little sister had murmured.

"Yeah, it's one I learned on my trip," Bron had told her, tucking her in bed beside King.

"Bron? I'm really happy no one hurt Killian." Moira tangled her fingers into King's fur. "He's your friend, isn't he?"

Bron frowned. "What makes you say that?"

"He makes your eyes smile, even if your face isn't. That's how I know when you really like someone."

"Well, don't tell anyone."

"I won't. I want him to come back."

Yeah, me too. Bron had kissed her head, patted King, and got out of there before Moira said anything else to emotionally kick her in the guts.

Bron stared at the map on the table in front of her and tried to pull her head away from Killian, but she ended up wondering if he was doing okay.

Of course, he was okay. He had all of his magic back and had his brothers and their beautiful mates to look after him. Lovely mates, who she had felt like putting daggers in when they had wrapped themselves around Killian.

Irrational. Everything, where he was concerned, was fucking irrational.

"Hey! Bron!" Imogen said, waving a hand under her face.

"What? Sorry?"

Imogen's face came into focus. "What the hell, sis? You looked like you were a million miles away. I was talking to you, and you were glazed over."

"Sorry," Bron repeated, rubbing at her eyes. "I was lost in my own head. I'm still messed up on Faerie time, I think." Imogen didn't look like she believed her for a second. She put a cup of coffee down beside her. If Charlotte caught them with hot drinks in the library, she would lose her shit. Bron thought it worth the risk just for the caffeine boost.

"Thanks, Gen."

"What are you working on?"

Bron turned back to the map of Ireland and the red markers she had been drawing on it. "I'm trying to map all of the gateways that are in Ireland. It's not just standing stones and burial mounds that I'm concerned about. It's all the places that aren't obvious."

"What do you mean?" Imogen asked, leaning over to scan the notes Bron had been making in a journal.

"The gateway Killian and I came through from Faerie. It dumped us in a churchyard. There was nothing that marked it as a gateway site. You know that marker stones and mounds were originally put up as a warning that it was a weak place where Faerie touched the human world, but what about the weak places that no one found, or the sites that have been built over or lost to time—"

Imogen put a hand on her shoulder. "Hey, calm down. This has got you really worked up."

"Because Morrigan is coming, Imogen! I was in her castle. I've seen shit that would give you nightmares. The full moon is a fortnight away, and we have no idea how she's going to get through to the human world," Bron said, almost shouting at her poor sister.

"I don't think you're lying about that, but this is eating your brain away. You can't come up with a good tactical plan when you can't think straight." Imogen sat down on the edge of the table. "The princes will be all over this too. I'm sure your Killian would have told his brothers all about Morrigan, and they are way more equipped to deal with a war goddess than us mere mortals."

"We can't leave it all up to them. It will take everyone to fight the horde if they come," Bron argued. "And he's not my Killian. He's his own Killian."

Imogen's smile grew wider. "Sure, sis. I didn't see Mr. Sexy Wings kissing *my* hand goodbye."

"For the love of the saints, please don't ever call him that to his face. He's insufferable enough," Bron begged. It wasn't inaccurate, though. The feather in her pocket seemed to hum in agreement.

Bron didn't know why she was carrying the damn thing around like a token. When she was thinking or anxious, she found herself stroking the silky dark feather, and it would calm her down. She wanted to ask him why the edges of his wings were going black again. She wanted to know why he gave her the damn thing to begin with.

"You know what we need? A night out," Imogen declared, jumping down off the table.

"What? No."

"We do. You especially. We haven't celebrated you making it back, and you *need* to get out and be amongst some life. I was meant to meet up with a few friends for drinks tonight in Temple Bar, so you're coming," Imogen said, tugging Bron away from the map.

"I don't know, Imogen, it seems irresponsible to go drinking when Morrigan—"

"Shut up. It's only a few drinks, not Bacchanalia." Imogen's face went serious for a second. "Although...no, you're right. A few drinks is a better idea."

"But—"

"Come on, let's find you something to wear." Bron gave in and let Imogen pull her away. One night out wouldn't be the end of the world, not yet anyway.

∼

Bron tried not to kick her high heels off under the sticky table she sat at. Imogen had made her wear one of her black halter dresses, and Bron only agreed to it because it had pockets.

Bron was wearing makeup for the first time in three months and was worried she would forget and smudge her black eyeliner into panda's eyes.

She took another mouthful of cider and tried to enjoy the music and noise of the bar. Imogen's friends were people she had met at university and had no idea what she did as a day-to-day job. Bron had never been able to hide who she was, and it meant that she always felt alone in a crowd of ordinary people.

"Imogen finally got you out. I can't believe it," the guy beside her said. "We've all heard so much about her amazing big sister." His name was Samuel, and he worked in some kind of project management. As soon as Bron had been introduced to him, she knew that Imogen was trying to set her up. *Should've known better.*

"I've been traveling," Bron said, drinking more cider.

"Yeah? You're lucky. I need to get out of Ireland for a bit, but work has been crazy," Samuel replied. He had sandy blond hair and kind hazel eyes and wasn't bad to look at. Bron might've gone with him for a one-night stand at some point, but now the idea made her feel uncomfortable.

Don't think about why.

"Tell me about your job," Bron said quickly, knowing people loved to talk about themselves. Samuel was no different, and it meant that Bron could politely nod and smile where necessary and didn't have to speak.

A glimmer of black and silver danced in the corner of her eye, and her head snapped around, heart pounding.

"You okay?" Samuel asked.

"Yeah, sorry. I thought I saw someone I knew. Will you excuse me for a second?" Bron got up and headed for the bathroom. For once, there wasn't a massive line, and she washed her hands in the small sink to stop them from shaking.

You're actually losing it. Bron checked her reflection in the mirror and put on some lip gloss. She was adjusting her long hair when she heard voices outside the small window.

"I've never hooked up with one of the fae before," a woman giggled. "Is it true what they say about your staying power?"

"All the rumors are true," a male replied with a charming laugh. "You want to try something that will get you higher than you've ever been?"

"I don't do drugs, especially magic ones." The woman didn't sound so confident now.

"Just a hit won't hurt—"

"I said no. Hey!"

Bron was moving before she could think it through. She pushed her way through the staff-only exit and out into the alley behind the bar. The fae male had the woman against a wall.

"Hey! The lady said she didn't want any," Bron called, making both of them freeze. The woman's dress was hitched up her thighs, and her eyes were swimming with tears.

"Why don't you mind your own business?" the fae said, his expression turning vicious. "Unless you want to join us."

"You couldn't keep up with me," Bron said, trying to keep his attention off the woman. She was edging away from the male, then she turned and ran. The male hissed.

"That was impolite."

"So was trying to force drugs down her throat," Bron replied, her feet sliding slowly into a fighting stance.

"Lucky you're here to keep me amused instead." The male moved, quick as lightning. Bron twisted to the side to dodge him.

"You really don't want to pick this fight," Bron growled.

"Maybe I do. I love a woman who fights back."

Bron kicked off one heel, catching it with her right hand. The ridiculous shoes were good for something, after all.

When he rushed her again, Bron blocked his reaching hands and smacked him hard in the temple with the spike of her heel. The fae cursed her, touching the amber blood that trickled down his face. He let out a laugh, licking the blood from his fingers.

"Now we are talking."

Bron didn't take her eyes off him as he started to circle her. "You can still walk away."

"I want you to run, little human. I want you afraid."

"Not going to happen."

The fae snarled and lunged for her as Bron swung. Her heel didn't connect as the fae stopped dead in his tracks. Hot amber splattered her upraised arm, a black sword suddenly sticking through the fae's chest. Blood bubbled out of his mouth as the sword sliced part of his side, and he slumped to the ground.

Bron's heart was in her throat as Killian flicked the amber blood off his sword. He was dressed in a black suit and silk shirt, so in conflict with the sword in his hand and the furious expression on his face.

Bron gripped her shoe harder, every part of her fighting not to throw herself into his arms in relief at seeing him. Killian's emerald eyes shone as he stared down at her, the scary as hell expression on his face shifting to a smile.

"Bronagh Ironwood, what a pleasure to see you again," he purred.

"What are you doing here?" she demanded.

Killian gestured to the body on the ground. "Looking for this piece of shit. He was one of the fae that drugged me for Morrigan. The question is, what are *you* doing here? That doesn't seem like suitable hunting attire." He looked her over, and goosebumps spread up her arms.

"I heard him trying to force drugs on a human woman and intervened," Bron replied. "We need to get rid of his body before someone sees."

"Easily done." Killian held a hand out over the dead fae, his magic curling over the corpse, dark as shadows. It dissolved, leaving nothing behind.

"Well, that's handy." Bron slid her shoe back on and cringed at the amber blood on her arms. "You missed a spot."

"I live close by if you want to get cleaned up," Killian offered. He looked at the back door to the club, lips pursing. "Unless you have a date waiting for you."

"It's Imogen that will be pissed." Bron looked at the club door and back to Killian. He was out hunting for Morrigan's spies, which meant he had information she didn't. He looked amazing in that suit. The giant sword he was holding only heightened his hotness. Anxiety fluttered in her belly as his smile widened. Curiosity to see what his place was like won her over.

"I'm sure Imogen will get over it eventually," Bron said, taking out her phone and shooting her sister a message.

Bumped into a friend and going home to hang out with them. Have fun, don't wait up. Bron turned the phone on do not disturb and tucked it back into her pocket.

"Lead the way, prince," she said.

Killian's sword disappeared, and he held an arm out for her to take.

"I don't want to get blood on your suit," Bron tried to object, but he wrapped her arm over his anyway. She might have moved a little closer so she could breathe in his too-appealing sandalwood and belladonna scent.

"The suit will survive. This way, Ironwood."

20

As a character trait, Killian had always thought self-control was overrated. Unfortunately, it was the only way forward where Bron Ironwood was concerned.

A dirty alley in Temple Bar was the last place he had expected to bump into her. He had been hunting in a haze, mind solely focused on his enemy for days. Then he got a whiff of her scent, mixed in with his prey, and he had lost his mind.

Bron, of course, was taking care of herself. Now, she was on his arm, smearing a suit that he liked in fae juice, and he couldn't have been happier.

Killian fished out his keys as they stepped through the gate leading through the garden and to his door.

"Do you need to do anything like run about and hide dirty clothes or your porn stash? I can wait," Bron said, letting his arm go.

"Very funny. I happen to be old enough to keep my house clean," Killian replied.

"I'll remember to take my shoes off."

"Please don't," he said before he could check himself. Seeing her wield the black pumps like a weapon before walking home in them was all kinds of sexy.

Killian tossed his keys on a side table. "Bathroom is through there if you want to wash the fae off you." *And every other male scent.*

"Thanks," Bron walked down the hall, heels tapping on the polished floorboards.

"You want a drink?" he called after her.

"Sure."

Killian retreated to the kitchen and took off his jacket. He breathed deeply in and out a few times to center his scattered brain before taking out two water bottles from the fridge. He wasn't sure if mixing alcohol and Bron in that dress was a good idea.

"I have to say, I'm impressed. You didn't lie about it being clean," she said, sliding onto a barstool. She took the bottle of water from him and had a mouthful. "This is a really nice place. Did you decorate it?"

"Don't act so surprised," Killian replied. For some reason, the fact she liked it made something glow inside of him. He looked her over slowly. He couldn't help it.

"Hot date?"

"It wasn't hot. Imogen thought I was working too hard and that it would be a good idea if we went out to have drinks with her friends. She set me up on a blind date without me knowing," Bron replied, a bit of color spreading up her neck.

"It must've been going bad if you chose to go and fight in an alley."

Bron shrugged. "It's not his fault he was boring. Anyway, you were the one that told me I should let people in."

Me. Not other men. Killian tried not to look as irritated as he felt. He turned back to his fridge and got out a half-eaten tub of double chocolate fudge ice cream.

"I can't imagine some normal guy would be enough to challenge you anyway, Ironwood," Killian said, passing her a spoon. "And we all know how you love those."

"So I've been told," she replied, digging her spoon in first. "Ice cream?"

"Something tough to get in prison, as it turns out. I can't stop putting it in my mouth." Killian ate a spoonful. "What are you working so hard on?"

Bron tapped her spoon against her full bottom lip. "I'll tell you if you tell me how your own hunting efforts are going."

"Deal. You first."

"Gateways," Bron said, not fighting him about it. "I'm trying to find all the known passages between Ireland and Faerie, where Morrigan can come through. I've been digging about in the library and online to find other sites that used to be ancient temples or sacred sites that have had churches built on them."

"Like Templecorran."

"Exactly. We dropped out where the site used to be. Stands to reason that there are other places like that," Bron said, giving him a smile before having more ice cream.

"That's very clever of you." Killian rested his forearms against the counter, digging his spoon in the tub. "I've been tracking down the assholes that drugged me and those that might be working with Morrigan. I want her to lose all of her little spies."

"How's it going?"

"The one I killed tonight was one of the main trio. The other male I, ah, questioned gave up some names, so I've been running them down."

"With a really big sword. Subtle." Bron looked him over. "Where is it hiding anyway? It looked beautiful."

"It's in my bedroom. Kian made me put wards on it so I could summon it any time I need it. He worries about me."

Ask me to take you to my bedroom to look at it.

"That's understandable. You did disappear on them for years. If one of my sisters had been taken, I would be the same." Bron huffed out an irritated breath. "I'm still kind of annoyed that they hired us to find you and made it so cloak and dagger."

"That's Kian's way. He didn't think your mother would help out if she knew who she was working for. I bet she was pissed."

Bron laughed softly. "You have no idea. Don't worry, her mercenary side won out. She won't turn down work for Kian."

"Good, we need allies when Morrigan comes," Killian replied. "Her followers have all confirmed that she's on her way. I'm hoping any of the others I track down will cough up some more useful information."

Bron's dark eyes gleamed. "You want help hunting them?"

Killian's heart skipped a beat at the offer. "Yeah, I really would. You want to share that map you're making of the gateways? Kian is hustling people to set up watches at all of them, an early alert system."

"Sure, that's an excellent idea." Bron stuck her spoon into the ice cream and left it there. "You know, it was embarrassing when your brothers turned up for you, but I'm glad it was them. And that you're not dead." The color was creeping across her neck again. "And that we bumped into each other tonight."

Killian leaned over and whispered teasingly in her face, "Missed me bad, huh?"

"Yeah, actually, I kind of did," she admitted, surprising him.

"Really? How much?" he blurted.

Bron kissed him, a soft press of lips that made him freeze. She had *never* kissed him, not once. She pulled back, and he almost growled at the loss of her. "That much."

"So not as much as I missed you then," he said, and her dark eyes widened.

"You missed me too?" Bron managed to say before he was kissing her again, tasting her sweet chocolatey lips.

"A lot." Killian kissed her again. "All the time." Bron grabbed him by the front of his shirt, pulling him in between her thighs. Her hands pushed into his hair, fingers twisting in his silver streak.

"If that's true, then stop moving your mouth away," she said. Her next kiss was demanding, so he put his arms around her, bringing her up against him.

This was the itch he hadn't been able to scratch for days, and the fury in his veins calmed the longer he was touching her. It was like he could finally think again.

"If you keep kissing me like this, I won't be held responsible for what happens next," Killian warned breathlessly.

Bron's expression turned coy. "Why? What's going to happen?"

"I don't think you want to know."

Bron tapped her ear. "If you're shy, you can whisper it to me." Her unexpected playfulness sparked all kinds of mischief in him. Killian kissed the edge of the offered ear, teeth nibbling her lobe and making Bron's hands tighten on his shoulders.

"I'm going to take your clothes off, bit by bit, tasting as I go," he whispered. "And I won't be as polite about what I want like I was the first time around."

"Before you do that." Bron slid her hands down his chest and gently pushed him back. "I need to know if you missed me for me and not because I'm the only woman you can touch."

Killian skimmed his thumbs over her cheeks. "I would miss you even if I couldn't touch you. That's not on my list of reasons at all."

"Why did you miss me then?" Her large dark eyes were full of emotion, and he almost told her that she was his mate, his perfect opposite and other half. Killian wanted to, but if she was already unsure of his motivations, then it would make it worse. Through their growing bond, he felt her emotions like a kick in the guts. Bron needed to believe that she was worth choosing, and he'd be damned if he let her think that she wasn't.

Killian kissed her cheek. "Because you're brave." The curve of her jaw. "And fearless." The tip of her nose. "You see through my bullshit and call me out on it." Her other cheek. "Because the more time I spend with you, the more I want to know you." He kissed her lips. "You're strong enough to stand by me and not behind me. Actually, come to think of it, you could probably fight all my battles for me. That would be quite handy."

"Hey." Bron pinched him, making him laugh. "You were doing so well."

"I haven't even gotten to your physical attributes yet." Killian was silenced as she kissed him. Her tongue touched his lips, and he opened for her. As soon as that tongue moved against his, desire exploded through him, and he pulled her closer, needing more of her against him.

"Stay with me tonight," he begged as they broke apart. "Please."

Bron's fingers stroked his cheeks, and she whispered, "Okay."

Her hair was soft and heavy in his hand. Her head tilted back so he could deepen the kiss further. Bron's legs came around his hips, the skirt of her dress riding up.

Killian's hands skimmed down the dark hose she was wearing and pulled her heels off, letting them drop to the floor.

"Thank God. I hate heels," Bron replied. Her own hands were getting busy, untucking his shirt and running her fingers over his skin. "Are you going to pop those wings out for me or what?"

Killian chuckled. "I will later. They would just get in the way for what I have planned." He lifted her off the chair so he could tug her hose down and pulled them off, revealing her soft brown thighs. "That's better."

Bron unbuttoned his shirt, dragging it off his shoulders. "Yeah, it is." She kissed the center of his chest and rested her forehead against him. "You always smell so good."

Killian smiled and undid the halter of her dress. He kissed the back of her neck, letting the top half of her dress fall down. She was wearing a dark green, lacy strapless bra, and tucked into her cleavage was... "Well, knock me down with a feather," he gasped, and she swore, trying to snatch the black feather sticking out of the side of the cup. "And what's that doing in there, Ironwood?"

"None of your business," she said firmly.

"That's my feather, love. It's absolutely my business," Killian teased.

Bron looked flustered and a little anxious. "If you must know, I thought if I got into a jam, I could use it to summon you. That's what it does, right?"

"Alas, it's just a feather. I gave it to you so if you really wanted to find me, your magical sister could use it in a tracking spell. I didn't have a phone number to give you." Bron groaned in embarrassment, but he was too excited on too many levels to let her wallow in it.

Killian grinned like a fiend as he pulled her off the barstool and carried her off towards his bedroom. "I fucking *love* that my feather has been living in your bra. I'm getting hard just thinking about where else you've put it for safekeeping."

"I can tell," Bron said, sliding slowly down his body and back to her feet. Killian sat on the edge of his bed and tugged her dress the rest of the way off. She was wearing matching green panties, and a happy growl rumbled through him.

"You're even wearing my color. You *must* have missed me," he said, pressing his lips over her thrumming heart.

"Happy coincidence," Bron said, gasping as his mouth closed over a lace-covered breast. Her fingers twisted in his hair as he unclipped the front of the bra and tossed it aside.

"I've noticed that I'm the only one getting naked, Killian," Bron commented. Her grip on his hair tightened, and she tilted his head up.

His mouth retook hers, robbing the words off her tongue while he slid her panties off.

"I don't need to be naked for this," Killian said. Bron squeaked in surprise as he turned her and pulled her down on the bed on top of him. She was backward with her knees on either side of his head, right where he wanted her.

"Killian, what are you—oh God," Bron gasped as he licked right down her center.

Fuck. She tasted better than he remembered.

"I told you I was going to taste you everywhere. I always follow through on my promises," he said, hands gripping her hips to keep her from sliding forward. He didn't give her a chance to reply and put his lips on her again. Bron's warm breasts brushed his lower abdomen as she tried to find her grip on either side of him.

"Fuck, Kill," she groaned. Then her hands were unbuckling his belt and pants. "Two can play at this game."

"And you're welcome to," he said as she pulled his dick free. His confidence jolted as her hot, wet tongue ran down his shaft before taking him in her soft mouth. Killian sucked her clit, and Bron's groan vibrated straight through him. It took every ounce of his self-control not to come right then and there.

Killian felt the second the emotional bond opened between them, and her pleasure tangled with his. His grip on her ass tightened, and he started to fuck her with his tongue. He worked her relentlessly until her arms and legs were shaking over him and she was coming hard and loud, Killian licking her all the way through it.

"I can't...I need to catch my breath, Kill, stop," she whimpered. He did, lazily stroking her thighs.

"Tell me what you need, love," he said. Bron slid forward and pulled at his pants and boxers.

"I need you naked and inside of me right now," she replied irritably.

"Done."

21

Bron laughed as Killian lifted her off him, pinned her on her back, and settled his large body between her thighs.

"God, I love how strong you are," she said breathlessly, every part of her humming and sensitive. Bron's nails dug into his shoulders. "Now, where are those wings?"

"You have a wing kink, you know that, right?" Killian joked, his smile pure sin.

"Did you ever stop to think that *you* are my kink?" Bron asked, kissing him. "And that maybe I want your true self on top of me?"

"You keep talking like that, and you're going to undo me," Killian murmured. His wings spread out behind him, and she sighed.

"There you are." Bron ran her hand over the soft arch to the silver talon at its tip. "Beautiful."

Killian's eyes softened. "Yes, you are. Every part of you."

Bron couldn't handle the emotion that welled up in her, so she pulled him towards her lips. Killian kissed her, taking his time as he eased inside of her.

Bron stroked the tattoo on his chest, her hands memorizing the shape of him, the feel of his large body moving against hers and making it sing.

She was skirting the edges of another orgasm when he grabbed her legs, put them over his shoulders, and drove back into her. Her vision burst with light as she came hard, crying out his name as she broke apart.

"Oh shit, was that a good sound or a hurt sound?" Killian asked, hand cupping her face. She opened her eyes, saw his genuine concern, and smiled up at him.

"Good sound. Fuck." Bron tried to think of something else to say and couldn't form the words. "Fuck."

Killian looked positively delighted. "Got you good, didn't I?"

"Shut up." Bron shifted her legs off his shoulders, but he stayed where he was. Then he started to move again, and she was clinging to him, her body matching his rhythm. Her grip tightened as a flash of sensation wrecked her, and she wasn't sure if it was her pleasure or his that she was feeling. Killian picked up his pace, and her brain stopped caring, too caught up in him to think of anything else.

His body, his eyes, his wings, his mouth, everything was made for sin, for decadence...for her. The next time she came, he went with her, and his magic danced over them, lighting her up with fae runes.

"One...day..." she panted as they collapsed on his sheets. "You're going to tell me what all of these mean."

"They say 'Killian was here,'" he replied breathlessly. Bron hit him with a pillow, and they both started laughing. He rolled onto his side and smoothed the damp hair back from her face. "Bath?"

"A bath would be perfect." Bron held up her arms to look at the runes. "They are kind of beautiful, aren't they?"

"They are. I'll be right back." Killian kissed a rune mark on her shoulder and headed for the bathroom, giving her an excellent view of his perfect ass on the way out. The sound of running water and him humming drifted toward her, making her smile widen.

Bron was almost slipping into a sex coma when Killian reappeared.

"Oh dear, I finally killed her."

"You wish," Bron said.

"Your bath awaits, Sleeping Beauty." Killian helped her up and steered her toward the bathroom.

Bron had spotted the huge tub when she had washed her hands. She figured it had been custom-made to accommodate his wings because she had never seen a bath like it. As she had lain in bliss, he had not only filled it with hot water and bubbles but had lit some candles and poured them both some wine.

"A girl could really get used to this," Bron said as she sank into the hot water.

"A girl is welcome to use my tub whenever she likes," Killian replied, climbing in the opposite end. He found her foot in the water and started to massage it. "What else have you been up to in the past five days?"

"Trying to remember how to live in a house with my boisterous family," Bron replied. "Eating to make up for all the weight I lost and trying to get my training schedule back in place."

Killian frowned. "Already? I thought you would have a few days off at least."

"We can't all bounce back as quickly as the fae," Bron said, gesturing to his body. "I don't know how you've gotten bigger in a few days."

"Elise forced healing potions down my throat, and Freya messages me three times a day to check I'm eating," Killian replied. "I've never had sisters, and they are both fussing. My brothers are even worse."

"Can I swap? Imogen showed she cared by making me a few coffees. Charlotte grilled me about how her glamours and other devices worked. Moira won't stop talking about you. Layla and my cousins Lachlan and Ciara haven't returned yet, but I'm sure I'll be forced to go over every detail of my trip with them too." Bron sipped her red wine and hummed in approval. "I'm tempted to hide out here in your tub with your wine collection."

Killian pulled her slowly towards him, their wet bodies making it easy for her to slide into his lap. "As tempting as that is, you promised to go hunting with me. Once Morrigan is dead, then you can hide in here as long as you like. As long as I'm invited."

Bron placed her glass down beside his and put her hands around his neck. "I need someone to pour my wine and massage my feet, don't I?"

Killian gave her a dirty smile. "You forgot screaming orgasms."

"I'll definitely need a few of those by the time this business with Morrigan is over." Bron toyed with the wet ends of his hair. "She's really going to give us hell, isn't she?"

"Yes, if she can. She will want to take revenge on you most of all. You are trained for a fight, but promise me you won't argue if I get between you," Killian said, deadly serious. His screams from the day Bron saw him tortured rose in her mind, and she tightened her grip on him.

"I won't let you fight her on your own."

"It's not about that. The sword you saw tonight, it's the only weapon I know that can actually hurt her, maybe kill her if we are lucky."

Realization dawned on her. "You and the sword are the big gun."

Killian nodded. "The only reason Morrigan managed to get me is that she drugged me. In a proper confrontation, she knows I have the strength to kill her. It's why she was so determined to get me on her side. She wanted me to cover the world in darkness and destroy it."

"You could do that?" Bron's mouth went dry as Killian nodded. "I suppose that explains why the cuffs I used on you didn't work that great."

"Does that knowledge scare you?" Killian asked, his eyes suddenly ancient and unknowable.

Bron considered the question carefully before answering, "No, I don't think it does. How do you know you could turn the whole world dark?"

"That was a part of the original plan when my brothers and I returned. If Kian's revenge and Bayn's ice didn't sway the humans, I was going to block out the sun."

"Your power was their end game."

Killian sighed. "My power is everyone's end game. It's one of the reasons that I used to play the charming dilettante courtier. I hoped everyone would forget what I was capable of."

"You didn't want them to be afraid of you?" Bron guessed, and he nodded.

"Not unless it was required. My father had the same power as me and taught me to control it and that it's always better to be loved than feared." Killian had a mouthful of wine. "He and my mother died keeping Morrigan locked up. I have no intention of letting anyone else I care about die because of her. So you promise that you'll get behind me."

Bron rested a palm on his cheek. "I promise."

"Good." Killian leaned into the touch. "Thank you." There was a tightness around his eyes that Bron couldn't stand to see, so she grinned.

"No need to thank me. I'm happy to use you as my living shield. One question, though. Can I inherit this bathtub if you die?"

Killian laughed. "Who would've thought such a smart ass lay under that grumpy exterior, Ironwood? You better watch out, or I'm going to start to think you have a sense of humor under there."

"I do, but don't tell anyone."

Killian kissed her smiling lips. "Wouldn't dream of it."

22

It had been a long time since Bron had been forced to sneak into the Ironwood manor. She had kissed Killian goodbye and fought off his sleepy attempts to make her stay.

"Come by late afternoon, and I'll show you what I've been working on," Bron had whispered before getting out of there.

She had been more than a little tempted to stay curled up under his wing, exactly where she liked it. The growing warm feeling that fluttered under her ribs every time she looked at Killian too long was the reason she had to leave.

Bron needed space to process it, figure out if it was just the sex making her feel this way...or something else.

After a shower, Bron dressed in her usual outfit of cargo pants and a long-sleeved thermal. Her hair was a bundle of knots from having it out the previous evening, and it took a good fifteen minutes to brush it out, braid it, and pin it up, out of the way.

"Should I ask who the owner of that coat is?" Charlotte greeted her as soon as she stepped out of the bathroom. Of all the sisters, she was the early riser. She was also studying the blazer that Killian insisted she wear home to keep her warm.

"Probably best if you don't. What has you up so early?" Bron asked, accepting the cup of tea her sister held out for her.

"You know me. I woke at dawn, and my brain exploded," she said with exasperation.

Charlotte was twenty-six years old, tall and willowy, with curly brown hair that she usually had pinned up in a messy bun. She was the calmest presence of all the Ironwood's and preferred fighting with magic than with blades. Her fingers were permanently stained with ink and chalk, and she always had a distracted look in her eye like she was constantly thinking of something else...usually magic.

Imogen had stopped trying to get her out on dates because, in Charlotte's mind, no man was as interesting as magic.

"Layla, Lachie, and Ciara are due back today," Charlotte said as they wandered towards the kitchen.

"How did the hunt in Germany go?"

"Good, I believe. You know Ciara loves hunting rogue werewolves. Layla complained loudly about freezing her ass off in the middle of the Harz Mountains because Ciara went tracking crazy," Charlotte replied with a small laugh at their younger sister's discomfort.

"Pretty sure I can one-up her on that after hunting through Faerie and Tir Na Nog," Bron replied.

"Big sister, you're going to have one up on everyone for a long time with that one."

Bron went straight to the fridge, eating grapes and cheese and anything else she could get her hands on. With a sigh, Charlotte moved her out of the way.

"Go and sit down. I'll cook you something. You clearly had a big night of...whatever."

"I went out with Imogen and ended up in a fight, if you must know," Bron said around a mouthful of apple. Charlotte wasn't as judgmental as Imogen, so Bron told her about the fae pushing drugs, bumping into Killian, and heading over to his place to compare notes on Morrigan's followers. Bron didn't mention screwing his brains out, and Charlotte didn't seem like she cared to ask.

"He's coming around later so I can show him the map I'm working on," Bron said. Charlotte placed a plate of bacon and scrambled eggs in front of her. "Have I ever told you that I love you and you're my favorite sister ever?"

Charlotte smiled. "Only when I feed you. You have a worried thinking face. What else is on your mind?"

"We need to put the word out to other hunters, see if they are available to help out when the full moon comes. If nothing else, we need to warn people that Morrigan and her horde could try and get through the gates." Bron ate a few mouthfuls of eggs. "You know anyone that can help out magic-wise? Wizard friends or something?"

Charlotte rolled her eyes. "Wizard friends? Come on, you know I don't do people. I will assist in any way I can. If I must, I will send out a text to some of the covens I know of, and they can spread the word."

"What about that Greatdrakes that gets around?" Bron asked.

Charlotte flushed with instant annoyance. "Reeve Greatdrakes is a disgrace to the magical arts and will be no use to us at all. The best he could do is jump in front of a horde creature and get eaten as a distraction while other people got away."

Bron didn't get a chance to ask about Charlotte's uncharacteristic outburst because Imogen stumbled into the kitchen, pastel hair a mess on top of her head and wearing a silk kimono.

"Jesus Christ, Charlotte, why are you yelling?" Imogen groaned, fumbling to turn the kettle on.

"Bron suggested getting that good for nothing Greatdrakes involved in our business," Charlotte said primly.

"Lay off Reeve. He's a cool guy," Imogen replied. She pulled out the ground-up coffee beans and dumped a heap into the glass plunger.

"He is *not* a cool guy."

Bron shot Imogen a confused look. "Am I missing something?"

"Charlotte is offended that Reeve has a natural affinity for magic, and she has to work at it."

Charlotte turned bright red with indignation. "I am not! He and his so-called trash magic are ridiculous."

"I once watched him make a cloud of silver butterflies at a party out of two gum wrappers and a straw. The dude is a freaking genius," Imogen argued. "And he's hot. Like a young Johnny Depp, Bron, I shit you not."

"Wait, *21 Jump Street*, young Johnny or *Don Juan DeMarco* Johnny?"

"The latter, mixed with a solid amount of *Chocolat* Johnny." Imogen, a shit-stirrer even with a hangover, waggled her eyebrows at Charlotte.

"I'm not listening to this. I have work to do," she said, getting to her feet.

"Don't be like that, little sis. I wasn't trying to upset you."

"You didn't. And just so you know, Bron spent the night with Killian," Charlotte said before storming out.

"Hey, not cool!" Bron called after her. "Wow, I've never seen her get so worked up over someone like that before."

"She'll be fine. Reeve gets her all antsy in her pantsy because she's so uptight." Imogen sat down in Charlotte's empty chair and helped herself to what was left of her bacon and eggs. "Killian was the mysterious friend you took off with last night, wasn't he?"

"Yeah, we bumped into each other when we were killing a fae in the ally."

Imogen huffed out an angry breath. "You were meant to be having a night off!"

"It wasn't intentional." Bron filled her in on the night, but unlike Charlotte, Imogen didn't ignore the fact she had slept over at Killian's.

"Are you shagging the Night Prince, big sister?" she asked over the rim of her mug.

"Would you tell anyone if I was?"

"I would be impressed because he's *the fucking Night Prince,* Bronagh. How did this even happen?"

Bron shrugged. "Just did. I like him."

"Must be a bit more than just *like*."

"Maybe it is. I don't know. I'm trying not to think about it too hard," Bron said. She got up to steal some of the remaining coffee. "He's going to come around today to look at the map I've been working on. If you see him, don't make it weird."

"Weird? Me? I don't know what you're talking about," Imogen said, pulling faces at her.

"And don't mention it to Kenna whatever you do." Bron gave her a serious look. "Please. Until I know how to define it, he's an ally."

"Okay, okay, I'll be good, I promise. Bumping uglies with the Night Prince, I don't think I've ever been so proud of you."

"Focus, Imogen. I need you to reach out to any hunter friends of yours. We need to warn them that Morrigan is coming. Her servants that Killian has questioned in the past few days have all said that she'll be here by the next full moon."

"I will shoot out some messages and emails," Imogen said, the teasing going from her face.

"Good, I'll be in the library," Bron replied and left her sister to nurse her hangover. She had things to do before Killian arrived, including coming up with a way to soothe Kenna's inevitable temper when he got there.

~

KILLIAN ARRIVED at the Ironwood manor at three o'clock on the dot. He had texted Bron about ten minutes beforehand, and butterflies had exploded in her chest.

On my way, I hope your wards let me in.

Bron smiled. *I suppose if you want to see me, you'll figure out a way through them.*

The alarms had been triggered and were loud enough to rattle the stones. Bron made it downstairs in time to see Kenna open the front doors. Killian was dressed in black jeans and an overcoat, somehow looking polished even when he was casual. Despite that polish and his charming smile, he still projected a hint of power and danger that made every part of Bron pay attention. She suddenly had a profound and violent need to kiss him.

You like him way too much.

"Lady Kenna, how lovely to see you again," Killian greeted her with a charming smile.

"What are you doing here, prince?" Kenna asked, eyes narrowing, one hand drifting to the dagger at her side.

"I was invited." Killian's eyes rose to Bron, and his smile somehow went from charming to dazzling. His emerald eyes seemed to heat with dark promise, and she gripped the banister, her knees threatening to give way.

"Hey, Killian. Thanks for coming," Bron greeted, her voice smooth despite the tremble inside of her.

Kenna whirled on her. "Bronagh?"

"Killian has kindly offered some information on the movements of Morrigan's servants. I asked him to come and have a look at the map I'm creating." Bron held her mother's penetrating gaze.

"You could have consulted me," Kenna said.

"We are allies. I didn't think I needed to," Bron replied innocently. Kenna looked from Killian to Bron and back again.

"I spoke with Bayn this morning, and he's got two friends, a light elf called Arne, and Torsten, one of the Úlfhéðnar, coming to join us. Kian wanted to see if you were open for a meeting of allies so everyone is on the same page?" Killian asked, smooth as silk.

"That would be fine. We have recalled my daughter Layla, as well as my niece and nephew from Germany. They will arrive tonight." Kenna turned to Bron. "We will speak later, daughter."

"I have no doubt. The library is this way, Killian, if you would like to follow me." Bron turned away from her mother's withering look and made for the stairs.

"Have a pleasant day, Lady Kenna," Killian said before catching up with Bron.

"I do believe she's warming up to me," he whispered, and Bron swallowed down a laugh.

"I wouldn't count on it, prince," Bron replied.

"Back to prince, are we, Ironwood?"

Bron pushed open the library door. "And what am I meant to call you?"

Killian's eyes heated again. "Oh, I could think of a few things."

Bron carefully ignored the thrill that shot through her belly and walked him around the stacks to her worktable.

"This is a nice library. Is there anyone else working in here?" Killian asked, looking around.

"No. My other sisters are busy doing their own thing."

"Good." Killian pulled her behind a set of shelves and kissed her hard and deep with just the right amount of bite. He gave, so she took until her hands started wandering under his shirt, and she forced herself to pull her mouth from his.

"What was that for?" she asked, trying to get her breath back. He loosened his grip on her braid.

"I wouldn't have been able to focus on a damn thing if I hadn't. I'm still sulking that you ran out on me this morning. I had so many things planned, Bronagh."

"Is that so? Like what?"

Killian bit his bottom lip. "Pull down your pants, climb halfway up that ladder, and find out."

Bron stepped back from him so she could breathe. "Maybe I'll take you up on that offer next time the manor is empty, and we are not going to get interrupted by one of my sisters."

"Good point. There are things a child shouldn't witness. Dark, dark things."

"Stop terrorizing me when we have work to do," Bron scolded and moved to her map. "These are the places that I had pegged as potential gates that Morrigan could come through. They all have had reports over the centuries as places with strange activity."

Killian took some photos on his phone. "Good job, Bron. I'll send these to Kian and see what he can do. He's been setting up watches at the hot spots in Britain and Wales. Bayn has taken Scotland."

"I still think if she comes in anywhere, it will be here in Ireland."

Killian folded his arms. "I agree, but what's your reasoning?"

"Her power, her cult, it was the strongest here. If you were a goddess that had been banished, you would want to go back to your old home first," Bron explained. "What was your theory?"

"We are here, and she will want to deal with us first. Both theories are good ones." Killian bent closer to the map, frown deepening.

"What is it?" Bron asked.

"This name... Clonmacnoise. One of the fae I questioned babbled it in the end. I thought it was a nonsense word because he was choking on his own blood. Ah, I mean..."

"Stop. Whatever excuse you're about to make, you don't have to, Kill. We have all interrogated people. You don't have to hide it from me," Bron assured him, placing her hand over his.

"Thank you, Bron," he said softly, his fingers tangling with hers. Bron looked back at the map, refusing to get distracted.

"There are ruins of a monastery in Clonmacnoise founded by Saint Ciarán," she said, letting his hand go so she could search on her phone. She found a photo and passed it to him.

Killian studied the picture, his frown deepening. "Want to go and check it out?"

Bron smiled up at him. "I thought you'd never ask."

"I want to come too!" Moira said, jumping out from the shelves and giving Bron a heart attack.

"You can't. You're too small," Bron said.

Moira raised her chin. "If you don't take me, I'll tell Mom where you went and that you were holding hands, making love heart eyes at Killian."

"Moira, it's going to be too dangerous that's why—"

Killian rested a hand on Bron's shoulder. "I got this." He crouched down beside Moira. "Little one, if you keep your mouth shut and let me take your big sister out of this mansion, I'll put a spell on you so you can understand and talk to King."

"You can do that?! King!" The dog in question trotted up and sat beside Moira attentively.

"I can do lots of things."

"Prove it."

"Not until you shake on it." Killian held out a gloved hand to her. Moira looked at it suspiciously for a few seconds before she shook it hard.

"Deal. Now, stay very still." Killian murmured softly under his breath. Moira giggled as emerald and black magic swirled around King and then her. "There you are. Try it out."

Moira turned to her dog and asked, "What do you think we should do next?" King's head tilted tail wagging. He let out a small series of sounds, and Moira giggled.

"You *always* want to sniff around the kitchen," she complained. She gave Killian a gap-toothed grin and then ran away with the dog.

"Hey! You forgot to say thank you!" Bron called after her.

"Thank you, Killian!" Moira shouted without stopping. He chuckled as she disappeared.

"She's cute."

"She's a pain in the ass. Why my mother decided to have another baby after sixteen years is beyond me," Bron said with a pained sigh.

"Babies are blessings, even the ones that aren't planned," Killian replied. "There's a good two hundred years between my brothers and me, but it wasn't going to stop my mother from having them."

"Here's hoping Moira can keep quiet long enough for us to get away."

Killian smiled. "She will."

"And for the record, I wasn't making love heart eyes at you."

Killian's own eyes were now glittering with amusement. "*Sure* you weren't. Now, show me the best way to sneak out of this place so I know how to get back in if I need to."

"And why would you need to do that?" Bron asked.

Killian pressed a brief kiss to her lips. "I wouldn't want to ruin the surprise."

23

Killian was a good boy and didn't follow Bron to her bedroom to retrieve her favorite weapons and coat. Honestly, if he got Bron behind a closed door, he wasn't sure what would happen.

No, that was a lie. He knew exactly what would happen. He'd pin her to the nearest surface and pull her hunting gear off to get to the delectable softness underneath.

The mating bond is going to drive you crazy if you don't tell her soon.

"Well, well, never thought I'd see you in my library," a woman said as she wandered through the stacks. She had multicolored hair and was wearing shredded jeans and a sweatshirt with a grinning skull on it.

"Let me guess, Imogen, right?"

"Fifty points to Slytherin," she replied. She looked him over and clicked her tongue. "It's not that I don't understand your appeal, but I'm surprised as hell that she would go for you. Or you for her, for that matter."

"You don't think I'm her type?" Killian asked.

"Bron's type is more for a night where she can forget their name and have no attachments."

"Maybe she's just been waiting for the right male."

Imogen crossed her arms. "She avoids complicated, and you, prince, are all kinds of complicated. If you're looking to fuck about, I'd ask you not to do it with my sister."

Imogen might not look like the other militant Ironwoods, but there was no denying the cold hunter in her eyes.

"I'd be lying if I didn't say I have an agenda when it comes to Bron, but it's not a malicious one in any way. You know enough about me and my reputation, so you have a right to worry, but I'm not playing her. I like her. I respect her. And I would do anything to protect her," Killian said honestly. Imogen's face broke into a crooked smile.

"Good. Bron hides it, but her heart's involved, and if you break it, I'll make Morrigan look like a fucking peach."

Killian laughed. "Understood. You Ironwoods really know how to bust a guy's balls."

"It's our specialty." Imogen's smile turned feline. "You know, Bron has dreamed about you since she was a baby. I thought she was going to kill you. There really must be a fine line between hate and love."

"Rest easy in the knowledge that my feelings towards her are the latter," Killian replied. He had known it in his bones when he had woken that morning, felt it thrumming in him every moment since. Imogen's face lit up with a combination of surprise and delight.

"Does she...have you told her?"

"And risk scaring her off?"

Imogen nodded. "Good point. Wow, the things you learn."

"What things?" Bron asked, placing her coat over her arm as she came in. Killian opened his mouth, but Imogen beat him to it.

"Do you know there is a creature in Faerie that has four dicks? That's astounding," she replied. In that second, Imogen became Killian's second favorite Ironwood.

Bron's eyes turned heavenward. "Saints have mercy. Why would you tell her that, Killian?"

"It kind of came up."

"I don't want to know."

"Where are you two sneaking off to? I disabled the cameras in the southern wood if you're looking for a secluded spot," Imogen asked and waggled her eyebrows.

Killian grinned, but Bron's glare warned him to keep his mouth shut.

"We are going to check out one of Killian's leads. Don't tell Mom until you can't avoid it."

Imogen nodded. "Noted. I have to say, Bron. I like this rebellious streak the fae is bringing out in you."

"He's definitely a bad influence, which is why I'm taking him far away from you. God knows what would happen if you were left unattended." Killian and Imogen shared mischievous grins, and he knew he would have an ally in at least one Ironwood.

Instead of using the main entrance, they went out of the mansion by a narrow wooden staircase and out the back to where Killian had parked his black Jaguar.

"We aren't flying?" Bron asked, disappointed.

"I'd prefer to conserve my stamina for other pursuits," Killian replied. "You don't like the Jag?"

"All depends. Can I drive?" she asked. Killian tossed her the keys, and she caught them with a surprised squeak. "Really?"

"Go for it." Killian climbed into the passenger seat. Bron put her sword and coat in the back and got in.

"I can't believe you're letting me drive," she said, putting on her seat belt.

"Why? I know you're a good driver, and I have no ego when it comes to handing a woman the keys."

"Wise male." Bron pressed the ignition button, and Killian swore he'd let her drive any time if it meant she smiled that way. They didn't go out the front gates either but kept driving through the parklands.

"I didn't realize how big this place is," Killian commented as they passed a shooting range.

"You need a lot of space to train child hunters. These woods were a fun place to hide." Bron was checking the branches above her, but for what, Killian didn't know. They came to another gate, but instead of going through it, she pulled into a spot underneath the trees and turned the car off.

Killian frowned. "What are we doing here?"

"This." Bron took his face in her hands and kissed him hard.

"What did I do to deserve that?" he asked, moving back from her.

"Nothing at all." Bron's hands threaded in his hair and pulled him to her mouth again, any tentativeness gone and only driving need remaining. Killian unclicked her seat belt and then his own so he could shift towards her. Bron started wriggling in her seat, kicking off her boots and then her pants.

Oh, holy gods. Killian caught a glimpse of a black lace thong before the scent of her arousal smacked him in the face. His self-control snapped, and he picked her up and dragged her over onto his lap.

Bron's hands skimmed the ends of his hair, down his chest, her legs tightening around him. Their kisses turned savage, a tangle of tongues and teeth.

Killian's hands gripped the soft curves of her ass, dragging her up against the rough fabric of his jeans.

Bron unbuckled his belt and pulled his dick free, stroking him roughly enough that he hissed. Running his fingers under the lace of her thong, he pulled it to the side.

Killian cursed as Bron lowered herself down on him, fitting him inside of her hot, wet body.

"Fucking hell," he gasped.

Bron brushed his black hair from his face. Dark eyes locked on his as she leaned in and kissed him. If Killian wasn't sure he was in love with her before, he sure as hell knew it now. Dark gods spare him.

Bron began to ride him, and nothing else mattered except for her scent, heat, taste. No one had ever felt this good, this perfectly right. If he had doubted that mates were made for each other, being with Bron obliterated every doubt.

Killian's mouth found her sensitive neck, and she groaned, gripping his hair harder with every thrust and grind of her hips.

Runes appeared over them, and the sight made them both pick up their pace. Their hands, tongues, and teeth were everywhere, greedy for skin and every little gasp and groan the other made. Killian's heartbeat was thunder in his ears, breath tight in his lungs.

"Kill," his name was a breathy moan on her lips, nearly sending him over the edge.

Killian's hand tightened hard on her bare ass, the other found her breast, and she cried out, her whole body shaking as she came. Killian pulled her harder against him, hips thrusting up to meet hers as his own release had stars dancing through his vision.

Bron's head rested against his, both of their bodies heaving as they tried to calm their breath.

"God, Killian," Bron whispered as she pulled free of him and fixed her underwear back into place. "I didn't mean to attack you."

Killian let out a mad little laugh. "Attack me anytime and anywhere you like, love." He kissed her worried face until she was smiling shyly. Gods, it killed him when she went shy. Bron slipped out of his grip and back into the driver's seat.

"Remind me to send Imogen a nice gift for disabling the cameras in this part of the wood," Killian said, fixing up his jeans and watching her wriggle back into her own.

"You ever tell Imogen about this, and she'll be calling in favors for a year," Bron replied, sliding her feet back into her boots. She gripped the steering wheel and took a few deep breaths. "Where were we going again? Clonmacnoise. Fuck. Okay."

"Do you want me to drive?" He couldn't resist asking.

"No. I just need a second to get the stars out of my vision."

Killian put his chair back and placed his hands behind his head with a satisfied sigh. "Always happy to be of service, Ironwood."

24

Bron didn't know what the hell was wrong with her. She kept her eyes firmly on the road and tried to make sense of what she had just done. She had only meant to kiss him. A brief peck before heading out. It was like a whole different Bron had woken up, hungry and demanding, and had taken over.

Goddamn gorgeous fae messing with your mind.

Killian was acting like that sort of thing happened all the time. Probably because before his curse, it had.

Bron's world was a place of routine and control. Ever since she had seen him in an arena in Tir Na Nog, she hadn't had either.

As if sensing she was about to freak out, Killian placed a warm hand on her knee, and after a second, she gave in and wrapped her fingers in his. She didn't know how to define what the fuck was going on between them, but she was pretty sure the madness was mutual. Killian was a prince. She doubted he would do anything he didn't want to.

A prince powerful enough to block out the sun and who is also holding my hand like he's my sweetheart.

Bron had never been sweet with anyone. She was actually convinced she didn't have the capability, but here she was.

Goddamn it. Moira was right. I do have love-heart eyes.

"Penny for your thoughts?" Killian asked.

I think I might want more from you than what you're willing to give, and it scares me more than Morrigan and her horde taking over the world.

"Wondering what we are going to walk into. It could be nothing, but if Morrigan's follower coughed it up while he was dying, he must've thought it had some value," Bron replied.

Killian's thumb brushed over the back of her palm. "Or he's sending us into a trap. No point worrying about it until we get there and see for ourselves. Don't worry, I got your back, Bron."

"Just be ready to summon your big sword if we get into trouble." Bron regretted her words as soon as she said them. She could *feel* Killian's grin at the innuendo.

"My big sword is always ready to come to your aid, Ironwood."

"I'm not even going to touch that one."

"You just did more than touch it."

"I'm regretting taking you hunting."

Killian lifted her hand and kissed the inside of her wrist. "You're going to learn I'm the best hunting buddy you've ever had."

∽

THE RUINS of Clonmacnoise sat on the outskirts of a bog, beside the River Shannon. It was going into winter in Ireland, so the sun was already down by the time Bron turned down the road.

"Looks like we are going to a party," Killian commented. The ruins were surrounded by parked cars, and people were milling about.

"This isn't what I expected," Bron said, pulling into a spare space.

"That is more like it." Killian pointed to a group dressed in red and black robes, their hoods up to protect their faces. "I'll be back."

Killian got out of the car and hurried after them. Bron was pulling on her overcoat and contemplating taking her sword with her when Killian appeared again.

"They smell like incense and blood, but it can't be helped," he said, passing her a red robe. His expression was cold and severe. "Something weird is definitely going on. Not like Renaissance Fair weird, but magic. I can feel it messing with mine, so be alert, and don't get lost."

"I won't," Bron promised and put the robe on. The smell of it was cloying, the sweetness and iron making her skin crawl. Killian was so big that his robe only made it to his knees. "Here's hoping they don't look at your feet."

Drums started thrumming over the noise of the fae and humans gathering. They were all wearing cloaks now, some with gold or black masks. Killian took Bron's hand, leading the way.

"They are gathering near the cathedral over there," Bron said, pointing. Her heart began to race as magic pulsed in the air. She wasn't as sensitive to it as Charlotte, but all of her hair was starting to stand up on end as chanting added to the drums.

"What are they saying?" Bron whispered.

"They are petitioning elements around us for aid, the land, the stones, the air, the water," Killian replied, drawing her in front of him, his body protecting hers.

Light filled the cathedral as power rolled out of the earth around them. The drone of the music continued as everything else seemed to still.

Bron held her breath as a portal opened. She felt it in her blood first, a simmering heat of the madness of battle, her adrenaline spiking to find the enemy. She could taste blood on her tongue, in the very air around them.

A tall figure emerged through the portal. He was dressed plainly in black leather, a sword on his back and a staff in his hand. Curly chestnut hair fell around a striking face, with burning amber eyes and an aquiline nose. He didn't have the pointed ears to mark him as fae, but there was a shine of the supernatural about him.

Bron wanted to kneel, to beg him to look at her, to offer him her blade and body and her life. Nothing else mattered.

"Fuck," a deep voice said behind her, but she couldn't tear her eyes away from the man with the staff. A strong arm went around her waist, and Bron took a shuddering breath as her head cleared. *Killian.* He was there with her. "Move, Ironwood."

Bron's feet were like lead, but Killian tugged her through the shouting crowd and out of the cathedral.

"Who...who was that?" Bron gasped, almost tripping over a gravestone.

"One of Morrigan's generals," Killian replied, voice low and vicious in a way she had never heard before.

"Stop! We have to go back! We have to stop him—"

Killian wasn't listening. He grabbed Bron tightly to him, his wings snapping out, and he launched them into the sky.

Bron could do nothing but clutch to Killian. He had never flown so fast with her before. In the light of the rising moon, she could make out the darkness trailing them, hiding their position in the sky. Bron buried her face into Killian's neck to keep it warm.

Morrigan's general. The people at the cathedral had been welcoming him like he was some kind of god. Maybe he was.

They landed on the gravel in front of the Ironwood manor twenty minutes later, Killian setting her to her feet.

"We have to go back," Bron demanded. "We can't lose him!"

"No. You aren't going anywhere near Aneirin, do you understand me?" Killian growled.

"You don't get to tell me what to do! How could you pull me out of a hunt like that?"

"How could I not?" Killian got up in her face, fury pouring off him. "Aneirin War Gull is not a fight you can win! I'm sorry if I love you too damn much to watch you die in some bullshit blaze of glory against a general!"

Bron reared back. Generals. Morrigan. The world. All of it fell away. "Did you just say you love me?"

"Yes, I did. That's why I'm not letting you go back and get yourself killed in the blood bath he's going to cause." Killian pushed his hands through his hair in frustration. "Stay here. I need to talk to my brothers, and I can't worry about where you are. Please, love, just stay. I'll update you, but I need to go."

"Okay," Bron managed to squeak. She wanted to tell him she loved him back. It should have been a happy realization, but Bron felt as freaked out as Killian looked.

"Be safe." Killian pressed a hard, fast kiss to her mouth and then was gone.

Bron's legs gave way, and she sank to the gravel. Imogen found her minutes later, sobbing and staring at the empty sky.

"What the fuck happened?" Imogen gathered her in her arms and pulled her to her feet.

"Imogen." Bron shook in her embrace. The fear of what she had seen finally hitting her. Bron had a strong will, but she had been ready to worship the man in the portal. If Killian hadn't been there, she would have. "One of Morrigan's generals has come to Ireland."

25

Killian didn't let himself think until he got into the safety of his own apartment and behind its wards. He put his hands over his face and cursed in three different languages. He should never have taken Bron to Clonmacnoise, involved her in his shit. Now he had made it worse by telling her that he loved her.

"One disaster at a time," Killian told himself. His phone started ringing, and he jumped to answer it.

"What the fuck is going on? I got smacked by your magic right in the middle of a meeting," Kian said urgently.

"Where are you?"

"London."

"Get Elise and get over here," Killian replied, pacing up and down his kitchen. "It's starting."

"What happened, Killian?"

Killian's phone started buzzing, and he saw Bayn was calling. "Hang on, I'm adding Bayn to this."

"What the fuck, Killian!"

"Yeah, yeah, I know. Bayn, you and Freya need to come to Ireland. Use ice, I don't care, get here." Killian grabbed his bottle of whiskey and had a mouthful. "I just watched fucking Aneirin come through a portal."

Both of his brothers were so quiet, Killian checked they were still connected.

"I had hoped he was dead," Kian said eventually.

"Of course he isn't dead! Morrigan wouldn't let anything happen to her favorite battle bard."

"Any idea why he was sent first?" Bayn asked.

Killian had another drink. "He is Morrigan's War Gull. If I had to guess, it's to herald her arrival. He'll be using his magic and battle poetry to stoke her red fires of madness, get everyone frothing and ready to fight whoever Morrigan aims them at."

"What about her other two generals? Any sign?" Kian asked. He had slipped into the emotionless warrior that Killian needed.

"No, but I didn't stick around." Killian told them about the informant, Bron's maps, and what they had seen at the cathedral ruins.

"You took your mate into that kind of danger? What the fuck is wrong with you?" Bayn demanded.

"I didn't know there was going to be any danger at all. And she's a hunter. I thought it would be good to have someone watching my back. As soon as I realized what was happening, I got her out of there."

"And let the War Gull get away."

"Oh, fuck you, Kian. You would've done exactly the same thing if it had been Elise. I wasn't about to get into a confrontation with Aneirin with all of those people around."

"They were Morrigan's followers. Our enemies. They are not innocents," Kian replied.

"We don't know that. They probably have no idea what they are worshiping or greeting with open arms. The humans of this time have forgotten the stories, the fear of the gods." Killian sat down, his leg jumping. "So will you come?"

"Of course we will. You're just going to bollocks it up without us," Bayn said. "Arne got back to me. He and Torsten will land in Dublin tomorrow."

"What about the Ironwoods? Are they open to meet with all of us?" Kian asked.

"Yes, they have called in their own people. Kenna might try and kill me for taking Bron hunting tonight, but that's her right."

"Good luck with that, big brother. Freya and I will be there in a few hours. Keep your shit together until then." Bayn hung up, and Killian gripped his phone tighter.

"Kian? I need to talk to Elise."

"Why?"

"Because she's my sister, and I need her goddamn advice."

Kian made a sound of exasperation. "Claim your fucking mate, Killian. She's going to need your power to protect her, and you're going to need her to call you back from the abyss."

"Fuck off," Killian snapped.

"I thought you wanted to talk to me?" Elise replied.

"Shit. I'm sorry. That was for Kian." Killian's leg kept on bouncing as he drank more whiskey. He couldn't get trashed like he wanted to, but he needed something to settle him.

"What's wrong? Out with it, I have to go pack."

"I may have lost my temper and told Bron I loved her," Killian said, a mad laugh coming out of him.

"Oh." Elise was silent. "Okay. Did you ask how she feels?"

"No, I left so I could call you all."

"Let me get this straight. You lost your temper and told her you loved her, and you left her just standing there?" Elise was suspiciously calm. "Kill, go and talk to her. She's probably freaking out. I know I would be after everything that happened."

"She's going to put a knife in me."

"You don't know that for sure."

"I can't handle Aneirin returning and rejection from my mate in the same night, Elise."

She sighed a long, long sigh. "How do you know she's going to reject you?"

"Because she's not the kind of girl to fall in love with someone in a couple of weeks."

"Maybe. It's a risk you're going to have to take, I'm afraid," Elise replied. Her voice lowered, and the tenderness in it hurt him more than yelling.

"Kill, you wanted to talk to me to get permission. Here it is; it's okay to love her. The mating bond only goes so far, but it can't make you love someone. You did that on your own. Go and talk to her. You're not going to get many peaceful nights in the coming weeks."

"Fine, I'll message her," he said weakly.

"No, you go and see her. We can make the calls and get everyone hustling over there. We have a few warriors already there. They can head out to the church ruins and see what's going on," Elise replied, a thread of iron in her gentle tone.

Killian knew she was right. It didn't make what he had to do any easier.

"Okay. You do that, and keep me posted. Tell them not to get too close because Aneirin's influence will mess with them."

"I will. I'll see you tomorrow morning."

"Night," Killian mumbled and hung up. He toyed with his phone for a few minutes before he gave in.

Are you awake?

Killian watched as the writing bubble disappeared and appeared a few times. Bron was entitled to be irritated with him. He would grovel if he had to. His phone buzzed.

Yes.

Killian huffed out a laugh. She always knew how to make him work for it.

Want some company? He held his breath. A part of him wanted her to say no, help buy some time to...

If you can get through the wards without waking everyone up.

Killian smiled. "That's my girl."

∾

BRON HAD SPENT the rest of her evening getting yelled at by Kenna. She had taken it, right up until Kenna had gone for Killian.

"Has he got you in some kind of a thrall that you would go off with him without telling me?" Kenna demanded.

"Killian would never do anything like that," Bron hissed. "We went to check out the church as a mutual decision."

"You should have checked with me first!"

"I'm a thirty-year-old woman. I don't have to check with my damn mother for everything I do!" Bron shouted back. On the mezzanine above her, she heard all of her sisters take a breath.

"You haven't been yourself since you came back from Faerie. What happened to you to want to throw in with this prince?" Kenna's gazed sharpened. "Please tell me you aren't sleeping with him. If he forced you—"

Bron growled, a deep feral sound. "Killian didn't do anything to hurt me and never will. We have bigger things to worry about than my relationship with him. I saw one of Morrigan's generals tonight. He's here in Ireland. Put your anger and efforts into fighting our real enemy, and leave Killian the fuck alone."

"You were always so determined to kill him. What could he have done to change your mind so quickly?" Kenna asked, her anger giving way as her voice cracked.

"I saw that he's *not* our enemy. Do you know our illustrious ancestor slaughtered babies? Little children in their beds. This house, our name, everything is based on the fact he *killed babies*!" Bron was shouting now and couldn't stop.

"You back the fuck off Killian, or I'll walk out of this house and go and fight Morrigan alone." Bron didn't wait for Kenna to reply but stormed up the stairs and past the pale faces of her sisters.

Two hours later, Bron had stopped crying but was still feeling lousy. She had never yelled at Kenna, never stood against her on any subject. She had drawn a line in the sand and put herself firmly on Killian's side.

Now that her anger was gone, she knew he had been right to take her out of the cathedral ruins. It was stupid pride that made her think she could take on a general and all of his followers alone.

You wanted to worship him. How could you have fought him?

All of that was nothing compared to the churned-up feelings she had about Killian telling her that he loved her. He was the Night Prince, and she was no one. It didn't make sense.

She had been curled in a tight ball in her bed when Killian had finally messaged her. She wanted to snap at him, to tell him to stay away, but she couldn't. She needed to see him if she was going to sleep at all that night.

Because she was Bron, she wasn't going to make it easy for him. She had unlatched one of her bedroom windows and had gotten back into bed.

"You know, I can't remember the last time I had to sneak into a lady's bed chamber," Killian's voice purred from the shadows.

"Good thing I'm not a lady," Bron replied, slowly sitting up. He had changed his clothes and looked scruffy around the edges from the wind. Her heart ached just looking at him, and all the indecisiveness that had plagued her that day vanished. She knew exactly how she felt about him.

"Kian is sending men out to the cathedral. Hopefully, they will be able to pick up a trail on Aneirin. Bayn and Freya turned up as I was leaving," Killian said, his gaze everywhere but her face.

"I'm sorry for yelling at you. For leaving you after you had been hit with Aneirin's influence. For telling you that I loved you in such an unromantic manner. Despite what the stories say, I'm not always as charming as my reputation claims."

"I could have told you that," Bron replied.

Killian laughed softly. "You rob me of all my tricks and good sense. It's like I can't pull any of my usual bullshit on you, and I don't want to. It's one of the reasons I love you."

Bron's mouth was dry, her chest tightening. "Are you sure this isn't a combination of stressful situations and getting sex regularly for the first time in years?"

"Stop trying to give me an out, Bronagh," Killian growled. "I'm over two thousand years old. I know my own fucking mind and heart. I've waited my entire life to find someone that makes me feel like this, so stop trying to convince me that I'm making a mistake. It's okay if you don't feel the same. I don't mind taking the time to convince you I'm serious."

Bron knew he was telling her the truth. He would wait it out and give her space if she needed it. She didn't.

"Thank you for the offer, but it's unnecessary. I don't need time to figure out if I love you back because I know that I do," Bron said. She lifted the side of her blankets up. "Now, are you going to come and kiss me or not?"

Killian's smile was the best thing she had seen in her entire life. He took off his jacket and boots before climbing in beside her.

Killian stroked her cheeks and jaw with heart-breaking tenderness.

When he finally kissed her, she could feel it all the way to her toes. Bron wrapped her arms around his neck and pulled him closer.

"I wasn't ever meant to love you," she whispered.

"I know, but you really shouldn't be so surprised. From what I keep hearing, I've always been the man of your dreams."

"The cheek of you."

"You love it. And me. You love me. Sorry, not quite over it." Killian kissed her hard and deep, and she forgot any comeback she tried to formulate. "What else were you up to tonight?"

"I yelled at Kenna." Bron told him about the fight and how sick she was feeling about it. Killian's arms tightened around her.

"Your mother will come around. She has a right to be worried. She's not going to understand about the generals or the horde until she sees them for herself," he said, stroking her hair. "She's never faced anything like Aneirin."

"What *is* he? I felt possessed just by looking at him. It faded as soon as you touched me, but I've never felt magic like that before," Bron said.

"He used to be a man," Killian replied. "He was from Wales and was a battle poet and a bard. He had a lot of magic for a mortal. Morrigan is the goddess of battle verse, so he worshiped her and got her attention. Even before her dark power changed him, he could whip men into a fighting fury. The power she gave him magnified that. He's called the War Gull, Morrigan's Raven, her Blood Sorcerer, because he can cause a frenzy before a battle. That's why she sent him first, to ignite her followers to violence, create her an army before the horde even steps foot in the human realms."

Bron curled further into him. "How are we going to stop him?"

"The same way we are going to stop Morrigan." Killian kissed her forehead. "Together."

26

The following morning, when Bron went downstairs, she found her younger sister Layla and two cousins Lachlan and Ciara fighting over bagels in the kitchen.

"Bron!" Layla plowed into her. She was twenty-four years old and was the only blonde in the family.

"New tattoo?" Bron asked, twisting Layla's arm to look at the swirling pattern of Celtic knotwork on her wrist. Her tattoos were fast turning into a sleeve of brilliant and beautiful colors.

"Yeah, I got this one a few weeks after you left. I was tempted to get a little headstone with RIP BRON on it," Layla teased. "It's good to have you back. Kenna might actually get off everyone else's ass."

"Out of the way, Layla," Lachlan complained. He was the only male Ironwood sibling in the house and would tell anyone who would listen that he was henpecked. Tall, well built, with dark hair and blue eyes, Lachie was a heartbreaker that Bron tried not to be overprotective of. At twenty-nine and thirty, the cousins were Bron's age, and yet, she felt like their big sister as well.

"Hey, baby cousin," Bron said as Lachlan squeezed her.

"I'm so happy you're home. Never send me on a hunt with Layla again," he replied, kissing the top of her head. Layla threw part of a bagel at him that he caught and ate.

"She wasn't that bad, but never take her camping."

"That's because camping is code for being cold, wet, and uncomfortable. I don't get all misty-eyed over the beauty of a dark, damp forest, unlike Ciara."

"That's because forests are beautiful." Ciara pushed in between them. She had dark hair like her brother, which was constantly dyed a dark purple that matched her violet eyes. She had lines of pretty silver studs up both of her ears and was the best werewolf hunter in the family. The smirk on her lips was pure trouble. "What's this I hear about you hooking up with the Night Prince?"

"I am going to kill Imogen!"

"Actually, it was Moira," Layla chimed in. "When you said you were going to kill him, I never knew you meant fucking him to death."

"That's because you haven't met him," Bron replied, and they all started jeering at her.

"When is he due to come around again?" Ciara asked.

"Today. He's bringing his brothers and some friends that are going to help us deal with Morrigan and her general." Bron caught them up as quickly as she could on what had happened the previous day and what she had witnessed of the horde creatures.

"Big game hunting by the sounds of it," Layla said thoughtfully.

"Going to need something that can penetrate hard shell if those scarabs turn up," Lachlan added. His eyes glazed over. "And something that can take out their wings first."

Bron found herself smiling. This was what she needed, people making plans and not doubting the threat.

Lachlan was always thinking up new weapons and designs and would have the best idea on how to take out anything that Morrigan might throw at them.

"What are you grinning at?" Ciara asked.

"Nothing. I just missed you guys, that's all."

"Any word on what these friends are? More fae?" Layla said, sitting down beside Bron.

"I'm assuming so. Bayn's friends are a light elf and one of the Úlfhéðnar if rumors are to be believed."

Ciara dropped her fork. "Úlfhéðnar? Are you fucking serious?"

"Yes?" Bron didn't like that look on her face one bit. It was like she had gone laser-focused. "Why?"

"Because a wolf berserker might not like the 'Wolf Killer' hunting with them."

"I don't think Torsten is going to care. You have only killed the troublemakers," Bron said. She gave Ciara a nudge with her shoulder. "I'm sure if you show him your charming self, he might be less inclined to hold your reputation against you."

"Whatever the case, Morrigan is more important. If you want to have a pissing match with him, then do it after our mutual enemy is stopped," Lachlan said.

"I'm more worried about Kenna trying to start fights with the Night Prince than Ciara getting into a tussle with a wolf," Layla added with a laugh. "We also heard about the fight you two had. Did you really growl at Mom?"

"Yeah, I did. I think I spent too long in Faerie, and some of that rubbed off." Bron cupped her mug in her hands. At least, that was what she was trying to tell herself when in reality, it was Killian's bad influence.

Layla lifted her mug. "To Bron, may she always cause this much chaos in our lives, and may we not all die in the next few days."

Bron laughed and tapped her mug against hers. "Morbid little shit."

∽

AFTER LUNCH, cars began to arrive at the Ironwood estate, and Kenna was a flurry of commands. If Bron didn't know better, she would think her mother was actually nervous. Bron had left her hair out but had dressed in hunting gear to make sure she looked professional. They had arranged the dining room table with extra chairs to prepare for the princes, their mates, and whoever else they brought with them. As soon as the cars arrived, they assembled in the main foyer to greet them.

"I feel like the Queen is coming," Imogen murmured to Bron and patted her pastel hair.

"If she were, I would hope you would dress in something without holes in it," Charlotte said with a raised brow at her sister's jeans.

"What are you talking about? These are my good pair."

Killian arrived in another slick black suit, looking so good, Bron wanted to rub herself all over him and purr.

"Jesus, good job, Bron," Layla whispered a little too loudly.

"Every time I arrive, more Ironwoods seem to appear," Killian greeted with a low bow. "Lady Kenna, thank you for hosting us." Kenna looked like she was about to tell him off when Kian, Bayn, and their mates came in.

"May I properly introduce Elise and Freya," Killian said quickly. Both women's attention went straight to Bron, small grins appearing on their faces.

"We have heard so much about you," Elise said, moving to shake Bron's hand.

"Nice to meet you too," Bron greeted, feeling a little awkward.

"Wow, what a place," a new voice said, and a black woman came in. She had springy brown hair and a bright pink coat on. "Hey everyone, I'm Chrissy. Aren't you a ridiculously good-looking family?"

"Yes, we are," Lachlan said, with a charming grin.

"Chrissy is our friend and human advisor," Kian explained as she joined Elise.

Bayn stepped forward and nodded to the men at his side. "This is Arne Steelsinger and Torsten. They have come from Norway to assist us." Arne was a tall elf with black hair and a sharp profile. Torsten was a massive bulk of Viking muscle and long blond hair.

"You must be the Úlfhéðnar," Ciara said, looking him over.

"And you must be the one and only, Ciara Wolf Slayer," he replied in a deep voice, eyes appraising her. "You are smaller than I imagined you would be, considering your reputation." Ciara's lips lifted in a challenging smile.

"Now, now, don't start, you two," Layla said, stepping forward. She surprised Bron by bowing elegantly and greeting Arne in perfect Elvish. Arne's eyes widened, and he bowed and responded in return.

"And what is your name?" he asked, his golden eyes assessing her.

"Layla. It's so nice to finally meet an elf," she said, giving him a bright smile.

"The pleasure is mine, Layla Ironwood."

Beside Bron, Charlotte stiffened, her blue eyes going cold as they found a man lingering in the doorway. He had a dark goatee and hair tied back in a short ponytail. Tattoos of runes crept from underneath a navy-blue scarf and up his tan throat.

Young Johnny, Bron's mind prompted unhelpfully.

"Am I late?" he asked, pushing his ringed hands into his pockets.

"You're unwelcome," Charlotte replied, and Imogen elbowed her.

"Not late at all. Everyone, this is Reeve Greatdrakes. He's a magician here in Dublin," Imogen said, coming to Reeve's rescue. He nodded his hello. His bright hazel eyes landed on Charlotte, and a lazy grin stretched over his face.

"What's up, Charlie Belle?" he greeted. Charlotte turned on her heel and walked off towards the dining room. Instead of being offended, the magician's grin only widened.

"Well, now that everyone is here, let's get this meeting started," David said with a too-bright smile. Killian somehow managed to slide over to Bron's side.

"No murders or arguments yet," he whispered.

"*Yet*," Bron said.

His eyes danced over her hair. "You left it out just to mess with me, didn't you?"

"I have no idea what you're talking about." Bron flicked it slowly over one shoulder. "Coming?"

Killian took a seat beside Bron, completely ignoring Kenna's frown. He and Kian had some kind of silent argument, but Killian refused to move.

Imogen winked at them from across the table. She knew he was marking his territory, and Bron was surprisingly reluctant to stop him. When his fingers found her hand, she twisted them in hers and held on.

"Let's start with what we know," Kian said, taking control of the meeting with ease. He went through his family's history with Morrigan, Killian's kidnapping, the knowledge that Morrigan's bonds were breaking. When he got to Aneirin arriving through a portal, he opened a tablet and placed it in front of Kenna and David.

"I sent some men to investigate the church at Clonmacnoise only hours after Killian and Bron saw the general come through. This is all that remained of his followers. From what we can gather, Aneirin used his influence and got them to massacre themselves."

Bron's hand tightened on Killian as she thought of the people's smiling faces at the ruins, all clueless to what Aneirin had planned for them.

"Sounds like what you did in London," Lachlan said. Elise and Chrissy both narrowed their eyes, but Kian didn't seem the least bit offended.

"It is, but not on the same scale or with the same purpose. This was a sacrifice in honor of Morrigan, to give her a power boost, probably to break the final bonds holding her."

"It seems like a waste of allies to do that to your own followers," Arne said, looking over the photos before passing the tablet to Layla.

"A sacrifice of the faithful would contain more magic than random people pulled off the street," Reeve clarified.

"And how would you know that?" Charlotte asked archly.

"Come on, Charlie, that's Ritual 101."

Imogen smirked. "Yeah, *Charlie*, everyone knows that." Charlotte stared down her nose at her for a moment then focused back on Kian. Bron shot Killian a pained kill-me-now look, but he was too busy trying not to laugh.

Kian went on to talk about hot spots around Dublin and the likelihood that Morrigan would choose the city to make her first appearance.

"But why Dublin? It doesn't make sense when she could pick anywhere around Ireland. Maybe somewhere less obvious," Kenna asked.

"It's because Bron and I are here," Killian answered. "We embarrassed her when we escaped her castle. She knows who Bron is and will come for her out of revenge."

"If that's the case, Bron, you're to stay on the estate grounds until the dispute with Morrigan is resolved. Now, moving on to—"

"No. I won't stay on the estate. I know what to expect from the horde creatures and Aneirin's influence, and you don't. I won't hide," Bron said firmly.

"You will do as I say, or you will be locked up."

"I wouldn't recommend that," Killian said coldly.

Kenna whirled on him. "She wouldn't have even been at Clonmacnoise if it wasn't for you."

"Bron offered to come. She will do as she likes. She knows more about Morrigan than any of you humans. Locking up your best asset is ridiculous."

"Don't you dare tell me what to do with my own daughter, fae," Kenna snapped.

"Oh, I fucking dare, woman."

Kenna straightened, outrage in every line of her face. "I am the Matriarch of the Ironwood family. Bron will do as I say. You have no authority here."

"No authority? Bronagh is my fucking mate! And I'm telling *you*, she will do whatever the fuck she likes!" Killian shouted. The whole room went deathly silent. Bron was shaking in her chair, the force of Killian's anger knocking the wind from her.

"My daughter will *never* be your mate," Kenna hissed.

"Killian! Don't!" Kian shouted as Killian's wings shot out, and darkness flooded the room. Everyone started yelling, but Bron stayed in her chair, torn between shock and anger.

A commotion of flying fists and grunts came from beside her, and the darkness vanished. Bayn and Kian were pinning Killian to the wall, his face a snarling, feral mask of inhuman fury.

"Go and fucking walk it off," Kian commanded. "You are frightening her." Killian's eyes snapped to Bron, and whatever he saw in her expression made the shadows vanish from his eyes. The beast receded until only Killian remained, pale and furious.

"Let's go," Bayn hissed, taking Killian by the arm and pulling him towards the doors.

"Trying to keep me from my mate will be the worst mistake you ever make, Kenna Ironwood," Killian said before Bayn wrangled him out. Bron made to rise, but Freya shifted into Killian's chair and stopped her.

"Let them go," Freya whispered, her hand on Bron's arm. "He has to cool off. Did Killian tell you about being his mate before this?"

Bron shook her head, too numb to speak. *I'm his mate.*

Kian started talking again, but Bron didn't hear a word of it.

27

Bron couldn't handle sitting at the table a moment longer. This time when she got to her feet, Freya and Elise followed her.

"Where are you going?" Imogen whispered.

"Bron has offered to show me the library," Elise said, giving her a meaningful look.

"Yes, I need to grab the map with the sites on it," Bron added in a daze. Kenna looked like she wanted to stop her, but David placed a hand on her shoulder. Kenna focused her attention back on Kian.

"God, your mother is a battle-ax," Freya commented once they were out of the dining room.

"I know. I'm sorry about her display. She likes to think I'm twelve years old still," Bron replied, anger lacing her words.

"That's parents for you."

Bron didn't know if she felt like crying, laughing, or finding a dark corner to get drunk in. Possibly all three.

"Wow, I was hoping to get to see the library," Elise said, giving the rows of shelves in front of her a wide smile.

"We'll have to watch her. Otherwise, she will get lost in here for hours," Freya added, rolling her gold and blue eyes.

"Don't pretend that you wouldn't do the same, cousin."

"I definitely would, but I have the decency to wait until I'm invited."

Bron laughed softly at their bickering. "You two are cousins and mates to two brothers. That's got to be complicated."

"It's a good thing you've come along to spice the gene pool up a bit with Vortigern's blood," Elise said. "Did you see Killian's wings just now? His feathers are almost all black again. Soon, his curse will be lifted altogether, and I might actually get to hug him without gloves on."

"Are you saying I'm breaking his curse?" Bron asked, sitting down on a reading couch before she fell down.

Freya flopped down beside her. "Wow, that bastard really didn't tell you anything, did he?"

"He told me he loved me, does that count?" Bron said weakly. Both Freya and Elise got soft looks on their faces.

"Yeah, that counts," Elise said.

Bron put her head in her hands. "Okay, give it to me straight... What the hell is going on with this mates business, and what precisely did you mean about me breaking his curse?"

Elise and Freya shared a loaded look. Then Elise told her everything; about mates being the only things able to break the curses, and how if she accepted Killian, she might end up with some of his magic and immortality.

"I got some of Bayn's magic," Freya said, holding her palm out and forming a perfect ball of ice.

"Kian thinks that the abilities will continue to manifest as time goes on," Elise added. "I haven't grown any horns yet, but I can keep on hoping. Did you not wonder why he could touch you and no one else?"

"Of course I did. I thought it was because of the vow he made to not do me harm. And he let me believe that," Bron added darkly.

"When Killian told us that you were his mate, his biggest fear was that you would cut him out of your life. He wanted to date you, have things progress naturally, so you wouldn't feel like he was trying to take your choices away." Elise gave her a small smile. "As you saw earlier, he is rather protective of you being free to make your own decisions. No matter how much it hurts him not to claim you."

Bron's eyes welled unexpectedly, and she swallowed back the tears. "It's hurting him?"

"A bit," Freya said, ignoring Elise's warning frown. "It's like he's fighting the animal instinct to claim and protect his mate. Never forget that he's not human, Bron."

"If he already loves me, why didn't he say anything about being his mate?" Bron asked. That was one thing she couldn't figure out.

"That's something he's going to have to answer himself. I do know that being mated will make him stronger in his fight against Morrigan. He knows it too and still hasn't pressured you about it. That more than anything should tell you about the strength of his character," Elise replied. She rested a hand lightly on Bron's shoulder. "He'll be back, so maybe hear him out before you jump to too many conclusions."

"I'll try, but I might have to kick his ass first." Bron looked at Elise and Freya, who would end up being a part of her family if she accepted Killian. "You know, I don't really need any more sisters."

Freya laughed. "No, you don't. Something tells me you need some friends, though."

Bron managed a smile. "You're right there."

"Are you three coming back? Because it's really rude to disappear and leave me to fend for myself," Imogen said, charging in and turning on Bron. "I don't care if you are having an emotional crisis because a super-hot fae wants to be your fuck buddy for life. Boohoo, however will you cope with a gorgeous male worshipping your mean brown ass? Pity party is over, now get moving."

Bron pointed at Imogen and told Elise and Freya, "This is exactly why I don't need any more sisters."

⁓

Bron went upstairs after dinner, once everyone had left for the night. She could tell Kenna wanted to talk to her, but she wasn't up for an argument. She locked the door to her bedroom, changed into some tights and a loose shirt, and went into the training room. She needed to move, or she would scream.

Taking down one of her favorite swords, Bron started to work through her drills. The meditative quality of the exercise began to work, which allowed her to dissect the events of the day.

They had a plan for the full moon, and Kian had put watches on the gates they knew about. Most of the hunters in Ireland would be coming to Dublin if there was an attack. Lachlan and Charlotte were working on weapon ideas. To Charlotte's considerable disapproval, Reeve was going to reach out to the magician freelancers.

Bron had sat silent, letting them plan all around her while she tried not to watch the door for Killian's reappearance. He hadn't showed. His brothers didn't seem to find it unusual, and Bron hadn't dared message him.

She was working through her fourth round of drills when something tugged in her chest. She paused mid-swing and stared at the beams above her head. A large figure was hunched in the shadows, and her heart leaped.

"Get down here so I can give you the kicking you deserve," she demanded, pointing the tip of her blade at him. Killian dropped to the mats, wings tucked in behind him. He kept a careful distance from her, face serious.

"I didn't think you were coming back," Bron said, feet sliding into a fighting stance.

"Never left," Killian replied.

"You've been hiding up there like a gargoyle all day?"

"I'm not about to leave you unprotected with Aneirin around."

"Because I'm your fucking mate, which you never bothered to tell me?" Bron shouted, raising her sword.

"You want a fight? That's fine with me, hunter." Killian pulled a sword from the wall. "It's not going to change the truth."

Bron attacked, and Killian defended. They circled each other, weapons clanging and muscles burning.

"You should have said something," Bron panted, dodging his lunge.

"Maybe I was worried you would attack me with a sword if I did." Killian hissed as she almost cut his thigh. "All you are doing is proving me right."

"You didn't give me a choice to react at all by saying nothing!"

"I wanted you to be open to the idea once your heart was already on board. If I had said anything earlier, you would have accused me of using fae tricks on you! That's just how you are," Killian retorted. "I wanted to know what we felt for each other was real and not some reaction to being mates."

"You can't possibly want to be tied to an Ironwood forever, Killian. You're a damn prince, and we were your enemy! Having Vortigern's blood makes me your enemy twice over."

Killian's face twisted in anger. "I don't give two shits whose blood is in your veins. You're not my enemy. You're the goddamn love of my life!"

Killian threw his sword to the other side of the mats and lowered himself to his knees. Bron was in front of him in two steps, the tip of her sword under his chin.

"I'm not fighting you anymore." Killian's eyes glowed in the dim light, but he didn't move. "Mate me, or kill me, Bron. The choice is yours."

Bron's hands were sweating, but she didn't lower her blade. "I could walk away."

"You do that, and I'm as good as dead anyway. I'd rather you kill me than become the broken soulless thing that Morrigan always wanted me to be." Killian closed his eyes. "It's okay. I'm ready to die."

Bron lowered her sword. "Do you always have to be so dramatic?"

Killian opened one eye, a smile forming on his lips. "You'll get used to it?"

Bron tossed her sword aside, took his face in her hands, and kissed him. Killian was on his feet and had Bron pressed against one of the support beams in a blink. His mouth hungrily tasted and bit, hands pulling off her sweaty shirt and tights.

"Never run out on me like that again," Bron said between kisses.

"I didn't want to frighten you." Killian's thumb brushed her cheek. "I'm sorry, love."

"Make it up to me."

Killian growled as Bron pulled the front of his shirt until the buttons popped off. His hot skin was pressed against hers as he lifted her up the beam and pinned her there. Bron ran her hands around his neck to the downy softness of his wings.

"Never hide these around me unless you have to," she demanded.

"I told you that you have a wing kink," Killian replied, the sparkle in his eye heating as she guided his dick to her entrance. Bron sucked his groan into her as he pushed inside of her.

"If you mate me, I promise to fuck you every single day," he said against her lips. "Any way you like."

"You say that like you would get nothing out of it."

Bron kissed and licked the sweat on his neck, gasping as he drove harder into her. She couldn't speak as heat burned up her spine.

One of Killian's hands wrapped around her neck, and he dragged her harder and rougher against him.

Bron screamed out his name as her orgasm hit her so swiftly, she couldn't hold it back. She fisted his hair in her hands, kissing him hard as he fucked her through it and found his release soon after.

"You know," he said, struggling to catch his breath. "I'm pretty sure your whole family would've heard that scream of yours."

"It might keep them from sticking their big noses into my business," Bron said. She pressed a gentle kiss to his forehead. "Now, what else will I get if I decide to mate you?"

∽

IN THE SHOWER, Killian poured some sweet-smelling gel in his hands and ran it over Bron's shoulders.

"Backwashing," he listed. His palms slid around to cup both of her soft breasts. "With bonus groping."

"Hmm." Bron leaned back into his chest, giving him an excellent view of his large hands over her.

"I would move you out of this house. I don't care where. Maybe I could take you back to the castle in Faerie where your family can't get to us."

Bron grinned. "Now you're just talking dirty."

"I would let you use my big sword that you admire so much. My real sword," he was quick to clarify when she raised a brow. "If we were mated, you would be strong enough to wield it, I'm sure."

Bron's grin turned into something deliciously violent. "I did like the way it cut through that fae like he was made of soft butter."

"I see I need to appeal to your violent streak more." Killian kissed her wet shoulder and up her neck. "You know, I have a whole armory at the castle you can take your pick from."

"Oh baby, say armory again," she whispered throatily.

The tone rather than the words had his dick trembling.

"*Armory,*" he purred. Her answering smile was lightning in his veins, then it slipped. "What's wrong?"

"You're the Night Prince." Bron struggled to find the words before trying again. "Even if Fate says we would be a good match, do you really want to be tied to a grumpy hunter like me forever?"

"More than I've wanted anything in my entire life," Killian replied without hesitation. He stroked the curve of her cheek. "We balance each other out. Two halves of the same attractive whole. The reason you've never felt like you belong anywhere, love, is because you belong with me."

"Stop saying the right thing. I don't know how to react to it." Bron's big eyes filled with tears but somehow managed to force them back.

She wrapped her arms around his neck and pressed her warm wet body against his until their hearts lined up and thrummed against each other.

"You're the best thing that's ever happened to me, Bronagh. Never doubt that," he said, hugging her tightly. The words to claim her were burning on his tongue, but he bit them back.

Not until she's ready, not—

"Killian, I accept you as my mate," Bron whispered. Killian gasped as the magic of the bond pulled them together, their skin burning with runes.

"I accept you as my mate in return, Bronagh Ironwood, until the day they burn my body and probably after that too," Killian replied, his voice breaking.

Bron's eyes were glowing with green fire, *his* fire, as she smiled shyly at him. Killian placed a row of gentle kisses along her jaw before finding her mouth. His heart was pounding hard enough to hurt as her beautiful, strong soul was bound up in his.

"You are worth every second I had to wait," he murmured, holding her tight to him and never wanting to let go.

"Killian, I can feel your magic inside of me," Bron said, awestruck.

"It's our magic now, love." Killian groaned as he tasted power on her lips. "I'll have to teach you how to use it before Charlotte gets any wild ideas about taking on your abilities as a science experiment."

"You will really have to take me to Faerie to stop that from happening," Bron said, pressing a kiss to his chest. She turned the taps off and stepped out of the shower. "But first, you need to take me to bed."

28

Killian woke the following day, with his naked mate stretched across him, and for the first time in a long time, all felt right in his world.

Even the threat of Morrigan couldn't dampen the golden swell of happiness inside him. He got out of bed as slowly as he could to not wake Bron and fished around for his clothes. He had twelve messages waiting for him, so he sent one back to Elise.

Guess who's mated? And trusted that she would spread the word to his brothers and Freya.

"Your wings are all black again," Bron said sleepily. She sat up and stretched.

"What?" Killian said, eyes glued on her naked body and sexy tumble of mahogany hair.

"Your wings," she said, pointing.

With considerable effort, Killian tore his eyes from her and to his wings. They were good as new, all the grey gone and looking better than ever.

"Which feather would you like to keep in your bra today?"

Bron got out of bed, wrapping a robe around herself. Like in her dream that seemed so long ago, she pressed a kiss in between his wings and wrapped her arms around his torso. A low sound of happiness rumbled through his chest as she ran her face over the feathers on his wing.

"Hmm, I've always wanted to do that."

"If you keep doing it, we won't be leaving this room today, and alas, we have to." Killian pulled her slowly around so he could kiss her. "Once Morrigan is sent into the abyss will be another matter. I intend to take you somewhere that no one can find us for a while. Maybe Egypt, if you want to go."

Bron's face lit up in excitement. "You better take me to Egypt. Now you've said it, there's no taking it back."

"I promise, love," Killian said. He kissed the top of her head. "We just need to figure out how to kill the goddess of war first."

"No. First, we need to go down to breakfast and deal with my family," Bron replied, cringing.

"When they get too much, close your eyes and think about me doing that thing you like."

Bron frowned. "That's not very specific. You do a lot of things I like."

"Then you should have a lot of material to work with," he replied, with a filthy smile.

∼

KILLIAN HUNG onto Bron's hand as they went downstairs and into a rowdy kitchen. Imogen, Layla, and Charlotte were arguing about involving 'rabble magicians' in their plans.

All three went quiet when they saw Killian. He went to let go of Bron's hand, but she hung on tighter.

"If you three want to say something, now's the time to do it," she said, eyes sparking with a flash of magic and challenge.

"I always thought you were going to die a virgin, so I'm happy to see that I was wrong," Imogen replied. She lifted a jug. "Orange juice, big brother?" He could've hugged Imogen.

"Thanks, that would be great," Killian said with a smile. Some of the tension left Bron's shoulders, and she finally let his hand go.

"God, I'm hungry. You three better have left me some toast."

"There's some more bread in the cupboard. So, Killian, have you told Mom that you've mated Bron yet? Because I want front row seats to that," Layla said, pouring him a coffee and placing it next to his juice.

"I can give you one of my shields to protect you from her if you like?" Charlotte piped up.

"I appreciate the offer, but if I can handle your sister, I'm sure I can handle your mother." All three sisters laughed at that. Bron threw him an exasperated look.

"Don't encourage them."

Layla refilled her own mug. "I don't suppose that hot elf is going to make another appearance today?"

"You're far too young for him," Charlotte said.

"He's probably hundreds of years old. Everyone is younger than him." Layla got a sly grin on her face. "What's up with you and Reeve Greatdrakes, *Charlie Belle*?"

Charlotte sniffed and focused on her porridge. "Absolutely nothing at all."

"Ah-huh."

Killian shared an amused look with Bron as the other women picked up their arguments where they left off. He had always wished he had sisters, and now he had an overabundance of them. Time would tell if it was going to be a good thing or not.

After breakfast, Killian gave Bron a lingering kiss, much to her sisters' amusement and jeering.

"I have to go and see what my brothers are up to, but can I come back later?"

"You better," Bron replied.

With his heart full, Killian headed out of the kitchen and found Kenna waiting for him outside the front door.

"Good morning, Lady Ironwood," he greeted politely.

"I see you and my daughter have mated," she said coolly.

"We have." There was no point in lying about it. Kenna pulled out a silver case, took out a cigarette, and placed it to her lips.

"Look, I'm not good at this, so I'm going to say this as best I can. I'm thoroughly confused by Bron's decision to go from hating to loving you so quickly." She blew out a silvery streak of smoke. "I don't know why it should surprise me because I haven't understood Bron since the moment she was born. Do you know what she calls David, a man that has been her stepfather for twenty-seven years?"

Killian shook his head.

"She calls him David. That's Bron." Kenna shook her head in despair. Killian tried not to smile.

"I've only wanted to protect her. For the last few years, I thought it was from you, so maybe you can understand why this mating thing doesn't sit well with me. I have a hot temper; she does too, so I haven't handled this as well as I should have," Kenna continued.

"I haven't either. Especially yesterday. I overreacted, and for that, I'm sorry," Killian said. Kenna nodded, taking another drag of her cigarette.

"In a way, I'm glad she has found someone who loves her so much. She's always been different from all my other girls. She was such a sad, quiet baby. The stories about you were always her favorite, you know? It was the only way my mother and I could cheer her up some days." Kenna raised a brow. "I suppose that makes sense now."

Killian laughed. "I guess so. I love her, Kenna. I'll do anything to protect her and your family. You have my word."

"I appreciate that." Kenna stubbed out her cigarette and picked up the butt. "Just keep making her smile, Killian." She turned and walked back inside.

Because he couldn't help himself, Killian called after her, "I will, Mom."

Kenna barked out a laugh. "Asshole."

Grinning, Killian stretched out his healed wings and took to the skies. He could feel his long, dampened power roaring through him. He had forgotten what it was like not to be cursed. He wanted to fly back to the Ironwood mansion and kiss Bron all over again.

Killian had to get changed, and then he would go and hug the crap out of his brothers. Like they knew he was thinking of them, his phone started buzzing.

"Hey Kian," he answered, dropping his speed so that the wind wouldn't drown him out.

"Congratulations, big brother," Kian said, his voice infused with joy. "Where are you?"

"Flying on non-cursed wings."

"Excellent. Elise and Freya are somewhat vocal about wanting to see you. Can you stop by, please?"

"I will. I just need to enjoy this for a bit longer and get some clean clothes. How about I meet you at the hotel in an hour? You can hold down Bayn for me, so I hug the pouty little bastard."

Kian laughed. "Will do. I'm really very happy for you."

"I know. Let's get through this fight with Morrigan and then celebrate properly."

"Sounds good. We will see you soon."

Killian was over his apartment in minutes and landed softly in the back garden.

Damn, it feels good to be whole again.

Killian went to his fridge for a celebratory beer when cold dread crept up his spine. He whirled as a spell hit him, driving him to his knees. His magic was draining out of him, and with a final shove, he sent a blast of power through the mating bond to Bron.

"Disappointing," a cool voice said. Killian dragged his eyes up from the tiles he was lying on.

"Morrigan finally let you out, hey, Aneirin?" he gasped. He was searching for a weakness in the spell that was holding him. He just needed to keep the general talking.

"She's a gracious goddess that rewards the faithful, something you would have known if you hadn't spurned her."

"Are you still jealous about that? Look, man, if she hasn't let you between her thighs by now, she's just not that into you," Killian said. The butt of Aneirin's staff hit him hard in the mouth.

"That's enough." High heels tapped on the floor, and Morrigan's terrifying and beautiful face looked down at him. Her red smile was cold and vicious.

"Hello, Killian. Where is your little mate?"

29

"You aren't lifting it high enough," Bron said from where she sat on a hay bale.

"Am too!" Moira snapped, but she still lifted the small crossbow up.

They were out in the grounds at the shooting range, rows of targets hanging from trees and straw men positioned around them. Bron was confident that Moira would be as safe as she could be in the mansion if Morrigan attacked. Moira knew every hiding place on the grounds and was under strict instructions to find one and stay there if they were invaded.

That didn't mean Bron wasn't determined Moira get as much practice in with a crossbow as she could.

"Layla said that you and Killian are like married now," Moira said, aiming the bow.

"Yeah, kind of. I'm his mate. You might like having a big brother."

"I think you should have a party and buy me a nice dress to wear," Moira said. Her tongue stuck out the side of her mouth as she aimed. "And King can wear a bow tie." The dog beside her barked in agreement.

"Tell you what, if you get the next shot, I'll have a party," Bron said. She needed Moira to have proper motivation.

"Okay." Moira released one bolt after another, all heart shots in the straw men. She gave Bron a smug little smile. "I'd like my dress to be purple."

Bron picked her jaw up off the floor. "You little shit."

"I practiced *lots* when you were away, Bron, because I want to be as good as you someday," Moira explained. Bron's heart squeezed, and she pulled Moira into a wriggling cuddle.

"Good! Because you know, you're going to have to protect the dogs if anything attacks the grounds."

"Me and King both will."

"Okay, how about you show me what you can really do, shortie?" Bron said, pointing to the other quiver of bolts.

Magic surged like cold darkness up through Bron, making her gasp and sink to her knees.

"Bron!"

She held out a hand. "No, get back, Moira! It's just Killian's power. Give me a second." Bron breathed slowly through it, the blood rushing to her head. It was like holding a burning star inside herself instead of letting it burst right out of her. Her hand started to pulse, and then the air around her tore, and the hilt of a sword appeared.

"What the hell?" Bron reached for the hilt and pulled a heavy black sword from out of the sky.

"Woah! How did you do that?" Moira asked.

"I have...no idea." Bron studied the sword before slowly pulling it from its sheath. The blade was matte black metal and inlaid with moonstones. "This is Killian's sword."

"Is it because you're his mate wife now?"

"Maybe. I don't know."

Moira started to bounce on the balls of her feet. "Try it out, Bron! That's the prettiest sword I've seen ever!"

Bron went over to one of the straw dummies and raised the sword. Hot power raced down her arm as she swung. There was no drag on the blade as it sliced through the thick dummy, and its top half slid to the dirt.

"Holy shit," Moira squeaked.

"No swearing," Bron said automatically, her eyes not leaving the blade in her hand. She shook herself and quickly sheathed it. "Okay, enough gawking, we are here for you to practice, not me." Moira pouted but got back to it.

Bron pulled out her phone and sent Killian a message; **We need to talk about your big sword. When are you coming around?**

She waited for the message bubble to appear, frowning when it didn't. Killian wouldn't miss an opportunity to send something back, laced with innuendo.

He did say he needed to see his brothers. Bron shrugged off her worry and focused back on training Moira.

∽

BY SUNSET, Bron's worry was back in full force. She checked her phone for the hundredth time before going to find Kenna. Bron had seen her talking with Killian that morning before she came into the kitchen, gave Bron a brief hug, and then went back to work. And that was that. Kenna's temper never lasted long, especially when she was in the wrong.

"I need Kian's number," Bron said, tapping on the office door. Kenna didn't look up from her computer as she rattled off the number. Her mother had a prodigious memory that was equal parts blessing and curse.

"Thanks, Mom," Bron said, typing the number into her phone.

"Everything okay?"

"I don't know. I've got a weird feeling, and Killian isn't answering."

"They are boys. They are probably rotten drunk celebrating his curse being broken."

Bron bit her lip as she typed. "I hope so."

Hey Kian, have you seen Kill? He's not answering his phone. Bron's phone rang almost instantly.

"Bron, are you telling me that he's not with you?" Kian asked.

"No. He said he was going to see you. I've been home all day waiting for him to come back."

"We assumed that he changed his mind and went back out to see you. The mating bond can be strong in the first couple of weeks. We thought you might be...occupied."

Bron's stomach plummeted. "No, he's not with me. I don't know if its relevant, but I had his sword appear out of thin air today—"

"Fuck. Stay at the mansion. Bayn and I will go check his apartment. Whatever you do, protect that sword with your life." Kian hung up without saying goodbye.

"What is it?" Kenna asked.

"He's not with them."

"I'm sure they will track him down, Bron."

"MOM!! Come quick!" Imogen shouted, loud and panicked. Bron and Kenna ran from the office and found Imogen in the TV room. On the flat screen were urgent news reports, images of burning torches, and a mob of people.

"This is happening in the city right now," Imogen said. "Look closely in the crowd."

Bron's hands tightened into fists. Amongst the wild-eyed people were the unmistakable curve of horns, black shells, and mutant animals.

"The horde is here," Bron said, dropping into her fighting calm.

"I'll call Kian. Assemble your sisters, Bron. We need to move on this." The three of them scattered.

Bron ran upstairs to Charlotte. She was in her lab with her goggles on, holding a smoking beaker.

"Leave it! The horde is here. Where's Layla?"

Charlotte started but didn't drop the beaker. "In her room."

Bron jogged over to the bedrooms and crashed into Layla, coming out at full speed. "Bron! The news!"

"I know. I saw," she said.

Layla grabbed her arm. "No! I was watching, and I saw Killian! Some tall guy with a staff was dragging him through the streets."

Cold fury filled Bron's veins. "Do you know where they were?"

"Not what street, but I recognized a tower of Christchurch Cathedral."

"Good. Now, get your gear and find Mom."

"What are you going to do?"

"Just do as I say, Layla!"

Bron went straight to her room and started to strap on her body armor that she only used when hunting feral werewolves. It was made of Kevlar and had reinforced panels over all her important places.

She wouldn't let her fear dig a hole in her brain. She clipped on her belts and holsters, carrying her knives, guns, and spells. Finally, she slung Killian's sword over her back and headed downstairs.

Imogen intercepted her at the door leading to the garage. "Where are you going? We are meant to meet Mom in the dining room, and she and David will tell us where to go."

"I can't wait that long." Bron pushed open the door and found the keys to her motorcycle.

"Bron! You can't go on your own."

"I have to, Imogen!" Bron shouted, even as her voice broke. "Aneirin has Kill. I need to go and find my mate."

Understanding flashed over her face, and Imogen pulled her into a tight hug. "Go get him, sis. We'll follow soon, so make sure you answer your phone."

"I will." Bron turned the key of her bike and roared out into the night, praying that she would get to Killian before Morrigan did.

30

Bron was riding past Phoenix Park when her phone rang and connected to the Bluetooth in her helmet.

"Bron, where are you? Kenna said you left the estate," Elise said, panic lacing her words.

Bron glided around two cars before answering. "The general has Killian. I couldn't find out where, but Layla spotted Christchurch Cathedral. I'll start there."

"You saw him? Shit. We are just leaving his place in Temple Bar and will start working our way towards the cathedral. For the love of God, drive carefully and watch yourself. It's madness here, and Killian wouldn't survive if anything happened to you."

"I will, Elise. I'll see you on the other side." Bron hung up and focused on the traffic. Cars were speeding in the opposite direction, trying to get out of the city. The sky was red and smoky in the distance.

"Fuck!" Bron slammed on her brakes as a stick insect monster the size of a horse appeared in the middle of the road. Bron pulled out her handgun and blew off two of its legs. It stumbled to the other side of the road just as a semi-trailer roared past, spraying the road with legs and purple goo.

Bron swerved around the carnage and kept going. Traffic was at a standstill. Cars were abandoned and trampled on. She wove in and out, trying to get as far into the city as she could. She rode up onto a footpath, dodging debris where the rioting had come through. They had been so wrong about Morrigan waiting until the full moon.

Bron slowed as she crossed over a bridge and into Usher's Quay. On the right side of her, the River Liffey was surging as a magician on the far bank pulled the water from it and shot it down a nearby street. As Bron got closer, she recognized Reeve, soaked and sooty.

"Hey!" Bron pulled up beside him and lifted her visor.

"Bron! About time you got here. Where the fuck is Charlie? Is she okay?" he demanded. His power was pulsing around him in crimson flames.

"She's on her way in. Call Imogen. I'm heading on."

"That water should have cleared the road for you a little. I'll keep them from coming up behind you," Reeve said.

"Thanks. Keep an eye on Charlotte when she gets here."

"On my honor as a gentleman," Reeve said with an elaborate bow.

Bron grinned. "You're not half bad, Greatdrakes."

"Tell your sister that!"

Bron turned to Lower Bridge Street and tried to dodge the puddles of water and drowned creatures. She hadn't seen one dead human, which was a blessing. Aneirin had no qualms about using them as cannon fodder, and Bron doubted the horde would differentiate between ally and snack.

Bron slowed as she reached the edge of a crowd. They carried torches and makeshift weapons and were heading towards the cathedral.

Horde creatures were roaming through the mob, hanging off the sides of the buildings and scuttling over rooftops. Bron gagged when she saw an arm hanging out of the side of the wolf hybrids mouth. She sometimes hated being right.

Bron abandoned the bike at St. Audoen's Park and headed out on foot. The sword on her back was thrumming with insistent power. She didn't want to start killing unless she had to.

She joined the tail of the mob and tried to wear the same dazed expression that all the other humans were wearing. The ground was sticky underfoot, and through the scant light, Bron could make out pools of blood and drag marks.

Oh God, Killian, please be okay. She didn't know how to use the mating bond to locate him. She had to trust that she could find him on her own.

You tracked him through three worlds. Dublin should be easy.

Drums were getting louder in the distance, a low humming drone of sound starting. Bron tried to hum along as she slowly walked near a scarab the size of a small car. Her hand itched to pull out Killian's sword and slice its ugly head off. She cut through the crowd, edging to the side, before slipping down an alleyway that ran behind the cathedral.

The few dazed people that were lingering about didn't give her a second glance as she climbed over an iron fence. The cathedral's bricks were rough, decorative, and easy to climb as she pulled herself up to one of the frames of a stained glass window. It had been covered in metal bars to stop vandals from breaking the windows to get into the church.

Bron didn't look down as she tested the covers with a firm rattle. Satisfied that she wasn't going to plunge to her death, she dug the toe of her boot into the metal grid and scaled up the window.

Her arms were burning as she pulled herself up the stone gutters and braced herself against the slope of the roof.

Bron looked around as she caught her breath. She had completely forgotten that the cathedral tower was getting restoration work done, and thank the saints and stars, the builder's scaffolding was still up.

"That's going to make it easier," she murmured. "Bless you, builders." She scrambled up the roof and along the ridge to where the scaffolding started. Bron used her lock picks to break the padlocks on the temporary fencing and started climbing up the ladder.

"People of Ireland, your goddess is about to return! Call for her!" Aneirin's voice reverberated around Bron, making her foot slip in surprise.

"Shit," Bron found her footing, adrenaline forcing her up the ladder faster. At the top of the tower, Bron climbed out of the scaffolding and hurried to the stone wall. Cold terror gripped her insides as she looked down.

Hundreds of people and creatures had piled into the intersection in front of the cathedral. The fence still stood, and Morrigan's fae guards surrounded a stage constructed of pilfered wood and metal. Killian was on his knees, covered in blood and his face pulped from a beating. Genuine fear pulsed through Bron as she gripped the crumbling stone.

"I'm coming, baby," she whispered and drew the sword from her back. It was singing to her in a song without words, the moonstones glowing softly and calling her to destroy the evil creatures of the world.

Ancient and terrible power burst from the square below. Aneirin had his staff raised and was chanting in an unknown tongue.

The drums and cries of the crowd got louder with every second. Power ripped the air open beside Aneirin, and Morrigan stepped onto the platform.

On top of her black hair was a crown of silver and black feathers, a red jewel in between her brows. She was wearing black leather and silver armor, black paint smeared over her eyes.

"My dark children! I have heard your cries from Tir Na Nog and have come to save you from the horrors of this world with no faith," Morrigan said, her voice full of love and authority. Bron trembled under the force of her power.

The sword's hilt started to burn, pulling Bron back from the spell that was woven into Morrigan's words. The goddess turned to Killian and placed her hands on his face to cradle it.

Bron couldn't hear what was being said; she only knew that the bitch-goddess who had tortured her mate for three years was now touching him.

My mate.

Morrigan bent down and put her mouth onto Killian's, and Bron's vision blurred red. The goddess had just made her last mistake.

Rage and heat ripped her new magic free with a shout. Power surged up through her, knowing what she wanted and responding to her desire.

Bron cried out in agony, sinking to her knees as the skin and muscles on her back opened and wings tore themselves free.

Spitting blood out on the ground, she heaved air into her lungs until the world stopped spinning and the pain lessened enough to focus.

Bron stretched out her bloody wings and climbed back to her feet.

Gripping the sword in both hands, she let its power draw on her magic. It had come to her that day for this purpose, and its song of blood and vengeance was booming in her ears.

Bron blew out a slow, steady breath and leaped from the tower.

31

One of Killian's lungs wasn't working properly. Each breath he took was painful, and Aneirin had done something to him to stop his fae healing.

The drumming of the fanatics around him was nothing compared to the gongs going off in his head. Kian would keep Bron safe. He was sure of it. If Morrigan had her, she would be gloating about it.

Aneirin was chanting something, his words blurring in Killian's busted eardrum. He had to get up and away from whatever the fuck the general was doing to stop his power.

A portal tore open, and Morrigan stepped through to make a grand entrance. Killian wanted to tear her pretty face off. He should've stuck the sword in her centuries ago. He had sent the sword to Bron with the last of his power. She was smart enough to get it to Kian.

"Oh darling, you have no idea how much it pains me to see you like this," Morrigan said, lifting his face.

"You're going to have to speak up. Your boy here fucked my ears," Killian replied. Morrigan frowned at Aneirin and sent the smallest amount of healing power into him. Bones and flesh knit, and whatever was bleeding internally stopped.

"Is that better?" Morrigan crooned, running her hands through his hair. "It's so nice to be able to touch you again. I'll have to thank that hunter for breaking your curse before I tear her throat out."

Killian growled so deep and feral that the guards pointed their spears at him. Morrigan only laughed, like it was all some great joke.

"Help me turn the world to darkness, and I'll let her live."

"Just kill me already. I don't know how many times I need to say no to you, woman," Killian snarled.

Morrigan leaned down, her breath smelling of cinnamon and blood. "Maybe you need a reminder of how good we were together." Killian's limbs locked down with her dark power, and Morrigan pressed her wet mouth to his. Killian gagged, trying to pull his head away. Morrigan held on, forcing her tongue against his teeth. She bit his lip hard, licking at his blood before pulling back.

"Still delicious as ever," she said.

Killian went to snap at her when he felt a deep pulse of familiar power. His eyes went to the top of the tower behind them.

"I refuse to believe you would choose a filthy human over a goddess who would make you king of three worlds," Morrigan said, her lips curled unpleasantly. "I can't wait to meet your little mate and see what the fuss is about."

"You're about to," Killian replied.

An angel of death was falling from the sky, a sword above her head and emerald green magic exploding out of her. Morrigan sensed it too late, black eyes widening as Bron landed on her, the black sword driving into the goddess's back.

Morrigan shrieked, a sound of horror so otherworldly that the spell on the crowd broke, and people fell, covering their ears.

Bron rolled to her feet and positioned herself in front of Killian. She screamed a battle cry right back at the dying goddess.

"My mate," Killian murmured, stunned and scared and unable to look away.

Dark power raced through the crowd, horde creatures screaming as Morrigan ripped her magic from them and back into herself. Blood poured from her mouth and eyes as she flailed, trying to remove the sword but failing to pull it free.

"How does it feel, you fucking bitch?" Bron snarled before shooting twice and blowing out Morrigan's knees. "That's for the spears you put in my mate's legs."

"Pull the sword free...and I'll give you the world," Morrigan groaned.

Bron aimed her gun at the goddess's head. "Killian *is* my world."

"Bron! Stop!" Kian shouted as he, Imogen, and Bayn pushed their way through the panicking crowd.

Morrigan screeched again, waving her clawed hands as she crawled toward them, hate driving her forward.

"Keep coming at me, I'm enjoying this." Bron put another two bullets in the goddess's chest, driving her back.

Morrigan's glamor keeping her beautiful tore away, and she became a creature of horror, her face barely in a form at all. Words full of power and terror rattled off her tongue.

God's speech. Killian had only ever heard it once and would never forget it.

A portal tore open, and a tall figure stepped out of a land of mist. Long black hair swirled around a pale face, a jagged black glyph tattooed on his brow. Eyes as black as the pit surveyed the mess in front of him.

"You...owe...me, Arawan," Morrigan gasped at him, bloody hand reaching for him.

The God of the Dead gave her a contemptuous look and heaved her up into his arms. Bron stepped forward fearlessly.

"That sword is mine," she said, and surprisingly Arawan waited for her to rip the blade free from the shriveling Morrigan. "Thank you."

Arawan turned towards the portal when his attention snagged on Imogen, pausing him mid step. His head tilted to one side, studying her, and he said in a husky, broken voice, "Hello, darling. What's your name?"

Imogen raised both of her handguns at him. "You can call me, Miss Go Fuck Yourself."

Arawan inclined his head, a small smile on his lips before he stepped into the portal with the dying goddess. Then he was gone.

Bron turned to Killian. "I hope I'm not always going to have to be the one to save you."

"You're going to fight all my battles for me. You're better at it," Killian replied, eyes filling with tears. "Nice wings."

Bron kissed him, forcing magic into him that began to heal all the damage Aneirin had done. Killian broke off the kiss as Kian cleared his throat.

"Not to hurry you two, but we have to get moving."

"Dumb ass getting yourself caught again," Bayn muttered, crouching down beside Killian. He gripped the manacles around his wrists, his magic freezing the metal until it crumbled.

"I love you too, little icicle," Killian said as Bayn hauled him to his feet. "Now, where the fuck is Aneirin?"

"Gone. I saw him disappear in the crowd as soon as Morrigan pulled her power from him," Kian said.

"He will still be dangerous even without it," Killian growled.

The people in the crowd were starting to wail, wandering around like panicked sheep. Horde creatures were dying and lashing out without Morrigan's power sustaining them.

"This looks like your time to shine, Kian. You're the one that deals with PR," Killian said.

"We need to make sure none of these creatures escape. You're helping." Bron rolled her eyes and passed him one of her daggers. Killian took it with a snort.

"That is *my* sword you're holding," he said.

Bron raised a brow. "You don't deserve to have a sword until you learn not to get fucking kidnapped." She jumped off the makeshift stage and sliced a creature's head off.

"That's my mate," Killian said. Kian and Bayn just shook their heads in an eerily identical move.

"Yeah, you're going to have a hell of a time." Imogen gave him a pat on the shoulder and went after her sister.

"Is anyone else worried that she caught the eye of Arawan?" Bayn asked.

Kian frowned. "Lucky she is family now, and we can keep a close watch on her. I didn't know Arawan was still...around."

"Well, he certainly is now that Morrigan fucking woke him." Killian looked at the dagger in his hand and groaned at the pathetic blade. Kian took pity on him and handed him one of his swords.

"Come, brothers, we have work to do."

"Gods, are you ever going to stop sounding like a noble wanker?" Bayn asked.

"Are you ever going to try acting like a prince?"

Killian laughed at his baby brothers and went to find his mate.

32

Bron hated wearing dresses with a passion. She adjusted the top again, worried that she showed way too much cleavage for a family event.

The dress had arrived at midday with a note that said, *Dreams really do come true.*

It was a black dress with a scattering of shimmering black gems that made it look like a piece of the night sky. It was the exact dress she had worn in the dream she had in Faerie.

She didn't know how Killian knew about it, but she would interrogate him after she had gotten through the dinner.

It had been a week since the attack in Dublin, and she had worked through it in a sleep-deprived daze. They had all fought the horde in groups.

Ciara had been saved by Torsten, and now she was forced to be polite to him. Charlotte had teamed up with Dublin's magicians, and they were working on finding where Aneirin had gone. She still had little tolerance for Reeve, but Charlotte had little tolerance for everyone.

Layla and Arne had led a group of hunters into the heart of the city and had been fighting their way to the cathedral when everyone's compulsion had been shattered.

Ireland was still a mess. They knew some of the horde creatures that were far enough away from Morrigan had managed to sneak off. Kian and Elise were worried about the creatures making it across the water and into England. It was going to make their lives busier than ever.

In response to a week of madness, Elise and Kenna had declared that they were having a night off, so the princes and their friends were all congregating for dinner at the Ironwood manor.

Bron fidgeted with the dress again, wondering if she could sneak away with no one noticing.

"Damn, you're going to make me semi-hard all night in that dress." Killian was watching her from the doorway, looking like sin.

"Only semi?" Bron asked. Killian made a helpless sound in the back of his throat. He moved to stand behind her and bent to kiss her in between her wings.

Bron hadn't quite figured out the magic to hide them away and had been too focused on other things to try. They were a dark green that sheened black, the tips of her feathers ending in gold. Killian touched them any chance that he got.

"What did I do to deserve such a beautiful mate?" he murmured, his arms coming around her.

"I don't know. What did I do to deserve such a troublesome one?" Bron groaned as he nipped her neck. "You're playing with fire doing that. We have your family and mine waiting downstairs for us."

Killian ran his hands down her breasts, sending fire straight to her core. "Let them wait."

"No, no, stop that," Bron wriggled out of his grasp.

"Fine, but just so you know, I'm going to do downright filthy things to you in that dress tonight," Killian said, voice full of delicious promise. Bron ran her hand down the front of his pants as she kissed him lightly on the lips.

"You better. Nothing semi about it." Bron gave him a teasing pat before stepping away. "Come on. If I have to suffer through this, then you do too."

Killian ran a frustrated hand over his face. "Fine. Yes. Okay." Bron grinned and took his arm.

Downstairs, everyone was drinking and chatting in the main

entrance hall. Freya spotted them at the top of the staircase and wolf-whistled loudly. Killian, never one to pass up an opportunity to be the center of attention, dipped Bron low and kissed her hard and long.

Bron forgot about being embarrassed as desire curled her toes and made her go boneless in his arms.

"Let her breathe already," Imogen shouted. Killian lifted Bron back upright, and all the blood in her body rushed to her face.

"Menace," she said, wiping her lipstick off his bottom lip. Killian's grin only widened.

"Bron! Bron! Look how pretty my dress is!" Moira said, racing to them, King hot on her heels.

"Wow, you look like a little princess," Bron replied, laughing as Moira twirled in a daze of purple and glittering diamantes. King was wearing a matching bow tie, and they looked cute enough to hurt.

Imogen passed Bron a glass of something fizzy and red. "We are never going to get that off her," she said as Moira tore away again. Bron looked at Imogen's leather pants and silver top.

"Where's your dress?"

"Don't need one when you look this good," Imogen replied with her cheerful fuck you smile.

Killian had voiced his concern about her catching Arawan's attention, but Bron wasn't going to bring it up with her tonight.

Imogen was strong enough to handle whatever was thrown at her, and if she wasn't, she now had three big fae brothers that would step in.

Bron hated gatherings, but with Killian's hand resting on the small of her back, they weren't all bad. She spotted Reeve in the crowd and raised her glass to him. He grinned his devil may care smile in acknowledgment before his eyes slid back to where Charlotte talked with Kian.

"Do you think she knows what she's doing to him?" Killian whispered in her ear.

"I can say with a hundred percent certainty that she doesn't."

David and Kenna came over to them, both wearing happy but tired smiles. "Well, Bron in a dress. Wonders never cease," Kenna said.

"You look great, sweetheart," David added.

"Thanks."

"David, I've been meaning to speak with you," Killian said, arm going around Bron. "Kian and I have been talking about your injuries, and we think we know some fae healers that may be able to help." Different emotions flickered over David's face, words failing him.

Killian looked at Kenna. "Ah, only if you are interested. I just wanted you to know that the offer is open."

"Thank you, Killian, that would be...I would be grateful," David said. Kenna gave Killian the slightest smile, which from her was untold gratitude.

After dinner, Killian took Bron's hand, and they slipped out into the gardens for some peace and quiet.

"Remind me again why we didn't run away to Egypt when we had the chance?" he asked, pulling her close.

"Because you wanted a big family gathering to celebrate finally being mated. I would've settled with a week in your castle in Faerie, but no, you had to go with family dinner."

Killian chuckled, tilting her face up. "Sorry, next time we go with your plan." He kissed her, fingers gliding down her bare skin to the curve of her breasts. Bron's wings shot out, startling her and making Killian throw his head back and roar with laughter.

"Oh, little hunter, what fun we are going to have with that," he said.

"Shut up. You do it too," Bron huffed, her literal feathers ruffling. Killian lifted her up and planted a kiss on her pout.

"You fucking glorious beast," he purred. "I love you so much it hurts."

"I love you too, even if you make me want to stab you at least once a day," Bron replied. She curled her arms around his neck and breathed him in. "This isn't going to end with the death of Morrigan, is it?"

"No, love. Not until Aneirin and the other two generals are dead. Without Morrigan to control them, my brothers and I don't know what will happen. It's a good thing we love a fight and now have a tribe of Ironwoods to help us." Killian's arms tightened around her, his lips creating a line of tingling desire down her neck. "But we have no generals to fight tonight, so tell me what would you like to do?"

"Take me flying?" Bron's wings flapped of their own accord. She wasn't very good solo but could glide easily with Killian helping her. She had found that flying was now her second favorite thing to do with him.

"We can always mess up this dress after our flight," she added, nibbling his ear.

Killian's soft chuckle made heat pound in between her thighs. "Oh honey, I plan on showing you how I can do both."

Bron kissed him as they shot into the sky, the night and stars belonging to them alone.

EPILOGUE

After an attack from a goddess, the world changed again. Humans and fae had stopped worrying about getting betrayed by the other and started worrying about what else might come out of the darkness.

Aneirin, sorcerer general, was the number one most wanted in the world. Only the fae princes and their human counterparts worried about the two generals that hadn't made an appearance in the Dublin riots.

The world now knew gods still walked amongst them. Some thought it a good thing; the ones old and wise enough knew it wasn't. Others began to hunt them down, eager to brush against the Divine.

In Ireland, Aneirin War Gull began to crow a different song of blood and magic.

Deep in a forest in Wales, the God of the Dead stepped into the human realm for the first time in centuries.

Dark elves began to plot, their centuries-long revenge against their light brothers starting to come to fruition, with intrigues and sharp smiles.

Buried deep in a cave in the north of Sweden, fanatics began digging, searching for the lost god of their bloodline.

All of them had forgotten that when it came to magic, power, and gods alike, all three demanded sacrifice...and it was always the one thing you never wanted to part with.

ABOUT THE AUTHOR

I believe that all monsters and villains deserve their happy endings. I prefer my clothes black, eyeliner winged, and books full of hot romance.

Come say hi to me on Instagram, or keep track of all of the gossip early by subscribing to my blog newsletter at:

https://alessathornauthor.com/alessa-news/

Or, alternatively Follow Me on Amazon to get all the Newest Releases directly to your inbox.

Thank you for reading '**Wrath of the Fae**,' if you loved it please consider leaving me a short review or a rating on Amazon as it helps other readers find my books.

This series continues with IRONWOOD, about our favourite hunting family.

ALSO BY ALESSA THORN

GODS UNIVERSE
THE COURT OF THE UNDERWORLD
ASTERION

MEDUSA

HADES

HERMES

THANATOS

CHARON

EREBUS

GODS OF THE DUAT
SET

THOTH

ANUBIS

FAE UNIVERSE
THE WRATH OF THE FAE
KISS OF THE BLOOD PRINCE

HEART OF THE WINTER PRINCE

WINGS OF THE NIGHT PRINCE

WRATH OF THE FAE (Box set Audio Book Edition)

IRONWOOD
TRASH AND TREASURE

GOD TOUCHED

ELF SHOT

LUNA CURSED

IRONWOOD (Box set Audio Book Edition)

THE LOST FAE KINGS

DANCE OF THE FOREST KING

SONG OF THE SEA KING

MERCENARIES AND MAGIC

DARKEST NIGHT

SHARPEST EDGE

TOUGHEST DEAL

DEEPEST CUT

Printed in Great Britain
by Amazon